DC501450

FEB 08

SPUD

Rave Reviews from South Africa

"A witty, sharp and thoroughly entertaining book . . ."
—www.southafricawriting.com

"*Spud* is a benchmark for comedic writing in the country and one of the most enjoyable reads I have had this year."
—Lauren Cohen, *EP Herald*

"Funniest book of the year."
—Julia Paterson, *The Citizen*

"Funny, fast-paced and wonderfully observant. . ."
—Book Shelf, *The Daily News*

"It's funny, well written and deeply moving."
—*Natal Mercury*

"Achingly funny . . ."
—Michele Magwood, *Sunday Times Lifestyle*

"*Spud* is one of those books which could easily be dismissed as nothing more than an adolescent read at first glance, but once you pick it up it's almost as if the pages turn themselves. All in all, a wonderful book."
—*Metrobeat*

"*Spud* is a delicious piece of writing, full of invention and very very funny."
—Derek Wilson, *The Argus*

SPUD

John van de Ruit

razor
bill

Spud

RAZORBILL

Published by the Penguin Group
Penguin Young Readers Group
345 Hudson Street, New York, New York 10014, U.S.A.
Penguin Group (USA) Inc., 375 Hudson Street, New York, New York 10014, U.S.A.
Penguin Group (Canada), 90 Eglinton Avenue East, Suite 700, Toronto, Ontario, Canada M4P 2Y3 (a division of Pearson Penguin Canada Inc.)
Penguin Books Ltd, 80 Strand, London WC2R 0RL, England
Penguin Ireland, 25 St Stephen's Green, Dublin 2, Ireland (a division of Penguin Books Ltd)
Penguin Group (Australia), 250 Camberwell Road, Camberwell, Victoria 3124, Australia (a division of Pearson Australia Group Pty Ltd)
Penguin Books India Pvt Ltd, 11 Community Centre, Panchsheel Park, New Delhi – 110 017, India
Penguin Group (NZ), 67 Apollo Drive, Mairangi Bay, Auckland 1311, New Zealand (a division of Pearson New Zealand Ltd)
Penguin Books (South Africa) (Pty) Ltd, 24 Sturdee Avenue, Rosebank, Johannesburg 2196, South Africa

Penguin Books Ltd, Registered Offices: 80 Strand, London WC2R 0RL, England

First published by Penguin Books (South Africa) (Pty) Ltd 2005

10 9 8 7 6 5 4 3 2 1

Library of Congress Cataloging-in-Publication Data

Van de Ruit, John.
 Spud / John van de Ruit.
  p. cm.
 Summary: In 1990, thirteen-year-old John "Spud" Milton, a prepubescent choirboy, keeps a diary of his first year at an elite, boys-only boarding school in South Africa, as he deals with bizarre housemates, wild crushes, embarrassingly dysfunctional parents, and much more.

 ISBN-13: 978-1-59514-170-5
 ISBN-10: 0-14-302484-1
 [1. Boarding schools–Fiction. 2. Schools–Fiction. 3. Choirboys–Fiction. 4. Family life–South Africa– Fiction. 5. Diaries–Fiction. 6. South Africa–Fiction. 7. Humorous stories.] I. Title.

PZ7.V28396Spu 2007
[Fic]–dc22
                                          2007006065

Printed in the United States of America

For my family, who taught me to laugh

'cknowledgements

Over my journey of the three years it took from Spud's first
rds to where this book now stands, numerous people have
ectly or indirectly guided my and Spud's travels.

Deafening applause to the wonderful crew at Penguin Books
for their faith, generosity, and absolute professionalism, especially
Alison Lowry, Jeremy Boraine, and my editor, Jane Ranger.
Thanks also to Hayley Scott and Claire Heckrath. My literary
agent, theatrical guru, and friend Roy Sargeant for his belief and
wise counsel. Tamar Meskin for her huge editorial input on the
early drafts and without whom this book might never have been
written. And of course Dave, Roz, Cathy, and Ash, who are my
rocks.

Thanks also to Sue Clarence, Julia Clarence, Anthony Stonier,
Murray McGibbon, Ben Voss, DMR Lewis, Rich (Fuse) Mylrea,
Janet Stent, Guy Emberton (who isn't really a banana vandal)
and Vampy Taylor. Finally, thanks to Ben Schrank, Jessica
Rothenberg, and the team at Razorbill.

–John van de Ruit

Dramatis Personae

Family	Mom
	Dad
	Wombat
Crazy Eight	John "Spud" Milton
	Robert "Rambo" Black
	Charlie "Mad Dog" Hooper
	Simon Brown
	Vern "Rain Man" Blackadder
	Henry "Gecko" Barker
	Sidney "Fatty" Smitherson-Scott
	Al "Boggo" Greenstein
Girls	Mermaid
	Amanda
	Christine
Prefects	Head of house – P.J. Luthuli
	Julian
	Bert
	Grant "Earthworm" Edwards
	Gavin, the weird prefect
	who lives under the stairs

Teachers	Headmaster - Mr. Glockenshpeel (The Glock)
	Housemaster - Mr. Wilson (Sparerib)
	English – Mr. Edly (The Guv)
	History – Crispo
	Drama – Mrs. Wilson (Eve)
	Play director – Mr. Richardson (Viking)
Sports coaches	Under 14 D/E rugby – Mr. Lilly and Mrs. Bishop (Reverend Bishop's wife)

When I consider how my light is spent,
Ere half my days in this dark world and wide,
And that one talent which is death to hide
Lodged with me useless, though my soul more bent
To serve therewith my Maker, and present
My true account, lest He returning chide . . .

"On his blindness," Sonnet IX
–John Milton

1990

Monday 17th January

04:30 I am awake. The first streaks of light peep through the sides of my old-lady curtains. I think I feel nauseous. The sheet under my legs is sticky and my heart is beating like a bongo drum. I can't get up yet.

04:48 The neighbors' dogs seem to be the only ones awake as they bark savagely at the rising sun.

04:50 Dad's awake. I just heard a loud shout come from his bedroom window. The dogs bark even louder. Dad stomps down the passage muttering to himself. (He hates our neighbors because they never seem to notice their dogs barking all night. He's always threatening to sue them or thrash them within an inch of their lives.)

05:00 The neighborhood erupts as Dad fires up his supersonic heat-seeking rose sprayer (which sounds like a ski boat hitting a sandbank at full throttle). The machine is so powerful that it blew Wombat's (my grandmother's) Queen Elizabeth rosebush out of the ground on its first tryout. Dad, wearing only his Cricketing Legends sleeping shorts (my Christmas present) and a surgeon's mask to protect himself from the deadly chemicals that he's now spraying into the atmosphere, points his machine at the neighbors' yard and dances like a loon on the lawn in front of my bedroom window. Maybe boarding school won't be so bad after all.

05:01 I watch from my window as my mother stalks into the garden in her faded lemon nightgown and screams something in my father's ear. He stops his loony dance and switches off his supersonic rose sprayer. He follows my mother inside. Seems like the neighbors' dogs got the last bark after all.

05:30 My father's exhausted after his early morning madness. I can hear him snoring loudly while my mother verbally abuses the policemen at the gate. The sight of my mother in her faded lemon nightgown must have frightened the policemen because they end the discussion by heartily apologizing to her and scuttling off to the protection of their police van.

06:00 It's time. I get out of bed. Next to the door stands my huge metal army trunk, my cricket bag, and my trusty Good Knight duvet. My uniform hangs from an old wire coat hanger. I reach for the blazer—it feels hot and heavy.

08:00 I'm courageously trying to swallow a mouthful of greeny scrambled eggs (including shells). I would have thrown it out of the window, but Mom was watching me like a hawk. She said I should have some nourishment before leaving for boarding school. Mom's notorious for her dreadful cooking—Dad refused breakfast because he's nursing a bout of the runs after last night's roast pork. (I think it was roast pork.) I'm too nervous to eat anyway and manage to scrape most of the egg into my napkin, slide it into my pocket, and then flush it down the toilet.

08:30 Dad's put his back out trying to load my huge metal trunk into the car. He clutches at his back like he's just been stabbed, collapses on the grass, and then squirms around in agony. With the help of Innocence (our trusty maid), I lug my trunk to the car and squeeze it onto the backseat. Mom gives Innocence a shifty-eyed look when she plants a big goodbye smooch on my lips. (Mom's convinced Innocence is running a brothel from her quarters in the back garden.)

08:36 My father's ordered to change his clothes as it seems he's rolled in something smelly during his dramatic writhing on the grass.

We're now running late. Mom taps at her watch and glares at me like it's my fault. Suddenly my terror overtakes my excitement and I start wishing that we could just cancel the whole thing and all go back to bed.

08:42 All set—Mom in her bright red smock, Dad in a tweed jacket and bow tie, and me in my new blue blazer, charcoal pants, red tie and white shirt (which felt too big in the shop but now seems to be strangling me). Dad blasts the hooter as he reverses our 1973 Renault station wagon into the road—the neighbors' dogs hit back with some ferocious barking. Dad throws his head back and laughs maniacally and then screeches us down the road into the oncoming traffic.

There's no going back now.

11:00 An African guard salutes us and then opens the huge white school gates. We pass through and drive along a beautiful avenue of trees called Pilgrim's Walk toward the school's gigantic redbrick buildings, which are all covered in green moss and ivy. My father is so busy pointing out a pair of mating dogs to my mother that he doesn't spot the speed bump that savages the underbelly of the car. Our station wagon limps up to the school and slides in between a Rolls Royce and a Mercedes-Benz. To announce its grand arrival, our rust-infested jalopy vomits up a couple of gallons of oil onto the ancient cobblestone paving.

We are met by two older boys wearing the same red tie as I am. They introduce themselves as Julian and Bert. Julian is skinny and confident, with blue eyes and wavy hair. He has a skippy walk and a cheery manner. Bert is massive—really massive (he looks nearly as old as Dad), with crooked teeth, vacant eyes, and a snorting guffaw of a laugh. Julian explains that they are prefects in the house in which I'll be living.

As they carry my trunk through the giant archway into the perfectly trimmed quadrangle, my mother trots out a long list of my amazing talents. (Scholarship winner, cricket star, prefect at primary school . . .) When she tells them about my beautiful soprano singing voice, Julian licks his lips and assures my mother that he is very fond of choirboys. Bert lets out a giant guffaw and elbows Julian in the ribs, making him drop the trunk on my father's left foot. Dad makes a funny squeaking whine and then assures everyone that he is "tough as teak" and "right as rain." I do my best to blend in, but it feels like the Boswell Wilkie Circus has just pulled into town.

The main quadrangle is surrounded by buildings, which remind me of those medieval castles in our old history books at primary school. We head toward a building that looks older than the rest. Its red brick has faded to peach brick and the moss and ivy are as thick as a hedge. The prefects lead us up a dark narrow staircase, through a long dormitory containing about fifteen empty beds, and into another dormitory, this one dark and creepy with low-hanging wooden rafters and dark brick walls. It is small and cramped, with space for just about eight beds. It feels spooky and smells like old socks and floor varnish. One of these eight beds is mine.

The dormitory is divided into cubicles by five-foot wooden partitions, which separate one cubicle from the next. Each cubicle has two wooden beds, two cupboards, two footlockers, a blanket, pillow, and mattress. Under each bed there are two drawers with golden door knocker handles. A few new boys wearing the same red tie as me are unpacking their clothes into their lockers under the watchful eyes of their mothers.

We arrive at a bed that has my name pasted onto the locker. The bed next to mine says *Blackadder*. At least I have a window.

My father, still limping around, and my mother, still puffing from the exertion of climbing the stairs, then have a huge argument about which drawer will house my socks and which my underpants. All the other parents stop what they are doing to stare at us. I kneel down and pretend to pack something into my footlocker.

On the way down the stairs we pass the whitest human being I've ever seen. In the dim light of the stairway, his paleness creates a strange luminous light. He is also wearing a red tie and he studies the floor closely as I pass by.

After a short sparring session between my parents in front of about twenty people outside the house, we make our way to the Great Hall, where we are addressed by various VIPs, including the local government official, our head boy Marshall Martin, and our rather frightening-looking headmaster, named Glockenshpeel. At first I think his name is a joke, but judging by the expression on his face, his name is no laughing matter. Glockenshpeel keeps referring to the school as an "institution" and the boys as "subjects." He also keeps repeating himself about discipline and stern punishment for wayward subjects. My father, nodding in agreement, eventually lets rip with an embarrassingly loud "Hear, hear!" This causes a moment's hesitation while over four hundred people stare at my nodding father and mother and a schoolboy who has turned beet red and is desperately thinking up a plan to dissolve into the covering of his seat. The school chaplain, who goes by the name of Reverend Bishop (destined for greater things?), makes a speech about the spread of Christianity in schools and the need for an open heart and an open mind. My father and mother agree that the Reverend Bishop is either homosexual or a communist, or possibly both.

13:00 Yet more embarrassment follows at the buffet lunch on the green lawn outside the library. My father, after seven gin and tonics, sneezes terribly loudly and then opens Mom's handbag to look for a tissue. As he unzips the bag, three sausage rolls, two gherkins, a string of Russian cocktail sausages, and a round of egg sandwiches launch themselves onto the lawn in full view of the headmaster, who coughs politely and pretends not to notice. I sidle up to some other people and pretend that they are my parents instead.

15:00 At last my parents depart, my father now in the passenger seat and Mom cramped up behind the wheel with a long strip of red smock caught in the door. After a hundred and fifty meters of pushing, the engine fires and they disappear around the bend in Pilgrim's Walk. I stand on the cobblestones staring at the driveway. I look around at the massive buildings and tall trees, which seem to surround me. I've never felt so small in my life.

18:00 Julian leads the eight new boys in our house down the stairs and into the common room (moth-eaten carpet, a few old red couches, a TV, and a notice board). There's a boy called Sidney who must weigh over 330 pounds and the luminous boy I saw on the stairs earlier who still looks like he's on the verge of death. (There must be healthier-looking corpses. . . .) Thanks to this sickly looking dude, I escape being the smallest boy in the house. It turns out that the lumo guy's name is Henry Barker. Our head of house is a black boy called P. J. Luthuli, who looks incredibly serious and is neatly dressed. He gives us important tips about the school like, "Don't run in the quad," and "Stay off the grass." He then tells us to get ready for bed. I think this is the first time I've ever taken instructions from a black person.

21:00 Lights-out! My first night away from home. A big muscular fast-talking boy with dark eyes and jet black hair called Robert Black seems to have appointed himself the king of the dormitory. He includes enough swearing in every sentence to satisfy the group that he means business and is to be heartily respected and hero-worshipped.

I'm sleeping next to a deranged individual called Vern Blackadder, who looks slightly brain damaged. He also has the nasty habit of pulling out large clumps of his own hair with a loud thunk.

I lie in bed listening to assorted snores and mutterings, the odd thunk of Vern's hair being ripped out, and the never-ending trickle of Pissing Pete (the concrete statue of St. Peter), who stands proudly in the fish pond in the quadrangle with water dribbling out of his sword.

Tuesday 18th January

06:15 Awoken by a terrifying siren. I jumped out of bed and called out, "Mom," before I could stop myself. Thank God nobody heard me. I followed the long line of boys stumbling their way down to the showers. As I reached the foot of the stairs a door opened, revealing a tiny room filled with smoke and candles. A strange-looking guy staggered out, stark naked, with a towel draped over his head and his willy pointing at the ceiling. A pimply boy called Al Greenstein said he's a weird prefect called Gavin who lives under the stairs.

The bogs (toilet area) consist of ten showers on a gray concrete floor with six basins and four toilet stalls. The floor felt slimy under my feet and the smell was foul. Julian and Bert, the two duty prefects, watched us showering and Julian made comments about everybody's willy. He described mine as "a runty silkworm with an eating disorder." I was shocked to see that every boy had body hair except me. Even Mr. Lumo has sprouts of black hairs around his groin. Bert shouted something that sounded like "Vulva," which means that our showering time was over. I got out quickly with my back still covered in soap.

Robert Black has the hugest willy. After his time was up, Bert shouted "Vulva" and Robert ignored him. Julian then shouted, "Time's up, Meatloaf!" much to the delight of Bert, who screeched out a song called "Bat Out of Hell" (which was about the speed that everybody charged out of the showers).

06:30 Roll call. (We have to start every day with this just to check nobody has run away or died in their beds.)

I nearly missed roll call because an older boy told me that it took place in the common room and that I should report there immediately. When I arrived in the common room, I found it completely deserted. Stupidly, I sat on one of the old red chairs thinking I was the first to arrive when actually it turned out that roll call was taking place outside in the quad. Luckily, I heard two boys run past in a blind panic and followed them out to where the house was lined up. It seems that when your name is called out, you have to shout "Sharks" in reply (nobody can explain why). P. J. Luthuli read out a name and then glared at its owner for some time before reading out the next. I waited nervously until . . . "Milton . . . John?"

"Sharks!" I squeaked. Everyone laughed.

Luthuli has a faint lisp, which was severely tested by the name of the fat boy Sidney, whose surname is Smitherson-Scott. After a number of attempts at getting it right, he glared at Sidney and rechristened him Fatty. (Most people call each other by nicknames here. Not sure who decides your name or how and if I've been given one yet.) The roll call then moved on to the older boys, but my brain was already panicking about finding the dining hall again.

The tall blond boy with railway braces called Simon Brown told us a story about an abattoir over a breakfast of egg and sausages. Lumincus Henry (already nicknamed Gecko) turned a pale green, ran outside, and vomited in the flower bed. This brought on a loud cheer from our section and a stern look from a miserable-looking teacher seated at the top table.

Bert, Julian, Luthuli, and Gavin (the weird prefect who lives under the stairs) spent the day showing us around the school and telling us what everything meant. The school consists of years one to three, matrics, and post-matrics, who only do university subjects and play sports. There are seven houses. Every house has four prefects and a head of house. The head of school is always a post-matric and he spends most of his time making speeches, meeting parents and old boys, and raising money to make the school richer.

It seems that every room has a code name and every quadrangle is identical, no doubt designed to completely confuse new boys. Our lesson timetable was like reading a page of hieroglyphics and I had to ask Julian to write down my lessons for me. My first lesson is English, which starts at 06:40 tomorrow.

17:00 The entire house gathered in the common room. About fifty boys stared at our cartoonish housemaster, Mr. Wilson, who's just like a goblin. He has big bulging eyes (one of which is squint) and a shoulder that looks like something's taken a huge bite out of it. He speaks in a rasping voice through clenched yellow teeth, and despite his small size he looks wickedly fearsome. He announced his seven commandments with a flourish of his cane:

1. Thou shalt not disobey those in authority.
2. Thou shalt not behave in a depraved fashion.
3. Thou shalt not tease my cat. (This is apparently a Siamese called Roger.)
4. Thou shalt not waste toilet paper.
5. Thou shalt not play with yourself (or others) after lights-out.
6. Thou shalt not go night swimming.
7. Thou shalt not play darts (a bit strange considering the lack of a dartboard).

Robert Black, who's nicknamed himself Rambo, told us after lights-out that Wilson's nickname is Sparerib and that a savage lion in the Kruger National Park bit off half his shoulder when he was a youngster. The doctors then took out one of his ribs to repair his shoulder. Everybody whistled and looked impressed.

Vern, my cubicle mate, has developed a nasty habit of going to the bogs every half hour for a piss and a sip of water. This wouldn't be a problem if he didn't set his alarm clock every time.

A tribunal made up of Fatty, Simon, Rambo, Al "Boggo" Greenstein, and myself found Vern guilty of moggy behavior and confiscated his alarm clock. Boggo Greenstein (a greasy-looking boy with big teeth and a bad case of pimples) has also rationed Vern to three visits to the bathroom per night. Vern didn't defend himself and handed over his alarm clock.

Can't sleep. I lie in bed, homesick. (I even miss Mom's cooking!) It feels like there is a lump of lead in my tummy. My new home is like a war zone, and while I take heart in the fact that there are two easier victims than me in our dorm (Gecko and Vern), I have the uneasy feeling that my time is coming. Every siren terrifies me because unlike everybody else, I never seem to be sure what happens next. I spend all my time looking for and following familiar faces around the school in the hope that they know more than me. I wonder what my parents would say if I gave up my scholarship and came home. Tomorrow school proper begins. Maybe I'll die in my sleep and miss it completely.

I dreamed lions were trying to bite my shoulder off.

Wednesday 19th January

05:50 Vern wet his bed during the night. His desperate attempt to change his sheets before the rising siren was foiled by Charlie Hooper (nickname Mad Dog) returning from an early morning bat-hunting expedition with his catapult. Mad Dog hasn't spent much time in the dormitory and seems to do a lot of hunting. Mad Dog stole the yellow stained sheet and hung it up from the rafters out of Vern's reach before raising the alarm.

When a snively Gecko returned from the phone room after a chat with his mom, he discovered Vern's soiled sheet hanging above his bed and charged down to the bathroom with his hand over his mouth. Mad Dog and Rambo exchanged a high five and some raucous laughter.

06:30 Roll call. Bert referred to Vern Blackadder as Vern Slackbladder, which dissolved the entire roll call into chaos. The hysterical backslapping and chanting was brought to an abrupt halt by a high-pitched cry from Sparerib, who looked like he was quite keen to slaughter someone.

06:40 Our first lesson was English with an extraordinary teacher called Mr. Edly (nickname The Guv—a nickname he said he was given when he was a boy at the school). He has a very posh English accent and strides around with a walking stick, swearing like a maniac. His long legs and bulging eyes make him look like a giant praying mantis. He had some spectacular outbursts (within five minutes he'd threatened to shoot off Boggo's head with a shotgun). The highlight of the class was when he threw a pile of Henry James novels out of the window and called the author "a boring poof." We all applauded; he bowed and then told us to get lost.

I like The Guv—and strangely enough, he seems to like me. After class he asked me to stay behind. His great bulging eyes studied me closely over the top of his old-fashioned horn-rimmed glasses.

"So, Milton," he said, "welcome to paradise lost." With that he roared with laughter and told me that anybody named after the greatest writer that ever lived must have fine literature in his blood. He presented me with a play called *Waiting for Godot*, written by an Irishman called Samuel Beckett. He prodded the book with his finger and said, "Nothing happens, old Johnno, but it's a raving blast. Now piss off; it's breakfast time."

I couldn't help smiling—it's the first time I've been called by my name since I've been here. (Everyone else calls me Spud because my willy is tiny and my balls haven't dropped yet.) Made a mental note to check out this other John Milton character and his book *Paradise Lost*.

08:30 Mad Dog told me that I was in his class for maths. I followed him down a series of corridors until we reached our classroom. The teacher was a kindly-looking man called Mr. Rogers. Unfortunately, it turned out that it was the remedial class. Mad Dog snickered into his rucksack as I packed my things, excused myself, and sprinted around in a blind panic looking for my maths class. All the buildings and quadrangles look so similar that it's easy to become completely disorientated (which I did).

Ten minutes ticked by on my old Remex stopwatch. I felt a huge lump in my throat—I was about to start sobbing. I wanted to go home. I wanted to run out of the school and keep going until I saw those old rusted gates and the giant acacia tree in our front garden. Suddenly there was P. J. Luthuli, marching along the corridor, looking important. Half sobbing, half panting, I asked him for directions. He patted my shoulder and led me to my maths classroom.

As I entered, I was faced with the most shocking silence. I stared at the dark figure standing at the blackboard and recognized the scowling face of the miserable-looking teacher from breakfast yesterday. He grinned a mean, thin-lipped grin and then said in a low, cold voice, "Milton, you're late. Report to the staff toilets after lunch." With a flick of his academic gown, he continued with his lesson on the basics of algebra. The teacher's name is Mr. Sykes (nickname Psycho).

16:20 After spending the afternoon cleaning the staff bogs with a scrubbing brush and an old pair of underpants (with the name Brett Ballbag scribbled on them with an ink marker), I returned to a completely deserted house. My heart sank—what had I missed this time? Then I saw the message on the notice board:

Touch Rugby 16:00 on Trafalgar!

Where the hell was Trafalgar?

I eventually made my way to the rugby field after getting lost again and ending up at the workshop instead. A greasy-looking mechanic in blue overalls gave me directions.

Trafalgar is surrounded by huge sycamore trees and smells of freshly cut grass. Spread out across its length was the largest game of touch rugby in history (easily fifty a side). I joined one of the teams without anyone noticing. The only recognizable face nearby was Gecko's, who was desperately trying to avoid the action by sprinting away from the ball as fast as his toothpick legs would carry him.

After what seemed like forever, the ball was hurled across to our side of the field and by some freak chance (and I mean freak!) it landed in the hands of Gecko. Gecko hurtled off without even realizing that he was in possession and darted through a gap between two third-years. A circus ensued as about twenty boys galloped after the terrified Gecko, who was making a beeline for the swimming pool. Eventually it was Mad Dog who flattened him with a crushing tackle just a few feet short of the pump house. Gecko hit the ground with a thud and immediately started writhing around on the concrete shrieking with pain. Bert helped him to his feet, and it was then that we saw Gecko's left arm hanging limply at right angles to his elbow. Bert picked him up and sprinted off to the sanatorium.

18:00 Gecko's left arm is broken. Mad Dog returned to the dormitory after a series of "meetings" with Sparerib, looking depressed. In the morning he has to see the headmaster, Glockenshpeel—he's worried he'll be expelled. Boggo reckons that Mad Dog could set a record for the fastest expulsion ever—after only three days at the school.

Couldn't sleep because Mad Dog kept whining and groaning.

Thursday 20th January

08:00 Mad Dog is still with us. Glockenshpeel has given him a severe warning and he has been ordered to write a letter of apology to Gecko's parents.

08:45 Had our first history lesson with Mr. Crispo. He is wickedly old—Simon reckons he may be ninety. He told us he fought in North Africa during the Second World War. This term we are studying the Anglo-Zulu wars of 1878–79, but instead Crispo showed us an old Second World War video on Dunkirk. Halfway through he blew his nose like a foghorn and then shook his head and muttered something to himself. At the end of the video he switched off the television and let us go five minutes early. From where I was sitting, I could see his eyes were full of tears.

14:30 Cricket trials. Although I was the best cricketer at my primary school (not that difficult considering most of the school was girls), I felt very nervous about my first go at high school cricket. The under-fourteen cricket coach is The Guv (much to my delight). He stalked around with his pipe and a shooting stick, making crazy comments like, "Greenstein, that forward defensive is about as porous as a whore's drawers!" Simon is an excellent cricketer and he smashed my first leg spin delivery out of the nets and onto a nearby field. To my horror, I realized that the ball had come to rest in the middle of the first-team practice session. The cricket gods all stopped and glared at me as I picked up my ball. I just about managed to squeak out an apology and then tore back to the nets.

Mad Dog is a fearsome bowler (fast and wild). He nearly killed Vern with a vicious bouncing delivery that reared up at my terrified cubicle mate. Rambo charges in to bowl with real aggression and savagery but lets the ball go rather slowly. The Guv told him he should take the fridge off his back, which made us all laugh. Rambo glared at me and my laughter fizzled out instantly. (This school is turning me into a coward.) At the end of the practice The Guv told us we were the crappest bunch of cricketers he'd seen in years. The first match is at the weekend and the side will be announced on Friday. Crossing fingers.

18:30 Prep (two-hour nightly homework session) was interrupted by Fatty's farting, which led to a complete classroom evacuation. Fatty pleaded that the beef stroganoff was off and the terrible smell was not his fault. Bert was so livid that he ordered Fatty to shut up and then beat him savagely on the fingers with a blackboard duster. This form of torture is called "finger tongs."

Mad Dog handed me a first draft of his apology letter to Gecko's parents. He reckons that because I won the scholarship, I was the ideal person to check his effort. Here follows the original:

Dear Mister and Missis Geko
 I am sorry about what happend to yor son Gecko. I broke his arm buy mistake with a wiked crash tackle. It's not my folt Gecko is bilt like a twig but I'm sorry for Mongreling his twig (his arm)

Sinserily
Mad Dog

21:15 I rejected Mad Dog's first draft and we composed a new draft together. (Mad Dog held the torch; I did the composing.)

Dear Mr. and Mrs. Barker,
 I wanted to take this opportunity to profusely apologize for acci-dentally breaking your son's arm. However, in spite of the damage and pain that our friend Henry has gone through, I am still con-vinced that I saved him from further, and possibly life-threatening, injuries. It is my belief that Henry panicked in possession of the rugby ball and sprinted toward the pool in a blind panic. I brought him down meters short of deadly danger, unfortunately causing him some pain in the process.
 Once again I apologize.

Yours sincerely,
Charlie Hooper

PS If Henry is there, tell him to get back quick—school just isn't the same without him.

Mad Dog was wickedly impressed with the new version. He especially liked the pool bit and how it sounded like he'd saved

Gecko's life. He wasn't sure about the PS because it's common knowledge that Gecko's in the sanatorium and not at home. I told Mad Dog that this was a perfect example of emotional blackmail. He seemed blown away with this and has vowed to call me "Brains" from now on. To repay the debt, he invited me on a pigeon hunt at 05:00. When I declined, he looked dangerous, so I told him that I loved eating pigeons but that I'm getting a sore throat.

On his way to bed Mad Dog poured a glass of water over Vern's sheet and then woke up the dormitory, who all sneered and mocked poor Vern while he changed his bedding again. I remained silent and then felt guilty for hours for being a coward and not standing up for my cubicle mate.

Friday 21st January

Vern tripped over somebody's foot at breakfast, which sent him and his jam on toast flying across the floor. There was riotous laughing and chanting until a grumpy old biology teacher called Mr. Cartwright banged the gavel and announced that there would be no condiments for two days. Fatty was distraught at the thought of no butter on his bread, no jam, honey, salt, vinegar, and tomato sauce. He has vowed deadly revenge on poor old Vern.

11:00 Checked out John Milton in the library. Actually, I first walked into the staff room by mistake thinking it was the library—only to see a big bearded teacher tossing peanuts into his mouth. He glared at me, so I closed the door and sprinted away. Turns out that Milton is an old seventeenth-century poet and *Paradise Lost* isn't a novel but a long and boring poem that doesn't seem to make much sense.

11:30 I'm in! I've made the under-14A cricket team! It looks like I'm down to bat at ten. Simon is captain. Also on the side is Mad Dog, and Rambo was chosen for the B side. I phoned my parents to tell them the good news. Mom told me that Dad spent the night in prison and that she was on her way to bail him out! She gave no explanation for his arrest. My dad could be a murderer!

12:00 Our first drama lesson was with Sparerib's wife, Mrs. Wilson, who's nicknamed Eve. (Eve is said to come from the spare rib of Adam.) She has six rings in her ears and one in her nose. Her hair is braided and today she wore a long earth-colored dress with dangling beads and thick silver bracelets. Eve looks at least ten years younger than Sparerib. (I can't believe this beautiful woman who looks like a forest fairy could have married Sparerib.) Boggo rates her breasts as incredible. I must admit they are impressive. I couldn't help notice that Boggo was staring at them with glazed eyes and at the same time sneakily adjusting his trousers.

Drama was awesome. We did all sorts of funny things like pretend we were animals, thunderstorms, and thumbtacks. Once everybody had stopped being shy, we had an absolute blast. Even Vern did a fair impression of a snake giving birth to a seagull.

Unfortunately, the lesson was ruined when Eve made us hold hands and tell each person that they were valuable and that we loved them. The sight of Boggo and Simon holding hands was too much for Rambo, who stormed out of the class in disgust. Eve burst into tears and told us that our class had bad karma (which also explained why Gecko had a broken arm). She then caught up with Rambo and called him into her office after the class, where she tried to teach him how to meditate.

19:30 Fatty's on the brink of suicide. Hamburgers and chips for dinner tonight (no salt, vinegar, and tomato sauce). He spent the meal glaring at Vern and muttering curses under his bad breath.

Eventually he stormed out of the dining hall without so much as touching his chips. It may just have been the light, but I could have sworn that I saw the hint of a smirk curling around the corner of Vern's lips.

22:45 Bert woke me up and said that somebody was shouting from downstairs that I had an urgent telephone call. My heart sank as I remembered my father. (Was this his final phone call before his imprisonment?) I stumbled down to the phone room and discovered a note pasted above the telephone: *Meat me in the storeroom under the stares. Mad Dog.* (With spelling like that, he needn't have signed his name.)

I crept past the room occupied by Gavin, the weird prefect who lives under the stairs, and opened the creaky door to the storeroom, which looked a bit like a dungeon. A flame burned in the far corner of the room, and standing over it was Mad Dog, surrounded by feathers and holding the charred corpse of an impaled bird over a gas cooker.

"Said you liked pigeon," he muttered, and held the crispy bird out to me. I took a small bite. Mad Dog nodded and I nodded back and there we sat, nodding, grunting, and chomping rock pigeons under the stairs in the middle of the night.

Saturday 22nd January

10:00 The 14A cricket team was victorious in our first match despite our opposition (Westwood College) having a rather dodgy age restriction. (The captain of their under-14 team arrived in his own car shortly before the match.)

17:30 Mom and Dad made a noisy arrival in the old lime green station wagon and immediately set out deck chairs and uncorked two bottles of wine. I finally discovered that my father had been arrested for indecent exposure. He wouldn't go into the details, but it seems that he was caught naked in the neighbors' garden at three in the morning. He says that it's all a load of bull and that he's getting the best damned lawyer in the country to represent him. My mother remained tight-lipped at my father's explanation and then abruptly got into the car and announced that they were leaving. My father packed away the chairs, shook my hand, and got into the car. After half the team pushed the old goat for about two hundred meters, it started with a bang and a plume of smoke and roared off down the driveway.

If I had the money, I would buy my folks a Mercedes for Christmas.

20:00 Watched *Pretty Woman*, starring Julia Roberts, in the common room. She is perfectly beautiful. Wickedly envious of Richard Gere. When I leave school, I will drive around looking for prostitutes like Julia.

For the first time this week I didn't feel worried before dropping off to sleep. Can't believe I have only been here for six days—it feels like a lifetime.

Sunday 23rd January

07:30 Awoken by some obscenely loud chapel bells, which seemed to be ringing from inside my locker. Upon closer inspection, I discovered that the giant bells are within a stone's throw of my window. To prove the point, Mad Dog shot one of them with his catapult, which struck a horrible note in the middle of "Amazing Grace."

08:00 Full-school Eucharist. Reverend Bishop rattled off a whole series of Latin verses, which sounded something like, "Bent the speakers, kill the cat," but like everything in this place, I didn't dare question. I just looked serious and as holy as possible. The chapel is brilliant—like a huge old Gothic cathedral with stained glass windows and an impressive altar that has a sculpture of a man with a sword stabbing a giant lizard on it.

A squeaky fart from somebody in our row interrupted Glockenshpeel's second New Testament reading from St. John's Gospel. Simon giggled, Fatty blushed, and Rambo elbowed Boggo in the ribs. And then as one they all glared at Vern, who hung his innocent head in shame. Glockenshpeel paused, the chapel fell silent, and for an instant it looked like The Glock was about to blow his lid, but after a few deep breaths and a wicked glare, the great man continued with his reading on forgiveness.

On Sundays all the boys have to leave the school for the afternoon (excepting matrics and post-matrics). This is called free bounds. According to Luthuli, free bounds is apparently enforced so that we will explore the surrounding areas. The real reason, says Boggo, is to give the teachers some peace and quiet and allow them to use the tennis courts. Not sure what to do or where to go. Will I get lost again and never find my way back to school? Think I'll follow the crowd and see where it leads me.

Spent the afternoon swimming at the dam. A friendly game of water polo with a tennis ball dissolved into an inter-house mud fight. Standing proudly like soldiers from one of Mr. Crispo's old war movies, we pelted the first years from Barnes House, driving them back into the reeds. The sight of Rambo, Fatty, and Mad Dog leading the charge made the Barnes cowards take flight. Unbelievably, Vern panned one of the enemy in the eye with a mud ball and the wailing wreck had to be carried to the sanatorium. Rambo gave Vern a pat on the back, causing my demented cubicle mate to grin like a psychopath.

17:00 Gecko has returned from the sanatorium. His arm has been set in a cast with a sling around his neck. Mad Dog was so relieved to see him that he gave Gecko a friendly thump on the back, which unfortunately propelled him right off his feet and into a nearby locker. Luthuli led the bloody-faced, broken-armed, sniveling Gecko back to the sanatorium.

Mad Dog has packed his trunk and said his last goodbyes. He's convinced that this night will be his last. With tears in his eyes he gave me his lethal catapult and told me I was his best friend. We shook hands and felt embarrassed.

I dreamed about Julia Roberts.

Monday 24th January

06:20 Mad Dog is still with us. Rambo told P. J. Luthuli that Mad Dog bumped into Gecko by mistake and then made up a convoluted story about a stray rat in the dormitory. Luthuli accepted the story with some suspicion. Rambo's theory is, "If you're gonna lie— lie big!" Rambo is now Mad Dog's best friend and Mad Dog has reclaimed his catapult.

12:00 Eve (Mrs. Sparerib) made us do the death scene from William Golding's *Lord of the Flies*. She chose me to be the victim who is torn apart by the gang of crazed youths. She gave me an old T-shirt to wear and told the group that the shirt was a metaphor for my body. After being kicked in the ribs and badly roughed up, it soon became apparent that nobody knew what a metaphor was.

Eve told the class to engage with our feminine sides and to play with our chakras. Boggo's convinced she wants us to bonk each other.

After the class Eve dabbed my wounds with cotton wool and disinfectant. As she leaned over me, I could smell her sweet breath and couldn't help but notice her beautiful breasts peeping out at me. I felt a strange shiver travel through my body—I could swear I nearly wet my pants! As I was leaving her classroom, Rambo brushed past me and asked Eve for some reading matter on William Golding. Eve was thrilled and ushered him into her office.

17:15   The first-years were called to a meeting with the prefects, who told us that our week of grace was now over and that life was about to get tough. They said that we now have to "slave" for a prefect (this means perform menial chores and behave like a servant) and that we were now open for initiation from older boys. We were told that respect and honor were to be valued and it was immoral to tell on another boy or to admit to being bullied or initiated. Looks like we are quite literally slaves after all.

I've been assigned to a tall stringy prefect called Grant Edwards (his nickname is Earthworm, although I have to call him Mr. Edwards). Earthworm is incredibly clever and a first-team cricket player.

A horrible-looking third-year boy called Pike woke us all up and informed us that he was our worst nightmare. He ominously declared first-year hunting season open, peed in our rubbish bin, and left.

Tuesday 25th January

My first day of slaving. Here follows my daily schedule, which Earthworm has written out in green, red, and blue ink and pasted on his wall:

06:20	Serve (Lord Earthworm) his tea—two sugars, no milk
06:22	Shine shoes
07:30	Clean room, make bed, and organize books
07:50	Take dirty clothes to the laundry
10:45	Made more tea and a slice of toast—anchovies, no butter
13:45	Clean room
14:00	Fetch clean laundry
14:12	Clean cricket boots
17:30	Clean room, more tea, un-crease bed after late afternoon nap
20:45	Pack books away, more tea (this time with milk), ready books for morning lessons

Earthworm doesn't speak much but watches me like a hawk while I'm working in his room. I suspect he could be a psychopath. (Could make a good combination with Vern.)

Vern and Gecko are slaving for Luthuli, Mad Dog and Fatty for Bert, and Simon and Boggo for Julian. Rambo is not happy about slaving for Gavin, the prefect who lives under the stairs, who, Rambo says, smells funny and spends most of the time breeding cockroaches and blowing into a long pole called a didgeridoo.

Had a dream that my mother was Julia Roberts and then woke up feeling homesick. I had a powerful yearning to run away, jump on the night train, and go home.

Wednesday 26th January

06:20 Severely reprimanded by Earthworm for making his bed

with the duvet buttons at the top. He says the cold buttons keep him awake and give him a rash.

06:40 The Guv instructed the class that lesbian writers are to be taken with a pinch of salt. He says they are "frustrated sex-crazed rug munchers with underarm fur and we should therefore dismiss the work of women called Woolf, Renault, and Agatha Christie.

Rambo asked him if we should study Shakespeare since he was a pillow biter. The Guv then accused Rambo of being homophobic and said that he had nothing against dykes and poofs. He even confessed that he wouldn't mind giving Martina Navratilova a jolly good rogering.

14:30 Choir auditions. Although it's seen as naff to be in the choir, it's still regarded as a lesser evil than cadets, which involves marching around the fields in the blazing sun. All of the first-years have to try out for the choir. The choir mistress, Ms. Roberts, seemed embarrassingly excited about my voice and placed me in the treble section (also known as the Spud section). Julian is the head chorister and sings lead in the tenor section. He ruffled my hair and told me that he adored my voice and that he'd take me under his wing. (If it weren't for the nasty snigger that followed, I might have found his offer quite comforting.)

Simon's the only other boy from my dormitory in the choir. Fatty came close, but I think the fact that he unknowingly drools when he sings counted against him.

23:15 Rambo informed us that he's in the process of planning a highly illegal night swim in which we're all invited to join. (For "invited," read "forced.") After some debate we agreed to listen to his plan. Once he'd casually mentioned the armed security guards and their savage Alsatian guard dogs, Rambo was hit with a flood of dissenters, led by Boggo Greenstein and myself. Order was finally restored when Rambo threatened to murder anybody being cowardly. (Needless to say, we all cowardly backed down.) Rambo's theory was that if we all took the plunge, then there was unity in numbers—and nobody left to rat on us. Friday has been declared D-day.

I watched Vern for ages as he chatted to his toiletries. It seems that each item in his toiletry bag has a different name. I pretended to be sleeping but couldn't help listening in on his nutty chatter. Am I the only person that knows he's mad? Am I mad for watching him? After what seemed like hours, he bade all his toiletries good night, switched off his torch, and went to sleep.

Thursday 27th January

11:30 Witnessed my first beating during Afrikaans class. Fatty's non-stop farting finally drove Mr. van Vuuren over the edge and he gave him a furious beating of two lashes with a sawn-off hockey stick in front of the class. I found the whole experience shocking. Fatty was wickedly brave and took the beating without so much as flinching. This angered van Vuuren even more, so he gave Fatty detention and the whole class extra homework.

Spent the afternoon reading *Waiting for Godot*. It's a play about two tramps living in a ditch and waiting for a guy called Godot—who never comes. They meet a clown called Pozzo and his slave, Lucky, who come and go, then come back again, eventually leaving the tramps to their never-ending wait. The play is wickedly odd. (Irish?) I have no idea why The Guv suggested I read it.

A fight broke out as Pike (hiding in the rafters of our dormitory) spat on Simon's head while he was listening to his Walkman. Simon flew at the miserable Pike and bit his arm; Pike pulled out a Swiss army knife and tried to stab Simon in the leg. Luthuli broke up the fight and gave both of them three sessions of hard labor (washing Sparerib's car and chopping firewood).

22:00 Final preparations and planning for the night swim. Boggo reckons we'll receive four lashes each if we get caught. (Apparently Sparerib beats like a sadist. No doubt forever avenging his tragic encounter with the lion.) Vern looked terrified and began pulling out his hair by the clumpful.

Friday 28th January

05:30 Woke up to find Vern changing his sheets again—I pretended to be sleeping. I've decided to be nice to Vern. (My uncle Aubrey once told me to always stay on the right side of demented people.)

08:00 Discovered a small column in the paper about my father's court appearance. I cut it out (and out of all the papers in the day-room) and set fire to them in the prefects' room's toaster. Here follows the article, which I copied before burning:

> MAGISTRATES COURT, DURBAN
> PETER EDWARD MILTON APPEARED IN COURT TODAY ON A CHARGE OF INDECENT EXPOSURE. HE WAS NOT ASKED TO PLEAD, AND THE CASE WAS POSTPONED UNTIL MARCH 6TH. MILTON WAS FOUND NAKED ON A NEIGHBOR'S PROPERTY. JUSTICE

LEIGHTON HAS ORDERED MILTON TO AN UNDIS-
CLOSED FACILITY FOR A PSYCHIATRIC EVALUATION.

Great. My father's not only a sicko but a nutter as well! Why do I feel like I'm surrounded by dementia? They say the first sign of madness is thinking lunatics surround you. (Am very troubled.)
Think I may have destroyed the prefects' toaster.

11:00 Haven't been dropped from the cricket team. Rambo's been included for the injured Steven George.

Read *Waiting for Godot* again and it made more sense. I actually found it quite amusing. Perhaps I'm falling into madness! (Make a mental note to keep checking if I'm talking to myself.)
Gecko's back from the sanatorium again. He looked his usual self (including cast, sling, plastered face, and unhealthy color). I noticed a terror in his eyes when an overly concerned Mad Dog approached him to offer another round of apologies. Gecko seemed pleased to see me again and told me about his adventures in numerous hospitals, clinics, and sanatoriums.

Saturday 29th January

01:15 All awake and ready for the night swim. Poor Gecko has been forced to take part despite some desperate whimpering and sniveling. Rambo insisted that (in a low menacing voice) "there can be no witnesses."

Rambo led us through the dormitory window and onto the vestry roof. I dared not look down at the quadrangle twenty feet below and shuffled along the precipice holding on to the elastic of Boggo's underpants. The roof creaked loudly as Fatty (bringing up the rear) landed on the old tin roof. Simon held the terrified Gecko with one arm as our intrepid group skulked along the roof to the chapel window. After some squeezing, pushing, and prodding we forced Fatty through the window and into the gallery of the chapel. With a solitary candle burning, the chapel was wickedly freaky. I could hear my heart thumping and Fatty's heavy breathing behind me.

Rambo led us down the stairs and along the aisle of the chapel. As we crept past the 134-year-old altar, Rambo jumped into the pulpit, spread his arms out like the Pope, and said, "Ladies and gentlemen, welcome to hell!" This terrified the blazes out of Gecko, who tried to make a break for it, only to be grabbed by Vern, who muttered, "No witnesses, Gecko," in his squawky, demented voice.

For some unknown reason we all then collapsed into fits of laughter. (Even Gecko was unable to contain himself and let out a shrill squeak that only made us more hysterical.) Then Vern was laughing uncontrollably. In fact, it was impossible to say whether he was crying or laughing as tears poured down his cheeks, his whole body shaking and convulsing.

After we recovered, Rambo led us into the pitch-black crypt under the chapel. The crypt is the home of the Monday night Christian Fellowship (happy-clappy Christians) and it's also meant to house the school ghost. The hilarity was soon forgotten as we crept on our hands and knees across the crypt's woolen carpet toward another door, which opens onto the school rose garden. From the rose garden it was over a small fence and across Glockenshpeel's lawn. His huge double-story mansion stood like a massive monster against the half-moon, a bit like one of those old castles in vampire movies.

While huddling under The Glock's lemon tree, Rambo gave us our final instructions. There we stood in our underpants, teeth chattering from fear. The night was thick and still and humid; away to the west there was the distant sound of great booming thunder over the Drakensberg Mountains, which only made the whole thing even more terrifying.

After a whispered countdown we sprinted as one across the rugby field (the most dangerous part of the expedition) and into the bushes near the bog stream (the stream that encircles the grounds). We then climbed through a barbed wire fence and suddenly the dam was directly in front of us, dead calm and beautiful in the moonlight.

One by one we slid into the cool water (apart from Gecko, who couldn't wet his plaster cast), feeling the soft mud squelch between our toes. We swam in complete silence until Mad Dog and Rambo tried to dunk each other. This soon turned into a mad dunking fight with everybody trying to dunk the next person. I managed to half dunk Simon, who retaliated by holding me under the water for about three minutes.

Suddenly Boggo hissed us to silence. Across the far side of the dam, a torchlight flickered across the path. And then another and another . . . We all stood stock-still in the water, a cold fear creeping over us. Silence. There was a clap of thunder and the wind began to gust with an eerie whistling moan. And then the dogs began to bark . . .

As one we launched ourselves out of the water and bolted for the fence and the rugby field. The guards must have released their dogs because suddenly their barking and growling was all around us. Rambo was shouting and Mad Dog was trying to shoot the dogs with his catapult. It sounded like he hit one because there was a horrific squeal. Despite the cast and sling Gecko leaped over the barbed wire fence like a springbok and scorched through the bushes like a man possessed. We all galloped across the rugby field, through the rose garden, into the crypt, up the stairs, into the chapel, back down the aisle, up more stairs, and into the gallery. Finally through the window, along the roof, through the dormitory window, and into my bed, muddy feet and all.

And then—dead silence, barring the sound of heavy breathing, the odd sniff from Gecko's bed, and the rumble of the thunderstorm. In the distance we could hear the guards whistling for their dogs. After about five minutes of silent panic, there was laughter and excited chatter. We all knew that we were safe, we'd made it, and we hadn't been busted. Excited personal accounts of the adventure flew around the dormitory, stories of dog chases, each more frightening than the last. By the time it got around to Rambo's turn, the guard dogs made the Hound of the Baskervilles look as threatening as a three-legged poodle with false teeth.

Gecko was convinced that a savage German shepherd had bitten him on the arse. After we all inspected his bum with the aid of Vern's torchlight, it was decided he was the victim of Mad Dog's catapult and had not been gored by a rectum-eating dog. Mad Dog denied the charge and Gecko refused to believe it had been a stone.

It was only after about half an hour of wild storytelling that we realized that we were short by one member. Fatty was missing. Rambo reckoned he had been caught by the guards; Simon said he was probably hiding somewhere. We tried to remember where we last saw him. I remembered trying to dunk him in the dam, but after that?

Mad Dog offered to go and find him, but once again Rambo insisted that we all go. Poor Gecko's eyes nearly popped out at the thought of having to repeat the process. For the second time we scrambled out of the window and onto the now very slippery tin roof and there we stopped. Our mission was complete . . . well, nearly.

Vern's torchlight lit up a gigantic backside half covered by shredded blue underpants sticking out of the chapel window. Fatty had got stuck coming back through the window. (Not sure why he was reversing through the window in the first place.) After some hushed cackling and a few cruel comments, we set about trying to free Fatty. After the seven of us pulled his legs (excuse the pun) for some time, Mad Dog decided that the only way to free Fatty was to push him forward back into the chapel (work that one out). Unfortunately, the big guy just wouldn't budge. With every push and prod Fatty groaned in pain, and to make matters worse, it began to pour with rain.

An emergency dormitory meeting was held to solve the Fatty problem. Mad Dog offered to rip the entire window out. Simon offered up his hair gel to lubricate Fatty and slide him out. Mad Dog suggested tying a rope to Fatty's foot and then attaching the other end of the rope to the school bus, which would drive off, pulling Fatty out. After exhausting all other options it was decided that we would work in shifts, two people per shift, and the rest would sleep. Myself and Vern took the first shift.

05:45 Rambo called another meeting. Things were now getting serious. Rising bell was only half an hour away and we were all in a lot of trouble. Fatty was in agony and he'd lost feeling in both his legs. It was still pouring with rain.

06:00 It was decided that we would all deny the night swim and Rambo would be our spokesman. He retired to his bed to brew up a story to explain the entire circus. Boggo and Mad Dog told Fatty that Rambo was cooking up a story and I was sent to wake P. J. Luthuli.

The grumpy head of house wasn't impressed with his early wake-up call. He was even less impressed when he saw Fatty's backside dangling out of the chapel window. He glared at all of us, whistled, and then said, "You bastards are toast!" Gecko sniveled and Vern pulled out some hair.

A sequence of events viewed from my window

06:07 The prefects and Sparerib stand in the main quad looking up at Fatty, shaking their heads and pointing occasionally. Sparerib does not look amused.

06:16 The rising bell has brought a small crowd into the quad, who all stare in astonishment at the chapel window.

06:30 Roll call is canceled as most of the school is now staring at Fatty's arse. Lewd comments are made as excitement spreads around the school. We watch the huge crowd standing in the drizzle and start to realize the enormity of the situation. Still no sign from Rambo's bed.

06:36 The crowd is dispersed by Glockenshpeel, who looks wickedly vicious. He snaps at Sparerib and the pair march into his office.

06:42 The school handyman, Rogers Halibut (his real name), sprays Fatty with lubricant oil and tries to yank him free. Fatty doesn't budge.

06:48 Rambo emerges from his cubicle, nods at us, and says, "Gentlemen, I have a plan." With that he strolls out of the dormitory, into the main quad, past the crowd of teachers and ground staff, and into the chapel.

06:55 Rambo exits the chapel, speaks to Sparerib, and they both walk into Sparerib's office.

07:13 The fire brigade has arrived. Somehow they maneuver their fire engine into the quad and raise a giant ladder up to Fatty, who has by now lost feeling in his entire body.

07:16 Rambo exits Sparerib's office and they disappear into Glockenshpeel's office.

07:23 Reverend Bishop hurries into the headmaster's office.

07:42 The fire brigade wrenches Fatty free and lowers him to the ground with the help of a winch crane.

07:43 Glockenshpeel, Sparerib, Reverend Bishop, and Rambo are there to meet him on his return to earth. Reverend Bishop holds his hand and says a prayer as Fatty lies on the stretcher. Glockenshpeel glares at Fatty and Sparerib gently pats his shoulder. As they wheel Fatty toward the sanatorium, Rambo leans over and whispers something into Fatty's ear. The big fella grins and is then wheeled away.

07:50 Rambo has performed a miracle (literally). A fourteen-year-old boy has convinced the chaplain that Fatty underwent a massive religious conversion in the night. Rambo's story goes that after speaking in tongues (whatever that means), Fatty stripped off his clothes and forced his way into the chapel, whereupon he was confronted by the Holy Spirit. After his spiritual conversion Fatty tried to return to the dormitory to spread the good news. Unfortunately, he was cruelly trapped in the chapel window.

Rambo has instructed us all to say that we were sleeping and have no idea what went down in the middle of the night. He reckoned that Sparerib and Glockenshpeel didn't believe the story at all and knew we were night swimming, but they didn't have the heart to ruin Reverend Bishop's moment after the idiot wept tears of joy in the headmaster's office.

08:00 The story has spread like wildfire. At breakfast a number of older boys kept sidling up to our table to shake Rambo's hand and beg for a retelling of the unbelievable events inside the headmaster's office. With each retelling, the story became more exaggerated and by the time we were noshing our egg and bacon, it had reached epic proportions.

Due to the rain, all cricket practices have been canceled. Despite my heroics of last week I am hugely relieved and plan a day of sleep and recovery.

Pike woke us up sometime before lunch to tell us that he knows that we were on a night swim and he's going to blow Rambo's story wide open. He left us with a malicious snigger and the image of him scratching his bollocks.

Rambo demanded five bucks from each of us and then sprinted out of the dormitory.

Rambo has bribed the guards into keeping silent. (He reckons they are the only loophole in his story.)

17:15 We all visited Fatty in the sanatorium and took him a bar of chocolate and some biscuits. Reverend Bishop was sitting at his bedside whispering quietly to him. Fatty seemed to be sleeping. The Reverend left when we arrived and beamed proudly at us as if we were Fatty's disciples. As soon as he was gone, Fatty woke up and told us that the idiotic chaplain hadn't left his bedside all day. He reckoned he would rather have been beaten by Glockenshpeel than listen to the rantings of the loon.

He seemed to be feeling better, though, and wolfed down the bar of chocolate and box of biscuits without chewing. He said he would be released in the morning. After a few minutes nobody could think of anything else to say, so we all shook his hand and left.

I called home to find out about Dad's court case and visit to the mental asylum. Surprisingly, he seemed in great spirits. He told me that the neighbors have dropped the charges against him because they say their point has been made. Dad reckons he was considering defending himself in the trial. He's convinced that he'd know what he was doing after re-watching three episodes of both *L.A.*

Law and *Matlock*. Unfortunately, the magistrate has ordered Dad to have six months of rage counseling. During this time he is forbidden to move or leave the country.

Mom cried when she heard my voice and promised they would be at next week's cricket match. After hanging up I had another desperate running-away moment, which was broken by Earthworm ordering me to make him his tea and toast and straighten his bed.

20:00 The whole house gathered in the common room for the Saturday night movie, which was *Rain Man*, starring Tom Cruise and Dustin Hoffman. Hoffman was brilliant as the retarded brother who can add up numbers faster than a calculator. After about twenty minutes somebody shouted out, "Hey, check, it's Vern Blackadder!" There was a brief pause and then the whole house erupted. Poor Vern pretended to be sleeping in the darkness of the corner, but everyone knew he was faking it. At last moggy Vern has a nickname.

Monday 31st January

06:15 Entered the showers to find Julian examining Gecko's bum. Bert and Julian shared a wink and then Julian ordered Gecko back to the sanatorium immediately. Gecko's wound has gone septic and he's still convinced it's a dog bite. Rambo warned him not to tell the sanatorium sister that he was bitten by one of the guard dogs and told him to say it was a bite he got over the holidays.

06:30 Rain Man wasn't at roll call. His bed was made, but there's no sign of him.

08:00 Word has spread of Rain Man's disappearance. Everybody has their own story. Mad Dog reckons he's hiding somewhere in the hills. Rambo says he could be under the house and Simon is convinced that he's an alien and never really existed in the first place.

Boggo played a nasty trick on Mr. Crispo during our double history lesson. After watching the video of Dunkirk again, Boggo asked the kindly old fossil a question really loudly. Crispo immediately adjusted his hearing aid, but Boggo then spoke in a soft whisper. Rambo joined Boggo in the ruse, which eventually turned the lesson into a complete farce. Poor Crispo became so upset that he ripped out his hearing aid, threw it on the floor, and jumped on it in a fit of blind rage. (Deaf rage?) He then dismissed us sadly. Once again I could see his eyes grow watery as he watched us trudge out of his classroom.

After English, I returned *Waiting for Godot* to The Guv and told him how much I liked the play. He was thrilled that I loved it and we got into a long conversation about the themes and characters. He asked me who I thought the mystical Godot character was. I told him I reckoned he was a slave trader.

His theory is that Godot is actually God and that the entire play is about modern man, who has gone spiritually bankrupt and destitute. According to The Guv, human beings are forever waiting for a spiritual entity to give some meaning to their lives. I wasn't sure if he was talking about God or other things like ghosts and spirits, but I didn't have the guts to ask because he might have laughed at me and called me a cretin. He called this double meaning *allagree* and told me to write the word down and use it as often as possible.

Our discussion went on for ages, only for me to realize that I had completely missed lunch. The Guv invited me back to his house, where his wife (a sweet lady, with blue eyes and warm smile) had made roast lamb. The Guv insisted that I have half a glass of wine, saying it's not every day he has the great John Milton over for lunch! By the time I'd finished my half glass, The Guv was already on to his second bottle of Boschendal Cabernet Sauvignon

1987 and was reciting Shakespeare's sonnets with his terrified cat (Ophelia) clinging to his cardigan.

After his second bottle of wine he led me to his study, which was covered wall to wall with books. He gave me *Catcher in the Rye*, by an American called J. D. Salinger, and said he wanted it finished within the week. He made me rinse my mouth out with toothpaste before leaving and ordered me not to tell anybody about the wine. I walked back to school, holding my book close to my chest and trying not to breathe.

Earthworm threatened me with punishment for neglecting my afternoon duties.

18:00 Still no sign of Rain Man. Sparerib has called his mother. (According to Boggo, his father died when he was young—which could explain why he's demented.)

20:00 Sparerib called us one by one into his office to ask us questions about Rain Man. I told him that he was quiet and a bit weird and that he was eating a sock last night but that I didn't think he was on the verge of a breakdown (which is a lie, but I didn't have the heart to tell him that Vern is plain demented). He asked me if Vern was ever bullied emotionally or physically. I shook my head. (Another lie. This place is turning me into a complete fraud!)

Pike paid his nightly visit and told us we were to blame for the disappearance of Rain Man. He reckoned that Rain Man had committed suicide and that his ghost would return to the dormitory for vengeance. He spat a huge greeny onto the wall and then left making eerie ghost noises.

I have survived January. One month down—only ten to go!

Tuesday 1st February

Still no sign of Rain Man. Sparerib seems to spend all his time in meetings with Luthuli and Glockenshpeel. Reverend Bishop even held a prayer session in the crypt for my missing cubicle mate. We all felt obliged to attend—which predictably moved the Reverend to tears. He was especially happy to see Fatty and invited him to read from the Bible.

After spending ages poring over the gigantic library dictionary, I finally discovered that The Guv's word is spelled *allegory*. It means a parable, symbol, or metaphor.

Julian informed us at lights-out that Gecko has had a large stone removed from his bum at Greys Hospital in Pietermaritzburg. He asked us to keep Gecko's bum in mind, adding that it was never far from his own thoughts. With a chuckle he flicked off the light switch and skipped away singing ABBA's "Gimme Gimme Gimme a Man after Midnight."

Wednesday 2nd February

Still no news of Rain Man. The school is split on the issue. Half the boys believe Pike and say he's dead. The other half believes Simon, who says he's an alien and never existed in the first place. I reckon he jumped the night train and headed toward home, but with Rain Man, I have learned to expect the unexpected.

The entire school was ordered to report to our common rooms because the new president, F. W. de Klerk, was delivering his open-ing-of-parliament speech. The bald Afrikaner told the country that he was going to change South Africa and dismantle apartheid. With one flick of his podgy finger he unbanned the African National Congress (ANC) and declared that he would free Nelson

Mandela. Mostly for the white kids staring at the TV, this didn't seem to matter much, but judging by the faces of the four black boys, including our head of house, Luthuli, this was something huge and incredible. After the speech groups of older boys stood outside the house, with hands in pockets, deep in conversation about the speech. Gavin, the prefect under the stairs, looked angry and spoke quietly to Greg Anderson while absentmindedly stroking Barry, his pet frog. Luthuli and the other black boys marched across the quad as a group, chatting excitedly to each other. A hot wind blew papers and leaves around the cloisters, and everything seemed sticky and on edge.

17:00 Rushed through my homework so that I could get back to *Catcher in the Rye*. It's a great book about a guy who doesn't fit in and runs away from school. Makes me think about Rain Man. I wonder where he is right now and whether he's happier there than he was here. It could be so easy to be a Holden Caulfield—to run away and venture out into the great beyond. My wild imaginings were brought to a screeching halt by Bert challenging Rambo to an arm wrestle. Rambo won, and an irate Bert ordered him to write a five-thousand-word essay on respect.

Thursday 3rd February

Glockenshpeel called an emergency school assembly in the Great Hall. Expecting some tragic news of Rain Man, we trudged into the hall fearing the worst. Instead our headmaster unleashed a tirade about vandalism and destruction of property. He looked wickedly savage as he studied the rows of faces in front of him. Nobody could meet his gaze, which made us all look as guilty as hell. He roared on about how someone had stuck a banana in the exhaust pipe of his Toyota Cressida and when he had switched on his car, the engine exploded. I stared at the floor for fear of catching somebody's eye and bursting into fits of laughter. The staff seated behind him looked grim, although I could detect a hint of a smile on the smacker of The Guv, who was as desperate not to crack up as we all were.

Glockenshpeel demanded that the vandal raise his hand immediately and take his punishment like a man. Surely nobody in his right mind would raise his hand in the face of this raging madman. A long silence followed as everybody looked around the hall for the culprit. No confession was forthcoming, so the enraged Glockenshpeel sat in a chair and said we would all wait in the hall until the criminal came forward.

09:00 Still no sign of the vandal. The school sat in awkward silence except for The Guv, who cheerfully unrolled the morning newspaper. Great news is that we've already missed twenty minutes of Psycho's double maths class.

09:45 Still waiting. Very jealous of The Guv's newspaper. Wished I had *Catcher* with me. Sixty-five minutes of maths gone. If the criminal could just hold out for another forty-five minutes . . .

10:06 A small boy near the front tentatively raised his hand. Four hundred boys, fifty teachers, and Glockenshpeel fastened their eyes on the terrified youngster. Glockenshpeel was out of his seat. "Yes?"

The poor boy gulped and then said in a thin voice, "Please, sir, I need the toilet." Glockenshpeel's eyes narrowed, and without so much as a word he picked up his papers and stormed out of the hall! The teachers followed, and so the great siege was broken. The hero's name was Ben Thomas, a first-year in Woodall house, nickname Tadpole.

15:00 Sparerib ordered us to stay in our dormitory because the police were coming to investigate the disappearance of Rain Man. As soon as he'd left, Mad Dog dived into his locker and threw four pigeon heads out of the window. He reckoned they might think he was psychotic and had murdered Rain Man.

Two very big policemen with great bushy moustaches rifled through Vern's stuff. The one called De Kock kept asking me questions and making notes. He was very interested in the fact that Vern wet his bed. Mad Dog asked if he could fire the policeman's gun. The policeman refused. He then asked if he could handcuff me to my bed. The policeman refused. He asked the policeman if he'd killed anyone. The policeman stared at him and then said that he only killed people who asked too many questions. Mad Dog then (stupidly) asked, "Why?" De Kock nudged his partner and said, "No wonder the poor kid ran away."

Simon caught Boggo wanking in his rugby sock. (Boggo's sock, I mean, not Simon's.)

18:00 The entire school sang the chanting song "He's a Wanker" as Boggo entered the dining hall. Mr. Crispo, no longer wearing his hearing aid, didn't hear a thing and continued eating his macaroni, unaware of the chaos around him.

Crept down to the showers after lights-out and examined my willy in the mirror. Still no hairs and no sign of becoming like the others. Rambo told me that when my balls drop, I'll get another nickname. Wonder when I can start wanking. Pulled my willy a few times but nothing happened, so I went back to bed and read another chapter of *Catcher* under my duvet using Rain Man's torchlight.

Friday 4th February

Gecko's back from the hospital. He can't sit down, so he has to eat and attend class standing up. He proudly showed us the stone that was taken out of his bum, although he's still convinced that it's a dog's tooth.

The story of Rain Man's disappearance hit the front page of the evening paper. There was a big color picture of him with a bizarre Christmas hat on. He looked completely moggy. The article took a dig at the school, trying to blame it for Vern's disappearance. It said, "It is unbelievable that a boy could walk out of one of the top private schools in the country without so much as a trace. What kind of establishment is this, a school or a luxury hotel?" (If this is their idea of a luxury hotel, then they can't have much of a life.)

18:15 Pike was lashed six strokes by Sparerib after Luthuli caught him smoking in the drying room. We applauded every stroke and laughed like maniacs when he flew out of the office rubbing his behind. In his seething rage, he chased after Boggo and tripped and fell in the gutter. (There has to be a god out there!)

It's been a week since the epic night swim and Fatty still hasn't returned to his normal bubbly self. Every afternoon he lopes off to the archives room and busies himself among pages and pages of clippings, articles, and pictures. He's lost his appetite and doesn't talk to us anymore. Maybe he really did have a conversion in the church after all.

Saturday 5th February

17:00 Feeling homesick, so I called the folks. Mom said Dad was in the garage and had been acting strange since De Klerk announced the unbanning of the ANC and the release of Nelson Mandela. They reckon South Africa is about to go up in flames.

Boggo said he heard a story about Rain Man on the radio. (Boggo always listens to the English First Division results over the radio. He's a rabid supporter of Manchester United.)

Watched *The Revenge of the Nerds*, which had everyone rolling around on the floor. (Bert even chipped his tooth after head butting a third-year called Guy Emberton by mistake.) Poor Gecko had to remain standing throughout the movie because of his infected bum.

Eerie discovery: Rain Man's laundry bag is full of dirty clothes. I'm sure it was empty yesterday. His pajamas, toothbrush, and torchlight are also missing. I could swear I used his torchlight the other night—somebody must be wearing his clothes! Rambo reckons the culprit is most probably Julian, who's been known to wear other people's clothing. (On Monday he ran around the showers with Lionel Jarman's sleeping shorts on his head.)

23:20 Still awake and thinking about Rain Man. Also wondering what will happen to South Africa. What will this Mandela be like? Is he really a communist? (To be honest, I'm not quite sure what a communist is, but Dad's terrified of them.) Took *Catcher* down to the bogs to read for a couple of hours.

Sunday 6th February

02:15 Earthworm caught me reading in the bogs and ordered me to remake his bed, brew him some tea, and clean his cricket boots.

Back in bed but can't sleep because Mad Dog's snoring. It sounds like a herd of buffalo grazing in our dormitory. I hurled one of Rain Man's school shoes at him but hit Simon by mistake. Simon leaped out of bed and shrieked with fright. I quickly pretended to be sleeping and did a fairly realistic snore with my mouth open and just a hint of drool on the side of my lower lip.

08:00 Julian did a beautiful solo of the hymn "Abide with Me." His voice is amazing. I confess to getting goose bumps. Reverend Bishop spoke about Rain Man and told the story of the lost sheep and the shepherd. We then prayed for him and his safe return. I put in an extra prayer for Rain Man just in case the big man upstairs wasn't tuned into Reverend Bishop's frequency.

21:15 Discovered the disappearance of Rain Man's pillows. Not sure if I should tell a prefect—I wouldn't want to rat on somebody by mistake—so I have decided to keep it to myself.

Finished *Catcher in the Rye* just in time—a great book in my opinion.

22:45 Rambo and Boggo are doing teacher impersonations. If you close your eyes, you would think Rambo is The Guv. Boggo enacted a whole scene involving Crispo and his hearing aid; it was wickedly cruel but wickedly funny!

Monday 7th February

One week since Vern's disappearance; still no word on his whereabouts.

The Guv invited me over to lunch again. This time we had beef stroganoff—delicious. Once again we drank wine together and discussed politics and literature.

The Guv reckons De Klerk's speech was one of the most amazing moments in South African history. He says I should document this moment to reflect on in years to come. I told him I keep a diary. The Guv was mightily impressed and said I was on the path to being a great writer like my namesake. He then said he was anxious to see what Nelson Mandela looked like. (He's been in prison for twenty-seven years for sabotage.) He's pretty sure that he will be our next president. I wonder what it will be like to have a black president?

We chatted for hours about *Catcher in the Rye*. He told me that it was the only meaningful book that Salinger wrote and that the man has become an absolute recluse from society. (I think I will one day become a reclusive writer, marry Julia Roberts, and live in a mansion near a swamp.) After finishing a second bottle of wine, The Guv delivered Hamlet's "To be or not to be" speech. It was brilliant. Unfortunately, when going on about the mortal coil bit, he swung his arm around and knocked over a lamp, which shattered all over his study floor. His wife cleaned up the mess and told me it was time to go. As I was leaving, I watched her half carrying The Guv to bed.

17:00 Earthworm gave me finger tongs with the blackboard duster for continually neglecting my duties. My middle finger feels like it could be broken. I didn't show any sign of pain despite the fact that my fingers felt like they were smashed. Instead I defiantly stared into Earthworm's beady little eyes while he was doing it. I think the glass of wine gave me confidence.

Boggo has a dirty magazine but has refused to say where he got it from. We all pored over the pictures of large-breasted women in naughty poses and sexy underwear. Rambo told me that I was wasting my time looking because I was only a spud and that my only hope of wanking was with a pair of tweezers. Everybody laughed. I felt the blood rushing to my face and tried my best to laugh along. I then went back to my cubicle in disgrace and felt humiliated.

Tuesday 8th February

06:15 I woke up and discovered that Vern's duvet and pillows have now also disappeared. I couldn't help but shout out in shock to the others, who charged over to my cubicle and then all began arguing over what happened. P. J. Luthuli, on a dorm check, overheard the commotion and learned the mysteries of Rain Man's bed. He shouted at me for not telling him earlier and strode off to find Sparerib.

Fatty told us at breakfast that he had unearthed some interesting stuff in the archives about an English teacher who hanged himself in the chapel in 1944. He says he'll fill us in after lights-out.

The Guv was absent from school today. The replacement teacher, Mr. Linton, looked remarkably like a chicken and told us that The Guv has the flu. (A hangover, more like it.) Mr. Linton told us all about Nelson Mandela (who'll be released tomorrow). He spoke of Mandela like he was a saint or a god or something but warned us that any man locked up for twenty-seven years for doing what he felt was right must be pretty pissed off. He advised us not to be scared (chicken), though, and to face the dawn of a new South Africa with hope and an open mind.

During drama Eve said that she'd fought all her life for freedom in South Africa and now it was upon us. She warned us of people close to us (including staff) who would try and poison our minds about black people and the new South Africa. She then made us hold hands and taught us the words to a freedom song called "Nkosi Sikelele." It was all in Zulu, so none of us knew what we were singing. (I have no doubt that Dad would call Eve a bleeding heart communist.) Rambo refused to hold hands with anyone, so Eve asked him to stay behind after class. Rambo reckons Eve is concerned that he's "affection phobic" and is determined to release him from his inhibitions.

Sparerib took our cricket practice in the absence of The Guv. He looked pale and distracted. What with Fatty, Rain Man, the childhood lion attack, and having a communist for a wife, I'm not surprised.

Reverend Bishop held a candle ceremony for our country. He also lit one for Rain Man and asked God to bless his soul. It seems that even the people of God are starting to lose hope that Vern is still alive. Around the school all the talk is about Rain Man and Mandela—Mad Dog's dad (Dad Dog) phoned to tell him that the civil war begins tomorrow.

Fatty is still gathering information about the teacher who hanged himself and said that he'll only reveal all once he's satisfied that he's covered all possible sources. It sounds wickedly interesting. Rambo's started calling Fatty by the name of Jessica, after the TV detective Jessica Fletcher. I reckon Fatty is trying to string us along with old murder stories and actually has no juice at all.

Wednesday 9th February

11:00 Crammed into the common room to watch the release of Nelson Mandela. The huge crowd outside the Victor Verster prison in Cape Town screamed as an old man with a gentle face and a huge smile walked free, holding the hand of his wife, Winnie. (Dad says Winnie is worse than Satan.) I felt all choked up with emotion—I couldn't believe that this smiling old man was really a communist terrorist. Around me the white boys just stared blankly at the screen. Floods of tears were rolling down Luthuli's face.

Pike suddenly threw a science book at the TV and shouted, "Well, there goes the country!" Luthuli leapt over the couch and grabbed Pike, roughly forcing him up against the wall. For a moment he seemed certain to hit him, but then his body relaxed, he smiled, and went back to his seat. (Let's hope Mandela will

show us whites the same mercy.)

I feel wickedly guilty about being a white person. I'm only thirteen, but I wish I'd known about apartheid and fought it like Eve. Rambo said that Eve told him during one of their meditation practices that she was arrested as a student in the seventies.

15:00 Dad phoned in a blind panic. He's just stocked up with supplies to last a year, nailed the doors and windows shut to keep out the communists, and he's got his spade ready to dig himself out of trouble like the Jews in Nazi Germany. He's also fired our maid, Innocence, who he says might be a terrorist. He then screamed and said the barbarian communists were at the door and slammed the phone down.

15:02 Dad phoned back to say that it wasn't the barbarians but my mother, who was locked out. He warned me that there are communists under every bush and that anarchy is upon us. I told him my drama teacher was a freedom fighter. He screamed and slammed down the phone again.

15:03 Mom phoned to tell me that Dad's been under a lot of stress lately and not to pay too much attention to his mad ravings. She apologized for not coming to my cricket match but said Dad had been too busy digging a trench in the back garden.

Boggo ran in to supper to tell us that they've found Rain Man alive. We rushed outside and saw Luthuli and Sparerib leading Rain Man across the quad toward the sanatorium. Sparerib's cat, Roger, followed closely behind with his tail raised like a TV antenna. Rain Man was wrapped in a blanket, his face black and his eyes as wild as ever.

Boggo got the scoop from Luthuli that Rain Man had been found under the crypt. He's been living there in absolute squalor and scavenging food from the rubbish dump. He would occasionally creep back into the dormitory at night to take things from his

locker. Apparently he'd spent the nine days under the crypt with only Roger for company. Boggo reckons the school counselor, a weird-looking man called Dr. Zoodenberg, took Rain Man down to the Town Hill loony bin for observation.

Thursday 10th February

Haven't spoken to Earthworm the entire week. I perform my duties in absolute silence and answer his questions with nods and grunts. He looks wickedly guilty and even offered me a bite of his tuna snackwich—which I gallantly refused.

08:15 Loud shouting interrupted The Glock's opening prayer during assembly. Gordon Wrexham, a final-year matric, had an epileptic fit and then abruptly fell asleep. Nobody seemed overly concerned (apparently this happens regularly). They just laid him out in the aisle and The Glock continued.

The Glock announced that Vernon Blackadder was safe and resting quietly. He also told us rather formally that the school, which has apparently always supported multiracialism and liberalism, welcomed the release of Mandela and looked forward to a bright future for South Africa. Eve led a standing ovation, her armful of silver bangles sounding like a tambourine. A couple of teachers refused to clap, including the frightening Mr. Wade (nickname Norm), Mr. van Vuuren, and Mr. Crispo, who obviously didn't know what was going on without his non-faulty hearing aid.

The Glock brought the applause to an end with a vicious swish of his academic gown. Like a giant vulture lurking over a carcass, he reminded us that he was still hot on the trail of the banana vandal and that he would not rest until the criminal had been apprehended.

The Guv dropped a book into my lap at lunch. It's called *Catch 22*, by Joseph Heller. The others at the table (Fatty, Rambo, and Boggo) ragged me about being The Guv's pet. I dare not tell them about the Monday lunch visits.

Inside the front cover The Guv left a note that read:

Dear Milton,
Sorry about that tawdry business on Monday. What did I tell you about this Mandela chappy? Destined for greatness, I'd say. This Catch 22 *is a masterpiece—absurd, funny, shocking. Get stuck in, boyo. I look forward to more debates next Monday!*

The Guv

22:00 Boggo reckons that Vern's undergoing brain scans in the nuthouse. He said that in all probability, he would be in a straitjacket right now. Rambo then joined in and the pair did a wicked impersonation of Rain Man and a psychologist in the nuthouse. Felt guilty to be laughing my head off.

Friday 11th February

Innocence, our former maid, has been to the labor court and is planning to sue for unfair dismissal. Dad is in a wicked panic.

11:00 Rambo's been dropped for Steven George (whose ribs have been repaired). Tomorrow we play Arlington High, a school in Pietermaritzburg that everyone says we should easily beat. The Guv's warned us about overconfidence. He said if we cock this up, then we'll all be disemboweled with a pair of rusty kitchen scissors. Mad Dog asked The Guv what "disemboweled" meant. The Guv said he would gut him like a fish—Mad Dog whistled and looked impressed.

Double drama (my highlight of the week) saw us doing improvisations (where you make up a scene and a character on the spot). Boggo was excellent. He pretended he was a drunken doctor trying to amputate Fatty's left leg. I pretended I was a butterfly collector in the South American jungle looking for a rare specimen. Rambo said he was a sex maniac and chased Eve around, who screamed and giggled like a little girl. At the end of the class, in an attempt to vent all our anger and frustration, she made us scream as loudly as we could. Mr. Lilly, the art teacher, whose studio is below the drama room, sprinted in with the first aid kit thinking there'd been a horrific accident.

Saturday 12th February

I found a chocolate on my bed and a note from Earthworm that read:

> *Sorry about the finger tongs. I was having a bad day.*

Victory is mine!

Sunday 13th February

Spent the day reading *Catch 22*. Some passages are so funny and absurd that I couldn't help chuckling out loud. In the afternoon, during free bounds, I crossed the railway line and stretched out and read under the pine trees. Some minutes later I noticed Boggo creeping through the fence carrying his porno magazine. He looked around suspiciously and then snuck into some thick bushes. I pretended not to see him.

Middle of the night. Woke up to wild screams. I disentangled myself from my Good Knight duvet to discover that Simon was on fire. Pike had set him alight with a lighter and a can of deodorant. Pike's sidekick, Devries, then poured an entire rubbish bin of water over my cricket captain before sprinting out the dormitory cackling and jeering.

Simon, Rambo, and Mad Dog sat together and discussed revenge. When I joined the group, Rambo stopped talking, stared at me, and said, "I don't remember inviting you over here, Spud." I gulped and blushed and went back to my cubicle, feeling humiliated.

Monday 14th February

Four days to the long weekend!

Valentine's Day. All the boys eagerly await letters and cards. I don't know any girls, so I joined the ranks of those who pretended to be busy at break time.

Simon got five cards, Rambo two, and Mad Dog got one, although judging by the spelling and writing it's most likely that he sent it to himself. The envelope was addressed:

Deer Mad Dog

And there was no stamp.

One of Simon's cards was erotic. The girl said she wanted to get hot and steamy with him. The card smelled of perfume and was signed *Your Horny Admirer*. Boggo asked Simon if he could have the card. Simon refused. Boggo asked if he could borrow it briefly. Simon refused. Boggo then offered Simon free use of his porno magazine. Simon handed over the card.

Lunch again with The Guv. This time he only had a single glass of wine. He said he really likes my parents and called them humble people. He reckons that money is the world's greatest corrupter. We chatted about *Catch 22* and he asked me to read some extracts aloud. We both cackled away at the "Major Major" section and the hilarious wit of Yossarian.

On the way back to the house I noticed Roger the cat prowling around outside the crypt. He looked dreadful. He's all skin and bones and half his fur has fallen out.

Everybody's talking about what they are going to do on the weekend. (Friday is our midterm break and we all get to go home for a long weekend.) Rambo, Simon, and Boggo are returning to Johannesburg. Mad Dog's going to Mozambique on a fishing trip with his older brother (Bad Dog). Fatty and I return to Durban, and Gecko's staying at school because his folks are overseas. Rain Man is still at home, and Boggo reckons that he probably won't be coming back. I kind of miss the odd thunk of hair being pulled out and the general weirdness of my cubicle mate.

Tuesday 15th February

Three days to go!

08:00 Glockenshpeel called an emergency assembly. As he swept into the hall with his dark gown flaring out behind him, I couldn't help but notice the faintest glint of a smile across his lips. After a prayer and a few announcements he told the school about Mad Dog's hat trick and then called him up and shook his hand. Mad Dog made a funny bow to the boys after shaking the big man's hand and received some raucous laughter and a few hisses. Unfortunately, it wasn't the bow that was stirring up the crowd but rather the fact that Mad Dog's fly was down and he was wearing bright red underpants.

Once the hilarity had faded, The Glock stared grimly at us and then said slowly, "I believe my investigations into the banana vandalism affair have borne fruit. Would Stott and Emberton report to my office immediately." With that he stalked out of the hall with long strides and a great air of triumph. After a deathly hush we all began to whisper among ourselves. Emberton, a third-year from our house, smiled and gave the "V" sign in defiance. Stott, a third-year from King house, looked pale and terrified.

Break-time news was that Emberton and Stott were ratted on by a first-year called Peter Scrawley (now named Rat Face and worse) from King house, who saw Emberton and Stott leaving the house late at night with a bunch of bananas. A hit has already been placed on his head. The two suspects spent the morning in meetings with Glockenshpeel.

18:00 Emberton and Stott have been suspended, pending expulsion. This means they've been ordered to go home and their expulsion will become finalized once Glockenshpeel has consulted with the board of governors.

Rumor has it that Scrawley was found unconscious in the King house bogs. Apparently, somebody clubbed him from behind with a cricket bat. Boggo says he's been sent home.

22:00 Emberton, dressed in civvies, is talking quietly to Mad Dog in his cubicle. (Boggo says they're second cousins.) The whispering goes on long into the night.

Wednesday 16th February

Two days to go!

The Glock told the assembly that Emberton and Stott are to be expelled and that their parents have already removed them from the school.

Mad Dog lowered the house flag to half-mast after assembly. Sparerib saw him and gave him hard labor.

13:00   A big notice on the house board read:

> SCHOOL PLAY. THIS YEAR'S SCHOOL PLAY WILL
>   BE *OLIVER*. SINGING AUDITIONS WILL BE HELD
>   TOMORROW AFTERNOON IN THE MUSIC CENTER.

Drama was canceled and we were told to read three chapters on medieval theater history instead under the watchful eye of Mr. Cartwright. Eve has rushed Roger to the vet after he collapsed outside the crypt, where he's been waiting for Rain Man.

Pike pissed on Gecko in the showers. Devries was waiting with his camera as Gecko charged into the toilet with his hand over his mouth. Bert was there but thought the whole scene absolutely hilarious.

Mad Dog told us he was going bat hunting and skulked out of the dormitory. From my window I watched him creep around the cloisters of the main quad and then slip down toward the exterior door of the crypt.

After no more than ten minutes, Mad Dog crept back into the dormitory looking pale and nervous. He said that he couldn't find any bats and that he wasn't feeling well. I felt strangely uneasy tonight—been thinking about Vern and Roger the cat and the expulsion of Emberton, who seems like a good guy with much spirit and humor.

Thursday 17th February

One day to go!
Woke up wet. Rain was pouring through my open window. The first chill of autumn is about and for the first time I put on my gray polo-necked jersey.

Our third assembly in a row. Glockenshpeel entered the hall in a furious rage. Another banana had been planted in his car's exhaust pipe. This time he'd spotted the dangerous fruit before any damage was done. He was so steamed that he threatened to expel the whole school if he had to. With that he stormed out of the hall, leaving everyone staring after him in fear and amazement.

15:00 Even more terror shot through me as I discovered a long line of boys waiting to audition for the school play. After an hour of waiting I at last had my chance. I entered a small room and there stood Eve, a savage-looking master called Mr. Richardson (nickname Viking), and Ms. Roberts, who sat at the piano. Eve greeted me with a warm smile. On her lap lay a half-bald Roger, who stared vacantly at the ceiling.

Viking said, "Right, Master Milton, let's see what you can do." He then asked me to sing a song called "I'll Do Anything," which I vaguely knew from primary school. I suddenly felt terrified, and my voice came out all weak and shaky like it was coming from somewhere other than my own mouth. After a few lines Viking stood up and shouted, "Thank you. Next!" With that any hopes for a career as an actor were obliterated. The next minute I was outside and walking slowly back through the gray drizzle to the house. I felt crushed; my first and only audition had been a complete disaster. I moped into the common room, sank into a chair, and tried to watch the soap operas.

Boggo reckons that Emberton and Stott may not be expelled. They were clearly not at school last night and now have a stronger case for their innocence. (Emberton's father is also an influential sugar farmer who has donated thousands to the school. Apparently he's furious and considering a lawsuit.)

I think I know who planted last night's banana.

Friday 18th February

Long weekend!

11:00 Hundreds of luxury cars lined Pilgrim's Walk. Under the trees to the left of the driveway were two old smoky buses that looked older than Crispo. I boarded the Durban bus and through the dusty window I saw Rambo being hugged by a strong-looking man with a shaved head. The two of them then jumped into a green sports car and sped away. I sat next to Fatty (and nearly fell off the tiny edge of the seat that was left). The 158-kilometer journey seemed endless. Fatty fell asleep and breathed fish paste breath all over me. I didn't mind because I was going home but made a mental note not to sit next to him on the trip back to school on Monday.

Mom picked me up at the Westville shopping center looking hot and bothered and not at all pleased to see me. She said Dad was being impossible and had charged off to buy guns. She reckoned his fear of communists was excessive even by apartheid standards. When I arrived home, I could see that Mom wasn't exaggerating. Dad has converted our house into an army bunker. The garden fence is now barbed wire. The gates are ten feet high, and every window and door has been barricaded up with wooden planks. Dad has enforced a strict lights-out rule from sunset to sunrise. (When else do you use lights?) Inside the house, hundreds of candles flickered, making the place look like a palm-reading center. Dad reckons the first thing the terrorists will go for is your electricity.

It took ages for us to clamber up the ladder and squeeze my

bags down through the trapdoor in the roof. Mom kept shaking her head and mumbling under her breath about madness following her wherever she went. We then struggled down another ladder and found ourselves in my parents' bathroom, which had a burning gas lamp perched on the toilet bowl.

Seated at the dining room table, my father was furiously trying to put together the pieces of his new rifle, which he had just taken apart. In the dim candlelight he looked terrible. Unwashed hair, thick stubble, creased clothes, and a mad look in his eyes. I suspect he failed to recognize me because he looked up at me, nodded vaguely, and said, "Howzit, Bob," before returning to his gun.

Besides all the weirdness it was good to be home, to enjoy some peace with no sirens and bells ringing every half hour. This peace was unfortunately shattered a little after four when Mom ordered Dad to clean himself up and stop behaving like an idiot. My mother's book club was arriving at 19:00 and she wanted my father to take the planks off the doors so that her guests wouldn't have to clamber onto the roof and into the toilet to get into the house. Dad sensed that he was on the brink of losing the argument and ran into the bathroom and locked the door. Mom continued shouting vile obscenities at him through it, but my father stayed silent, defiantly refusing to retaliate.

19:00 My mother's book club cronies filed in, each trying to talk louder than the next. Mom had me serving drinks (a full-time job). Every time I entered with more drinks, the room went quiet, and then as I left, the raucous conversations flared up again. (As if I didn't know they were talking about their husbands and sex.)

I entered the lounge for about the twelfth time carrying a tray of drinks when suddenly I was struck dumb by a sight so lovely, so . . . unreal, that I very nearly lost control of the tray. Standing before me was a mermaid (without a fishtail), a girl so beautiful that a sharp pang shot through my body and made my left leg go numb.

"Johnny, this is Marge's daughter Debbie." The introduction

came from my mother, but her voice sounded miles away. This creature with big green eyes, golden skin, and long wispy blond hair smiled at me with perfectly shaped gleaming white teeth and said one word that nearly flattened me with its beauty.

"Hi."

"Jean, I promised Debs a swim in your pool, if that's all right," said Marge to my mother. My mother swung her hands wildly and whiskey sloshed over the side of her glass. "Of course. Johnny, get Debbie a towel and show her the pool." I gulped, trying desperately not to look at the creature standing opposite me. I could feel my cheeks flush and knew that my face was as red as a stop sign. Eventually, I mumbled something and the creature skipped off to my room to change. The thought of her taking her clothes off in my room made me feel weak. I remembered that my planes-and-trains underpants were lying on the floor in full view. I felt nauseous. I wished I had a video camera in my room to record the moment forever, just to prove it actually happened. (Besides, I could probably make a fortune peddling the tape to Boggo.)

I took ages to choose the right towel for Debbie, and then I waited in the passage for her arrival in a complete state of terror. I didn't have to wait long. She skipped past me, yanked the wrong towel from my hands, and slipped through the back door and into the pool before I had time to move or think or even pinch myself.

"Come on, Johnny, it's warm." She giggled and splashed me with water. I did the only thing a thirteen-year-old boy could do in such a situation and that was attempt a very macho Olympic dive. What followed was a catastrophic belly flop (a groin flop would be more specific). I sank to the bottom of the pool, where I let out a howling scream of agony bubbles. I took my time floating to the surface—and there she was. The Mermaid. Staring at me with her enormous green eyes. And then . . . laughter, the sound of angels. She was laughing at me, but not with the cruel laughter of school. This laughter seemed beautiful and soft and warm, like the sound of a flute. Then I was laughing too, and the world was spinning and for once this wasn't a dream. I would not suddenly wake up in a cramped little cubicle with a siren screeching in my ears. I was home.

Saturday 19th February

06:00 Mom woke me up and said I had to search the garden for Dad.

Found Dad sleeping in some shrubs at the bottom of the garden. Around him were two empty wine bottles and a Kentucky Fried Chicken bucket filled with bones. (Not sure if wine and Kentucky qualify as living off the land?)

Mom threw a bucket of water over him and ordered him to bathe. After disentangling himself from the shrubbery, Dad loped off to the house shaking his head and talking to himself.

I went back to bed and tried to remember every detail of last night. Unfortunately, it all seemed a blur. I struggled to remember the Mermaid's face. I must be in love. (Haven't felt like this since the morning after *Pretty Woman*.)

Spent the afternoon watching cricket on TV. Unfortunately, because of apartheid, we don't play international cricket (sometimes rebel sides come out and play against us, but it's not the real thing). Today it's Transvaal against Western Province, but it's a four-day game, so everything happens really slowly. Dad joined me, looking surprisingly normal again. He said he was sorry for his behavior and mumbled on about being under stress.

Our family is going out to dinner. (No doubt my father's trying to prove his sanity to us.) Mom looked far happier and even kissed Dad before we left.

We arrived at a steak house called Mike's Kitchen. Dad announced that from now on, he's going to try to give black people a chance and attempted to talk to our waiter in pidgin Zulu. Unfortunately, our waiter was a dark-looking Indian who grunted angrily and then stormed off, never to be seen again.

I tried to casually slip the Mermaid into the conversation, but as soon as I did, my parents winked at each other and my mother said, "I think our little Johnny has a crush." I felt myself blushing and was about to change the subject when to my horror I realized that the dreaded Pike was sitting at the far side of the restaurant with his parents and his younger brother (who looks just as ugly). I pretended to ignore the monster and buried my head in the menu.

Halfway through our meal I looked up to find Pike standing at our table with a wicked grin on his face. Here follows the conversation:

PIKE	Hey, Johnny, man, what a surprise!
ME	[*muttered*] Hello, Pike.
PIKE	And these must be your folks. Hello, Mr. and Mrs. Milton. I'm Leonard Pike, a mate of Johnny's from school. [*They shake hands.*]
DAD	[*Knocks over his wineglass*] Always nice to meet a friend of Johnny's.
PIKE	Ah, Johnny's a legend. We all love him to bits. Well, I've got to run. [*Runs his steak knife up and down my back*] I'll pop round for a little chat on Monday night, Johnny. Oh, and enjoy those spuds! Goodbye, Mr. and Mrs. Milton—it was an absolute pleasure.

With that he sauntered back to his table. My folks commented on what a nice friend I had made. I bit my lip and said nothing—school is still two days away, and two days is ages.

Sunday 20th February

Innocence is back. She gave me a smooch on the lips when she arrived and ordered Dad to carry her suitcase to her room. Dad made a funny noise and then obeyed. It seems that Innocence, with the law behind her, is now in some sort of position of power around the house. Mom and Dad have decided to bide their time until they catch her in the act of brotheling and then fire her once and for all. I'm glad she's back and hope she sticks to the rules—after all, she did carry me around on her back for the first four years of my life.

12:30 Lunch with Wombat, my mother's mother and my father's nemesis. For some unknown reason she insisted on calling my father Roy and me David. Every ten minutes or so she would point at me and tell my mother how handsome I was and that thankfully I didn't look anything like my father. Dad, who was taking ages to light the barbecue, whistled loudly to himself.

12:38 My father managed to set himself alight after pouring paraffin over the smoldering coals. All I heard was a bloodcurdling scream and then a splash as he threw himself in the pool. It was like something straight out of a *Lethal Weapon* movie. I jumped up to rescue Dad in case he was hurt, but he seemed okay and managed to scramble out of the deep end and onto the rock garden. My mother, without even asking if he was all right, told him to stop fooling around and to change his charred shirt.

While chewing on a very tough, paraffin-flavored piece of steak, Wombat informed us that somebody had broken into her flat and left a ten dollar bill on her dining room table. No matter how hard we tried to convince her that no self-respecting thief leaves money at the scene of a crime, the senile old bat would hear nothing of it and said Buster Cracknell (the supervisor of her block) was her chief suspect.

After lunch the conversation drifted toward politics. Since De Klerk's speech and the release of Mandela it's become the major topic of conversation in the Milton household. Wombat said she hoped that she would be dead before the blacks took over. Dad said he hoped so too. I could almost hear my mother's lip clatter to the grass. Dad's back where he belongs—in the doghouse.

Received a weird phone call from somebody with a squeaky voice who immediately hung up. I swear it sounded like Gecko, but I guess it could have been a crank call or, even worse, Pike.

Monday 21st February

Woke up feeling depressed. Tonight I return to school, and the thought of it makes me ill. Dad went off to work for the first time in ages, and Mom dragged me around the shopping center with her. My heart did a break dance when she said she was meeting Marge for tea, but then I remembered that the Mermaid goes to a government school and would probably be in the middle of geography right now. I spent my time in the sports shop testing out different cricket bats while Mom had tea with Marge.

On the way home I swallowed my pride and asked Mom if Marge had mentioned the Mermaid and me at all. Mom hesitated and then said that the Mermaid liked me very much. My heart sank—my mother's a terrible liar.

17:30 Fatty asked the small boy sitting next to me on the bus to swap places with him so that we could chat. Thankfully, the big fellow didn't smell like fish paste this time. Fatty reckoned he'd unearthed some information about an old teacher called Macarthur, who apparently hanged himself in the chapel in 1944. The story goes that Macarthur's ghost still roams the school at the dead of night searching for salvation.

The bus chugged its way up the hills into the Natal Midlands, the lights on the road flickered dimly, and every mile made my body feel heavier. I thought of the Mermaid and my mom's lie. Did the Mermaid think I was a fool, or ugly, or didn't she even care? An older boy sitting in front of me was telling his mates about having sex with his sister's friend. The story sounded a little rough around the edges, and soon his friends called his bluff and accused him of sleeping with his sister.

As the bus dragged its way closer to school, I became more and more anxious about what it was going to be like. Was Pike really coming to get me? Would I still have my old bed when I got to the dormitory? What had happened to the others? I closed my eyes and thought about the Mermaid, which only made me feel homesick. I could feel tears welling up in my eyes. I clenched my teeth and my fists and told myself to grow up. Thankfully, by then it was dark in the bus so nobody saw my moment of weakness.

21:00   After hours of agony, the return to school wasn't nearly as bad as expected. Everyone sat around comparing notes about the weekend and telling stories. Here follows a brief highlights package.

WEEKEND SCORECARD:

Rambo	Got into a nightclub
Simon	Felt a girl's breasts
Mad Dog	Caught a fifty-kilogram Zambezi shark in Mozambique
Fatty	Sleuthed the Macarthur mystery
Boggo	Returned with a harder-core porno mag
Gecko	Contracted chronic food poisoning and laryngitis and was back in the sanatorium
Spud	Met the most beautiful girl in the world

It seems that the school supervisor wasn't told that there was a boy staying in our house over the weekend and he'd locked up all

the doors with Gecko trapped inside. Boggo said the desperate
Gecko had screamed himself hoarse and then eaten what looked like
a piece of steak from Mad Dog's locker. Mad Dog said he didn't
have any steak in his locker but then admitted that there might have
been a few old pigeon carcasses lying around.

Simon was midway through telling us about the size of his girl's
breasts and what they felt like when the light switch snapped on.
The dormitory was flooded with harsh white light and there stood
the shocking figure of Sparerib. It was too late for us to bolt for our
beds, so we all just froze on top of Simon's locker and stared
guiltily back at our housemaster.

"Talking after lights-out, I see," said Sparerib, squinting at us with
his wonky eye. "I'm sure you've many stories to tell." He strolled
toward us and lifted himself onto Fatty's locker. "I just wanted to tell
you," he continued, "that tomorrow Vern Blackadder's returning to
school. I'm sure you all know that Vern has been through a lot and
he's made a brave decision in coming back. Now I want you guys to
give him a break, make him feel welcome. And whatever you do,
don't ask him about his little . . . er . . . disappearance. Thanks, boys.
That will be all." With that he snapped off the lights and disappeared
into the darkness.

After Sparerib had gone, everybody began whispering excitedly
about the return of Vern. I'm quite pleased about Rain Man returning. I miss not having a cubicle mate, and Vern always supplies a solid
stream of moggy behavior to break the boredom. Boggo did a classic
Vern impersonation and we all laughed despite Sparerib's warning.

We continued talking about our weekends and I told the gang
about the Mermaid. Boggo was outraged that I hadn't spied on
her through the keyhole and everybody said I should have kissed
her. Simon was especially interested in my meeting with Pike at
the restaurant on Saturday night. Fatty refused to tell us about his
findings in Durban over the weekend and said he had a few things
to check out before he revealed any more evidence on the
Macarthur saga.

I lay awake listening to Pissing Pete and the sound of a goods train as it clattered off into the distance. All around me was heavy breathing and the odd snore coming from Mad Dog and Fatty. I drifted off to sleep, and in my dreams I saw Pike and the Mermaid holding hands. She smiled and then slowly they walked away from me.

Tuesday 22nd February

17:00 Today is Shrove Tuesday. Once again nobody seems to know what that actually means except that on this day, it's a tradition at the school to have an inter-house pancake race along the cloisters in the main quad. A boy from each year and the housemaster from each house make up the relay team, and each runner has to complete a lap of the quad before handing over the frying pan to the next runner. The rules are that the pancake has to be flipped at every corner, which often leads to a dropped pancake, which slows the runner down because he has to pick it up again, reflip, and then catch up with the other runners. The rest of the school stands in the middle of the quad and screams for their houses.

Rambo was chosen from our year, and he started the race and opened up an early lead. Sparerib was incredibly quick, and by the time he handed over the pan to our last runner, Bert, we looked to have the race all sewn up. Unfortunately, Bert, who is high on speed but low on coordination, dropped the pancake at every corner and our house came second last.

As the crowd drifted away, I spotted a lonely figure standing near the fountain watching the goldfish in the pond. The bald patch on the back of his head was a sure sign that this boy was none other than the infamous Vern Blackadder. I noticed Boggo and Rambo sniggering at him from the common room window. I walked up to Vern and tapped him on the shoulder. He turned slowly and I was shocked to see that he looked just like an old man. I held out my hand and he shook it. "Welcome back, Vern," I said. He flashed his demented smile at me and then turned back to the pond. I stood with him in silence for a while and together we watched the fish.

Wednesday 23rd February

At breakfast, Boggo announced that Gecko's making a recovery from his bout of pigeon poisoning and that he should be out of the san by Friday.

"Good," said Rambo. "Then he'll be fit for the night swim."

There was a long silence, apart from the sound of Fatty choking on his pork sausage.

"Are you mad?" cried Boggo after recovering from the shock and helping me thump Fatty on the back. "We are not doing all that again. It was a raging catastrophe!"

"This is not a debate, Boggo," snapped Rambo. He then smiled warmly at the rest of us and casually said, "Friday night, gentlemen, Friday night." And with that he took a final bite of his toast and sauntered out of the dining hall, leaving us all staring after him.

11:00 On the board was a notice that read:

OLIVER AUDITION. CALLBACKS!
14:30 AT THE MUSIC CENTER.

Underneath was a long list of boys called for a second round of auditions. I bounced around the common room like a loony kangaroo after seeing my name second from last. My acting dream is still alive—just!

14:30   A smaller group of about thirty boys crowded around outside the music center. This time Viking called us all into the big band room for a pep talk. Viking spoke at the level of a shout, and huge globules of spit flew out of his mouth, making him look like he'd just recently picked up a serious case of rabies.

"Gentlemen," he roared, "congratulations on making it to the second round! This play—should you make it—will dominate your year, your time, and your mind. I am a perfectionist—if I don't get perfection, then I get violent, not so, Barnes?" A small boy leaning on a pair of crutches, with his left leg in a plaster cast, nodded sadly. "Do I make myself clear?" We all nodded like dummies. Viking is burly and bearded and has savage-looking green eyes.

He began to pace like a caged lion. "An actor," he boomed, "has no room for fear! No room for modesty! And, most importantly, no room for his ego! I have the ego—you deliver the goods! Capeesh?" We all nodded again. "Right!" he shouted, making Ms. Roberts jump and clunk a note on the piano by mistake. "Let's do this!"

We all shuffled out and waited to be called. Ms. Roberts once again played the piano while Viking prowled around scribbling notes on a clipboard. When I walked in, Viking shouted, "Milton the Poet!" and told me to sing "I'll Do Anything" again.

This time I sang well. My voice sounded clear and I was more in control. Viking didn't stop me and wrote many notes while I was singing. When I was finished, he stared at me for ages and then said, "Thank you, Milton. Call in Stopfield."

Now that was more like it! At least I'd given a fair account of myself. I may not get a big role, but at the very least I should make the chorus.

On the way back to the house I met Vern, who's been reunited with Roger the cat. Roger sat on Vern's lap and purred happily to himself. Both of them looked just like concentration camp survivors from Crispo's Auschwitz movie.

18:10 Gavin, the prefect under the stairs, ordered all the first-years out of dinner to hunt for Albert, his pet rat. Mad Dog found it behind the fridge in the prefects' room. Rambo says his prefect is wickedly weird and breeds cockroaches to feed Albert and Victoria the house snake.

21:30 Pike and Devries left a dozen eggs under Rambo's duvet cover, which exploded when Rambo sat on his bed. After cleaning himself up, Rambo demanded that our dormitory wage a brutal war against Pike and Devries and that we agree that any action against one of us is an action against all. We all shook on it, including Vern, who looked deadly solemn and committed.

Mad Dog admitted to placing the second banana in Glockenshpeel's exhaust pipe and said that he did it to save his cousin. He also said that Stott and Emberton had been responsible for the first banana. We all congratulated him on his bravery and called him a legend. Mad Dog reckoned it was the power of Emberton's dad that finally swayed the board.

Fatty then rose slowly and said, "The board of governors are a sneaky lot, and trust me, gentlemen, I have proof of it." With that he farted loudly and called it a night.

Roger the cat jumped through my window and slept the night on Vern's bed. Vern talks to Roger in a strange language that makes him sound stark raving crackers. Roger responds by purring and rubbing his head against Vern's chin. As weird as their relationship is, Roger is probably the only reason Vern is back at school, so I don't mind all the jabbering away in cat language—after a while the madness becomes normal.

Friday 25th February

Full-school singing practice. Reverend Bishop left the school song for last. Everybody knew the words, so he didn't bother calling the hymn number. Four hundred voices nearly raised the roof off the ancient building. I had goose bumps all over as every boy let rip with as much passion and heart as he had. It was impossible not to feel like a huge band of brothers about to go off and thrash the living daylights out of the enemy. This feeling of unity and passion lasted exactly six minutes. Amazing how quickly a science class can suck every last bit of life out of you.

23:00 Night swim: Fatty was sent downstairs half an hour ago. If he was spotted, he was ordered to tell the prefects that he was feeling ill and needed some air. Once the coast was clear, the plan was for him to sneak across the quad, past the crypt, through the rose garden, and then to The Glock's lemon tree. He was then to give the owl hoot that Mad Dog had taught him. This would be our signal to follow.

We sat in silence waiting for the signal. Rambo paced up and down the aisle of the dormitory muttering to himself. Secretly, I was hoping that the call would never come and that the swim would be canceled. Outwardly, I assured everybody that I was looking forward to taking on the guards and their dogs.

Roger had already settled down on Vern's bed and looked rather put out by all the activity. He kept meowing at Vern, who clucked away at the cat in his own alien language. I may be wrong, but I'm sure Vern asked his pencil case if it wanted to go night swimming with him.

23:16 At last the hoot came (it sounded more like a constipated wolf than an owl) and we kicked into action. In all the commotion, Gecko made a feeble attempt to slip out of the dormitory but was hauled back by Mad Dog. We stripped down to our underpants and began the long tortuous journey to the dam.

We reached the lemon tree without alarm and found Fatty noshing away at a loaf of stale white bread that he'd found in a dustbin outside the prefects' kitchen. Rambo led us across the rugby field, over the fence, and into the dam. This time there was no fooling around. Everyone kept half an eye out for torchlight. Gecko grubbed around the water's edge, making ready for a snappy getaway. The water was colder than last time and there was no moon. All about us was deathly quiet except for the trickles of water running from our bodies.

Rambo whispered the command "Octopus," and we crept out of the water and began our return back to the house. Without the excitement of the chase or the threat of any danger, the swim seemed slightly hollow and pointless.

Rambo's plan was for us to return to the dormitory the same way we went out and for Fatty to wait, dry off, and change back into his clothes that he'd left under The Glock's lemon tree. Mad Dog would let loose the owl call when all was ready. Rambo reckoned that if Fatty was caught, the first thing the prefects would do would be check out the dormitory. According to him, nobody would be stupid enough to believe that Fatty would go on a solo night swim.

Our return was as simple as our journey out. No guards, prefects, dogs—not even a stray cat. I sprang back through my window and onto my bed, landing on something long and thick. At first I thought it was my cricket bag, but then the lump moved beneath me. The lump seemed quite a bit bigger than Roger the cat and its arms were holding me, strangling me. Then I was being pounded with a laundry bag. I shouted out in shock. At the same time there were other shouts and curses and then on flicked the light switch. Standing at the door bathed in light was the figure of Luthuli. The lump in my bed was Bert. Prefects and other matric boys were popping out of everywhere, laughing and shouting.

"I think you gentlemen are officially busted!" cried Bert. Even Earthworm seemed pleased with himself as he stood up holding Gecko over his left shoulder like a sack of potatoes. "I trust Fatty isn't stuck in the window again," said the head of house rather ironically. Nobody answered—there was nothing to say.

Julian asked Rambo where Fatty was, and before he could answer, I blurted out, "He's in the sanatorium!"

"Really?" asked Luthuli without believing me for a minute. "What's he come down with—another religious conversion?" I shook my head lamely. Luthuli rubbed his hands together and said, "Gentlemen—we'll deal with you in the morning, unless Mr. Black can think of another one of his ingenious excuses."

He then flicked off the lights and the prefects left the dormitory. There was a long silence. Somebody whistled softly. At last Rambo spoke in a deadly, menacing voice. "We've been set up. Somebody's sung a sweet song in the ears of Luthuli and, trust me, when I find that leak, I'll stop it for good!" Rambo was seething. It seemed the humiliation of the failed plan hurt him more than whatever savage fate awaited us. Another long silence followed. In fact, it went on for so long that for a moment I thought everybody had gone to sleep. But then I realized that everybody was probably thinking about our brutal punishment that surely lay ahead.

"I hope you've a got a plan up your sleeve, Rambo," said Boggo rather hopefully. Rambo paused and then spoke in a low voice. "No plan, Boggo, we're busted. We take our punishment like men."

"What will the punishment be?" I asked, surprising even myself. Boggo replied, "There are two options, Spud. The first is that the prefects deal with us, which will probably be a combination of punishments. Or else they'll hand us over to Sparerib, who will lash us four each." I heard Vern gulp next to me. The idea of four strokes from Sparerib was obviously as sickening to him as it was to me.

"Trust me, they'll take it to Sparerib," said Rambo, speaking as if he'd had great experience in such matters. "Technically, the prefects aren't allowed to beat us and they'll be worried that someone will blab."

The floorboards creaked as Fatty shuffled in. "Thanks for the owl hoot," he barked. "Luthuli caught me coming into the house."

"What did you say to him?" asked Simon.

Fatty spat out the window and then felt his way to his cubicle. "I told him I was feeling sick and that I went to the san."

"And what did he say?" questioned Rambo. By now Fatty had found something to eat in his locker and spoke with a mouth full of food. "He said all right and that I was a lucky bastard."

"You *are* a lucky bastard," cried Rambo. "You've just escaped a wicked thrashing!" Rambo and Boggo went on to describe the events of the evening. Fatty listened intently, all the while noshing away at something that sounded like pieces of metal.

After Rambo had finished, Fatty belched and stepped into his pajamas. "Well, I guess I'm owed one after last time," he said.

Rambo countered quickly in an accusing voice. "What do you mean, you're owed one?"

"W-well," stammered Fatty, "I got you guys off and did the whole religious conversion thing."

"If your big fat pig arse hadn't got stuck in the window, everything would have been perfect, you stupid shit!" Rambo was seething now. Kneeling on my bed and peering over the partition, it seemed that he had been waiting for a victim to lash out at and Fatty had just volunteered himself to be slaughtered. "Our motto is One for All. If we go down, you go down," said Rambo savagely.

"Well, I didn't see all you guys standing up there in the pulpit helping me out," replied Fatty in a whining voice.

"You ungrateful bastard!" shouted Rambo. "Who do you think got you out of that whole mess?"

"The same person who got me into the mess in the first place!" said Fatty, standing up to meet Rambo, who had slowly made his way over to Fatty's cubicle. For the first time our dormitory was the scene of some real ugliness. What followed was shocking. Rambo punched Fatty in the face. Fatty fell back against the locker. Mad Dog charged in and attacked Rambo, who bit a chunk of flesh out of Mad Dog's shoulder. Older boys streamed into the dormitory along with Luthuli, who flicked the lights on and managed to break up the fight. There was blood everywhere and Fatty was sobbing like a little boy. I felt like helping him. I wanted to put something over his nose to stop the blood. He lay on the floor like a great dying animal surrounded by curious onlookers. I felt sick. Blood was spurting out of his nose like Pissing Pete. An hour ago it was All for One; now it was Dog Eat Dog! (Or Man Eats Mad Dog.)

Saturday 26th February

06:00 This morning was dull and overcast. The bloodstains on the floor reminded me of last night. Fatty is in the san with a broken nose, Mad Dog is out hunting, and Rambo was seen striding off to the showers, his big jaw clenched in an expression of complete defiance.

Boggo grimly informed us at breakfast that Luthuli has reported us to Sparerib. Being it's the weekend, we have no idea when we shall be thrashed. It seems there is no going back and certainly no getting out of it. There's nothing left but to wait in vain for the pain! I wish I could get it over with now and not have to travel to Durban (cricket match against Lincoln High School) with this dark cloud hanging over me.

I chatted to Mad Dog on the bus about last night. He said that he didn't give a stuff about being beaten and that Rambo is a childish prick who wants to rule the dormitory and turn us all into Rambo worshippers. I nodded but said nothing. I wish I could share his confidence when it comes to being beaten. Mad Dog must have read my thoughts because he slapped me on the shoulder and said, "Trust me, Spuddy—when you're getting the lashing from Sparerib, just close your mind off and think about the best thing in your life. If you can focus properly, you won't feel the pain." I very much doubt Mad Dog's theory will work, but hell, it's the only plan that I've got right now!

It was a huge relief to see the folks already encamped when we arrived. They had their deck chairs laid out and the wine was flowing . . . or nearly. When the side filed past them, my parents didn't even seem to notice us at all. Dad had a wine bottle trapped between his thighs and Mom was pulling at the bottle opener with all her might. They were both grunting with exertion. Unfortunately, as we walked past, Dad had his back to us, so it looked like they were doing something dodgy. The whole team was still sniggering away by the time we got to the change room. Overall, though, the embarrassment was a small price to pay for the warmth and happiness I felt at seeing people whose official job it was to love me.

We batted first and, thanks to Simon scoring 102 runs, I was not called on to bat, so I sat with the folks and chatted about ordinary things like the neighbors' dogs and Dad's ongoing battle to keep our pool from going green.

We declared on 225 runs for the loss of three wickets. Simon and The Guv decided that was enough runs. We took to the field to some polite clapping from other parents and loud whoops and screams from mine. Dad even did a funny war dance around his deck chair to psych us up. Once the laughter had died down, Mad Dog took the new ball and bowled faster and wilder than ever.

I was fielding at mid-wicket when across the field I saw a girl with beautiful long blond hair skip through the school gates and onto the stands. My heart pounded—could it possibly be her? It was too far for me to see for sure. My concentration slipped and I dropped a simple catch, much to everyone's disgust.

My bowling, however, was inspired. I would love to say that it was due to the extra practicing with Earthworm during the week, but the truth is, I was bowling for the Mermaid.

After I took my fifth wicket, the blond girl walked up to my parents and spoke to them. It had to be her! Surely they didn't know any other blond girls? I began to get nervous and excited. I ran through a possible conversation in my head. How should I act toward her? What would the others think of her? Of me? I no longer cared how many wickets I took–I just wanted her to love me.

After bowling Lincoln out for 106, with my personal bowling tally being six wickets for 42 runs, The Guv called us into a huddle and told us we were now the mean machine and congratulated us on our "clinical" victory. I raised my head out of the huddle and the Mermaid was gone. Instead of heading for the change room, I sprinted toward the school gate, but there was no sign of her. I approached my parents, who sprang out of their seats and hugged me. Dad was utterly sozzled and wept tears of joy. (He's convinced I will play for South Africa one day.) There was no other way of asking the question, so I just said it.

"Who was the blond girl who was speaking to you?"

My mother paused as if confused. I could read her thoughts, which were about the reason for me wanting to know rather than the answer to my question. "Just some girl who wanted to borrow a lighter. Why?" I didn't answer. The girl was not the Mermaid and that's all I needed to know. I said goodbye to my confused parents and headed back to the change room.

21:00 Still waiting on the bus for The Guv to finish his after-match drinks with the Lincoln teachers. Unbelievably, my parents were also invited to join the party. I'm terrified at how drunk they must be by now. Mad Dog managed to steal a bottle of cheap red wine from somewhere and passed it around the bus. The bottle came around and I knew that I had a decision to make. Drink from the bottle and risk expulsion, or pass it up and be a naff? The bottle came closer, with each boy choosing a path. Simon and Mad Dog had drunk, but George, Stubbs, and Leslie refused. Then the bottle was in my hands. I thought of the Mermaid who wasn't. I thought of the night swim, I thought of Rambo, I thought about what it must be like to be Vern with no dad and no friends. I drank deeply. The wine tasted like vinegar. Mad Dog thumped me on the back and said, "Good one, Brains, your old man's wine is hectic stuff!"

Sunday 27th February

02:10 Arrived back at school at last and fell into bed. The dormitory was dead quiet (apart from Roger, who was purring louder than a sewing machine).

21:30 Rambo called the dormitory to a meeting in his cubicle. He apologized to Fatty and Mad Dog and said that we should all make peace with each other. We shook hands like the members of the United Nations, and with that, life was breathed back into the dormitory. Simon told the others about us drinking on the bus and we were warmly congratulated for our complete disregard for the school rules.

Typically, Boggo brought us all back to the stark reality of our thrashing. Rambo said he saw Sparerib playing squash and our housemaster winked at him and said he was warming his arm up for tomorrow.

Gecko whimpered and sat on Roger the cat, who'd also joined the dormitory meeting. Roger hissed, Gecko screamed, and we all laughed and jeered.

Pike and Devries arrived to gloat over the night swim and attempted to scare us with old stories about brutal floggings. Devries tried to join in, but with his jaw wired up he sounded like a retard. We laughed and squawked until they gave up. Pike pulled down his pants and mooned us and then ran out squealing like a pig.

Monday 28th February

08:00 Still haven't been thrashed. The terror is killing me. I reckon the worst thing about execution must be the waiting!

No history lesson because Crispo was absent. This gave me the chance to finish the final eighteen pages of *Catch 22*. Disappointed to find the ending was rather abrupt. I had to check that I hadn't lost a page of the book. Have to ask The Guv about this one. (No doubt he'll have some cunning explanation.)

13:45 The Guv's wife left us a delicious lasagne in the oven. He opened up a bottle of red wine and gave me my usual half a glass. He said I looked sad and distracted. I told him about the night swim and the fight that followed. My English teacher flashed a smile and said, "One day, young fella, you will have a great story to tell."

The Guv reckoned that there could be no classic ending to *Catch 22*. "It's too episodic, too crazed, too screwed up to end normally." I still feel that the last line of the book is a little weird.

After finishing lunch with The Guv, I took a stroll around the fields. Everywhere boys were playing cricket, kicking rugby balls, or hitting golf balls, while others were suntanning or just sitting and staring into space. I gazed up at the huge billowing thunderclouds rising up over the Drakensberg. Everything was clean and calm and perfect, like the picture on the cover of the school brochure that I was sent just before Christmas.

I thought about home and tried to work out in which direction it was. (Which only made me feel homesick, disorientated, and a little dizzy.)

Dinner: Still no sign of Sparerib and our thrashing. Maybe we've been let off?

No such luck! Sparerib called us all out of prep (except for Fatty and Vern). I felt my right leg shaking as we followed him to his office. He sat behind his desk and looked at us with a mixture of anger and humor. (Of course it could also have just been the fact that he has a wonky eye.)

"Right," he said, rubbing his hands together. "Our intrepid night swimmers." He studied us all in turn. My whole body was shaking now. I felt light-headed. Next to me Gecko swayed. Mad Dog gripped him with his left hand.

"I have decided to release Vern Blackadder from punishment due to his frail state," continued Sparerib. "Are there any objections?" We all shook our heads, and just for that brief moment I wished that I were Vern Blackadder in the warm comfort of the classroom and not Spud Milton standing in front of the executioner. I then remembered that Vern has no dad and his cheese is slipping off his cracker (so basically it was fifty-fifty). Sparerib opened a cupboard and took out three canes. After some consideration he chose the thinnest cane and returned the other canes to the cupboard.

"Gentlemen," said Sparerib with a forced sigh, "I don't take night swimming lightly. It may be a game or an adventure to you, but we staff see it as a dangerous pastime. While at school you are under my care, and so to prevent further episodes of this nature, I will be making an example out of you lot."

The siren wailed for the end of prep. I could hear boys shouting and running. Nearby somebody stumbled and hit the ground with a thud. A chorus of laughter followed. And then . . . a knock at the door. Sparerib shouted, "What?" After a brief pause the door creaked open and there stood Vern Blackadder staring at us, his face white with terror. Sparerib's tone softened. "Ah, Vern, you aren't called. You've been granted a period of grace."

Vern didn't move. He just stood there staring at Sparerib. After what seemed like ages, he lowered his gaze and said, "Sorry, sir, all for one." We stared dumbfounded at Vern as he continued to look at the floor. Rambo smiled and nodded to him with a look of great respect.

"Very well. Four strokes each, one at a time. Let's get this over with." As we shuffled out of the office, Sparerib pulled out a chair and took off his jacket. Rambo (who had chosen to go first) stayed behind. The door closed. After about ten seconds the beating began. It sounded truly horrific. Each stroke seemed more savage than the last. Rambo emerged from the office, walking casually, but couldn't hide the pain in his face. Mad Dog followed and sauntered out, smiling. A crowd of boys, many from other houses, gathered around to watch the show. Next Boggo sped out, rubbing his arse. Much to the delight of the growing crowd, he pulled down his pants and cooled his bum on the redbrick cloister wall. By this stage, I was all set to run away or wet myself. Then Gecko flew out of the office, screaming, and vomited in the gutter.

I staggered into the office and could hear the noise of the crowd outside. "Hands on the chair, Milton, and grit your teeth," said Sparerib as if he was offering me a cup of tea and a chocolate biscuit. I gripped the chair and stared out of the window at the starry sky. Mad Dog's words were screaming around my head. "Think of the best thing in your life and you'll beat the pain."

I could see the Mermaid. We were back in the swimming pool . . . WHACK! Her beautiful bright eyes, water droplets cascading down her face . . . WHACK! "Come in, Johnny, it's warm! It's lovely!" WHACK! "Hold your breath, Johnny, hold my hand, Johnny!" WHACK!

Then I was running. My backside was on fire. As I left the office, I remember catching a glimpse of Vern's horrified face. He was last. The crowd hooted and laughed. I kept running and running and running and then I was laughing and shouting. People I didn't know were thumping me on the back and laughing. Rambo shook my hand and Mad Dog threw his arm around my shoulders. There was Simon and Boggo and Vern and Gecko, laughing, talking rubbish. Tonight we were once again brothers in arms.

Tuesday 1st March

06:20 Julian lined us up in the showers to examine our backsides. He and Bert took their time going from one bum to another making observations and now and again prodding someone's butt cheek with the back end of Bert's toothbrush. Gecko's entire backside is blue, and Julian awarded him first prize. There was a flash of light, and before we knew it, Julian had taken a photograph of our naked behinds. (No doubt this photograph will surface in some seedy magazine when I'm rich and famous.)

After the shower (and photo shoot) we marched off to roll call, where the entire house was looking at us like we were celebrities (except for Pike and Devries, who were too busy trying to stab Roger the cat with a broken Coke bottle).

12:00 On the notice board: *OLIVER AUDITIONS*. Then there was a list of ten names, including J. Milton. The auditions are tomorrow at 15:00.

At dinner The Guv strolled past my table and said, "A word, Milton." I followed him out of the dining hall, and together we strolled out through the archway and down the path toward the fields. The sun was just setting, and streaks of pink and orange shot across the pale blue cloudless sky. After walking in silence for some time, The Guv lit his pipe and said, "I didn't give you a book yesterday." In all the commotion about the night swim I had completely forgotten. "I thought you looked rather distracted and ill at ease." I told him about the flogging and he chuckled to himself.

We turned on the path and began the slow amble around our cricket field. In the fading light it seemed different and kind of lonely. "Johnno, you ought to be aware that this is without doubt the best damned book any man could ever write. As far as I'm concerned, this book is the ultimate proof that God exists. And trust me, these are strong words coming from a devout atheist!" He opened his sling bag and pulled out the thickest book I've ever seen.

My heart sank. Surely The Guv wasn't giving me the Bible to read. (I'm not against the Bible, but I wouldn't like to read it cover to cover.) The book was pale green in color, and on the cover was a huge eagle flying over a snow-capped mountain. "Do take good care of it, Milton. It was my twenty-first birthday present from my parents." The Guv patted me on the back and strode off down the road in a cloud of pipe smoke. In the dim light of the early evening I ran my fingers gently through the pages. The book is called *The Lord of the Rings*.

Wednesday 2nd March

Gavin, the prefect who lives under the stairs, dropped a letter into my lap while I was trying to find my *Modern Basic Mathematics* textbook. I didn't recognize the handwriting on the envelope and thought that it was perhaps some mistake (nobody has ever written me a letter at school). I opened it rather slowly, trying not to tear the envelope. It was written on pale peach-colored paper in smooth and flowing handwriting. My eyes immediately glanced down to the name signed at the bottom of the page. It read:

Love, Debbie

I think I nearly fainted. My heart was pounding like a gigantic bongo drum. I quickly packed up my books and sprinted up the stairs to the safety of our deserted dormitory. I opened the letter and began to read:

Dear Johnny,

I'm sorry I haven't written sooner, but things have been really busy what with moving house and all. My new room is much bigger than before, and I have a beautiful view of the sea. School is boring as usual (except for art and history).

I think of u often and really enjoyed our night together. When are u coming back home? I think we should have more adventures in your pool.

Keep well.
Love, Debbie

PS Have u heard the new INXS tape? (Gorgeous)
PPS My new address is
4 Strathmore Avenue
Durban North
4051

The bell rang for the end of break. I folded the letter and slid it carefully into my back pocket and then sprinted off to Afrikaans, prouder and happier than I can ever remember being.

15:00 Viking grandly announced to the ten of us that we are being considered for the title role of *Oliver*. He then ordered us to line up outside the music room. (I still had the Mermaid's letter in my pocket—I must have read it over thirty times in four hours.) I was second last in the queue and news filtered down that we would have to sing a song called "Consider Yourself." It's one of those tunes that I seem to know although I can't ever remember having learned it.

I read my letter one last time before striding into the music room. It's amazing what the most beautiful girl in the world can do to you. One moment you feel lower than a squashed dwarf and the next you feel like you're the king of the mountain.

Viking nodded and greeted me formally. "Right, Milton," he said. "Down to the last ten." He scratched his beard and studied me closely. "I very much liked your last audition. A little bland in the face, but the voice was bewitching. Now 'Consider Yourself' is probably the best-known song from the score. It's full of life and vitality, and for the first time in the play we get a vision of a better life for Oliver."

I decided to be as expressive as possible and launched into the song like a maniac. After one line he shouted me to a stop and told me I looked like a retard.

In total he made me sing the song five times, and after each attempt he would ask me to add something new to the next attempt or to stop doing something that I had added. At last he seemed satisfied and before dismissing me from the room, he told me to keep a sharp eye on the notice board. I skipped my way back to the house up the familiar pathway, and for the first time I truly thought of the crazy idea that I could play the lead role of *Oliver*. While skipping away like a fairy, I nearly crashed into Devries, who was on his way to the sanatorium for a "cheeck up." (Ha ha!)

All in all, a perfect day in the life of Spud Milton.

Thursday 3rd March

My run of good luck continued when the boy who sits next to me in English (Geoff Lawson) invited me to his parents' horse farm on Sunday. He's promised to take me fishing. I thanked him for the invite and we made plans to meet at the old gates, 07:00 sharp. (He says his farm is about an hour's walk from the school.)

Saturday 5th March

The Lord of the Rings is fascinating. I'm reading all about these crea-
tures called Hobbits who live in a place called the Shire. In the first
chapter, a hobbit called Bilbo Baggins has a big party to celebrate his
eleventy-first birthday (111) and then disappears rather dramatically
at his own birthday bash. Forty pages down, 1,002 to go.

Have written twelve letters to the Mermaid. Not sure which one
I should send.

20:00 The Saturday night movie was *Days of Thunder*, with Tom
Cruise. It was all going great until a huge storm struck, which
brought on a power failure. A groan echoed around the school as
we were all plunged into darkness. Rogers Halibut brought in a
small generator that made a huge noise and little difference. The
movie was canceled and we were ordered to bed.

Sunday 6th March

07:00 Met Geoff Lawson at the old gates and together we walked
along the road. Geoff looked concerned and ill at ease, glancing suspiciously at every car that drove past. After about ten minutes of
walking, he pulled me off the road and down a dust track that led to
a distant farmhouse on the hill. The next minute an old white farm
truck sped off the road and stopped next to us. I followed Geoff as
he leapt onto the back of the vehicle. A black man dressed in a white
uniform jumped out of the driver's seat and covered us with a sheet
of tarpaulin. The truck did a quick U-turn and took off back down
the road. Geoff explained that what we were doing was highly illegal
but it was a lot better than walking ten kilometers to his farm. The
black man who'd picked us up was their housekeeper, whose English

name was Joseph. (Generally African people have an English name because white people can't pronounce their Zulu ones.)

After about twenty minutes the truck stopped. Joseph pulled back the tarpaulin and I was greeted with the most extraordinary sight imaginable. I was gaping at a mansion as only seen in Hollywood films. A huge white house with a thatched roof and green leafy sycamore and oak trees. Everything was perfect, and this farm (if you could call it that) was a lot like what I always thought heaven would be.

"Breakfast is waiting, Master Geoff," said Joseph with a gentle smile, and led us inside. The dining room was larger than our living room, kitchen, and dining room combined and we were treated to eggs, bacon, tomatoes, toast, and fig jam.

Geoff and I spent the day paddling around the dam in a small boat, fishing, laughing, and talking nonsense. Geoff managed to catch a small rainbow trout, but I only succeeded in catching a tree and the anchor rope. We chatted about school and English and life in our houses. He seemed very interested in the goings-on of our dormitory, especially the truth of Fatty's conversion and the Vern disappearance saga. He says that his house is boring and that our dormitory has become known around the school as the "Crazy Eight." He reckons everyone, including some of the teachers, thinks we're stark raving mad. I don't think they're far wrong.

He went on to say that his parents live in Johannesburg but also have homes in Montreal and London and that they seldom visit the horse farm except to see him. For an instant he looked sad, but then he quickly changed the subject to other things.

Geoff was wickedly impressed that I was reading *The Lord of the Rings*. He reckoned he had once got the book out of the library but was too scared to open it.

17:00 Joseph dropped us off where we had met him and waved goodbye. Tired, satisfied, and with a belly full of luxurious food, we strolled happily through the old school gates, up Pilgrim's Walk toward the great redbrick buildings in front of us.

Monday 7th March

Still agonizing over the Mermaid. I have now written about twenty letters to her, none of which I like. If I don't post one of them by tomorrow, she'll think I'm not interested. I long to see her; even a picture of her would do. I spend the evening composing my twenty-first letter to her in three days.

Dear Mermaid,
I think of you constantly. I love you so much that you occupy just about every waking and sleeping moment of my life. I long to see you, watch you, and kiss you (and if I wasn't a spud—a whole lot more). I thought I saw you last week while I was playing cricket, and I turned into a useless bundle of nerves. I have read your letter 124 times and searched every line for hidden meanings or clues as to how you feel about me. I am terrified that you don't love me.

With all my heart,
Johnny

PS I confess I dreamed about you stark naked . . . Sorry.

After a brief read I decided that the letter was perhaps a bit honest and I opted for a less radical approach. Also, I can't call her Mermaid to her face—she'll think I'm childish or mad!

Dear Debbie,
Thank you for your letter. It was good to hear from you again. I

*really enjoyed that night in the pool and look forward to many more.
School is great and I am doing absolutely fine. I enjoy drama, history, and especially English (mainly because my teacher is a raging
madman). Otherwise, I have auditioned for the school play, Oliver,
and have made it through the first couple rounds of auditions.*

> *Keep well.
> Hope to see you in the holidays.*
>
> *Love,
> Johnny*

PS *Write soon.*

After reading all twenty-two letters twice over, I have finally
decided to send the above version in the morning post.

Tuesday 8th March

The letter has been posted. My hands were shaking badly when
I pushed it down the chute. I then had second thoughts about
sending it and tried to slide my hand down the chute only to be
shouted at by the head boy, Marshall Martin, who thought I was
trying to steal letters. I told him I was checking if I'd put a stamp
on my envelope. He eyed me shiftily and told me to get lost.

How long until I get a reply? Sparerib saw me talking to myself
and looked at me strangely with his squint eye. He then shook his
head and trudged off. I think Sparerib rates me as a bit of a border-
line nutter.

Crispo has definitely lost the plot. He brought Boggo up in
front of the class to demonstrate a Nazi interrogation strategy.

Crispo attempted to be vicious, but his poor German accent made us all laugh. Even Boggo snorted and giggled in the face of the old geyser's dodgy ham acting. Boggo's laughter came to a screeching halt, though, when Crispo brought out some dangerous-looking apparatus that he called The Sausage Machine. He plugged it into the wall socket and then asked Boggo to take his pants down so that he could attach the rusty old electrodes to his testicles. A shocked silence spread across the room as we all realized that the old maniac wasn't joking.

Fortunately, sensing danger, the quick-thinking Boggo jumped up and informed Crispo that the bell had rung and that the lesson was over. Poor Crispo looked at his watch and shook his bewildered head in a fog of confusion.

The Guv canceled lunch because of a staff meeting. Spent the afternoon with Mad Dog trying to shoot red-winged starlings with his catapult.

Once again I set my work aside and spent prep reading *The Lord of the Rings*. Worried that this book may mean the end of my scholarship.

Thursday 9th March

17:45 Rambo told me that a matric boy called Greg Anderson has a sister who was the top sprinter in South Africa. He said she held the All Africa 100-meter sprint record. He said that Anderson loves talking about his sister and that I should go up and ask him how fast she runs the hundred meters. It all sounded a bit bizarre but, hoping to make a new friend, I approached the big matric, who was sitting in the common room reading the papers. He smiled as I greeted him and asked me how I was doing. I then asked him how fast his sister ran the hundred meters. He stared at me dumbly and then suddenly tears welled up in his eyes. He looked away, wiped his face on his shirt, and shook his head sadly. His newspaper dropped to the ground and suddenly I felt myself lifted off my feet and thrust against the wall. The wind shot out of my body like a popped balloon. I was gasping and staring into the ferocious face of an enraged animal.

Gavin, the prefect under the stairs, put down his didgeridoo, and tried to calm Anderson down. Anderson ordered him to stay out of it, and with a shrug Gavin returned to his didg. Anderson stared into my eyes for some time and then said in a broken voice, "My sister lost her legs in a car crash last year. You bastard!" With that he released his grip and stormed out of the common room, slamming the door behind him. The first face I saw was the leering Pike, who shook his head and said, "You have just made the hugest enemy of a first-team rugby player. You are so dead, man. If I were you, I'd pack my bags and get out before you're killed." I stumbled out of the common room, still heaving heavily, and saw Rambo laughing his head off in the cloisters. I tried to hurl abuse at him, but he just laughed and strolled off to supper with Boggo.

Never in my life have I felt so awful. I felt homesick and sad and ashamed. I walked slowly to the dormitory and started packing my trunk.

Friday 10th March

06:30 After a night of very little sleep I've decided to confront the demon head-on and apologize to Greg Anderson. I've also decided to unpack my trunk and fight on!

07:30 Anderson refused to let me apologize. He said that he was too disgusted to talk to me and that he didn't want to see me ever again. I retreated from his bedroom door with a heavy heart.

Instead of moping, though, I decided to be proactive and verbally attacked Rambo at breakfast. Unfortunately, he just laughed at me and said that he'd been joking and that any person with half a brain would have known it. After breakfast I scribbled an apology note and slid it under Anderson's door.

Mom phoned and said that Dad had run over one of the neighbors' dogs and was trying to convince the mourning neighbors that it was an accident and not an assassination. Mom said that it was a gruesome sight and that after the collision the car was making a strange clanking noise and so they would probably not risk driving up tomorrow. She asked me if I was all right. I lied and said I was fine. Looks like a black day all around for the Miltons.

Saturday 11th March

Still no word from Greg Anderson. I know I've scarred him really badly. To add to my woes, I had a disastrous match against St. Julius. Luckily, we hung on for a draw as the mist and drizzle came down around 15:00. Simon and Mad Dog bravely held out until The Guv ordered everybody off the field, saying he couldn't see through his glasses anymore. The opposition coach seemed less than pleased to go off for such a light drizzle, but The Guv walked him off to the staff room to drown his sorrows. He must have had many sorrows because a number of the St. Julius boys watched the movie (*Wall Street*) with us and only left at about 22:00!

Still racked with guilt about Anderson, who's been making a point of savagely glaring at me at every possible opportunity. Made a mental note to say a special prayer for him and his poor sister in chapel tomorrow morning.

Sunday 12th March

09:00   Reverend Bishop's sermon stuck me in the guts! It was about humiliation and speaking harsh words to people. He told us that we must not let Satan in the door, and then, with a wild swish of his hand, he knocked over a vase of roses, which shattered on the floor at the foot of the pulpit. He stared at the debris and then shouted, "Damn you, Satan! Get out of God's house!" He looked wickedly vicious, so nobody laughed, except for Pike, who quickly pretended he was clearing his throat. The Reverend rabbited on for another half an hour and then took a giant swig of wine from the communion cup before giving some to The Glock, who also looked thirsty.

Geoff asked me if I wanted to go to his farm again. I was tempted but felt too depressed to go, so I lied and said I had work to do.

Spent free bounds reading, but not even the greatest book in the history of the world could hold my focus.

I had a desperate urge to call the Mermaid but chickened out at the last moment.

18:30   Had the first laugh of the weekend while watching a National Geographic program about baboons. A large male baboon with big bollocks was beating his chest and trying to look scary when Emberton shouted, "Hey, check, it's Glockenshpeel!" The whole house hooted with laughter, especially when the baboon then tried to mate with a terrified smaller baboon with a bright pink bum.

I was sitting alone outside on the house bench when suddenly a large figure sat down beside me. My heart leapt with fear as I realized it was Greg Anderson, no doubt coming to get his revenge.

"Spud," he said gently, "I have to tell you something." My heart sank. No doubt he was going to tell me about the pain and anguish he was going through, or, even worse, he was going to give me the graphic details of the accident. He stared into my eyes for what seemed like ages but was probably only a few seconds. I could see the pain and anguish—the horror of having a crippled sister. I think if I had a crippled sister, I'd also be protective over her and help her all the time. He leaned close and said:

"I don't have a sister."

With that he got up and sauntered into the house. I was speechless. I felt the most overpowering feeling of relief and then pure anger. My entire weekend had been ruined by a stupid sick joke. I was ready to lash out at anyone (a dangerous idea when you're an undersized first-year spud). Luckily, the first thing I saw was Roger the cat and I chased him all the way back to Sparerib's garden, all the while making crazed noises. (I think I'm becoming a replica of my father.) Unfortunately, I nearly ran into Reverend Bishop, who was leaving a prayer session in the crypt. He muttered sadly to himself and then went about his business. In hindsight I'm relieved that Vern wasn't around or he might have freaked out or stabbed me with a pair of scissors for terrorizing Roger.

This night shall be remembered for the longest fart ever recorded. (Simon clocked Fatty's feat at 28.6 seconds on his stopwatch.) Fatty said he would try to better his record the next time there were baked beans for dinner.

Monday 13th March

Had a great lunch with The Guv. We went on for hours about the first book of *The Lord of the Rings*. The Guv did a brilliant impersonation of Gandalf, and together we reread the Hobbits' escape from the Black Riders. Once The Guv uncorked his second bottle of red wine, he began to talk freely (mostly about what awaited me in future chapters). He then stopped abruptly and stared at me.

"Johnno," he said with a slight slur, "if rumors are to be believed, you may soon make quite an acting debut." A thrill of electricity shot through my body, but no matter how much I pressed him for details, he refused to say any more, quickly changing the subject to my dismal form on the cricket field last Saturday. I told him that I was under great stress with the sick joke about Anderson's imaginary sister and her missing legs. The Guv let out a giant guffaw and clapped merrily. He reckoned he fell for the exact same crack thirty-five years ago. Except they let him stew for a month before coming clean! It's hard to imagine The Guv as a boy at the school (and a head of house). It seems that he would never have fitted in— I suppose in those days everything must have been different.

After lunch I strode off back to the house but was soon stopped in my tracks by a loud shout of, "Milton!" Crispo was calling me from his veranda. Before I could even explain why I was hanging around the staff houses, he had me seated next to him in a wicker chair and his maid, Gloria, set down some tea and biscuits and smiled warmly at me.

"Lovely girl, that Gloria," said Crispo once she had left. "Taken care of me since my Sybil passed away. Look at those beautiful lilies she planted. Arum lilies. As you get older, it's the small things that make one happy, Milton." For the first time I noticed a huge bed of white flowers, with a long yellow stem peeking out from the middle of each bloom. Crispo was right—just looking at them made you feel happy.

Soon Crispo was telling me brilliant stories about the war and how Montgomery outwitted Rommel in the desert.

Afternoon became evening. Reluctantly, I excused myself, but Crispo refused to let me go. "Who's your housemaster?" he asked.

"Spare—er, Mr. Wilson," I said. Crispo called for Gloria and she brought out the telephone. He called Sparerib and informed him that I would be working at his house that evening. And so it was done. Gloria brought out a blanket and spread it over Crispo's legs to keep the autumn chill out of his bones, and on we waded into the darkness of 1942.

After gorging myself on my second meal of roast beef of the day, we retired to the comfort of the log fire in his living room. The room was covered with maps and charts and war memorabilia.

We stared into the fire together and said nothing. After a while Crispo turned to me and said, "I hear they call you Spud." I nodded and felt the blood rushing to my face. Then he smiled and said, "That's what they called me too. A late bloomer, I was." I looked at Crispo and tried to imagine him as a Spud. It was impossible—he was too old.

Another long silence followed and then Crispo spoke again. This time his gaze didn't shift from the roaring orange flames and his voice seemed strangely distant, like a voice that used to be his and had long since faded away. "Remember, boy, God gave us the greatest gift of all. Not love, health, or beauty, not even life. But choice. God's greatest gift is choice."

He looked at me for a moment and then his attention returned to the flames. The grandfather clock chimed yet again. 22:00! I leapt out of my chair and thanked Crispo for his hospitality. The old man seemed lost in the fire and nodded without looking at me. I turned and walked to the door. As I pulled the swing door open, Crispo called after me. "Come back again, dear boy, there's still so much left to tell." I thanked him again and left him to his fire.

Tuesday 14th March

12:00   On the notice board:

OLIVER AUDITIONS. SMITH, WINTER,
AND MILTON PLEASE REPORT TO THE MUSIC
ROOM AT 17:00.

Bada bing! Three left standing; who will be king?

The day went by in a daze. I kept having daydreams about killing Winter and Smith and taking the lead role.

17:00 The three contenders met outside the music room. Smith is a tallish boy with a cheeky face and a cocky manner. He told us that the auditions were a farce because Viking had already promised him the role of Oliver. For a first-year he was incredibly arrogant. (I reckon a night in our dormitory would wipe that smug grin off his smacker.) Winter looked small and fragile and a lot like a girl. Blond hair and blue eyes and a very Oliverish look. With my brown hair and olive green eyes, I have to say I thought my chances were slim.

Viking ushered us into the band room, and sitting faithfully on the piano stool was Ms. Roberts, who could always be relied upon to smile warmly and blow her nose on a pink tissue as a result of her allergies.

"Right, gentlemen, as you can see, we're down to the wire. I won't bugger you about. One of you three will get the role of Oliver. The sixty-four-million-dollar question is, who?" Smith smiled and ran his fingers through his floppy blond hair. I am already beginning to loathe him. Winter looked nervous and had eyes like saucers, which made him look even more perfect for the part. God knows how I looked, but my mouth was dry and I was sweating.

Over the next hour we sang constantly. Sometimes we all sang together; at other times we sang duets or solos. We sang all sorts of songs and tried different voices. Viking even made us read poetry and recite a monologue. It soon became obvious that Winter's voice was dodgy, but his look was perfect. Smith had a lot of confidence and bravado but an average voice. I had a good voice, but I didn't look at all like Oliver.

On the way back to the dining hall, Smith rabbited on about his acting exploits and how he was on a television advert for some diet margarine that neither Winter nor I had ever heard of. He once again assured us that he had the part wrapped up and that Winter and I were fighting it out for the role of his understudy. As we were nearing the dining hall, a long stringy boy who looked about twenty-three ran up to us, hoofed Smith in the backside, and ordered him to sort out his room. The sudden change in Smith was unbelievable. He dropped the bravado immediately and became a whining little wimp scampering off to clean his prefect's room. It's hard not to love this life!

Thursday 16th March

Had an urgent call from Dad, who sounded ecstatic. He said that war had broken out between the ANC and the Inkatha Freedom Party (IFP). He reckons things are fine as long as the blacks are killing each other and not the whites. He's decided to de-barricade the house and donate his stockpile of canned food to the Salvation Army. More good news was that the neighbors can't press charges against my father because there were no witnesses to the slaying of their dog, and it would come down to my father's word against the dead dog's. Looks like Dad got the last bark after all.

Dad went on to say that his brother, Uncle Aubrey, has invited us up to his farm in Namibia for a week during the holidays, but it all hinges on whether Mom insists on bringing Wombat along.

Julian skipped up to me at break time and said, "Well, well, well, guess who's the lover boy!" and dropped a red envelope into my hands. I immediately recognized the Mermaid's handwriting and sprinted up to the dormitory to read the letter. The dormitory was deserted apart from Roger, who was napping in a shaft of sunlight on my bed. He looked rather irritated at the disturbance and hissed at me.

Dear Johnny,

Thanx for your letter. It was great to hear from you again. I was getting worried u weren't writing back. I'm glad school is going well, I'm sure u will have some stories for me when I see u. When are u coming home? The weather is getting cooler and if u take too much time, swimming season will be over.

My friend Liezl and I have started modern dancing lessons—I plan to become a famous dancer and singer like Madonna. School is boring as ever and I'm counting down for the holidays. What are u up to?

I'm not sure if u knew this but my mum and dad are getting divorced. They are fighting all the time. Dad has moved out and Bruce and I see him at the weekends. It makes me sad and I'm still hoping they will be able to fix things up and for Daddy to come home. You don't realize how lucky u are to have a normal family until it's gone.

Must go now—have to do maths (yuck) homework and feed Brutus (our boxer).

Miss u.
Love,
Debs

I carefully folded the letter after reading it for the fifth time and swaggered out of the dormitory.

Friday 17th March

Four pairs of my underpants are missing. The laundry denies losing them in the wash. (Having just two pairs of underpants left could lead to a lot of washing or a rather unhygienic final week.) I thought about telling somebody but chickened out—I might end up ratting on someone by default and get clonked on the head like rat-faced Scrawley.

14:10 Just before prep Rambo called us together and told us that today was Boggo's birthday. The sneaky villain hadn't told anybody for fear of being initiated (it's a school tradition to make a birthday boy's birthday as unpleasant as possible). After prep Rambo and Mad Dog leapt on Boggo and wrestled him to the ground. The rest of us seized an arm or leg and dragged him screaming to the bogs. What followed was disgusting. The mob carried Boggo into a toilet stall (I put myself in charge of his left foot) and Rambo shoved Boggo's head into the toilet and then Mad Dog flushed the chain. Boggo choked and thrashed violently but we were too strong for him. Once released, the now fourteen-year-old puked and then collapsed onto the bathroom floor, retching his guts out. Most of the house turned out to laugh at him. I felt desperately sorry for poor Boggo and more than a bit guilty for my hand in his bogwashing. I ran upstairs and fetched his towel and some clothes and brought them down to him. The crowd had scattered and Boggo was sobbing on a bench in the showers. I gave him his things, thought about cheering him up but then felt embarrassed, so I gave him a pat on his shoulder and left.

I hurried upstairs to check my calendar and to my horror I realized that my birthday (April 20th) will fall during term time. I shuddered at the thought of what terrible fate awaits me.

Sunday 19th March

A day of perfect relaxation. Me, Tolkien, and my writing pad. Wrote eight different letters to the Mermaid. Here follows the chosen masterpiece:

Dear Debbie,

Five days until the holidays (private schools get an extra week's holiday). Things have been quite hectic at school, with lots of ups and downs. Our cricket team was unbeaten this term, and yesterday we had a big celebration. Otherwise, the fight for Oliver is down to three of us (one of the opposition has already been on TV, so I'm not getting my hopes up). My dormitory is hot on the heels of an old murder/suicide that happened forty-six years ago, but I will tell you the whole story when I see you.

I'm sorry to hear about your parents. I'm not so sure about my parents being normal, but I take the point. Are you going away for the holidays? My dad wants us to go to see my uncle Aubrey in Namibia.

> *See you soon.*
> *Love,*
> *Johnny*

PS I dreamed about you last night.

I reckon I have just the right mix of news, interest, sympathy, and passion. Already worried about the weekend. I have to see her, but I'm scared to phone. (Make that terrified.)

Monday 20th March

I know you're not going to believe this, but Vern and Gecko are in serious trouble. They've both been hauled before Glockenshpeel and beaten six each for breaking into the biology laboratory. A security guard caught them sneaking through a half-opened window in the middle of the night. Since they were only on their way in, they were not accused of stealing but just of trespassing; otherwise they might well have been expelled. The beatings took place while we were in geography, so I cannot report on whether Gecko cried or vomited.

After lights-out, the entire dormitory crammed into Vern's and my cubicle to hear Gecko's telling of the story. Since his decision to take a beating for the team and now after this latest mission, Vern's shares have gone through the roof and everyone's stopped calling him Rain Man altogether. Gecko loved his moment in the spotlight and added enough suspense and exaggeration to impress both Rambo and Fatty, who demanded a retelling of the story, to which request Gecko happily obliged.

Gecko said that they broke into the biology lab to steal some of Mr. Cartwright's lab rats to feed Roger. They showed us their bruises and explained in great detail their sessions with The Glock. The gathering was broken up by Julian and Bert, who'd come to inspect "botties." After Bert had taken a series of photographs, he ordered us to bed, switched off the lights, and slapped Julian on the bum. Julian squealed in a high-pitched voice and the two ran out of the dormitory, giggling.

Before heading to bed, we all shook hands with Gecko and Vern. Rambo congratulated them for their courage and their disrespect for the school rules. They both grinned like idiots and looked incredibly proud of their achievement. Before switching off his torch, Vern shook Roger's paw and told him that he was a brave kitty. Roger purred, scratched his ear, and licked his balls.

Wednesday 22nd March

07:20 Dressed in our finest school uniforms, the Crazy Eight made their way through the archway, past the crypt, along the pathway, and through the headmaster's gate. Rambo paused under the lemon tree and winked at us.

We were on our way to breakfast with Glockenshpeel (a tradition since the school's earliest days). Luthuli had given us strict instructions to behave like gentlemen and to do the house proud. Fatty had already been to breakfast in the dining hall to avoid looking like a pig at the headmaster's.

The Glock's wife (a large woman with a wart on her chin) greeted us at the door and ushered us into the headmaster's grand mansion. We were shown into a beautiful large wood-paneled dining room. At the head of the table sat The Glock reading the *Financial Times*. He looked up and said, "Ah, so at last we get to the Crazy Eight." Simon laughed politely and we all sat nervously around the table. Vern and Gecko looked embarrassed and sank low into their chairs. The Glock studied us with a severe look and then smiled grimly. "Unfortunately, I seem to have met a few of you under vastly different circumstances." Gecko tried to clear his throat to hide his embarrassment and nearly choked. I silently prayed that he wouldn't vomit—this was definitely not the time or place.

The headmaster made us all introduce ourselves. When I stood up and said my name, The Glock raised his eyebrow and said, "So *you're* Milton?" He looked at me as if he expected more and then moved on to Boggo.

Miraculously, the breakfast went off without a hitch: Fatty turned down a second helping, Gecko didn't vomit, Vern didn't pull out any hair, Rambo was gracious, Mad Dog was polite, Boggo looked clean, Simon was as presentable as ever, and I was just me. The Glock wasn't nearly as scary as I thought he would be and, surprisingly enough, he even seemed to have a sense of humor. P. J. Luthuli was waiting nervously for us outside the house and seemed mightily relieved when we assured him that nothing had gone wrong. He punched the air with delight and breathed a heavy sigh of relief. One got the feeling that our head of house had been dreading our big breakfast for weeks.

Fatty canceled a previously scheduled Macarthur meeting because he wasn't feeling well. He reckons the breakfast with the Glock must have given him diarrhea.

Thursday 23rd March

Eve asked Rambo to stay behind after class to rehearse a scene that they plan to perform for the rest of the class sometime next term. Looks like Rambo is now officially the teacher's pet. Boggo thinks it's all a bit dodgy.

11:00 At last a stroke of luck! The entire house jostled around the notice board to read the message.

> OLD BOY J. G. COLE (1982–1985) HAS BEEN AWARDED A RHODES SCHOLARSHIP TO OXFORD UNIVERSITY AND WILL TAKE UP A DEGREE IN EGYPTOLOGY IN SEPTEMBER. IN ACCORDANCE WITH SCHOOL TRADITION, TODAY WILL BE A HALF DAY. THERE WILL BE NO LESSONS AFTER 11 A.M.

An enormous game of house touch rugby was immediately organized. Fifty boys streamed down to the field in a state of great excitement, and for two hours we sprinted around on a soft carpet of orange and brown leaves.

Just hours away from freedom!

Friday 24th March

08:00 We all marched into the final assembly full of the joys of autumn. Everywhere was the sound of laughter. Even The Glock seemed unusually happy. No doubt he was relishing the thought of three weeks of peace and quiet. After various announcements he reminded us that even in the holidays, we were ambassadors of the school and should behave accordingly at all times.

He then opened up a piece of paper and said, "As many of you know, this year we are mounting a major school production, *Oliver*, in conjunction with St. Catherine's school." (A few whistles and a deadly glare from The Glock.) "Mr. Richardson will be directing the production, and he has been conducting intensive auditions over the last six weeks or so. The casting has been completed and the lead roles are as follows: the role of Fagin will be played by Mr. Edly." (The Guv to play Fagin! My palms were sweating.) "Nancy will be played by Mrs. Wilson." (So Eve was Nancy. My guts did a somersault.) "Bill Sykes will be played by yours truly." (The Glock was playing the psychopath Sykes—talk about typecasting! I felt a desperate need to take a piss.) "The Artful Dodger will be played by Lloyd Croswell." (Loud applause and whistles. Why is my heart beating in my neck?) "And last, but certainly not least, the title role of Oliver will be played by none other than . . . John Milton!" (Applause, an elbow nailed me in the ribs, hands were on me, and everything was . . . was . . . slow motion.)

Suddenly I was surrounded by boys and masters and I was out-side in the sunlight pumping hands and getting back-slapped. Then I was in maths, staring at my textbooks. Then history and Crispo was crying and making speeches and shaking our hands. Then I was dragging my trunk to the storeroom. Then I was shaking hands with the Crazy Eight and Earthworm was there. Then suddenly I was on the bus and Fatty was going on about Macarthur, but I couldn't hear a word. All I could hear was applause, one gigantic standing ovation. Now I was hugging my mom and tears were rolling down my cheeks and I was sniffing and Dad was crying and digging in his pockets for his handkerchief—finally I was home and I didn't feel a day over four years old.

Saturday 25th March

Woke up with a raging headache from last night's celebrations. Dad forgot that I was only thirteen years old and kept pouring me gin and tonics.

12:30 Still no sign of my parents. I think it's quite possible that they have drunk themselves to death.

In my drunken haze I seemed to remember plucking up the courage and calling the Mermaid but then hanging up when a man answered.

My awesome run of luck continued when my mother (after finally waking) told me that she had invited Marge and the Mermaid around tonight. She said Marge is feeling stressed about the divorce and the Mermaid likes the pool (being a mermaid). With a cheeky smile Mom asked me if I would mind entertaining her for the evening. I did my best to look cool, but it obviously didn't work because she screeched with laughter and clapped before scurrying off to get ice for their pre-lunch drinks. I did the only thing a cool teenager can do in such circumstances. I turned around, swaggered to the bathroom, and vomited up my breakfast. (I think Gecko would have been impressed with my effort.)

Dad has started a neighborhood watch. He and his buddies cruise around the neighborhood in the station wagon looking for criminals. Dad takes his gun along but hasn't managed to shoot anyone yet.

18:00 Once Dad had driven off in his camouflaged army uniform with black shoe polish smeared on his face, Mom and I set about readying the house for the ladies. I'm glad they are only coming after nightfall so that the Mermaid won't notice the pool's turned into pea soup.

19:15 After a few moments of awkwardness (I attempted to shake the Mermaid's hand while she tried to give me a hug at the same time and I only succeeded in jabbing her left breast) we headed out to the pool. The Mermaid was different this time, sort of . . . less mermaidish. She seemed sadder and a little scared of me. She was still as beautiful as she was in my dreams. After some small talk we slowly relaxed, and soon we were lolling on the pool steps together, telling stories and cackling like hyenas.

She loved hearing stories about The Guv and Mad Dog and made me tell her every detail about the auditions. She predicted that I'd one day be a film star and we would go to the Oscars together and walk hand in hand down the crimson carpet with great flashbulbs exploding in our faces. Before I knew it, she'd slipped her fingers through mine and she was looking longingly into my eyes. This was the moment!

I got scared. I panicked and dived back into the water. Somewhere under the deep, cool, green water I let out a scream of agony—I'd just blown the chance of my first real kiss!

Sunday 26th March

All hell broke loose when Mom casually mentioned to Dad that Wombat is joining us on our Namibian holiday adventure, which kicks off on Tuesday. My father flew into a manic rage and screeched off in the station wagon. I retired to my room with *The Lord of the Rings* to avoid the latest outbreak of hostilities.

Dad returned sometime in the middle of the night and I could hear Mom ordering him to sleep in the living room. I then heard him stumble and crash into the telephone stool on his way down the passage. Welcome back to normality.

Monday 27th March

Dad's convinced that Innocence is running her brothel again. Every half hour or so an African man walks up the driveway carrying a packet and then disappears into her room only to emerge about twenty minutes later. Mom's wickedly scared of Innocence because she keeps threatening lawsuits against them.

Major embarrassment as I joined my mother on an underwear shopping expedition. With a loud voice she hollered to me (and to everybody else in the crowded shop) and held up a pair of leopard print scants and then erupted into shrill peals of laughter. I pretended to ignore her, but her hollering got louder, so I decided to cut my losses and take the embarrassment on the chin. Eventually, I escaped the shop carrying some ordinary white and blue underpants and sprinted toward the car.

Not sure if we're leaving for our holiday tomorrow or not. Mom and Dad are still not speaking, although Dad has been seen tinkering on the station wagon, which is a positive sign.

I called the Mermaid, and thankfully she answered the telephone. We talked for about an hour (although I'm not sure what we actually spoke about). I told her we would go out to the movies when I got back.

Tuesday 28th March

06:00 My parents have had yet another furious argument about my grandmother (Wombat) joining us on our holiday. Dad says Wombat is a senile old fart, and Mom says that Dad's brother, Aubrey, is a drunken maniac and a bad influence on me. So much for a happy family reunion in Namibia! Dad's also worried that the country (that he calls "South West") is now being run by blacks and will end up in chaos.

06:45 My parents have another argument about the amount of clothes my mother has packed. Two suitcases, a travel case, and a vanity bag for a weeklong trip to a farm in the Namibian desert. My father orders her to repack.

Mom eliminates the travel bag but gains an overnight bag. My father shakes his head, jumps in the car, tries in vain to start the engine, and then orders me to start pushing. The old goat catches fire about a kilometer down the street. Dad claps with delight and shouts, "Reliable as rain!" as Mom and I jump in the car huffing and puffing like two TB patients.

07:00 Wombat ticks Dad off for being ten minutes late. Dad does his nut routine when he sees Wombat's luggage (three suitcases and an overnight bag). He piles them onto the roof of the station wagon under the watchful eye of Wombat, who keeps saying "Do be gentle, Roy," and, "David, help your father, he's small of body and weak of mind." I won't mention what Dad is muttering under his breath, but I can assure you, it isn't pleasant.

07:15 We're off! The Milton Easter adventure has begun!

13:08 Wombat hasn't stopped prattling on since we left Durban. Her worsening senility means she's told us every story many times before. Mom doesn't allow us to tell her about the constant repetitions because it makes Wombat confused and anxious. In hushed tones, Wombat told us for the fourth time this morning that she suspects that Buster Cracknell is now stealing her yogurt. She reckons he's using the spare key to break into her flat and then gorges himself on her Woolworths strawberry delight. We all nodded and shook our heads. Mom promised Wombat that she'd investigate the situation. (Wombat apparently phones the police every morning to report the matter—they have threatened to prosecute her for crank calls.)

After passing Bethlehem (a small town in the Orange Free State and definitely not the place of Jesus' birth), my father burst into operatic song in the middle of the fifth repeat of the yogurt story. Wombat told my father that he was rude and unpleasant and that he should try to be more like David (me?). Mom shook her head at him and dug her nails into his leg. Dad stopped singing.

After eleven hours of sheer madness we finally arrived at the Holiday Inn in Kimberley in the Northern Cape Province. Wombat told us that her father made an immense fortune in diamond mining at the Great Hole of Kimberley. (Unfortunately, the mine was last used in 1908, when her father would have been just fourteen years old.) Mom reminded Wombat that her father collapsed and died after a sneezing attack and that he worked for an insurance company. Wombat wept bitterly and said she remembered the sneezing tragedy like it was yesterday.

Yet another family argument erupted after Wombat refused to share a room with me. She said she wouldn't have people thinking that she's "shacking up with a toy boy." My mother reminded her that I'm her grandson and just a boy of thirteen. Wombat replied that sleeping with an underage grandson was in poor taste and that she didn't care whether my balls had dropped or not, she wanted her own room. I felt my cheeks flush and a pressing desire to hit Wombat on the head with the hotel fire extinguisher.

19:45 I joined Dad in the lounge for a drink before dinner. He asked the waiter if there was anywhere he could get some rat poison after hours. The waiter said he would check the hotel storeroom. Dad then looked me squarely in the eyes and warned me never to get married, and if I had to, then I should marry an orphan.

Mom joined us in a panic and said that Wombat had disappeared. Dad cheered loudly and ordered a double whiskey to celebrate.

Twenty minutes later Wombat was found in the honeymoon suite watching television in bed. She refused to budge when the hotel staff asked her to return to her room and burst into floods of tears when the manager arrived and ordered her to vacate the suite. She then rummaged around in her handbag and showed the hotel manager a picture of her late husband and told him that this was where they had spent the first night of their honeymoon. The manager told her that the hotel was only five years old. Wombat pretended not to hear him and told him the yogurt story. The manager soon realized he was dealing with a nutcase, cut his losses, and let her stay in the suite at no extra cost.

Dad's convinced that Wombat's feigning madness to get her own way and tried to persuade my mother to leave her behind in Kimberley and pick her up on the way home. My parents then had yet another ripsnorting argument in front of everybody in the dining room. I cast my mind back to school and wondered how all the other boys were enjoying their holidays. Surely they had to be having more fun than the folks, Wombat, and me.

Wednesday 29th March

08:15 Dad has been refused entry into Namibia because the border control computer says he has a criminal record. (He doesn't—yet—

but he's still meant to be under psychological evaluation.) Dad, having driven for two days through blazing heat and endless repetitions of the yogurt saga, completely snapped and threatened to drive the car off the bridge and into the river. Wombat, who didn't know about Dad's run-in with the law, told my mother to file for divorce immediately. She went on to say that she'd always suspected that he was a criminal and that he had "mixed blood in his veins and close-together eyes like a monkey." Mom told Wombat to shut up and ordered her back to the car.

08:36 Suddenly the border post was open and a smiling official waved us through. My father returned to the car, whooped loudly, and merrily drove us into Namibia. After a long pause, he said, "Since I'm a criminal, I thought I'd act like one and try a little bribery." Wombat was outraged and said her Walter (my deceased grandfather) would turn in his grave were he to witness such horror. Dad retorted by saying that it would be no worse than the poor man's horror of living with Wombat for forty-two years. Luckily Wombat didn't hear him.

We finally arrived at Uncle Aubrey's farm. Uncle Aubrey, Aunt Peggy, a dog called Lion, and a pet sheep (called Baa) met us at the gate. Uncle Aubrey and Dad got stuck into some violent punching, wrestling, hugging, and backslapping. My mother and Wombat remained in the car. I got out and hugged my relatives. Lion jumped up and knocked me over. As always, they told me I'd grown and am looking more like my dad every day. Aubrey gave me a few friendly punches, and by mistake I landed a good one right in his stomach. I felt wickedly guilty as Dad and Aunt Peggy tried to revive Uncle Aubrey, who was doubled over on the fence. Once we were at the house, Mom got out of the car and shook hands with Aubrey and Peggy. Aubrey grabbed her hand and planted a big kiss on her lips and then smacked her bum. Mom blushed and quickly commented on the flowers. Wombat refused to get out of the car until the dog and the sheep had been locked away.

After a long drinking competition, Dad and Uncle Aubrey started a savage arm-wrestling bout. The arm wrestling became horseplay, horseplay turned into a wrestle, the wrestling soon became a shadow-boxing match, which then lost its shadow and turned into a boxing match, which at last became a full-on fight. Dad punched Aubrey in the nose and Aubrey pushed Dad over the couch, smashing a lamp in the process. I tried to break it up by turning off the lights, but this just made things worse when Dad ran into the glass sliding door and knocked himself out cold. Mom ran in and shouted at both of them like they were schoolboys. After my father had regained consciousness, the two brothers shook hands, hugged, and went to bed.

Could swear I heard hyenas whooping and cackling in the night. Decided to sleep with my head under the blankets for safety.

Thursday 30th March

05:00 Uncle Aubrey woke me up with strong coffee and told me to get ready for "the hunt." I think Uncle Aubrey must have been a Mad Dog in his day.

Armed with a shotgun, Uncle Aubrey ushered Dad and me into his weather-beaten old Toyota truck and drove us into the bush. As the older brother, Uncle Aubrey inherited the family game farm, which extends for miles across the dry semi-desert of southern Namibia. (My father, as younger brother, inherited his father's old clothes and the station wagon.) The alcohol fumes from the two brothers nearly knocked me out, so I braved the chilly morning air and opened the window. Uncle Aubrey passed around a bottle of headache tablets. Dad swallowed four.

After no more than five minutes Uncle Aubrey brought the truck to a screeching halt, jumped out, and took a shot at a springbok, which was grazing under a big camel-thorn tree. He missed the entire tree by meters. We then drove for ages without seeing anything. Dad complained that his bum had gone numb, so we stopped to stretch. I was then given a shooting lesson by my uncle, who showed me how to aim and use my shoulder as a shock absorber against the kick of the shotgun. I blasted an anthill with my first shot. Uncle Aubrey applauded and reckoned I have potential and was most probably already a better shot than my father. Dad bit his lip and gave a funny false laugh. Unfortunately, I missed most of what my uncle was saying because my ears were ringing and my shoulder felt like it had just been shot off!

A few minutes later we spotted a large herd of springbok. Dad sneaked out of the truck with the gun and whispered to us to follow. He announced to us that he would demonstrate how a real hunter goes about shooting a springbok.

After leading us in a broad circle, Dad pointed to the herd of springbok across the ridge and told us he was moving downwind of them so that they wouldn't smell us. When I pointed out that there was no wind, he hissed at me and called me a cocky bastard. Keeping close to the ground and stalking through the dry thorn trees, I felt like a real hunter. I could hear my heart thumping in my chest. Dad took the lead and communicated by strange hand signals, which neither Uncle Aubrey nor I could understand. After what seemed like ages, we crouched not more than fifty yards from the buck. Dad pointed out a male with big horns at the front of the herd and whispered, "His horns will be on my bedroom door." Then he said, "Now watch and learn," took aim, and fired. There was a huge explosion, and the springbok herd galloped away in a cloud of dust. My father sprinted after them, whooping and shouting with joy.

The three of us stood staring. My father grunted. Uncle Aubrey clicked his tongue. I whistled. Around us the African morning was full of birdsong.

Dad had succeeded in firing a hail of bullets through the truck's windscreen. We drove silently back to the farmhouse.

We returned to find the farmhouse in a state of chaos. Wombat was in tears, Mom was fuming, and Peggy was making tea. Wombat's third suitcase (carrying her underwear, petticoats, and her dead husband's gum boots) had been stolen in the night. Dad, with the gun slung over his shoulder, casually brushed the broken glass from his trousers and told everyone that he'd used Wombat's suitcase as a bribe at the border post.

17:30 I'm now officially the only person speaking to my father. We took an afternoon walk along a dry riverbed to watch the sun set. He asked me about school and I told him about Fatty and the night swim and Gecko, Rambo, Boggo, and Mad Dog and his pigeon hunting. He laughed at my stories and told me that he had hated boarding school. (He went to a government school in Upington in the Northern Cape.) He then gave me a sip of his beer and told me to never be ashamed of myself and that even the queen has to shit once a day. I nodded solemnly like I understood his point and stared out at the setting sun. After a long silence, Dad gave me another swig of his beer and then said he must go and apologize to everyone. I stayed out in the bush and threw stones at an old lamppost and for a moment, a very brief moment, I wished I were back at school.

22:00 Dad has miraculously calmed the troubled waters and we all sat happily around the fire laughing, chatting, and telling stories. Even Wombat emerged from her room to join the party. Mom cleverly placed Wombat next to Aunt Peggy so that she didn't have to listen to the first of many stories about the saga of the disappearing yogurt. Dad got me to tell the story about Fatty getting stuck in the chapel window. Everyone laughed uproariously at Fatty having to speak in chapel about his Jesus revelation.

Wombat drank too much sherry and started singing old British war songs. Uncle Aubrey sang a song in Afrikaans, and before long the two were arguing about the Anglo-Boer War of 1899–1902. Wombat steamed off to bed after Aubrey called the English a "bunch of Nazis" and then returned a minute later to call the Afrikaners a bunch of "racist pigs" for creating apartheid. What followed was a heated debate about politics and Nelson Mandela. Feeling brave, I stepped in and told everybody how pleased I was about the freedom of Mandela. After a shocked silence, my father called me a bleeding heart commie and sent me to bed. I felt wickedly rebellious. Perhaps one day I'll be able to call myself a freedom fighter.

Saturday 1st April

08:30 Absolute pandemonium has broken out. Wombat has been declared missing. Mom is beside herself with panic while Dad is trying his best to look concerned. Everybody has dispersed to various parts of the farm for a manhunt (Wombat hunt).

At a family meeting over coffee in the kitchen, it was decided that Wombat may not have returned from her walk yesterday. The police have been called.

Lunchtime: While chowing down on baked beans on toast, Uncle Aubrey suddenly jumped up, laughing, and shouted, "You little beauty!" like he'd just discovered fire. He took the pipe out of his mouth and knocked it savagely against the wall calendar. "April Fools' Day!" he declared, like it was the most obvious point ever. Nobody seemed particularly convinced by his theory since Wombat is partially senile and often forgets her own birthday.

Dad and I spent the afternoon searching the farm while the others waited for the police.

Teatime: More coffee and debate. I told everyone the story of the disappearance of Vern "Rain Man" Blackadder. Uncle Aubrey thumped me on the back and called me a genius. He then led the long line of Miltons under the house armed with a powerful torch and his shotgun. No Wombat but plenty of fruit bats.

The police have promised to begin searching in the morning should she not return.

18:45 My mother is already onto her fifth glass of wine. Dad says he's matching her glass for glass out of sympathy.

After some Sherlock Holmes detective work, I discovered that Wombat's toothbrush, pajamas, and overnight bag were missing.

20:00 I chaired the third family meeting of the day (because everybody else was too drunk). I told them that I thought Wombat had escaped and was not lost. I ordered Aunt Peggy (as the least pissed of the adults) to begin phoning hotels, guesthouses, bus services, and airports.

The Holiday Inn (Kimberley) informed Aunt Peggy that they had an elderly woman by the name of Elizabeth Windsor, who had checked into the honeymoon suite yesterday. (Wombat often thinks she's the queen nowadays and signs most documents Elizabeth.)

I phoned the hotel and asked the receptionist if the old lady in the honeymoon suite was the same lady who had caused chaos in their hotel on Tuesday. She giggled and said it was. Wombat has been found!

Mom, reeking of alcohol, kissed me a hundred times and called me a genius (should she be surprised?). Dad put on a brave face and tried to look relieved. After much kissing and fondling, Uncle Aubrey and Aunt Peggy said they had to check something in the bedroom and disappeared for fifteen minutes.

Mom called Wombat and started shouting at her over the phone. Wombat told her she was afraid of the dog and the sheep and didn't like the company. Mom started crying and soon they were chatting lovingly to each other.

Dad pulled me over and through gritted teeth he uttered, "I'll never forgive you for this, you little bastard!" With that he grabbed a bottle of whiskey, stalked into his bedroom, and slammed the door.

Think I may become a missing persons investigator when I'm older. At the age of thirteen I've already been involved in two cases, solved one, and am well up on police procedure. Spud Milton, PI—could even be a TV show!

Sunday 2nd April

It's been decided to leave Wombat in Kimberley until we pass through tomorrow. The details of her escape are not consistent with a senile old woman but rather a deceptively sly criminal. Apparently, before taking her morning walk, she packed a bag and called a taxi service, telling them to meet her on the main road. The taxi then drove her to Keetmanshoop, where she caught a coach to the Holiday Inn in Kimberley.

Had a lovely evening over a tasty roast lamb and mint sauce meal. (Fatty would have done his nut.) Dad and Uncle Aubrey recalled stories of their childhood on the farm. After dinner Uncle Aubrey tried to get a game of indoor cricket going, but this was abandoned after Lion ran away with the tennis ball and ripped it to pieces.

Monday 3rd April

05:30 We left, hooting, in a cloud of dust with Lion chasing our car for nearly a kilometer. (Haven't seen Baa the sheep since last night.) We were all in good spirits and Dad got us singing "Country Road." Because we were in Namibia and in a closed environment, I didn't feel embarrassed and even added the odd trumpet sound and my infamous drumroll.

06:00 Dad's still singing, but by now solo.

After off-loading another suitcase of Wombat's clothes, we slipped through the border without having to fill out a form or wait in a queue. Even Mom saw the funny side of Wombat's suitcases being used as international bribery currency.

Dad's mood plummeted after Kimberley. Wombat didn't stop prattling on about the poor service of the hotel staff and the fact that they were stealing her toiletries. Dad kept his eyes fixed on the road and both hands gripped tightly on the steering wheel.

After four hours of nonstop complaining and endless repeats of the yogurt story, Dad, with the whites of his knuckles showing on the wheel, stopped the car at a late night emergency pharmacy in Ladysmith. Ten minutes later he returned with cool drinks and a soda water for Wombat.

Wombat passed out. Her head lolled back and her mouth opened, displaying a set of yellow false teeth and a wickedly pale tongue. Dad let out a delighted chuckle and squeezed Mom's leg.

23:00 Home at last. Dad and I had to carry the comatose Wombat to bed, lock her flat, and throw the keys through the window. As we trudged through the flower bed he confessed that he had dropped seven sleeping tablets in her soda water and said he would stock up for future trips.

So endeth the Miltons' Namibian adventure of 1990.

Thursday 6th April

Have now completed a two-day period of rest and relaxation, much needed after our rather stressful holiday. I've advanced through the epic *The Lord of the Rings* at a rapid rate, only pausing to eat, swim, and talk to the Mermaid on the telephone. I have conquered *The Fellowship of the Ring* and am presently sweeping through *The Two Towers* quicker than Shadowfax the horse!

Mom says Wombat was unconscious for thirty-six hours and by the time she woke up, she had no recollection of ever even going on holiday! She called the police to report the theft of many of her clothes and suitcases.

19:30 After hours of my begging and pleading, Mom is allowing me to join Dad on his neighborhood watch. I promised her that I would stay in the car at all times. Looking forward to catching a few criminals or even witnessing a murder.

20:00 Dad and I set off for the neighborhood watch together. We picked up somebody called Frank, who has a permanently red face and talks without opening his mouth. Frank rambled on about a gang that's been "robbing the neighborhood blind" and reckoned that they stole Willy van Vuuren's BMW last night. Like Dad, Frank also wears "camo" clothing and has rubbed some sort of mud pack on his face. He says it's what the U.S. Army uses. Dad applied the mud pack to his face and then declared himself "ready for action."

The first two hours were uneventful. We gratefully accepted Frank's offer of some strong coffee from his flask, only to discover that the milk was sour. There was a moment of excitement when a stray cat managed to trap itself in a rubbish bin. Dad and Frank stalked the bin like it was a land mine. Frank eventually lifted the lid, and the crazed animal flew out like a demon. Dad screamed and dived into a hedge for cover and Frank screamed and fired three shots into the air. The gunfire seemed to wake up the entire neighborhood. A woman screamed and dogs started barking everywhere. Dad and Frank galloped back to the car and we sped off down the street like a bunch of criminals.

Later on we met Garth and Bob (also dressed like idicts), who said they had just foiled a possible house breaking. Dad and Frank were wickedly jealous and redoubled the effort to find some real crime.

The moment of truth arrived a little after midnight when we stumbled on a rather shady-looking character trying to open a car door with a coat hanger. The man was dressed in pajamas and a satin night robe and was feverishly working away at the side of the car. Dad flicked off the station wagon's lights and pulled the car off the road. He ordered me to stay in the car, and he and Frank pulled out their guns and began creeping toward the car thief, who was still desperately trying to prize open the driver's door. The thief was operating under a bright streetlamp, so I could easily see what was going on from the safety of the back seat of the station wagon.

Dad and Frank, using the car as a shield, were able to sneak right up to the thief without being detected. With a shout they ordered the burglar to drop his coat hanger and place his hands on the car. The burglar looked terrified (who wouldn't when faced with two armed middle-aged men in camouflage and mud packs?). Dad frisked the criminal but only succeeded in discovering a toothbrush, dental floss, and a tube of toothpaste. I heard him saying to Frank, "It's amazing how high-tech these criminals are nowadays!"

"Take the car, take everything!" cried the panic-stricken thief before Frank shut him up by jamming his revolver into the base of his neck. Meanwhile Dad returned to the car and radioed the police, triumphantly announcing that he had apprehended a car thief. His tone was nothing short of ecstatic and he gave me a wink before sprinting back to the scene of the crime.

Suddenly a large blond woman in a dressing gown walked out of the front gate of the house and onto the road. When she spotted Frank and Dad, she let rip with a gut-wrenching, bloodcurdling screech. They both aimed their guns at her and she screamed again and then fainted. Once the lady had recovered, she became angry with Frank and Dad and told them to leave her husband alone. Dad was immediately suspicious and ordered her to place her hands on the car. Frank frisked her and came up with a box of Smarties (a bizarre weapon for a criminal's accomplice). Dad looked like one of those Vietnam soldiers who had just captured a leader of the Vietcong. He kept his gun in the face of the criminals and spoke in a gruff voice. (A bit like Robert De Niro with a mud pack.)

Then a police van screeched up and two policemen jumped out and immediately pointed their weapons at Frank and Dad. The cops forced them to lower their guns and lie down on the road. I ducked down behind the driver's seat and watched the drama unfold through a crack between the driver's seat and the door. After some lengthy debate and much gesticulating it was finally established that the "criminals" were trying to break into their own vehicle because the blond woman had locked her keys inside the car. Therefore, the criminals weren't criminals at all but law-abiding citizens going about their own business. For a while it looked like Dad and Frank were going to be arrested (for aggravated assault), but finally the policemen dissuaded the irate man with the dental equipment and the angry lady with the Smarties from pressing charges. The man finally agreed to let Frank and Dad off with a wave of his toothbrush. To add insult to injury, the policemen confiscated Dad's and Frank's guns and took down their details.

Frank and Dad were fuming when they returned to the car. Dad ranted on about how the country was going to the dogs, and Frank threatened to emigrate to Fiji. To add to their woes, the station wagon started making a horrible clunking noise and the entire engine seized just a hundred meters from our house. Dad kicked a tire savagely and then limped home in silence with me following a few steps behind, desperately trying not to laugh.

Friday 7th April (Bad Friday)

I swear I could see tears in Dad's eyes as the tow truck drove past with the poor old station wagon dragging behind. After watching his pride and joy dragged around the corner, Dad limped inside and screamed loudly. I was about to run after him to see if he was okay, but Mom stopped me and said he was just letting off a bit of steam. Suddenly there was an enormous crash and then the tinkle of broken glass. Mom leapt to her feet and said, "Right, that's it!" She then stormed into the house to find that Dad, in his rage, had ripped the bathroom cabinet out of the wall, forgetting that it contained all of Mom's expensive perfumes.

The language that flew around our house for the next twenty minutes would have made The Guv blush. Eventually, Dad said he was moving out, packed a suitcase, grabbed the car keys, and headed to the garage. There was a howl of frustration when he realized that the car was gone. So he set off on foot, limping down the road with his suitcase dragging behind him.

I returned to my room and wondered why this always has to happen over the holidays. They've had all term to fight! I closed the door, but I could still hear Mom sobbing in the bathroom.

Saturday 8th April

Mom says Dad's moved in with Frank and as far as she's concerned, the marriage is over. Mom wouldn't say whether this was because of her perfume or because Dad has moved in with another man.

19:10 Operation First Date! Black shoes, blue jeans, white T-shirt, spiky gelled hair. The movie—*Ghost*, with Patrick Swayze and Demi

Moore. The mission—to seal the deal and have my first proper kiss (called a grab).

Marge picked me up in her Mazda and dropped us at the cinema. The Mermaid was wearing a short black dress, high heels, and with her makeup on, she was terrifyingly beautiful. I prayed that I'd meet somebody from school and they would see me with her. I struggled to think of anything to say. I was completely intimidated by this goddess walking beside me. After an awkwardly long silence we sat down at the Pizza Hut for a cool drink. The Mermaid asked me about the Namibian trip, and pretty soon I had her in stitches, telling her about Wombat and her missing clothes. (She thinks the yogurt story is hilarious—perhaps she hasn't heard it enough. . . .) I have never been so thankful for my weird dysfunctional family before. In front of me, the most beautiful girl in the world was laughing so much that her makeup had run and turned her perfect face into a honey badger!

Her makeup continued to smudge during the movie. We held hands all the way through. I only broke her grasp twice (to wipe my sweaty palms on the underside of the seat). The movie was a real tearjerker, so I decided to look manly and rugged and unaffected throughout. We chatted about *Ghost* over vanilla milk shakes at the Milky Lane and then, holding hands, strolled outside and sat under a big green leafy tree on the verge of the road.

Suddenly the talking stopped. The Mermaid was looking at me with that same intense stare that she had given me that day on the pool steps. This time there was no swimming away. I stared back and hoped she didn't hear the big thumping snare drum in my chest. Our lips met, my eyes closed, and then I felt her tongue in my mouth. After a moment's shock my own tongue met hers and we were joined in a mad tongue wrestle of love. We seemed to kiss for some sort of eternity and when it was over, I was instantly overcome with the most wonderful feeling of accomplishment. All I could think about was charging back to school to casually tell the Crazy Eight that I had kissed the Mermaid and she was now my girlfriend.

Sunday 9th April (Easter Sunday)

08:50 Mom and I filed into St. Margaret's Anglican church and found Dad already seated and seemingly deep in prayer. When he sat back in his pew, he looked totally disheveled. He was unshaven and his shirt was all wrinkled. (I guess living with Frank isn't all it's cracked up to be.) I enjoyed the hymns, many of which I had learned in the choir, and sang at the top of my soon-to-be famous treble voice. The old bat in front of me turned around during the sermon and told me that I had a splendid voice. The priest was much more charming and relaxed than our Reverend Bishop and didn't show any signs of psychotic behavior or any manic hand gestures during his sermon.

After the service Mom and I jumped into her rented car and headed off to Wombat's flat for the traditional Easter egg hunt. (This used to be exciting until I turned eight but has since become a bit of an ordeal.) As we were pulling out of the parking lot, I turned around and saw Dad waving pathetically. Mom bit her lip, pretended not to see him, and sped off down the lane.

Wombat was in a state of great agitation when we arrived. She said she'd hidden all the Easter eggs last night but couldn't remember where she'd put them. I checked all the usual places (booze cabinet, underwear drawer, windowsill, under the sink) but couldn't find them. Mom had to restrain Wombat from calling the cops and accusing Buster Cracknell of aggravated Easter egg theft. We assured her that they would turn up in due course (hopefully before they went moldy). After all, Easter Sunday is meant to be the day when things come back to life.

Wombat (in keeping with tradition) treated us to lunch at the Royal Natal Yacht Club. While eating my roast chicken and trying to ignore the shrill nattering of my grandmother, I watched a gigantic cruise liner sailing into the harbor. Four tugboats were leading it to its berth. I pointed it out to Mom, who reckoned it was the

QE2–the most luxurious boat on the sea. Wombat then became all snivelly and said that she had spent six glorious days of her honeymoon on the *QE2*. Mom winked at me–Wombat spent her honeymoon in Margate!

Dad was waiting for us when we got home, and he and Mom went to their room for a chat. I called the Mermaid and wished her happy Easter. We chatted for ages until Dad started cooking and singing opera in the kitchen (his sneaky way of keeping the phone bill down). Dad fried up an English breakfast for dinner, after which I escaped to my room to join Frodo on his journey toward Mordor.

Monday 10th April

Mom woke me up at 08:00 and said there was a man on the phone who needed to speak to me urgently. I answered the phone, my greeting rather croaky.

"Rise and shine, Milton, this is no day to be oversleeping!" The voice needed no introduction–it was Viking.

"Yes, sir, I mean, no, sir, I was awake." Viking chuckled and then told me that I may have got the part of Oliver, but that didn't mean I was a good enough actor to fool him.

"Listen, Milton," he continued in his great booming voice, "I wanted to congratulate you personally for landing the big fish! To think, after your abominable first audition I wasn't even going to line you up for the chorus. It was that little vixen wife of your housemaster's who insisted. And blow me sideways, that tart was right!"

I thanked Viking for giving me the chance, but he cut me off with, "Now listen, Milton, we need to do something with your look. How would you feel about curly blond hair?" I stammered out something and he said, "Good. Now whatever you do, do not cut your hair! I have obtained permission for you and the Fagin's gang chorus to grow your hair long. So if you cut your hair, you may as well go the whole hog and cut your head off as well!" I assured him that I wouldn't cut my hair and he told me we would start rehearsing as soon as we returned to school next week. Then he abruptly hung up.

My hands trembled as I put down the phone. Blond hair, thousands in the audience. Let's face it, dear diary, I'm only months away from being a star! Spent an hour looking at my features in the bathroom mirror. Unfortunately, a round face and a button nose are hardly the right assets for a heartthrob—perhaps the blond hair will turn me into a Patrick Swayze!

Wednesday 12th April

I decided to prepare myself for the limelight with twenty questions that the world will need to know about me.

Name:	John Howard Milton
Age:	13 (nearly 14)
Nickname:	Spud
Date of birth:	20 April 1976
Star sign:	Aries (although some dodgy astrologers insist on calling me a Taurus)
Favorite food:	Cheddar cheese
Favorite drink:	Vanilla milk shake

Favorite film:	*Pretty Woman*
Favorite actress:	Julia Roberts
Favorite actor:	Myself (ha ha)
Favorite book:	*The Lord of the Rings* (I haven't finished it yet, but The Guv said it is the best book ever, so I would rate it above *Catch 22*)
Worst book:	*The Secret Diary of Adrian Mole* (Any boy's diary written by a woman called Sue Townsend is not to be trusted.) Adrian Mole is a raving nerd who wouldn't last one day in our dormitory. Even Gecko is less cowardly than this Lucozade-drinking, pill-popping, pimply Brit! (I did think the book was hilarious, though.)
Greatest achievement:	Kissing the Mermaid—and I suppose winning a scholarship wasn't too bad
Favorite sport:	Cricket
Most embarrassing moment:	Any public gathering with my parents
Funniest moment:	Any one of The Guv's English lessons
Future plans:	To establish myself as a great actor, writer, and scholar

Something your fans wouldn't know about you:	I keep a diary.
Who would you most like to be:	Julia Roberts's boyfriend
Who would you most like to meet:	Nelson Mandela

Saturday 15th April

As you may have gathered (by the serious lack of diary entries), my holiday hasn't been as exciting as I'd hoped. The Mermaid is away at a Girl Guide camp. Dad is at work, and Mom always seems to be out on some errand. I've also decided against calling up old friends from my primary school. (After all the emotional goodbyes and handshaking, I still haven't heard a peep from any of them.)

Instead, I have spent the last few days practicing Oliver songs and reading *The Lord of the Rings*. I'm now well into the third book of the trilogy, called *The Return of the King*. The Guv's right—it is an amazing book that almost can't be explained. It gets five stars on the soon-to-be-famous Milton book-rating system.

It has just sunk in that on Monday night I return to school and, unbelievably, I can't wait to go back. The desire to start rehearsing and find out what everybody has been up to has me wishing that the weekend would just fly by. Also, three weeks of hanging out with my loony family has started me questioning my own sanity.

Monday 17th April

The Mermaid came around with Marge to say goodbye. We talked for ages in my room while I packed. We kissed until our tongues ached (with all the practice I'm becoming a maestro) and then the Mermaid cried and said she didn't want me to go back to school. She looked so sad that I almost burst into tears. I suddenly had a desperate urge not to go back. That deadweight in my tummy was stronger than ever and suddenly I felt terribly nervous and unsure of myself. Once the Mermaid had gone, I packed the last of my clothes, showered, and dressed in my school uniform. Ready . . . or not?

On the way to the bus, Mom took me to visit Wombat. When I arrived, she clapped and told me that I was extremely handsome. She asked me if I had a girlfriend, and Mom told her about the Mermaid. She shook her head sadly and warned me about settling down with a family too soon and said I must "spread my wild oats." Obviously, Wombat's forgotten I'm a spud.

Wombat then went on to tell us (in hushed tones) that the bank was stealing money from her accounts. She's gathering her evidence, and once her case is watertight, she'll then inform the Department of Finance. Mom abruptly stood up and said it was time to go.

Mom cried at the Westville bus stop, but thankfully she didn't do anything drastic like wave the bus off or chase it down the road!

The bus trip was totally boring. Fatty wasn't there and I knew none of the boys very well. A number of the first-years looked wickedly miserable and one of them burst into tears as the bus pulled away. As a punishment he was forced to sing all five verses of the school song to the giggling and squawking occupants. One of the older boys said that he liked the look of the young boy's sister and asked him if she "squatted for bus fare?" The young boy burst into tears again and was then ordered to sing the national anthem with his pants down. I shrank down low into my seat, worried that as the next-smallest person on the bus, I would be the next victim. Luckily, the older boys got bored and told the sniveling first-year to get lost. The poor sod returned to his seat and tucked into some delicious-looking sandwiches, perfectly wrapped by his mother in cellophane.

I stepped off the bus into a Midlands wind that was cold and biting. The trees had lost most of their leaves over the holidays. I walked through the archway into the main quad and there stood Pissing Pete pissing on his goldfish. Some things never change.

Earthworm was standing outside the house, sipping a cup of tea and looking smug. He said hello and then ordered me to unpack his trunk and bags. Suddenly there was a piercing screech and then a squeal as Julian sprinted past in his underpants pursued by Bert, who was brandishing a flyswatter.

The bus from Johannesburg was late, so most of our dormitory hadn't arrived. Only Vern and Fatty were about. Fatty was noshing a box of sandwiches and Vern was trying to unpack around a playful Roger, who kept jumping inside Vern's trunk and viciously attacking his socks.

21:30 Lights-out. The dormitory is at last assembled and it's like we've never been away.

CRAZY EIGHT HOLIDAY HIGHLIGHTS:

Rambo	Joined a gym. Got a blow job from a twenty-five-year-old woman. Went to six different nightclubs (three on the same night).
Mad Dog	Shot a goat on his farm.
Simon	Was invited to the Transvaal junior cricket academy and met South African cricket captain Clive Rice.

Gecko	Flew to London to see his folks and nearly got run over by a red double-decker bus. Reckons he hit a vomit count of seventeen.
Fatty	Broke his own cheese-and-tomato-sandwich eating record and wolfed down twenty-four at one sitting. He also says he's made some inroads into the Macarthur mystery.
Boggo	Bought a porno video.
Vern	Had to return to school midway through the holidays to collect Roger, who had gone on another hunger strike.
Spud	Kissed the Mermaid—who is now officially his girlfriend. Went on a dodgy family holiday to Namibia.

Tuesday 18th April

06:15 The rising siren launched me out of my bed like a Scud (Spud) missile. A huge groan sounded around the dormitory. As I padded along the cold floors toward the showers, I was left in no doubt that the holidays were now well and truly over. Afrikaans greeted us at 06:40. Seriously reconsidering my desire in the holidays to get back to school—think I may have been afflicted by a bout of Milton madness!

A new subject for this term is called religious instruction, with

Reverend Bishop, which is basically a class where we are supposed
to talk about Christianity but actually discuss anything we feel
like. Rambo spent the lesson taking the piss out of the Reverend,
who thought he was being sincere. He asked the chaplain if oral
sex was against God's law. Reverend Bishop said it was fine as long
as it was within a loving and committed relationship. Boggo then
asked the poor man if it was immoral for a woman to sit on a
police baton. The chaplain didn't understand the question and
said that women had a right to protect themselves. By then the
class was beside themselves. Larry Radford from Blake house tried
so hard not to laugh that he had a coughing fit and had to be
excused. Reverend Bishop asked Fatty to say the closing prayer
before dismissing us.

11:00 The notice read:

FULL *OLIVER* CAST MEETING
IN THE THEATER AT 16:30.

12:00 The Guv looked identical to my dad on Easter Sunday:
unshaven, crinkly clothes, and bloodshot eyes. He seemed distracted and mumbled his way through double English. He didn't
once make a joke or threaten anyone with a gruesome death. After
the lesson I went to say hello. He just said, "Greetings, Milton,
good holiday?" and stared distractedly out the window. I could see
he wasn't really interested in my reply. Disappointed, I excused
myself and slipped out of the classroom.

16:30 About fifty of us gathered in the theater to meet Viking.
(The teacher actors were absent.) The big black stage thrusts right
out into the auditorium, which seats about five hundred people,
and with the gallery overhanging the action it looks like a coli-
seum. Already the atmosphere was electric. I noticed that many
boys stared and pointed at me in private discussions. "TV star"

Smith looked away when I smiled at him. Winter just looked big-eyed and sad.

"All right, you bastards. I will be running a tight ship. In fact, this ship will be run tighter than a nun's $%&^#$!" I looked around. Did Viking just say what I thought he said? "This play will be your life for the next five months. This play will be no amdram wanky school production; this play will be good enough to grace any professional stage anywhere in the world. I demand endurance, discipline, and, most of all, creativity!"

Viking called up Lloyd Cresswell (The Artful Dodger) and myself and showed us off to the rest of the cast. "These are your stars. Give them all the assistance they need because by God, they're gonna need it!" I noticed Geoff Lawson among the cast and he gave me a smile and thumbs-up. It was a relief to see a friendly face.

Viking handed out scripts and musical scores to everybody, despite the fact that most of us can't read music. He then handed out rehearsal schedules. The cast is made up of three chorus groups, the workhouse boys, consisting of the youngest, smallest boys (like me), Fagin's gang of medium-size boys, and then the older London Town chorus, who are mostly third-years and matrics. Each group will practice twice a week. I have to be at just about every rehearsal, which is fine with me. Rehearsals will take place mainly in the evenings, Monday to Friday, from 20:00, and all day on Sundays. With special permission from Sparerib I've been granted leave of absence from prep from 19:30 every night and from free bounds on Sundays. Rehearsals begin tomorrow night!

When we arrived for lights-out, we found that everybody's bed had been moved out of the window and onto the vestry roof. Due to the steady drizzle they were all soaked. P. J. Luthuli was absolutely livid and immediately called in Pike and Devries, who denied responsibility for the prank. Sparerib had to get the laundry opened and we all marched off in our pajamas to get new mattresses. Luthuli has vowed to kill the offender (slowly and painfully).

Pike woke us up and asked us if we were having wet dreams. Rambo threw a shoe at him, which clonked him on the head. Pike squawked and disappeared and the rest of us cheered—according to our tally, the score is now 1–1.

Wednesday 19th April

After weeks of anticipation, the great day arrived for our first rehearsal in the music department. I was so nervous that my score and my voice were shaking like dried leaves in a hurricane. Thankfully, I didn't have any solos, and we worked on the grand intro "Food, Glorious Food" and the song "Oliver with the workhouse boys" chorus. Both Winter and Smith were there and made a point of ignoring me. Ms. Roberts and Mr. Sturgeon (the musical director) took us through our paces. Mr. Sturgeon, who is completely bald and a dead ringer for Kojak (hence the nickname), swung a baton in our faces and screamed if we were going too fast or too slow. Winter started crying for no apparent reason and Viking had to take him outside for a pep talk. After the rehearsal Viking patted me on the back and said, "I see tomorrow is your special day, Milton. Happy birthday . . . and, er . . . good luck."

I walked back to the house, gazing up at the stars. With all the excitement about rehearsals and the new term, I'd forgotten about my birthday completely. Tomorrow I will no doubt be put through some horrendous torture. (I sure hope it isn't a bogwash.) I eventually decided that whatever will come will come and calmly sauntered back to the silence of the sleeping house.

Thursday 20th April

Happy birthday, Spud Milton! Fourteen years old today. (A birthday shared with Adolf Hitler.)

I got calls from the folks and the Mermaid and a birthday card from Wombat in Mom's handwriting. Besides the above there was no other mention of my birthday from anyone. Not even a wink or a suspicious glance, nothing. Could the impossible happen? Could my birthday be forgotten? (Unfortunately, this seems unlikely as each boy is given a list with the precise age and birth date of every boy in the school.)

The Guv called our cricket team to a meeting in his classroom after lunch. He told us that we've been invited to a cricket festival in Cape Town over the July holidays. The Guv wanted to see how many of us would be interested in going. Eleven hands immediately shot straight up into the air. The Guv ran his hand through his graying stubble and grinned for the first time this term. "Why am I not surprised?" he said, and dismissed us with a wave of his walking stick. Our team gathered outside and chattered excitedly about the possible tour to the Cape. What a birthday present! As I headed toward the lunch queue, The Guv called me over.

"Happy birthday, Milton."

He slipped a present (badly wrapped, in Christmas paper) into my hand and strode off toward the staff room. I slid the present under my shirt and sprinted back to the dormitory, where I hid it at the back of my footlocker. I'll be damned if I'm gonna leave incriminating evidence of my birthday in full view of the Crazy Eight!

20:00 Rehearsal with Lloyd Creswell and myself. (He calls me Oli and I call him Dodge.) We worked on our solo pieces with Kojak once again swinging his baton around like a maniac. Viking looked on, occasionally making a point or asking us to try something different. Ms. Roberts clunked away on the piano without showing any ill effects from all Kojak's shouting and screaming, apart from the odd sneeze and the repeated blowing of her nose.

I walked with Dodge back toward the school. We talked excitedly about the play and about being cast in the lead roles. Eventually, Dodge said goodbye and followed the path that led around the front of the chapel through the parking lot and on toward his house. I figured I'd waste a little more time before hitting the dormitory in the hope that the Crazy Eight would have all fallen asleep by the time I returned. I followed the same path taken by Dodge, but instead of moving on to the parking lot, I snuck into the chapel.

Three candles burned on the altar and, unlike last term's night swim, the chapel felt strangely warm and inviting. I took a pew toward the back and listened carefully for suspicious sounds (supernatural or otherwise). Beside the rickety old 23:00 freight train, chugging its way up to Johannesburg, all was silent. I thought of the play, the Mermaid, the scholarship, the cricket tour. I thought about being fourteen years old, and I thought about frail old Mr. Crispo and his smiling face of tears. . . . And then I did a funny thing. I said "Thank you" out loud without really meaning to. My voice echoed around the empty chapel, sounding incredibly loud and full-bodied and not like a spud at all. Maybe this was a sign from God that my days of being a spud are numbered?

Unfortunately, I then thought about Macarthur's hanging in the chapel, and a sense of unease overcame me like a thick mist. I was convinced that I heard a deep voice mumbling in agony. I kept turning around to check the huge oak doors behind me, half expecting them to creak open. (Then I reckoned that a ghost wouldn't need to open the doors; he would just drift right through them.) By now I had completely terrified myself and scampered out of God's house, slunk through the cold concrete cloisters, and nipped into the house, up the stairs, through the second-years' dorm, and finally tiptoed into our dormitory. There was complete silence. I could hear the rhythmical breathing of sleep. The full moon cast yellow light through my window and onto my bed. Roger glared at me intently as I slipped off my shoes and socks, unbuttoned my shirt, and slipped out of my pants and underpants. I leaned forward to grab my pajamas from under my pillow . . . and suddenly the dormitory exploded! Boys were everywhere! Hands searched for me, held me, found me. In a blind panic I lashed out, but soon the powerful bodies around me had killed my fight and were picking me up and carrying me through the dorms and down the stairs.

I began struggling again as I was carried into the harsh white light of the bogs. The thought of a bogwash made me want to vomit. (Boggo said it was the most horrific moment of his life.) In the light of the bathroom, I realized that the mob was large. There must have been between fifteen and twenty boys there, including Pike, Bert, Julian, and even Vern and Gecko.

Instead of dragging me into a toilet stall, I was dropped onto the cold concrete floor, and it was only then that I realized that I was completely naked in the stark white light in front of so many prying and demented eyes. My hands instinctively tried to cover my groin, but strong arms pinned them to the floor. Above me was Rambo with a black shoe brush, and suddenly he was polishing my balls! Then there was somebody else viciously scrubbing my spudness. I screamed and screamed. A hand clamped my mouth shut, but still I kept screeching. Then Pike was there with a huge toilet brush and I could hear ugly laughter and then felt more pain. I closed my eyes—I couldn't look.

Lying on the cold floor staring up at the long fluorescent lights, I realized that no arms held me anymore. The shower clock read 11:31, the date April 20, 1990. Fourteen years ago almost to the minute I had been born, but then it had been my mother's turn to have the pawing hands, the pain, the terrible bright light. . . . I scrambled to my feet. The bathroom was deserted. I looked down at the black mess of my spudness. I opened the tap and tried to wash it away, but the black shoe polish wouldn't go. Even rubbing with soap didn't help. Eventually, I had to use the clean end of the toilet brush to scrape away at myself. And there I stood (in my birthday suit) scrubbing my balls as the last few minutes of my birthday ticked away.

In the last minute of my birthday, I crept back into the dormitory. All were asleep as before, except for Roger, who, in the moonlight, seemed to be looking at me with a mixture of pity and menace.

At least it's over.

Friday 21st April

I woke up to flaming red spudness. In various spots on my willy the skin had been broken. (Maybe this will speed things up down there.) I didn't shower (the thought of Julian and Bert inspecting my battle scars was not thrilling). Breakfast was as jovial as ever, with Rambo telling us how they had planned my attack with the utmost attention to detail. I think this was told to make me feel better, but it did little to help my shattered ego.

Sunday 23rd April

The Guv was on fire at the morning rehearsal. He shouted and performed and stalked around the stage like a psychotic loon. His singing is dodgy, but he gets away with speak-singing most of his words in a gruff Cockney accent. To hear him drop his hot potato Oxford accent for that of a London lowlife is alone worth the ticket price. He kept shouting out things like, "Cue!" or, "Don't upstage Oliver!" "They came to see me bat, not you bowl!" Even Viking didn't seem to have a clue what he was talking about most of the time.

Unfortunately, The Guv returned from the lunch break completely rat-faced. His breath stank and he became wild and abusive. After he had stumbled and fallen into the orchestra pit, Viking pulled him aside and sent him home. The entire Fagin's gang chorus watched in awkward silence as he staggered out of the theater still muttering away to himself in his Cockney accent.

Eve arrived for the afternoon rehearsal (she plays the prostitute, Nancy). When Viking told her he was going to make her look like an absolute slut, fifteen boys licked their lips and imagined our large-breasted drama teacher in skintight clothes and a leather whip (at least that's what *I* was thinking). Although I'm not sure if they had any skintights or whips in nineteenth-century England.

I proudly missed my first free bounds!

Monday 24th April

The Guv was back in top form in English today. He made Simon recite Keats's "Ode on a Grecian Urn" while savagely beating out the rhythm on the table with his left shoe, which he had whipped off his foot. Simon kept losing his place, causing The Guv to scream and beat louder on the table. A couple of curious onlookers gathered at the window to watch The Guv's circus. When our raving mad teacher saw them, he hurled his shoe at them. The boys scattered, and without batting an eyelid, The Guv pulled off his right shoe and continued his crazy drumming, which was only stopped by the shrill ringing of the lunchtime siren.

13:30 The Guv's house was in complete disarray. The sink was clogged with dirty plates, his bed was unmade, and the living room floor was covered in old newspapers, dirty socks, and empty wine bottles. Over a lunch of toast with peanut butter and red wine, The Guv told me that his wife had moved out during the holidays. He didn't say why, and I didn't ask him for any details.

After lunch we talked about the final book of *The Lord of the Rings* (I am on page 891 and am desperately trying to eke out the story for as long as possible). I could see that The Guv was thrilled that I loved the book. We read extracts of the "Siege of Gondor" together, with The Guv putting on a different voice for each character. We chatted about the cast of Oliver, and The Guv reckoned that Eve needed a jolly good rogering and that she wasn't getting any from Sparerib, who was a miserable sod born to be an undertaker. By then he was slurring quite badly, so I politely thanked him for the lunch and made my way back to the house.

Tuesday 25th April

Today's topic of discussion in religious instruction was "Love thy neighbor." Boggo kicked things off by asking the chaplain if you should love your neighbor even if she was a satanist. The chaplain considered the question carefully and then smiled sweetly and said, "God loves everyone, Alan (Boggo's first name). Even those who have turned against him." Then Rambo asked, "So are you saying we can have sex with our neighbors, then, Reverend?" The Reverend blushed and said, "Not sex, Robert (Rambo's first name), er . . . not unless you are married to your neighbor, of course. . . ." I decided to take the gap. "Why would your wife be living next door then, Reverend?" I asked in my most innocent spuddy voice. The chaplain knew I had him cornered and by the sound of all the snorts and giggles, the class knew it too.

"Er . . . I'm not sure, John (my first name)," said the Reverend. "I think perhaps we've drifted a little. . . ."

Then it got worse. Boggo asked Reverend Bishop if your willy would frizzle up if you had sex with a satanist. The chaplain said he wasn't sure. Rambo then inquired if the chaplain had ever had a threesome with two lesbians. Reverend Bishop looked at his watch in desperation and said, "Good God, look at the time!" and dismissed us fifteen minutes early.

Wednesday 26th April

08:00 Grim-faced teachers filed into the hall, some whispering among themselves, others staring out vacantly at us. The Glock followed, his academic gown blowing out like he was walking through a hurricane. He also looked bleak. When he reached the lectern, he felt for the microphone switch to check that he was live and then told us all to be seated.

"This morning the school flag flies at half mast." He looked sadly upward to the roof as if he'd spotted a leak. "This morning we mourn the passing of a great friend and servant of this school— a man who devoted his life to the spirit and ideals that we all hold dear. Teacher, friend, master, and servant. Today we mourn the death of John Riley Crispo. Let us all bow our heads in prayer."

I didn't pray.

It couldn't have been more than a month ago that I sat with Crispo on his veranda, looking out at the stars and listening to his old war stories. I remembered his visit to our rehearsal last week and how old and frail he looked. In my mind's eye I could see his wonderful old face so clearly. I wish I could have spoken to him again—

even just to say goodbye. But too late; Crispo's gone for good.

The prayer ended and we filed out of the hall. Most of the boys looked sad as they made their way to their classes. I walked off into the gray autumn mist, desperately fighting away an enormous lump in my throat.

Thursday 27th April

Still very disturbed about Crispo. Boggo reckons he died in his chair out on the veranda. His maid, Gloria, brought out his afternoon tea and couldn't wake him.

Received a letter from the Mermaid.

Dear Johnny,

I hope your birthday was great and that u didn't get some horrible things done to u. I have a present for u, which u will have to collect when u come back 4 the long weekend. How are the rehearsals going? Send news and gossip.

On my side, school is much better, although I would still rather be on holiday with u. We are going on a tennis tour to Empangeni next week. (I've never been there before, but I heard it's not much of a holiday destination.) I saw your dad on Sunday at the mall. He was wading around in the fountain outside the Wimpy. A huge crowd was gathered around watching him—I'm not sure what he was doing, maybe u can find out for me. I'm curious.

Otherwise, my love, I miss u terribly—why do u have to be so far away from me? Come home immediately.

Love,
Me

PS Don't be surprised to see me on the sidelines at one of your matches.

I called home and got Mom on the phone. She had no idea what Dad had been doing walking around in the fountain at the shopping center. I told her about Crispo, but I could hear from her tone of voice that she was busy and not really interested. She said they were coming up to watch my first rugby match on Saturday.

Just before lights-out P. J. Luthuli announced that we would be climbing a mountain called Inhlazane (Mother's Tit) on Sunday. The mountain lies twenty-eight kilometers from the school—we'll be leaving at 03:00 and returning well after dark. The "hike" is apparently a new boy initiation tradition at the school. Poor Fatty is beside himself with worry and plans to get a doctor's certificate from the sanatorium first thing in the morning. Gecko said he would join him, and even I could swear I felt the beginnings of a serious disease coming on.

Saturday 29th April

P. J. Luthuli pulled me out of breakfast and said that Glockenshpeel wanted to see me in his office immediately. At first I thought it was a practical joke, but one look at Luthuli's face told me differently. I marched across the quad toward the great man's office, my heart thumping and my body breaking into a sweat. I began replaying the last few days over in my head. I had to be in some sort of trouble or else this wouldn't be happening. The Glock's secretary ushered me into the headmaster's office and, no doubt noticing my terror, patted my shoulder before closing the door on her way out.

"Have a seat, Milton." The Glock was seated comfortably in his leather armchair with the newspaper spread over h.s desk. He gestured to a chair on the opposite side of the desk. "Can you believe this idiot actually believes Lincoln could beat us this afternoon? Gone are the days when the local paper was run by old boys." He sighed, folded his paper, and looked me squarely in the eyes. "Don't look so worried, boy. You haven't done anything wrong, have you?" I shook my head and uttered a squeak.

"Good. Now, you seem to have made some sort of impression on my dear friend Johnny Crispo. He requested that you sing a verse from his favorite hymn, 'Jerusalem,' at his funeral service. Ms. Roberts will coach you after chapel tomorrow morning. The funeral will be on Tuesday. Thank you, Milton, that will be all."

The Crazy Eight were still trying to figure out why I'd been summoned to The Glock's office by the time I arrived back at the breakfast table. Boggo had already taken two official bets. Rambo had placed a buck at 10–1 odds that I was being thrashed. Simon had also put two bucks on me reporting Pike for bullying at 20–1 odds. They all seemed astonished that I had been asked to sing at Crispo's funeral. While pocketing his profits, Boggo admitted that he would have given 100–1 odds on singing at Crispo's funeral. (In Boggo's opinion I'm five times more likely to be a rat than sing at a funeral!) Fatty confessed to eating my scrambled eggs and bacon while I was away, saying that he didn't think I would feel like eating after seeing The Glock. In truth, the idea of singing a solo at Crispo's funeral had devoured my appetite anyway.

Sunday 30th April

As good as his promise, Luthuli roused us for our 03:30 start to conquer the infamous Inhlazane. My legs felt like lead and my teeth chattered as I stumbled out of my warm bed. Roger whined in anger as he realized that Vern was moving out. We were each given a small plastic bag filled with supplies—a juice, a bun, an apple, and a bar of chocolate. In the pitch black we set out, following Luthuli, who marched ahead. All we could see was his white cap in the darkness. Our head of house set a cracking pace and Vern, Gecko, and I almost had to trot to keep up. Luckily for Fatty, his peptic heart had allowed him to stay at school.

We climbed out of the valley and onto the hill above the school. Unfortunately, it seemed that the path led ever upward. As the sun rose, we were tackling a range of mountains called the Seven Sisters (soon renamed the Seven Bitches). The Seven Sisters were surely created by God to torment hikers. As soon as you climb the first sister, then the next one rears up in front of you. And so it goes on—seven mountains and each one higher than the last. I can imagine what poor Frodo Baggins must have felt setting out toward Mordor in *The Lord of the Rings*—although I doubt the Misty Mountains were as savage as this!

Soon it started getting warm, and then hot. Our supplies were finished and there was no sign of any fresh water. The lack of water didn't seem to worry Luthuli, who kept up his cracking pace, making no allowances for uphill or downhill. Boggo was held back after getting tangled up in a barbed wire fence and Gecko, who had strayed off the path to take a piss, was charged by a randy bull with a giant boner and dived into a thornbush.

11:30 Luthuli led us around the back of the mountain and we began the final climb. We scampered along behind him, using rocks and grass to grip our way up through the crevices and gullies. Eventually, we hit the summit and were met with the most spectacular view I've ever seen. To the left lay the snow-lined peaks of the Drakensberg Mountains. To the right, the huge Midmar dam was spread out like a giant hand. Everywhere there were green pastures and grazing animals, clumps of trees with beautiful old farmhouses peeping through the nearly naked sycamore trees. A cool breeze

blew across the summit. Luthuli gave us half an hour to rest. I took
the opportunity to sit and enjoy the view and spent my break gazing at the Drakensberg (which, translated from Zulu, means the
Barrier of Spears). I thought about Frodo's journey into Mordor
again; I thought about the play, my birthday, the Mermaid, Crispo,
and The Guv. I thought about the thousands of men who've
climbed this mountain and sat on this very spot and perhaps
thought of similar things. I had a sudden longing for the Mermaid,
to sit and talk and listen and breathe and kiss.

Mad Dog discovered a beacon and ordered us to piss on it as
a bonding exercise. He said it would leave our mark and create a
new tradition. We all stood around the poor beacon and let rip.
(Except for Vern, who was overcome with a severe case of stage
fright.)

The return home was long and tortuous. Our legs were weary,
our skin was burned, and dehydration had set in. Luthuli led us on
a different path in an attempt to find water. We eventually drank
from a rather foul-smelling pond. On we trudged into the setting
sun. Simon fell awkwardly and twisted his ankle and had to limp
most of the way home. Rambo helped him on the down slopes and
privately worried that his under-14A half-back could be seriously
injured.

At last we stumbled into the house at 20:45, exhausted and
starving. Luthuli allowed us to make snackwiches in the prefects'
room, and after eating and showering the Crazy Seven collapsed
into bed and soon joined Fatty in slumberland.

Last thought before falling asleep: forgot to rehearse for
Crispo's funeral. (In fact, I haven't been to chapel either.) Have
decided to refer all complaints to Luthuli.

Monday 1st May

Woke up and joined my limping dorm mates on the way to the showers. Bert had to carry Gecko down the stairs because he kept falling and crying, and Simon's ankle was still badly swollen.

The Guv spent half of English moping on about how the rest of the world gets a public holiday for Workers' Day on May 1 except for us. He told us that if we were real men, we would organize a revolt and close the school down. Boggo stood up and told The Guv that our extra week's holiday made up for the lost public holidays. The Guv accused him of being "Thatcher's spawn" and called us a bunch of miserable proles with no backbone and then threw his dictionary out the window. I won't tell Dad about The Guv's Workers' Day demands or he might accuse him of being a communist!

20:00 Kojak was at his psychotic best during rehearsals, waving his baton around like it was a knight's lance. He spent most of the rehearsal screaming and thrashing his baton on the music stand. The more hostile he was, the worse my singing became. Eventually, Viking brought the rehearsal to a close as he could see that our musical director was frothing at the mouth and looking on the verge of another stroke. (His last stroke happened two years ago during rehearsals for *The Pirates of Penzance*.)

Ms. Roberts kept me behind after the rehearsal and coached me through "Jerusalem," the hymn for Crispo's funeral. I have to sing the first verse. The second will be sung by the choir and the final three by the congregation. The thought of singing over a dead man's body makes me want to vomit, quite frankly. (Made a mental note to ask Gecko for some of his anti-puking pills.)

Tuesday 2nd May

11:00 Crispo's funeral. The entire school answered the call of the bells and happily left their classes and filed into the chapel. The service was wickedly sad and Reverend Bishop was surprisingly composed and seemed to make a fair amount of sense in his sermon about Crispo's loyalty, love, and honor to the school. My solo was better than I expected, although it still sounded like my voice was coming from somebody else's mouth. (I wonder if this had something to do with Macarthur's ghost?)

Crispo's coffin was carried by a bunch of old codgers dressed up in army uniforms. Sitting in the front of the choir stalls, I was no more than ten feet from the coffin and I spent the entire service trying to imagine what his body looked like. Was his tongue lolling out? Were his eyes open? What was he wearing? Was his face a picture of fear and agony? Was he even there?

Gloria sat in the front row with one of her arum lilies in her hand. She didn't stop crying and placed the lily on Crispo's coffin as it was carried past her.

One of the old codgers stumbled while carrying the coffin out of the chapel. For a moment it looked as though the coffin would fall, but The Glock jumped in and held up the tilting side, thereby averting a certain disaster. A sneaky smile slid across Pike's snakelike face. (Was it a coincidence that he was sitting on the aisle seat where the old codger stumbled? I think not.)

Our last lesson of the day was religious instruction with the Reverend Bishop, who seemed to be on some sort of a high after the funeral service. We soon got into a heavy discussion about death. Boggo asked the chaplain if Crispo had gone to heaven. The Reverend got all emotional and said he was sure the old man was dancing with the angels as we spoke. Rambo said that he was sure Crispo had gone to hell because he had tried to fry Boggo's balls in history. Fatty then cleared his throat and asked, "What about ghosts?" The Reverend smiled and said, "The only ghost I believe in is the Holy Ghost."

"What about Macarthur's ghost?" asked Rambo. He then went on to explain to the Bishop about Macarthur hanging himself in the chapel. Reverend Bishop reckoned that the whole thing was an old wives' tale. The siren rang and Reverend Bishop did a bad job of hiding his relief.

Gecko still hasn't recovered from Inhlazane and has been given a pair of crutches by the sanatorium. Simon's ankle is better and much to Rambo's relief, he looks certain to play on Saturday.

Wednesday 3rd May

Finished *The Lord of the Rings*. I feel utterly depressed—the journey of Frodo has become a part of my life, but now it's all over and I have to return the book to The Guv and move on. Wrote a long letter to the Mermaid but still felt homesick so I called home and had a chat with Dad. He told me that he and Frank had been banned from Neighborhood Watch and warned against starting a renegade group of street guardians. He says the cops are watching him, so he's keeping a low profile.

Mom reckoned that Dad threw his change into the fountain in the shopping center for good luck and then realized that he had no money to pay for parking, so he groveled around in the water until he had recovered his two bucks. (I'm so relieved that I wasn't there. Just hearing the story was embarrassing enough.)

Big news is that Saturday is the junior social (first and second years) in the Great Hall. Busloads of St. Catherine's girls are brought up and one of the matric boys is chosen to be the DJ. The dormitory was abuzz as Boggo gave us all a great lecture on sex and

how to rape and pillage schoolgirls. He has offered up some great
rewards for scoring. They are as follows:

Kissing (grabbing)	. . . .$1
Squeezing breasts	. . . .$5
Touching her "Holiest of Holies"	. . . . .$10
Getting a blow job	. . . .$50
Sex	. . . .$100
Recording sex on videotape	. . . .$500
Threesome sex with two girls	. . . . .$1000

The only catch is that these acts have to be witnessed by two
other people. To enter the competition, we all have to give Boggo
five bucks. To avoid looking like a wimp, I paid up my money and
announced that I would shag a chick on Saturday. (Everyone
laughed and said that if the Spud managed to shag anyone, they'd
each give me a million.) At least if I don't score anyone, I can say
it's because I already have a girlfriend.

Thursday 4th May

Our new history teacher, Mr. Lennox, is wickedly clever and
spent the lesson talking to us about the ANC and the origins of
apartheid (which isn't in the syllabus). Looks like we are destined
to never learn our history syllabus. Mr. Lennox, with ginger hair
and bushy eyebrows, looks a bit daft but seems as sharp as a button and is truly passionate about his history. He was openly vicious
about apartheid and compared it to Nazi Germany. (I hope my dad
never gets to meet Lennox; they'll surely end up in a fistfight.) He
told us he was starting a new society at school, which will meet
every second Sunday night after chapel at his house. It will be

called African Affairs and will look at politics in South Africa. After class I put my name down and he told me our first meeting would take place this Sunday night. With all the excitement of the play I'd forgotten about my plan to make plans to fight the system. Nevertheless, I am about to take my first giant leap toward being a real freedom fighter!

14:30 Practiced tackling for the first time today. I managed to half tackle Geoff Lawson (he's about my size) but got out of the way if anybody big ran at me. I think just about everybody followed my example, and our overweight captain, Gareth Hogg (nicknamed Pig), managed to score thirteen tries in half an hour. Being the smallest, I managed none. (Further proof that, barring a miracle, I shall never play for the springboks.) Saturday's match is against Arlington High, who we demolished at cricket last term. At this stage they're not certain of making up an under-14D team—so if we do play, we are almost certain to win.

Rambo returned to the dorm well after lights-out. He said he'd been practicing his scene for the drama class with Eve. Boggo asked him if he would ever shag Eve. Rambo snorted and said he was crazy.

Friday 5th May

Had a rehearsal with The Glock today. Viking worked on the scene where Bill Sykes (the psychopath played by Glock) kidnaps Oliver from Nancy (Eve). Thankfully, it says in the script that Oliver is terrified—which isn't hard to do with The Glock shouting in my ear and dragging me along by the collar. Viking told me that I was superb in the scene and then criticized The Glock and told him to get rough and tough! He got up close to the headmaster and whispered, "Pretend this boy is the one who tampered with your car." A wicked glint shone in The Glock's eyes and his face became dark and menacing. We ran through the scene again and this time he was savage with me, pulling my hair and pushing me into the wall. I felt myself wanting to cry and instinctively bit my lip, but then I thought I would let myself go and I started sobbing. After the scene, I rubbed my eyes and smiled—just to show that I was only acting. Viking leapt onto the stage and pressed his face close to mine. "By God, Milton, if you can do that in September, we won't have a dry eye in the house." He then turned to The Glock and said, "Boss man, that was superb. But look out—I think we may have unearthed another Brando!" With that, the gruff director dismissed us.

I tried to walk ahead of the headmaster, but he called me back and walked with me toward the main quad. "Milton, I just wanted to congratulate you on your singing at Johnny Crispo's funeral. You have quite a voice, young man, and I thought you handled the moment very well. You know that he told me a couple days before he died that he spent an evening with you and that you reminded him so much of himself when he was your age. Rich praise indeed from a former head boy." I wasn't sure what to say—I felt proud, happy, awkward, and embarrassed (and probably a few other emotions as well). Before I could say anything, The Glock gave me a pat on the back and strode off to his office.

Suddenly there was a nasty slurping noise from the common room and framed in the window were the ugly faces of Pike and Devries. I ignored them and walked into the house. Unfortunately, they grabbed me and started dragging me toward the bogs. "Little brownnoser, why don't you just lick his crack next time!" snarled Pike, who had pinned my arms behind my back. I struggled frantically and managed to kick Devries' broken left arm. He wailed in pain but then recovered enough to launch his knee into my thigh. A surge of pain shot through my leg and then it went numb. Devries held my legs together and they carried me toward the stinking toilet stalls.

"If Spud goes anywhere near that toilet, I'll beat you two so hard your pictures at home will be crying!" Pike and Devries stopped dead in their tracks. "In fact, I'll beat you, and then I'll hand you over to Sparerib for more." I recognized my prefect's voice. Pike hissed and dropped me roughly to the floor. Devries followed and the two menaces loped out of the bathroom muttering to each other. I scrambled to my feet and began thanking the trusty Earthworm. He straightened me up and sent me off to make him a cup of strong tea. I thanked him again and ran off to make him the best cuppa ever made.

The inspiring intensity of war cry practice was broken by a first year called Ferguson from Woodall house who screamed at the wrong time. However, what made his error even more disastrous was the fact that his voice broke spectacularly at the same time, which made him sound like a cross between a wailing woman and a constipated donkey. Even Luthuli found the incident amusing and I noticed a quick flash of his gleaming white teeth. Although our chanting and shouting was loud, with the weak Arlington team visiting us tomorrow, there was more laughter and far less passion than last week.

After practice, Pike caught up with me on the way to the house and said, "I'll get you, Spud—a bogwash is nothing compared to what's coming your way." He spat on my jersey, cackled like a hyena, and then slunk off to join his mates. If ever there was one person who I would wish a sudden death . . . .

Boggo (now with thirty-five bucks of cash in his pocket) offered some further incentives for tomorrow night's social evening:

Presenting Boggo a bra $10
Presenting Boggo underwear $20
Presenting Boggo a G-string $40
Presenting Boggo a black G-string . .$50

Boggo told us that any other items would be evaluated before he made an offer, although he made it clear that he wasn't inter-ested in jackets, blouses, socks, hair bands, or tampons.

Saturday 6th May

10:00 On arrival it was discovered that the Arlington team only had thirteen men. (Their prop failed to turn up and the right wing was expelled yesterday for trying to steal a teacher's car.) There was a long discussion between their coach and Mr. Lilly about whether the match should go ahead. Eventually, it was decided that the game would kick off but would be stopped when it became embarrassing for the visitors.

11:00 Pig led us onto the field to the sound of loud cheering from my folks, Mr. Lilly, and our linesman. (The under-14D match, surprisingly, is not that well supported.) The Arlington team was obviously terrified and realized they were on a hiding to nothing. From the kickoff Pig caught the ball and charged right through the opposition and scored.

I placed the ball on a mound of sand and steadied myself for the goal kick. All was still. Before me stood the goal posts. This was my moment. I couldn't miss. I took my run up, my technique very much based on years of watching Naas Botha on the telly. I approached the ball like a pro and kicked it solidly. Unfortunately, it came out low and struck the crossbar and then rebounded savagely at me, striking me straight in the face. The medics and Mr. Lilly sprinted onto the field with the first aid kit and wiped the blood from my nose. Once I was repaired, I ran back to my team, who were doubled over with laughter.

My goal-kicking debacle must have given the opposition some heart because before we knew it, they had scored four times and were leading 20–4. We struck back just before halftime, when my pal Geoff Lawson scrambled over in the corner. This time my kick was from the touchline and virtually impossible (although I was in no danger from the goal posts this time). After completing my Naas Botha routine, I gave the ball a mighty thump, and when I looked up, I saw it flying high and true. The flags were raised and

I trotted back to my mark having salvaged some pride. My father did his famous rain/war dance and Mr. Lilly ran onto the field and tried to hug me while I was running back to my mark.

Unfortunately, that was our last highlight, and dear diary, I am ashamed to admit that we were humiliated by the thirteen-man Arlington team. The final score, 46–12! Not even Mr. Lilly's team talk under the tree could cheer us up. Worse was to come, as for the second week in succession the under-14Ds were the only team to lose. The first team won by a whopping 72–3.

I had hoped my moment of kicking madness would not make its way back to the dormitory. However, it didn't take long before a crowd of mocking faces surrounded me at dinner with ironic cheers and mostly jeers. My nickname seems to have changed from Spud to Boomerang.

20:00 Mad Dog was banned from attending the social after barking loudly as the St. Catherine's girls stepped off the bus.

The 180 junior boys (first- and second-years) all stood to the left side of the hall where the snacks were laid out. Fatty, who obviously had no plans of scoring, began loading mini sausage rolls and tuna sandwiches into a kit bag. We all spoke in loud and confident voices, mostly discussing the first-team rugby match while subtly eyeing the girls, who were milling around the cool drinks table at the opposite side of the hall.

The music started and the lights faded. A giant mirror ball reflected little patterns on the dance floor, but if the truth were told, our social had less atmosphere than Crispo's funeral.

It was Rambo and Simon who eventually broke the ice when they sauntered over to a crowd of girls and struck up a conversation. Soon Boggo joined them. Simon looked wickedly smooth and casual in his faded jeans and dark shirt, and all the girls were watching him, grinning like idiots in the hope that he would return their interest. One of the girls in the group was stunningly beautiful. She looked identical to Julia Roberts (although much younger and prettier and with golden red hair). She seemed to be the only girl not batting her eyelids and giggling at Boggo's raw jokes. Suddenly I realized that she was staring at me. I blushed and looked away and then quickly looked back to find her still staring at me. The funny thing was that she was just staring, like she was looking at a statue or a house (and a pretty crappy house at that!). I felt that dreaded thumping-heart feeling again. The moment was interrupted by Geoff Lawson, who came across to find out if I had recovered from my accident on the field. Geoff, like the rest of us, looked uneasy and frequently his chatter would fizzle out as his eyes followed a girl moving across the hall. He nudged me in the ribs and said, "That redhead's a killer. I'd give an arm and a leg to . . ." The rest faded away with the music.

Queen's "Another One Bites the Dust" at last caused a dance floor invasion. The dancing began as a huge circle of boys and girls and then broke up into smaller groups. Vern, Gecko, Fatty (dancing with his kit bag), Geoff, and myself moved to the far side of the dance floor and began dancing with a group of seven girls, who immediately whispered to one another and then stalked off. In hindsight, I have to admit we didn't make for the prettiest group. Vern's spasmodic dancing style leaves a lot to be desired and Gecko appeared to be constantly on the verge of some sort of fatal attack.

Time ticked by slowly, and the social nightmare of embarrassment plodded on like a lethargic snail. Simon and Rambo both left the hall holding hands with different girls. Mad Dog climbed up the drainpipe and crawled through the window to join the action but was kicked out after grabbing a large girl's buttocks and shouting, "Who's the man?"

Alphaville's "Forever Young" played and couples paired off and slow-danced together. Geoff and myself retired to the snack tables, which by now had been picked clean (including garnish). While Geoff rambled on about rugby, I couldn't help but look at Julia Roberts, who was dancing with a lanky second-year from Barnes house. Geoff nodded at the redhead and said, "Bet you a million bucks she's a stuck-up bitch." I think I nodded in agreement.

After the song, the beauty said something to her partner and then joined a group of girls near the DJ stand. I felt like I wanted to meet her but was too chicken to make a move. Eventually, the music stopped and the girls were ordered to the bus. Mad Dog managed a parting shot when he howled like a wolf from our dormitory window as they all crossed the quad. We watched them go and I was left with the vision of the beautiful redhead disappearing through the archway, never looking back.

HERE FOLLOWS THE DORMITORY SCOREBOARD (FINAL TALLY):

Simon	Kissed two girls and managed to return with a size 28A black bra. (Which according to him was undeniable proof that he had fondled a girl's breasts.) Boggo said that a 28A meant the girl *had* no breasts, so he only paid half ($5).
Rambo	Kissed twin sisters, each without the other knowing. (Boggo refused to pay out until the truth of this story had been established. Nobody had seen any twins, although Rambo said that was because they were identical.)

Nobody else scored, except for Fatty, who had made off with a kit bag full of snacks. Boggo claimed to have been on the verge of scoring when the girls had been called to the bus. Mad Dog has been ordered to see Sparerib on Monday after his dodgy behavior. I assured the dormitory that I had had numerous scoring chances but hadn't acted on them because of my girlfriend. (Never let the truth get in the way of a good story.)

Dreamed about Julia Roberts. (The one with red hair.)

Sunday 7th May

Viking smashed Smith on the head with a tin plate after he dropped it for the third time during the workhouse scene rehearsal. Smith collapsed like a lead balloon and burst into floods of tears. Viking showed no sign of remorse, ignored the sobbing Smith, and shouted, "From the top! And if I hear another plate drop, there will be bloodshed!" Smith realized that nobody cared much for his troubles (least of all me) and returned to the line of workhouse boys queuing up for imaginary gruel.

Monday 8th May

It's official. Three more pairs of my underpants are missing. This time I spoke to Vern about the situation and he said he was also missing two pairs. After making a few inquiries at breakfast, I soon uncovered a hornet's nest. Everybody (besides Fatty) is missing underpants and has been too nervous to say anything. Unfortunately, because I raised the alarm, I was unanimously elected to take the matter up with the prefects.

12:15 The Guv proudly announced that our cricket tour to Cape Town is officially on. Unfortunately, the cost is two thousand dollars per player. I will have to make a call home to ask the impossible.

Had another storming lunch with The Guv, whose mood is slowly improving despite the fact that his wife still hasn't come home. This time we wolfed down pieces of greasy reheated Kentucky Fried Chicken and drank Coke. I was pleased to see that The Guv's house smelled better and was far neater than before.

Apparently Gloria, who used to work for Crispo, is now coming to The Guv's three times a week to wash, clean, dust, and drive out rats and other small foraging animals. Gloria greeted me with a warm smile and I could see she was already caring for The Guv like she did for Crispo. She placed The Guv's neatly folded newspaper and his spectacles on the table next to him and switched on the lamp.

I told my English teacher that I thought *The Lord of the Rings* was without doubt the best book that I've ever read, and tears sprang to his eyes. He patted me on the head and muttered, "Blessed boy, blessed boy." I handed his gigantic book back to him and together we read our favorite bits out loud. The Guv (despite drinking Coke) seemed to be getting rapidly pickled. He moaned on about his wife and then began to weep. It was only when I went to close the window that I saw the half-empty bottle of Captain Morgan's rum teetering on the windowsill (cunningly hidden behind the net curtain).

While cleaning up Earthworm's room and checking the ink in all twelve pens in his pencil case, I casually mentioned the underpants problem. Earthworm studied me closely over the rims of his reading glasses (no doubt deciding whether I was trying to put one over) and then asked me a series of quick-fire questions. I told him that, in total, our dormitory had lost over twenty-four pairs of underpants. There was a long pause as my prefect studied me once more and said, "I'll take it up with the relevant authorities." He then returned to his chemistry notebook and not another word was uttered. I felt hugely relieved that the deed was done and the whole thing was now out of my hands.

Tuesday 9th May

07:30 The unthinkable has happened. With nighttime temperatures no more than two degrees Celsius and plummeting fast, Rambo announced at breakfast that there would be another Crazy Eight mission tonight. He said that it would only kick off after midnight. A groan passed around the breakfast table. Boggo shook his head, Fatty muttered unhappily to himself, Gecko looked pale, and Vern just looked demented. Who in his right mind goes night swimming after midnight in winter?

22:45 Once the house had gone quiet, Rambo brought the group into a huddle around his bed. He explained that he wanted us to raid the kitchen (i.e., break in and steal large quantities of food from the kitchen stocks). Rambo (who I'm sure has a great future as a Mafia boss) has bribed one of the kitchen staff to leave a window open, paving the way for the great kitchen robbery!

As always, it was Boggo who brought the great risk home to us. "If we're caught, we're finished, expelled, maybe suspended; if we're lucky—let's just say we'll be in deep you know what."

Boggo's warning was interrupted by Fatty, who leapt up and shouted, "I'm in!" looking totally inspired. "Me too," said Mad Dog without the faintest shred of fear in his eyes.

"That's three," said Rambo, eyeing the rest of us. "Gecko doing the san, one more vote will seal it." Silence. I shook my head and looked down—I could feel eyes boring into me, but there was no way in hell I was going with this one. Vern looked moggy and pulled out a clump of hair. Boggo told Rambo to go to hell. It looked like democracy had finally bitten Rambo in the bum. It was a classic Crazy Seven standoff, and for once it seemed that sanity would win the day. Roger jumped up onto the locker and let out a howl to announce his arrival.

"Good—Roger's in. That's four, then!" At first I thought Rambo was joking, but soon it became obvious that he was deadly serious. Roger had been given a vote. The die was cast. It took me a few moments to realize that a neurotic cat had quite possibly decided my fate! Vern hissed and clucked at Roger, who purred and repeatedly head-butted the edge of Vern's towel rail. Boggo was beside himself that a cat had swayed the vote on such an important issue. Unfortunately, our pleas for sanity were in vain and Rambo's imaginative plot was unveiled. Beginning to think that a subzero night swim might have been a more appealing option.

Wednesday 10th May

Midnight—the witching hour. My legs were shaking—hell, everything was shaking. I'm not afraid to admit that I was terrified. Perched on Fatty's shoulders with my head poking through the kitchen window, I was once again reminded why this school is a living hell. And as far as I was concerned, this was it. How do you explain to your parents that you were expelled for stealing food from the school kitchen when you're not even hungry?

As the smallest, I was unanimously voted to lead the break-in. (Despite Mr. Lennox's speech the other night, I am seriously beginning to doubt the idea of democracy.) Eventually, I was forced through the window and landed in a heap on the cold kitchen floor. I felt my way to the door, undid the Yale latch, and opened the door for six madmen and a cat.

Once inside, things ran fairly smoothly. Rambo knew the cupboards that needed to be opened and set about loading his cricket bag with packets of food. Roger thought the entire operation was a game solely for his benefit and quickly crouched down into stalking mode, pouncing on anything or anyone who moved. Fatty closed the window, and within three minutes the door was locked and the Crazy Seven plus cat were streaking barefoot across the frostbitten quad.

Once again I felt the terror grip me—I knew they would be

waiting. One of the prefects would be lying in my bed waiting for me to land. Once in the house, we crept up the stairs and tiptoed through the second years' dormitory. Somebody shouted and I went cold. But then, silence. It was only a sleep talker. I felt for my bed—it was still warm but empty.

STOLEN GOODS INVENTORY:

2 kg cheddar cheese
4 kg dark cooking chocolate
10 kg stewing beef
10 kg white rice (uncooked)
10 tins of tuna
3 loaves of bread
6 eggs (two broken)
1 spatula (nobody's sure how the spatula got into the bag)

We soon set about gorging ourselves on our stolen booty. Rambo wanted us to devour as much as we could before the rising siren (in case of a dormitory raid). Mad Dog fired up his portable gas cooker and soon he was stewing beef and using the spatula to good effect.

03:00 I lay on my bed, trying not to vomit. Even breathing was difficult. One by one the group slipped off to sleep, leaving Fatty with his cheese and bread and Roger to his tuna fish. Still wondering why we risked our futures for cheese, bread, and stewing beef—fell asleep without an answer.

08:00 Relieved that no emergency assembly was called. Too tired and stuffed to concentrate on lessons properly.

14:20 Called home and told the folks about the Cape Town cricket tour in July. Dad was thrilled until I casually threw in the bit about the two thousand dollars. What followed can only be described as a loud sneeze combined with an epileptic fit. After Dad had calmed down, I told him in my most innocent voice not to worry and that missing the tour wouldn't be the end of the world. This little bit of manipulation worked a treat because Dad suddenly shouted, "Over my dead body will my son miss his cricket tour to Cape Town!" He then slammed down the phone. The phone rang almost immediately and it was Mom demanding to know what I had said to Dad because he was walking around the garden talking to himself. After I explained, she told me not to get my hopes up and rang off.

I called the Mermaid, who sounded sad and depressed. She wouldn't explain why and answered all my questions with a "Yes" or a "No" or a "Dunno." Eventually, I gave up and said goodbye. As she put the phone down, I could hear her starting to cry. I felt awful. I took a stroll and ended up in the sanatorium visiting Gecko, who seemed over the moon to see me. I told him about the kitchen raid and could see in his eyes that he was envious and sad. He asked me to stay with him a while, but I knew that would only make me feel worse, so I made up an excuse and left. I continued my walk and ended up at The Guv's house, only to find it empty. I saw Mr. Lilly walking his poodle (with a tight pink sweater wrapped around its fluffy white body) but decided not to approach him.

The sun had already sunk behind the hills and a chill breeze bit at my nose and ears. I pulled my polo-neck sweater over my mouth and set off to the dining hall for a dinner of stewed beef and rice.

Tuesday 16th May

It is nearly a week since my last diary entry.
Today started off with a quote scrawled on paper and then

pinned to the house notice board, which read:

Suddenly the talking stopped. The Mermaid was looking at me with that same intense stare that she had given me on the pool steps. This time there was no swimming away. I stared back and hoped she didn't hear the big thumping snare drum in my chest. Our lips met, my eyes closed, and then I felt her tongue in my mouth. After a moment's shock my own tongue met hers and we were joined in a mad tongue wrestle of love. We seemed to kiss for some sort of eternity, and when it was over, I was instantly overcome with the most wonderful feeling of accomplishment. All I could think about was charging back to school to casually tell the Crazy Eight that I had kissed the Mermaid and she was now my girlfriend.

I knew where it was from, and by then I also knew that my diary had been stolen. I think this is worse than the first week and my birthday combined. I feel ashamed and wish I'd never kept a diary in the first place. I thought about telling Sparerib. I thought about telling Earthworm. I didn't tell anyone.

I found my diary this morning in my locker. Nobody's admitted to stealing it or bothered to apologize. I know it was Boggo, though. (I heard him bragging to Mad Dog that he'd taken it.) I looked back over what I've written and felt ashamed that everybody had read my personal thoughts and things. Why did I write them down? Was I stupid enough to think that they wouldn't steal the diary and read it? Boggo must have been itching to know what I've been writing every day.

I've thought about burning it or hurling it into the bog stream. But here I sit writing away—I guess I'm addicted.

I read my grandfather's (my dad's dad) gold inscription on the brown leather covering:

Every man's life, no matter how routine, will fill a chest of books, and if he's lucky, a million miles of film. Forget nothing lest yourself be forgotten.

(I still don't know if these were his words or someone else's. I was too young to ask him before he died. I've always just assumed they were his.)

I'm finding it hard to look anyone in the eyes. I'm not sure what they know and what they read.

Wednesday 17th May

LAST WEEK'S NEWS

There has been no mention of last week's kitchen raid. (Apparently the caterer thinks it was an inside job since there was no sign of a break-in.) Six more pairs of underpants have been stolen, including two pairs of mine. We lost our rugby match 66–0 to Weatherby, but thankfully we weren't the only side to lose (the under 15Cs lost 9–8). The first team crushed the opposition 42–12.

Gecko is once again in good health and made yet another triumphant return to the dormitory. (At least I know *he* didn't read my diary.)

Rehearsals are getting a little boring what with singing the same songs over and over and Kojak as demented as ever. I can't wait to start speaking dialogue and stringing the songs together. Viking reckons we'll only do that after half term.

19:00 A complete house search was carried out during prep. We were ordered to remain in our prep classrooms while the prefects rifled through our belongings. Word is that Sparerib is hot on the tail of the underpants thief. Boggo reckons our housemaster might soon have a dodgy sex scandal on his hands. We could hear the movements of the prefects through the ceiling as they searched the second years' dormitory.

21:00 Various boys have been hauled into Sparerib's office to explain various items found in their lockers. Pike was in possession of a fake ID and a nasty-looking scalpel. Devries' porno mags were confiscated and Fatty was questioned over a ten-kilogram bag of rice and three kilograms of rotting stewing beef that were found under his bed. He was forced to get rid of the meat but was allowed to keep the rice. But still no sign of the thirty-five-odd pairs of missing underpants. Whoever this pervert is, he must be crafty.

After lights-out, Fatty lit his candles and summoned us to his cubicle with his now familiar ghost buster routine. I reckon the entire Macarthur mystery is getting a bit stale. It's been weeks since we had any new information, and by the looks of things, the Crazy Eight (with the exception of Fatty) are starting to doubt that this hanging ever happened in the first place.

Sleep took a long time coming and I'm sure I woke in the middle of the night to the sound of somebody shrieking in terror—perhaps it was only in my dream, but the panic slept with me under my Good Knight duvet. Rambo rates it as the naffest duvet cover he's ever seen. I don't give a stuff!

Friday 19th May

11:00 Unbelievably, the under-14D team has remained unchanged. (I don't think Lilly had the heart to drop anyone.)

Received a depressing letter from the Mermaid. She says that she's been advised to see a psychologist so that she can be prescribed some antidepressants. I called her immediately, but Marge said she was sleeping. I have no experience in dealing with depressed people. (I'm only fourteen and come from a strong family line of madness, but no depression.) I called Mom to ask if she knew anything about the Mermaid. She said it was her parents' divorce that was eating her up. She said I must write to her as much as possible. Mom also said that Wombat had found the Easter eggs in the washing machine but had since lost them again.

Boggo nearly killed himself during prep. (Pity he failed.) Because he was cold, he had shifted his seat right up near the fire. Unfortunately, the back of his trench coat caught alight and soon the diary thief was engulfed in flames. Quick as a flash, Bert blasted the fire extinguisher at him, blowing Boggo right off his seat. Luckily for him he was wearing three sweaters underneath his trench coat and escaped any serious burns. Have a feeling that this is just part one in a series of horrors that Boggo will receive for stealing my diary. (It will be like the curse of Tutankhamen's tomb!) Bert has been credited with saving Boggo's life, and fires have been banned during prep.

Saturday 20th May

22:00 Julian lined up the Crazy Eight and beat us with his pink fly-swatter. He said the state of our dormitory was deplorable. After each stroke with the swatter he squealed with delight and skipped around like a fairy. Bert would then let loose a booming laugh and clap like a loon. The swatter didn't make us sore at all, but everybody pretended to flinch in agony in case he selected a more serious weapon. Fatty hammed it up so much that Julian apologized for hitting him too hard. Rambo's convinced that Julian is the infamous underpants thief.

Sunday 21st May

10:30 It would be a lie to say that the entire schoo. gathered to watch the female *Oliver* cast arrive for their first rehearsal. In fairness to the boys, the figure was closer to eighty-five percent of the school. With The Glock and Viking there to usher them through to the theater, nobody dared make any funny comments or barnyard noises. Much to everyone's relief, the group of twenty was not a bad-looking bunch. No doubt Viking had chosen wisely. I was anxious to see which girl would take the role of Bet (the girl Oliver sings "I'll Do Anything" with).

Viking called each girl up onto the stage to introduce her to the rest of the cast. They all blushed and smiled sweetly. The last girl he called up was Bet, a girl called Amanda Lawrence, dressed in a black coat and beret. She sauntered onto the stage, flicked off her beret with a flourish, and bowed. Long red locks of hair cascaded down and the snare drum kicked off in my chest. Bang! Bang! Bang! It was Julia Roberts!

Viking called Dodge and me onto the stage. I could hear the whisper of girls' voices. I forced a smile that made my cheeks hurt and felt myself blushing. Amanda Lawrence stared at me. I suddenly realized I am completely and utterly terrified of her.

We began with the London chorus songs "Oom-Pah-Pah," "Who Will Buy?" and "It's a Fine Life." The girls sang brilliantly, and combined with the elder boys' tenor voices, it sounded fantastic. Despite Viking's gruffness I could tell he was delighted with the sound. Kojak also appeared calmer—perhaps the girls' voices have a soothing effect on his psychopathic tendencies.

And then came the moment. Dodge and Eve, Spud and Amanda singing the song of love called "I'll Do Anything." My nerves were jangling. The entire cast was watching us with complete focus. Lloyd and Eve kicked off with gusto and then it was my turn, and then I was singing. The sound was full and clean; I noticed the transformation in Amanda's face. Instantly she'd become soft, loving, and even more beautiful. Was she acting or was she melting to the sound of my voice? She opened her mouth and her voice was strong and husky and beautiful, like a rock star. Applause and whistling.

Viking strode onto the stage and told us it was appalling.

During the lunch break Amanda sat alone on the grass outside reading a book called *Waiting for the Barbarians*. I couldn't see who the author was. Amanda has a definite DO NOT DISTURB aura about her. I munched on my apple and gazed at her from behind the fountain. Geoff Lawson sauntered up to her and tried to chat, but she kept reading and nodded to him while he was crapping on about some boring old anecdote. Eventually, he gave up and came and sat with me behind the fountain. Together we spent the rest of the lunch break watching her read. I think she's more beautiful than life itself.

20:00 African Affairs focused on Mandela. Lennox began by reading the statement that Mandela had read at his treason trial in 1963. We then watched a documentary on the great man and debated his future. It was agreed that, barring assassination, Mandela would be South Africa's first black president. What nobody was prepared to predict was exactly when he would achieve this and what would follow thereafter. When the issue was thrown open to the floor, I pretended to have a mouthful of scone and passed over to somebody called Gerald, who then made a complete arse of himself by saying that apartheid wasn't as bad a thing as everyone made out.

Linton Austin said that thus far Mandela has shown no sign of rage or anger (a bit strange after being locked up for twenty-six years!). Lennox expressed concern at the escalation in violence between Buthelezi's IFP and the ANC. Luthuli reckoned there was every chance of a black-on-black civil war. Lennox shook his head and scratched his reddy beard and shook his head some more. I left the meeting full of worry and fear. Would I have to fight in a civil war? Who would I fight for? Judging by what is said, Mandela has more street cred than Buthelezi and you can at least understand what he's saying in his speeches.

21:00 I strolled back to the dorm full of worries and questions about our country. But most of all I was stung by the image of a girl in a black coat and hat who, five hours before, had flashed me just the slightest hint of a smile before strolling across the quad and disappearing onto the bus.

Monday 22nd May

I awoke thirty minutes before the siren, racked with bone-mangling guilt over the Mermaid. I spent geography writing her a letter, telling her news, and letting her know that I can't wait to see her over the long weekend.

The Guv didn't touch a drop of booze at lunch. I asked him about *Waiting for the Barbarians*. He said it was a splendid South African novel written by J. M. Coetzee. He pulled the book from his shelf and handed it to me. The Guv seemed much happier about life in general and didn't mention his wife once. He reckons that the play's going to be brilliant and that if I didn't shag at least three girls over the next three months, I should consider myself a closet homo. I laughed despite my embarrassment—still no sign of becoming a man. I was hoping my birthday scrub down would have kicked my lunch box into action.

18:00 It takes a certain kind of person to get excited over baked beans for dinner, but for Fatty these beans were a passport to setting a new school farting record. (According to Fatty, the unofficial record of twenty-four seconds was set by a guy called Alf Thompson in 1981.) Fatty wolfed down six bowls filled with baked beans and then declared himself "carbo-loaded."

His first major test was to hold himself back until after lights-out. He seemed a bit worried about getting more finger tongs from Bert if he let one go by mistake during prep.

By the third session of prep Fatty was straining to contain himself. He was terribly bloated and his cheeks seemed puffier than ever. Miraculously, he held himself together and announced that the record fart would be let off at 22:00 in the comfort of his own cubicle.

21:55 The Crazy Eight, plus cat, gathered around Fatty's cubicle. Both Simon and Rambo held their stopwatches at the ready. Fatty was perched on about four cushions looking like some sort of grotesque Buddha. After a few minutes of excited chatter Fatty silenced the crowd and said that he was aiming for the thirty-second barrier and that he was dedicating his fart to the memory of Macarthur. He then seemed to concentrate incredibly hard, lifted his giant backside slightly, and breathed deeply. There were two beeps from the stopwatches. At first there was a low rumbling groan, like a big dog moaning in pain. The groan grew into a loud rumble. The loud rumble grew into something terrible.

Twenty, twenty-one, twenty-two . . . And on it went, only to be believed if heard. Twenty-six, twenty-seven, twenty-eight. Fatty's face turned purple. He lifted his bum even higher. Simon and Boggo raised the stopwatches, ready for the end. And then BEEP BEEP. A new school farting record of thirty-three seconds! Fatty was ecstatic.

I leaned forward to shake his hand but leapt back at the rancid smell. Suddenly there was a mad rush to open windows. Eight tins of deodorant were let loose on the atmosphere, but still the awful smell of Fatty's fart seeped into every nook and cranny of our living space, as it would for most of the night and probably the following week. Gecko vomited out the window and I nearly followed.

Fatty was delighted with his performance and demanded that I write a full account in my diary. The above account was posted (with my permission) on the notice board and serves as an official record to a legendary moment in the school's history.

Tuesday 23rd May

Still feeling guilty about Julia Roberts—I had a dream about her last night (Amanda, that is, not the Hollywood actress). To ease my guilt, I called the Mermaid and chatted for about ten minutes. I didn't know whether to bring up the depression thing or not, so I opted for the easy route and told her the highlights of Fatty's extraordinary farting performance instead. Surprisingly, she wasn't that interested and seemed a bit distracted, so I said I would see her soon and then hung up.

14:30 The grand rematch between the under-14Ds and the lowly Es proved more embarrassing than last week's grand title bout. This time we lost 32-12 (*and* they had only fourteen players, one of whom was Vern). Mr. Lilly said he was in a hurry to get to his etching class and left abruptly after the match. (I think it's fair to say that the coach has at last jumped the sinking ship.)

Simon and Rambo waited until Julian had gone to dinner and then conducted a thorough search of his room. Simon is Julian's slave, so there was no real risk of being caught out. Much to their dismay, they didn't find the missing underpants, but they did manage to come up with two pairs of women's panties, a pair of lacy stockings, and a bicycle pump! (A bit strange since Julian doesn't own a bicycle.)

22:15 Lay awake watching Vern having a conversation with his towel. At one stage the towel must have said something funny because he burst into fits of moggy laughter. Even Roger thought it was a bit weird and jumped onto my bed until the madness passed.

Wednesday 24th May

23:00 In addition to the usual candles, Fatty now had four mirrors planted around his cubicle for what he called "an enhanced visual effect." We all approached the scene with some hesitation—even Roger hung back (perhaps sensing the presence of the supernatural). The windows and doors were ordered closed (a pity since Fatty's school record still lingered strongly). We gathered around the big man's cubicle in respectful silence. Fatty produced two shiny glass balls, which he rolled around in his hands. He then placed his forefinger to his lips to indicate absolute silence and began kneading them around in his hands. He let out a low hum as if meditating and closed his eyes. Mad Dog had to wrap his hands around his mouth to keep from laughing and Boggo smirked and shook his head like he thought Fatty was bonkers.

Suddenly Roger sprang onto Fatty's locker, his fur standing bolt upright and his eyes wide like blazing comets. He was staring savagely at the dormitory wall on the chapel side and then he let out a terrible moan. Vern instinctively reached out for his cat, but Rambo stopped him. There was a bang and we all jumped as Simon's cricket bat fell to the floor. Then one of the candles sizzled and burned out.

I squeezed my legs together to stop myself from wetting my pants.

As quickly as it began, the moment was over. As if by magic, the strange energy of the room disappeared and Roger set about grooming himself as if nothing had happened.

A raging debate flared up between the believers (Fatty, Simon, Gecko, and Vern) and the non-believers (Boggo and Rambo). Mad Dog and I were on the fence. For the believers, what had just occurred was the ultimate proof that the ghost of Macarthur had just visited the Crazy Eight. The non-believers said that the cricket bat, which was leaning against the locker, had simply fallen, the candle had burned out, and Roger was deranged and neurotic. To prove their point, Rambo tried to relight the candle and couldn't, and Roger spent the next ten minutes pouncing on and trying to eat his own tail.

As always in these Crazy Eight debates, nothing was ever resolved. If I had to choose, I think I would side with the believers. In my view the likelihood of these three incidents occurring over a few seconds seemed a bit more than a coincidence. Also the look on Roger's face and the way his fur stood on end certainly wasn't natural. True or false, ghost or no ghost, interest in Macarthur has never been so intense. A truce was eventually called and we all went to bed—although I doubt anyone slept.

Thursday 25th May

Mad Dog found a dead cat while out hunting guinea fowl. He reckoned it was killed by a dog or a jackal. Just after prep he strung the carcass up above Vern's bed and we waited for Vern to return from the bogs.

Unfortunately, the gag didn't exactly work out as planned. When Vern saw the hanging cat, he freaked out and had some sort of epileptic fit, no doubt thinking that Roger had been assassinated. Then Bert stormed in, seized Vern, and tried to hold him upside down to prevent him from swallowing his tongue but succeeded only in dropping Vern on his head. With a thunk Vern crashed onto the concrete floor, which knocked him out cold. Julian ran in, saw Vern and the cat, screamed, and fainted. Gecko charged into the dormitory, took one look at the swinging cat, turned pea green, and galloped toward the window. He didn't make it and vomited on Mad Dog's bed. Mad Dog then charged after poor Gecko with his hunting and filleting knife, only to be stopped by Sparerib, who blew a fuse and gave Mad Dog a week of hard labor. Ho hum. Another day in the life of the Crazy Eight.

Friday 26th May

09:00 Speech and drama. Eve dressed Rambo up in a Shakespearian actor's costume and insisted on him wearing a gigantic codpiece. (Like a cricket ball box but bigger and stiffer!) She kept fiddling with Rambo's pants and adjusting his codpiece, much to the delight of the snickering class. For the first time this year Rambo blushed a bright crimson.

LONG WEEKEND

Sat next to a second-year boy called Morgan Govender on the bus down to Durban. He told me he was leaving the school because his parents are emigrating to England before the revolution begins. I told him Mandela would see us right—he just laughed and invited me to his house for curry.

Mom picked me up in the station wagon, which looked like it had been sat on by an elephant. She told me the hand brake had failed and the old goat had roared down the driveway and crashed into the old acacia tree at the bottom of the garden. Dad is beside himself as he's just had the car souped up. Apparently, the tree got away unscathed.

17:00 Visited the Mermaid. I found her lying in bed, dressed in her pajamas, staring vacantly out of the window. She looked awful. In fact, it took me a while to recognize her. She was horribly thin and wickedly pale. Her eyes were sunken into her head and they were badly bloodshot. There were dark rings around her eyes and her lips were pale blue in color.

I kissed her gently on the cheek and then she began to sob and sob . . . and sob. She was like a frail old woman dying of some horrendous disease. Where was the beautiful girl of my daydreams? Where was the firefly that lit up my world? She was gone. My Mermaid was gone.

I sat on her bed, holding her sweaty hands, and told her every story I could think of. Gone was the giggling beauty of before—now she could only frown or nod at my stories (even the funny ones). She refused to talk about herself, except to say she was fine. It didn't take a genius to figure out that she was anything but fine. It looked to me that there was something terribly wrong with her.

After what seemed like ages, Marge came in and said it was time for me to go. She kissed her daughter and so did I. The Mermaid started sobbing again as we left. Marge shook her head sadly and told me that she'd hoped I might spark some life into her. Marge drove me home and thanked me again for trying. I smiled and thanked her for the lift, but we were both feeling sad and disappointed because my visit hadn't made any difference to the Mermaid. I walked slowly up the driveway wishing that I had witnessed the unmanned station wagon tearing down the driveway on its date with the acacia tree. Now that would have been something!

Saturday 27th May

09:00 I took a stroll down to the shopping center to browse around and find a present for the Mermaid. I finally decided on a light prism that reflected all the colors of the rainbow. (It certainly wouldn't rate as a useful present but might make her feel better just to look at it.) I strolled back toward the entrance and stopped dead in my tracks. I could feel the blood draining from my face; my tongue lolled about uselessly in my mouth. Once I had recovered the use of my limbs, I bolted into a nearby Bessie's Butchery. From my hideaway I peered around the door just to check that my eyes weren't deceiving me—unfortunately, they weren't.

My father was noisily rattling collection money in a tin box and handing out large red stickers to every innocent shopper he could get his hands on. Behind him was a huge signboard emblazoned in thick red paint with the words SEND SPUD TO CAPE TOWN! To make matters worse, he was forcing people into parting with their cash. Like a loony circus ringmaster, he strode around shouting nonsensical slogans and harassing old ladies. I slipped out of the butchery and sprinted home.

Mom just smiled after I had finally related the horror that I'd just witnessed and said, "Isn't it wonderful? Your father has already raised over six hundred dollars for your trip and he hasn't even covered a quarter of the shopping centers in the city!"

My shame gave way to guilt—my dad is actually willing to beg to send me on a school cricket tour. This is proof that my dad is a marvelous father. (Perhaps I should donate him to a more deserving boy.)

12:00 Dad returned in triumph with 220 bucks and a plastic button in his money box. He looked wickedly proud of his efforts and I didn't have the nerve to tell him that I felt desperately ashamed.

I have begun reading *Waiting for the Barbarians*, which seems after ten pages to be a very strange book. I have, however, decided to persist with it. I'm sure it could come in useful to possibly spark a great literary conversation with my co-star or with the "brains" at the African Affairs meetings.

Sunday 28th May

12:00 What would a long weekend be without a lunchtime barbecue with Wombat? The grand old lady arrived in a faded green ball gown and a crimson smoking jacket (no doubt under the impression that her long-awaited invite to lunch at Buckingham Palace had finally arrived). Unfortunately, all she got was a termite-infested deck chair, a tough steak, and a piece of sausage!

Wombat's fuming because the policeman (who she called in to inspect the case of her missing bath mat) managed to make off with a jar of her strawberry jam. She's now lodged a charge of theft against the policeman. To make matters worse, Wombat's adamant that somebody's stolen her car. (Unfortunately, she doesn't own a car nor has she ever learned to drive.)

For an extra laugh I asked her about the Easter eggs. She moved closer to me and whispered that somebody had stashed them in the washing machine and then cunningly moved them to another location. (Talk about Inspector Wombat!) Dad said that it could be the Easter bunny. Wombat gave the matter some thought and then assured us that she wouldn't tolerate rodents in her flat—even if it were on a holy day.

Wombat asked me again if I had a girlfriend and then prattled on about me "spreading my wild oats." She told us that my grandfather had proposed to four women and left them all standing at the altar before finally tying the knot with her. (I wonder what the other four were like and if he ever regretted his decision.)

After lunch, Dad asked Wombat (who he says is "as mean as cat shit" and "wouldn't give you ice in winter") if she would like to enter a competition where the first prize is a trip to Buckingham Palace for a week. Wombat (who is apparently rolling in cash) bought ten tickets to the value of two hundred bucks. Dad winked at me and said, "Cape Town, here we come!" Mom shook her head in dismay and cleared away the lunch plates.

Visited the Mermaid again. This time she was sitting up in bed and looking a bit brighter. She still didn't say much but seemed happier and giggled when I told her about our lunch with Wombat. Unfortunately, I soon ran out of stories, so I just sat with her holding her hand. After a while, she asked me to sing her a song from Oliver. I sang "I'll Do Anything." Unfortunately, that started her sobbing again.

The sobbing turned into hysteria when Marge told me that I had to go. She gave the Mermaid some pills and told me to sit with her until she fell asleep. After she passed out, I kissed her pale, cool forehead, draped the blanket over her, and left. On the way home Marge explained that the Mermaid was going to see a psychiatrist for the first time tomorrow. I arrived home feeling sad and utterly depressed. That homesick feeling was starting up again—the great heaviness in my tummy—the dull ache in my bones. Tomorrow I'm getting back on the bus and going back—back to Mordor! (Okay, okay, so maybe it's not quite so bad!)

Mom was waiting in my room when I got home. She gave me a hug and said, "Girls are complicated, Johnny. Don't spend too much time working them out. Just listen to them and try and fig-ure out what they want." I nodded; Mom gave me another hug and walked out. She'd left a Snickers on my pillow.

Monday 29th May

I discovered that Innocence is selling home-brewed booze from her room. I followed one of her clients and hid behind a bush while the deal was going on. She charges one buck a bottle. The booze looks like a mixture of linseed oil and frothy piss. Decided not to tell the folks or they'll try and fire her again.

Spent another embarrassing morning buying underpants with Mom. This time she got into a long conversation with a fruity shop assistant on what happens to underpants in boys' boarding schools. (I haven't told her that there could be a sicko on the loose—I just blamed it on the laundry.) The shop assistant nearly convinced my mother that I needed something exotic. (Can you imagine the mocking if I revealed my brand-spanking-new tiger skin tanga to the Crazy Eight?) Thankfully, the assistant had to help another customer and I got away with the usual blue and white jocks. I wish this pervert would stop stealing my underpants—I'm not sure how many more of these shopping expeditions I can take.

17:30 Sat next to Fatty on the bus (in truth, I sat half under him and half off the seat). While noshing a bucket of fried chicken he told me that his mother wanted him to go on a diet. His parents are worried about him having a heart attack before he reaches twenty. I told him it was puppy fat and that he shouldn't worry. (Okay, I lied, but it made him feel better.)

CRAZY EIGHT WEEKEND SCORECARD:

Rambo	Smoked pot. He reckons it just makes you feel really pissed and a bit neurotic. He did say that he remembers laughing hysterically at things that weren't funny.
Simon	Watched seven videos and got pissed with his cousins in Zimbabwe.
Vern	Refused to say what he did. Judging from the size of his bald spot, he pulled out a lot of hair.

Gecko	Had a blood transfusion.
Boggo	Went to his first strip show. He said it was way overrated and the strippers were all butt ugly and had stretch marks. (Not sure what stretch marks are, so I just shook my head in disgust.)
Fatty	Stayed at home and ate.
Mad Dog	Shot a crow with a pellet gun.
Spud	Had lunch with his senile gran and tried to look after his neurotic girlfriend.

Nothing much has changed over the weekend, except for a rock pigeon that got trapped in our dormitory and shat on Simon's pillowcase. The bird was perched quite happily up in the rafters cooing contentedly to itself when Mad Dog killed it with one savage flick of his catty.

Wednesday 31st May

Boggo has drummed up enough support to be the house's AV monitor. This means that he has access (and a key) to the audiovisual room one week in every seven when our house is on duty. Not only will he be able to watch his porno movies at school but being the sly capitalist that he is, he plans to make a tidy profit from his screenings.

20:00 Bada bing! The real deal has begun. We have started with the dialogue and the action scenes of the play. Tonight we rehearsed the workhouse scene and I got to say the famous line: "Please, sir . . . I want some more," to the evil Mr. Bumble (science teacher Mr. Dennis). This is definitely more like the real thing—real acting—the real McCoy. Stand by, De Niro, here comes Spud Milton! (He must be quaking in his boots!)

Thursday 1st June

Looks like the Rain Man is back with a vengeance. Since returning to school, Vern has not slept in his bed. He slinks off late in the night with Roger clinging to his sweater and then returns just before the rising siren. I'm not sure if it was the dead cat or landing on his head that set him off, but either way he certainly isn't normal (not that he was ever really classically normal).

I'm concerned about bearing witness to another of Vern's Houdini disappearing acts. I casually informed Earthworm of Vern's odd behavior while sharpening his scissors. Earthworm stared at me over his reading frames until he was satisfied that I wasn't putting one over and then said, "I'll take it up with the relevant authorities." Feel a little bit guilty about telling on Vern, but demented people have to be watched closely!

During double drama, Rambo and Eve performed their scene from a Tennessee Williams play called *A Streetcar Named Desire*. Rambo played the young and aggressive Stanley and Eve played Blanche. In the scene Rambo responds to Blanche's flirting by trying to get it on with her—creating all sorts of tension. They were both excellent in the scene, and afterward Eve demonstrated to the class how one goes about approaching a stage kiss. She repeatedly kissed Rambo to demonstrate (she even showed the wrong way of stage kissing and stuck her tongue in his mouth). Boggo then asked to practice with Eve, but she said that we had run out of time. We were all wickedly jealous—Rambo just shrugged after class and refused to answer any of our questions. Spud smells a rat

Friday 2nd June

After lights-out Boggo accused Fatty of being a chicken because he refused to eat a tin of shoe polish. Boggo then did a loud chicken/rooster impersonation. Rambo joined in with a very realistic cow moo. I threw in a high-pitched sheep baa for good measure. Then followed the rest: Gecko barked like an old granny's poodle and Fatty shouted like a baboon. Simon tried a hippo but ended up sounding exactly like Viking. The barnyard musical dissolved into fits of cackling laughter (hyenas?) and into general Friday night chaos. Just as well Rain Man had already disappeared to his hideaway because the noise would have spooked the hell out of Roger.

Suddenly from across the quadrangle came a savage blast of animal noises. Barnes house first- and second-years replied with interest. Not to be outdone, the seven of us redoubled our efforts, raising new barnyards from all over the school. Soon Fynn, Century, West, King, and Woodall houses joined in with gusto. Suddenly the school was alive with the sound of domestic and other animals in a splendid display of late-night school spirit.

Then some idiot set off the siren. There's always one goon who takes things too far. Unfortunately, that idiot standing in the middle of the quad in his dressing gown with a lantern looked astonishingly like The Glock! We leapt away from the windows and dived into our beds. The other houses must have done a similar thing because suddenly it was only the Woodall idiots who were still mooing, barking, and bleating. (Woodall doesn't overlook the quad, so they obviously hadn't seen the danger.) The Glock, with his cane in one hand and a lantern in the other, strode off to ruin Woodall's night. The Woodall barnyard symphony lasted another two or three minutes and then stopped abruptly. No doubt The Glock was rounding up a few wayward animals for a savage thrashing.

Saturday 3rd June

The under-14Es (formerly under-14Ds) stormed to their first victory over the awestruck St. James side by a whopping 19–0 (Yours truly kicked seven points.) Mr. Lilly was so thrilled with the victory that he burst into tears and then hugged us each in turn. St. James lost every game (our first team won 18–7) barring one . . . that's right, you guessed it, the brand-spanking-new under-14Ds (formerly the under-14Es) lost 28–0. The curse continues!

18:30 Called the Mermaid, but Marge said that she was asleep and that she'd had a bad night. I asked her if the psychiatrist was helping. She sighed and said it was traumatic.

20:00 Saturday night's movie was *The Deer Hunter*, with Robert De Niro and Christopher Walken. The movie is all about Vietnam and is savage! Walken spends the entire movie playing Russian roulette until he finally runs out of luck and takes one to the cranium. Mad Dog said it was the best movie he'd ever seen. Enough said. (Not sure about De Niro quaking in his boots . . .)

Sunday 4th June

10:30 The girls are back. We spent the morning working on the funeral parlor scenes. The girl playing Charlotte (real name Jessie) is very funny and friendly. She treats me like I'm her brother and spends her life punching me or trying to punch me. She told me that she lives on a farm near Ladysmith and has four brothers.

As always, Amanda was aloof from the crowd and spent the morning reading her book. I walked past her on the way to the toilet and

I noticed that her new novel is called *A Dry White Season*. She must have finished *Barbarians*. It turns out that she's in standard eight (second year) and more than a year and a half older than me. Damn. Not that I was ever interested.

At lunch she walked past me without so much as acknowledging me and then spent the hour talking to some of her friends. I noticed Geoff Lawson joining the group and he spent the entire time perving over Amanda. In the afternoon session we did Fagin's scenes and sang our duet a couple of times. Once again, she instantly transformed herself into a loving, gentle creature and then, as soon as we were finished, marched off the stage like an iceberg in boots. Thank goodness I have the Mermaid or this ice queen would really be distracting me.

16:30 As the girls and boys said their farewells and headed for the bus, we locked eyes. I could swear that I saw the hint of a smile on Amanda's face—but to be honest, it was dark and immediately after that she sneezed. I shall keep watching and waiting . . . for interest's sake.

Monday 5th June

Sparerib is away for the week at a science symposium in Bloemfontein. Luthuli has assured us that he is fully in charge and has permission to beat anyone he chooses to as hard as he likes. To prove his point, he lashed Devries with his hockey stick for spitting a greeny in the gutter.

The Guv said *A Dry White Season* is a book about the "struggle" written by an Afrikaner called Brink. He rates it as the finest "struggle" book written thus far. The "struggle" is the word all the freedom fighters use when they talk about fighting against apartheid. When he asked about my sudden interest in political novels, I told him I wanted to be a freedom fighter and part of the "struggle." This is partly true, after all.) The Guv laughed and said I couldn't struggle myself out of a plastic bag. He ruffled my hair and we sat down to a lunch of tinned spaghetti. (The Guv's wife is still AWOL.)

23:10 On the way down to the toilet I passed Rambo coming up the stairs (he had been missing since lights-out). He said he'd been working in the library. This is a bit strange since the library closes at nine and he didn't even have any books with him. I didn't ask any questions, though, and he pushed past me and disappeared into the dormitory.

Tuesday 6th June

21:30 The dormitory's ablaze with gossip about Rambo and Eve. Somebody saw Rambo coming out of Sparerib's house late last night. Since Sparerib is now away and after the kissing sequence last week in drama, word on the street is that Rambo is bonking Eve. Everyone's green with envy—but still no word from Rambo, who's once again "working late." Boggo says he's taking even money bets that they are "doing something" and five to one odds that they are actually having sex. Nobody was brave enough to put any money down.

Wednesday 7th June

07:30 Called Dad to wish him happy birthday. He thanked me for the socks and the car wax (which I had apparently bought him).

He said he and Mom were going to the fish shop for dinner and were then going to watch *Matlock* on the telly. The last of the great party animals!

22:40   Rambo admitted there was something going on with Eve. I could tell that he was dying to tell us but was probably sworn to secrecy. Boggo plagued him for ages about Eve and even offered him large sums of cash in exchange for the scoop. Rambo refused and threatened to murder anybody who spread any rumors.

Mad Dog, who never really gives a damn about gossip, was snoring loudly throughout the entire conversation. In fact, it was so loud that it felt like the windows were rattling. As quiet as thieves, the rest of us slid into his cubicle and, obeying Rambo's command, each boy (besides Vern, who had disappeared soon after lights-out) picked up a part of his mattress and lifted Mad Dog skyward.

Surprisingly, he wasn't very heavy and kept on snoring. Not so much as a start. We carried the mattress through the second-years' dormitory and to the top of the stairs, where we had to put Mad Dog down because Boggo and Simon were overcome with giant snorts and strangled guffaws. Once they'd recovered, we picked up the mattress with the snoring Mad Dog still in a deep sleep and started down the stairs. Halfway down the stairs Fatty felt the pressure and farted. There was a mad rush to evade the stench and in the process we very nearly dropped Mad Dog. Unbelievably, he still didn't stir and we coaxed the mattress through the house door and out into the quad. We gently laid Mad Dog to rest on the frosty lawn next to the fountain, slap bang in the middle of the main quad, and then galloped back to the dormitory. For over an hour we watched the sleeping bundle from our dormitory windows. Gecko became concerned that Mad Dog would contract frostbite, hypothermia, or piles. Rambo collected up four blankets and skulked back into the quad and carefully tucked Mad Dog in. He reckoned the crazy bugger was still snoring when he left him.

Thursday 8th June

06:00 Mad Dog still sleeping in the quad, although all you can see is a huge pile of red blankets.

06:14 The boy on siren duty runs straight past Mad Dog without even seeing him.

06:15 Rising siren. Mad Dog turns over in his bed. The siren ringer stops and stares at Mad Dog for a moment and then sprints back to his house.

06:18 Mr. Cartwright walks across the quad and into the staff room without noticing Mad Dog.

06:19 Mr. Lilly strides across the quad, sees Mad Dog, stops, and stares. After a moment he shakes him awake. Mad Dog waves him away, turns over, and continues sleeping. Lilly trots off to the staff room looking terribly concerned.

06:20 Mr. Lennox walks straight past Mad Dog while reading the morning paper. He comes within a foot of tripping over the sleeping beauty. Wild hilarity erupts in the dormitory.

06:22 The Glock strides out of the staff room and across the quad. He walks past the body, stops, looks back, looks around suspiciously, and then approaches the bundle of blankets. He cautiously prods Mad Dog with his shiny black shoe and then kicks him. Mad Dog kicks out sideways and turns over, clearly irritated by the interruption. The Glock kicks harder this time. Mad Dog slowly sits up, opens his eyes, and stares dumbly at The Glock. He then looks around in total confusion, says something to The Glock, gathers up his mattress and his pile of blankets, and gallops into the house.

Mad Dog was too puzzled to chase or even threaten us. He just sat on his bed, shaking his head in utter confusion as he watched the rest of us howling with mirth, staggering around clutching at our stomachs. I asked Mad Dog what he had said to The Glock. "Morning, Mom," was the reply!

21:15 Guy Emberton caught Boggo wanking against the water heater behind the toilets. (What Emberton was doing lurking around there hasn't been established.)

Friday 9th June

08:00 Boggo received the infamous "wanker chant" again in the dining hall and turned a bright crimson. Mr. Hall, the first-team rugby coach, joined in the chant as Boggo attempted to hide his face in his porridge.

Middle of the night: Vern charged into the dormitory screaming, shouting, and gesticulating wildly. Mad Dog picked him up and turned him upside down so that he wouldn't swallow his tongue. (Luthuli has given us explicit instructions as to what to do if Vern has another fit.) It took some time for Vern to indicate that he wasn't having a fit and that he had urgent news to tell us. After Mad Dog turned him right-side up, he set about telling us, in a series of gasps and moggy gestures, that Macarthur's ghost had visited him and Roger while they were hanging around in the crypt. The ghost had apparently lifted Roger clean into the air and then whispered something that Vern couldn't understand, although it sounded something like "echo." Vern said Roger had shrieked in terror and disappeared into the night.

Nobody was quite sure whether the story was real or the mad ramblings of a gibbering cretin.

Saturday 10th June

I am officially word perfect. At Monday night's rehearsal I shall arrive without my script—no doubt earning a few extra brownie points from Viking!

My hair is starting to look long and shaggy. A couple of masters have seriously inquired over its length. After my telling them the whole spiel about Oliver, they have by and large grunted and then walked away muttering to themselves about falling standards of discipline.

Wrote a long letter to the Mermaid, who I am now addressing as Debbie in my letters. Am terribly worried that I'm no longer in love with her. I spend hours daydreaming about Julia Roberts (Amanda). Think I might be losing my grip. I took a stroll to the san after dinner and told Sister Collins that I was concerned about my life and was feeling a little odd. Before I was able to continue, she shouted, "For God's sakes, you aren't queer, it's just a phase." She then ordered me to gargle with some foul purple liquid and take a laxative.

Sunday 11th June

08:30 Released my fourth prisoner since taking Sister Collins's laxative. Next time I'll keep my troubles to myself!

20:00 Tonight's African Affairs meeting focused on the anti-apartheid activist Steve Biko, who was brutally murdered in police custody. The police said he had slipped and fallen out of the prison window—but how dumb do they think we really are? Mr. Lennox showed us a documentary about the murder, and it didn't take long for a heated debate to kick in. Stung with passion and guilt (and way too much filter coffee), I stood up without thinking and said I was ashamed to be white! Linton Austin sniffed and gave me a withering look over the top of his spectacles and told me that shame was a useless emotion. Luthuli jumped to my defense and said that South Africa needed more white people with a conscience. I flushed with pride and felt immensely relieved that at last I had said something and wasn't laughed at. On the way back to the house Luthuli told me he was proud of me and that his grandfather, Albert Luthuli, was a Nobel Peace Prize winner and a former president of the ANC. I looked at our head of house with a new sense of awe and admiration. No wonder he had tears in his eyes when Nelson Mandela was released. I said the first words that came into my head. "I want to be a freedom fighter."

Luthuli smiled at me and said, "Spud, by the time you finish school, the struggle will be over." With that he disappeared into the prefects' room and I slipped into the dormitory full of raging ambition to join the struggle. Under the soft warmth of my fluffy Good Knight duvet, I started plotting the downfall of De Klerk and his evil apartheid empire.

Monday 12th June

Woke up with a sore throat and a husky voice. Tonight the girls are being bused in for a rehearsal and Viking's plan is to "stumble through act one." I'm not sure how my voice will hold up. I tried to sing but sounded alarmingly like Wombat, so I stopped immediately.

19:00 Astounded! Amanda just cruised past me and breezily said, "Evening, Spud," and then disappeared before I had a chance to close my mouth and put my tongue away.

Surprisingly, my voice held up fine although the rehearsal was sheer torment. Kojak and Viking took turns shouting and screaming at us with Dodge and myself receiving most of their abuse. Even The Guv was shat on by Kojak for singing an entire song completely in the wrong key. The school band, who have been hard at work practicing the music, sat in and watched the rehearsal to get an idea about the show. Before long they were yawning, and after an hour and a half of them had fallen asleep. Not a very promising sign. Act one is meant to be an hour long: our effort came in at a shade under four—Dodge reckons he heard Viking screaming in the toilet after we had been dismissed.

Tuesday 13th June

My throat is in agony and I'm sneezing all over everyone. What if I have some terrible disease and I lose my role to the awful Smith or the drippy Winter? I will fight my germs in absolute secrecy! Unfortunately, when I sneeze, I do it in royal style and let rip with a continuous volley of eight or nine in quick succession, which then leaves me weak and faint. (Boggo reckons that five sneezes is the equivalent of an orgasm. I sure hope an orgasm feels better than this!)

After lights-out Rambo finally admitted that he's been having sex with Eve. He says she is like an animal and likes it in different positions. He swore that if the news leaves the dormitory, he will slit all our throats. Boggo was so overcome by Rambo's revelation that he sprinted off to the bogs for ten minutes. Rambo's shares have skyrocketed to hero status and we all shook his hand, and once Boggo had returned from the bogs, he even asked Rambo to autograph one of his porno mags.

I couldn't sleep with my sore throat and the thought of Eve and Rambo actually having sex together.

Wednesday 14th June

My condition has seriously deteriorated. I woke sometime in the afternoon to find myself in a bed in the sanatorium. Sister Collins said that I had fainted during maths and had been carried in by some worried classmates. She shouted at me for not coming sooner and then gave me a savage injection in my bum and kissed my forehead.

I woke in the night and found myself staring into the worried face of Viking. I tried to speak but couldn't—Viking panicked and woke up Sister Collins, who lambasted my director for waking her up and said, "Of course he can't speak, you fool, he's got chronic bronchitis!" Viking turned pale, left me a chocolate, and scuttled out of the sanatorium.

Thursday 15th June

Sometime during the course of the morning Bert came into the sanatorium with a dodgy complaint. He didn't seem to see me in the bed and I pretended to be sleeping. After much humming and hawing and clearing of his throat he admitted to Sister Collins that he had a problem with his willy. She ordered his pants off and then gasped when she saw that his giant penis was covered in what looked like a bright green slime. Once she'd recovered her composure, she set about inspecting his infected member with a pair of yellow dish-washing gloves and what looked like a huge pair of tongs. Eventually, she gave him some cream and told him to stop playing with himself so much. Bert nodded and then loped out into the sunlight.

I woke in the afternoon to find Gecko in the bed next to me. Gecko, who seems to have taken up permanent residence in the san, announced rather proudly that he'd contracted a rare form of schistosomiasis (although he didn't seem to know what this disease entailed or where he'd got it from). We spent the after-noon chatting, or rather Gecko chatted and I nodded. I have never seen him so relaxed and happy. Obviously, the sanatorium agrees with him.

THE WORLD ACCORDING TO GECKO:

Born in London.
His father is an entomologist (studies bugs and rare flies).
His mother was a ballet dancer but now does nothing.
Reckons that he was bitten by a foul bug (being studied by his dad) at an early age and that has led to a long string of diseases.
Has had forty-two diagnosed diseases/illnesses/afflictions and at least six unknown to medical science.
His parents spend most of their time in England because they think South Africa is dangerous.
Gecko senior is also an old boy of the school, a tradition that spans five generations.
His dad is waiting for his rich old mother-in-law to die. Then he plans to retire and run a bed-and-breakfast in a place called the Cotswolds.

Gecko surprised me by being completely open and quite intelligent. He reckons he hates everyone in our dormitory except for Vern and me. Although he did say that I often try and act like a "heavy" and then he doesn't like me. I felt guilty as I remembered all the times I've joined the group in ruthlessly ripping off Gecko and laughing at his projectile vomiting. Gecko also seemed dead certain that Macarthur and Crispo had been murdered and that The Glock was the murderer.

"I tell you, Spud, this place is like an insane asylum! There are maniacs in this place—even our headmaster's a maniac! Don't you feel it too? It's like there's always someone out to get you, or laugh at you or make you feel like an idiot or a coward or something."

Gecko is right—if you are on the wrong side of the fence, this place is hell. From the way he spoke, Gecko assumed that I was on the right side of the fence while I've always felt like I was on the wrong side with Gecko and Vern. Maybe I just sit on the fence and am neither in nor out?

Suddenly my heart sank. I scrabbled through my bag and was massively relieved to find my diary was still with me. I had just had the terrible image of it being passed around the house again while I was lying helpless in the san. I slipped it under my pillow and waited for my heart to stop thumping.

Gecko shook his head at the injustice of it all and looked sadly out of the window. He then turned to me suddenly and said, "Spud, you know when you sing, it's like . . . it's like . . . I dunno, this may sound weird, but it's like I know there might be a God out there." He then obviously felt embarrassed and rolled over and lay still.

There, among the white beds and sheets, pills, syringes, potties, and dull cream curtains, the most unlikely person in the world had said the most . . . unbelievable thing to me. The deadweight in my gut was back—I felt warm tears in my eyes and had to grit my teeth and fight them back. I felt terrible shame and guilt. I remembered all the times I'd jeered and snickered and mocked Gecko in front of the others, all because it made me feel stronger and part of the pack. But Gecko had real courage. To tell somebody that they're special takes courage. I reckon this vomiting, pale-faced Gecko has more guts than the rest of the Crazy Eight put together.

Friday 16th June

SOWETO DAY

Had calls from the folks and the Mermaid. Sadly, the Mermaid and I ran out of conversation and had a terribly long pause, which was followed by us both talking at once. I just didn't have enough energy to carry on with the conversation so I told her my throat was sore, hung up, and felt guilty.

Kojak stopped in for a visit after lunch and brought me his Walkman and a tape of the *Oliver* music so that I could keep myself up to date. He said the rehearsals are driving him mad and then managed to snake some free high blood pressure pills out of Sister Collins before leaving. I could hear him shouting at a boy outside for walking around with his shirt out.

Luthuli visited me at break and told me that today is the anniversary of the Soweto uprising, where the police shot and killed many innocent and unarmed marchers in 1976. I felt proud that my head of house shared that with me and made a big heading of it in my diary.

Sister Collins stuck a list called the Sanatorium Commandments on the front door. She said she's sick of repeating herself day after day.

SANATORIUM COMMANDMENTS:

1. No rugby boots to be worn in san!
2. If you are sick enough to miss school, then you are sick enough to be in san!
3. No checking into san without san Sister's permission! (Anybody caught disobeying this rule will have to drink COD LIVER OIL.)
4. No sleeping in dormitories during school hours without permission from your housemaster or the san Sister!
5. No missing sports unless in possession of an off-sport slip signed by the san Sister!
6. No smoking in sanatorium!
7. No visiting after visiting hours!
8. Hydrogen peroxide is for medical use only and not for hair bleaching!
9. If you have a sore throat, gargle red liquid and take two orange pills from the red bucket. Do not bother me unless you are on death's door!
10. No dying in sanatorium! (Please do this over the holidays.)

My health has definitely taken a turn for the better. Sister Collins reckons I could be out by tomorrow night. The chants from the war cry practice have made me anxious to return to the real world. I'm dying to get back to rehearsals—and to see what the rest of the Crazy Eight have been up to. Also, exams are only ten days away—I had better start learning to avoid any embarrassment over my scholarship (in truth, I'm not sure how I got it in the first place; there are a couple of other boys in my class who make me look like a complete brain donor).

Spent the evening in conversation with my new big mate Gecko, who also loves my Wombat stories. Perhaps I should write a book called *The Weird and Wonderful Adventures of the Wily Wombat*. A tragicomedy beginning with chapter one—"The Mystery of the

Disappearing Yogurt." I could feel the dark fog in my head lifting and the feeling of inspiration and happiness take over. It must have been the same for Gecko because he said he was feeling better already.

Sister Collins came to read us a story at about 21:00. She started reading from the Hardy Boys. I felt embarrassed—surely it had to be bad form for a scholarship winner to be seen listening to the Hardy Boys! I asked Sister Collins if she could read something a little more advanced. "Nonsense!" she barked. "Everybody loves the Hardy Boys—even my late husband got it when he was sick!"

And she was right. It was fantastic. Like two little brothers and their mom, Gecko and I lay in bed while Sister Collins read us stories in her deep, husky voice. When she had finished the chapter, she closed the book, tucked us in, gave us each a kiss on the forehead, and switched off the bedside lamp.

No wonder Gecko loves it here.

Saturday 17th June

Woke to find a small note on the table next to my bed. It was double folded and written on bloodred paper. Once my eyes were focusing, I opened the letter, which read:

> *To my darling Spuddy,*
> *Get better, baby. I miss you.*
>
> > *Love,*
> > *Your Million Dollar Bet,*
> > *AMANDA*

After I nearly fell out of bed, I held the note in my trembling hands and read it over and over and over and over.

After a quick shower, I read it another couple of hundred times, read it to Gecko four times, and then spent the rest of the morning daydreaming about Amanda. Think this could be trouble!

Mr. Lilly came bouncing into the san to tell me that the under-14Ds (formerly the under-14Es) had lost again. He sat down on Gecko's bed with a happy sigh. Unfortunately, he hadn't noticed that the bed was occupied and sat on Gecko's head. Gecko screamed, coughed, and vomited, narrowly missing the startled rugby coach. Sister Collins chased Mr. Lilly out of the ward by savagely brandishing a giant thermometer at him.

17:25 I have been released and declared partially healthy. Sister Collins has ordered me not to put any strain on my voice for at least three days. Wrapped in sweaters and a scarf, I took my first tentative steps out of the sanatorium and onto the crunchy brown grass. Mr. van Vuuren, our Afrikaans teacher, strode past. "Good evening, sir," I croaked with all the good cheer of Father Christmas. The bulky master with his huge bulbous nose glared at me and growled menacingly, "Get a bloody haircut."

As I strode into the house, I was bowled over by about twelve boys all shouting and pushing. Back on my feet, I realized that it was in fact the Crazy Eight (actually the Crazy Five but with some accomplices), who were carrying Simon out toward the fish pond. Our cricket captain landed with a splash and disappeared before launching himself back out of the pond with gallons of water cascading out of his school uniform. He trudged back toward the house. "Happy birthday," I said as he passed me.

"Stuff off!" came the reply.

Damn, it's good to be back!

Sunday 18th June

Amanda gave me a big hug when I arrived at rehearsals. (She did also hug Dodge, Geoff, and a few others.) Viking didn't allow me to sing but still wanted me to rehearse so that I could familiarize myself with some of the changes. Winter, who has been filling in for me while I was sick, looked miserable as he sat in the auditorium watching the real Oliver tread the boards. What can I say . . . you can't swim with the sharks if you piss like a guppy!

During lunch I tried to strike up a conversation with Amanda about *Waiting for the Barbarians*. Unfortunately, it didn't turn out as well as I'd hoped. She said she gave the book up after twenty pages and called J. M. Coetzee a morbid cynic without the faintest shred of subtlety in his writing. I agreed (I have, after all, only managed eleven pages in three weeks) and assured her that he was one of the worst novelists alive (despite his Booker Prize, which must have been a fluke).

There was great sadness as we said goodbye to the girls for the last time this term. Due to exams and the coming holidays, there'll be no more rehearsals. Before setting off, Viking put the fear of the theater gods into us by saying that the next time the full cast rehearses, it will be exactly six weeks until curtain up!

Monday 19th June

11:00 The under-14A cricket touring squad has been posted on the notice board outside the dining hall. The team is exactly the same as before, with Rambo added as the twelfth touring member. Fatty has also been included as the team scorer (our scorer used to be The Guv's wife). This means five of the Crazy Eight will launch an attack on the Mother City! We have our first practice tomorrow afternoon and set off for Cape Town next

Saturday, returning the following Sunday.

While I was in the sanatorium, gossip about Rambo and Eve had spread like wildfire. Apparently, Rambo was so angry that he hung Boggo out of the dormitory window by his feet until he confessed to starting the rumor. (He later denied his confession and blamed Vern, who disappeared for two nights and pulled out most of the hair on the left side of his head.) Rambo is now being called Adam, and Eve's private parts are officially known as the Garden of Eden.

According to Rambo, Gavin, the prefect under the stairs, has trebled the cockroach population in his room. He made Rambo remove the cockroaches from the dustbin and place them in a large cardboard box. Rambo is willing to pay someone to swap prefects with him. I told him I wouldn't trade Earthworm in for a thousand bucks.

Tuesday 20th June

16:00 I arrived at cricket practice in my rugby boots—it seemed very weird putting on the old pads and gloves. Mad Dog was so erratic that he bowled one of his fireballs into the wrong net and nearly killed Martin Leslie, who was caught unawares while adjusting his ball box. The Guv was back to his usual high spirits and hurled some spectacular abuse at us throughout the practice. He said my bowling "had gone from guile to vile." He also told Rambo that he was the slowest bowler in the world and should be prosecuted for bowling donkey drops without a permit. The Guv did receive his comeuppance when a classic straight drive from Simon smashed into his shins, causing the loon to fall off his shooting stick and let loose a volley of furious swearing.

Dinner: Luthuli handed Boggo the keys to the AV room (this week is our house's duty week). Boggo's eyes lit up and he snatched the keys from the head of house (reminded me of Gollum and his Precious . . .). The delighted Boggo wolfed down his lamb chops and sped off to check out his new porno control center.

Wednesday 21st June

15:00 During a learning break for exams, Gecko (who has ruthlessly annihilated his schistosomiasis) and I took a stroll across the fields, past the dam, and up into the hills. Gecko told me about the time he met Elton John at a cocktail party in Knightsbridge in London. (Elton passed Gecko on the stairwell and asked him where the toilet was.) We reached the top of the steep hill and sat on a flat, smooth rock that was warm from the sun.

Below us lay the school, all redbrick turrets and spires like a medieval castle. Shielding the buildings stood the bare trees and underneath them the dry frostbitten fields. In summer it makes a perfect postcard; in winter it seems a dry and desolate place. After a long pause, Gecko suddenly asked me to sing to him. I felt embarrassed and said that I was not allowed to sing for a while. He seemed disappointed and I felt guilty again. He said my singing at Crispo's funeral gave him goose bumps and that he hoped that I would sing at his funeral one day (provided that I didn't die before he did). I gave him my word and gradually felt the terrible weight of guilt ease away.

Thursday 22nd June

20:30 Boggo's porno debut. Rambo and Simon were invited to watch the premiere of *Randy Racks* with Boggo in the AV room. All three said it was a wicked experience. Being a spud, Rambo said the porno would be wasted on me because I "fire blanks." I felt the blood rush to my face and sank low into my mattress and desperately tried not to be curious. No matter how many times I'm teased about it, my spudness still kills me!

Friday 23rd June

Julian hauled myself and Gecko into the prefects' room and demanded to know if we were poofs. We assured him that we weren't. He looked dreadfully disappointed, canceled our tea and toast, and told us to get lost. As we were leaving, he told us to let him know if we ever had a change of heart. While climbing the house steps together, Gecko said his cousin was a poof but had since come right, got married, and opened up a sex shop in Cape Town. I told him that (together with the Elton John story) it probably was best not bandied about in these suspicious times.

War cry practice before the Kings College game traditionally takes place in the quad, which is seen as the holy epicenter of the school. This despite the quad's reputation having being somewhat dented by Fatty's window debacle and Mad Dog's night on the lawn. All week the school has been alive with stories and records about our meeting with Kings College. In over a hundred years we have beaten them only three times and last year they thrashed us 44–3! The last time we beat them was in 1977, when Kings claim they were laid low by a flu epidemic.

18:30 As is tradition, prep was canceled and all the boys were ordered to their common rooms to watch the video *The World's 100 Greatest Tries*. Our common room was packed. I captured a small piece of carpet in the corner. The lights were switched off; the video played. But instead of Naas Botha, Gareth Edwards, and David Campese we got two naked women kissing each other. It only lasted a few seconds, but the roar of approval from our common room and other common rooms around the school lasted several minutes. The video was hastily changed and Gareth Edwards was returned, but the damage was done.

Surely Boggo's error was fatal (that is, if it was an error). The video channel is beamed to all the staff houses as well as to most of the nearby farmhouses around the estate. Some staff member has had to have seen the beautiful ladies in action. I'll be surprised if Boggo lasts the weekend.

Dreamed of the Mermaid and Amanda kissing each other on my bed. Is that sick or normal? Rambo said that if he was a girl, he would be a lesbian. Come to think of it, so would I!

Saturday 24th June

A terrified Boggo consulted Rambo in our dormitory before marching off to meet The Glock (and presumably his death). We all huddled around Rambo's cubicle and spoke in hushed whispers. Boggo was terrified. In his trembling hands lay the porno tape in a white plastic box. We wished him luck before he shuffled out to meet his fate. The rest of us waited together in the common room as the minutes ticked by. Eventually, a smiling Boggo returned (without the tape), gave us the thumbs-up, and skipped up the stairs to the dormitory. Half the house galloped after him and found the scoundrel relaxing on his bed like a Texan billionaire. Here follows his account:

Obeying Rambo's instructions, Boggo decided not to deny knowledge of the tape but rather to bring the porno tape forward to The Glock. What he *did* deny was that the tape was his. He told The Glock that it was just lying there in the AV room and Boggo had mistakenly thought it was the *World's 100 Greatest Tries* tape. After some probing questions, The Glock gave Boggo the benefit of the doubt and confiscated the tape (Boggo reckons he slipped it into his bottom drawer). The Barnes house AV monitor was then brought in for questioning. Another grand escape for the Crazy Eight. One day Rambo's empire must fall. . . .

We lost 92–0 to Kings. The under-14Es lost 108–0 (Mr. Lilly has claimed it a victory!).

By 15:00 every single one of our teams had been swept aside by the menacing green-and-black tide. Kings College seemed invincible. Their first team, which looked twice the size of ours, took to the field in front of thousands of people. After a few minutes the inspired team in red-and-white-hooped jerseys sprinted onto the field to the sound of an enormous war cry. Kings College dampened the excitement by scoring in the second minute and by halftime had opened up a 12–0 lead. Our unbeaten record was on the rocks. It seemed certain that the great Kings College would be triumphant for the thirteenth time in a row.

But the second half was a different story. No doubt Mr. Hall had fired them up with his halftime speech/threats, which he had apparently conducted with a revolver holstered to his hip (according to Bert, that is). Unbelievably, Armstrong scored twice, and Brown kicked both the goals: 12–12. The score stayed like that for the rest of the half.

Then, with only seconds left to play, Kings intercepted a stray pass and their winger scorched down the sideline and scored under the poles. We hung our heads in misery as Kings erupted, hurling their straw hats into the air in a scene of mass celebration.

Suddenly there was cheering all around me. The ref had blown his whistle. Penalty to us! The ref adjudged that the Kings winger, who'd made the interception, was offside. The Kings College boos were silenced by their head boy, who brought the school to order with a savage wave of his flag.

Time had elapsed as Oliver Brown placed the ball on a small mound of sand. He took his familiar crablike steps backward and then to the side. And there he stood, examining the poles like a professor. Without doubt it was a difficult kick, from an acute angle and with the pressure of ten thousand people standing in eager anticipation. . . . THUMP. The ball flew high and directly at the right-hand upright. And then came that soft right to left curve like a bowling ball. The flags were raised and then chaos. A stampede onto the ground. The players lifted high, war cries, hymns, car alarms, dogs, babies, roosting birds . . . everything joined in. We had beaten Kings College! The Kings had been dethroned. Long live the Kings!

Sunday 25th June

After the excitement of yesterday, I set about learning theorems, reading poems, studying climatology, and brushing up on South African politics from 1908. Needless to say, a long nasty day without relief. I broke the monotony with a telephone call to the Mermaid, who was completely vague and bland and had nothing to say.

Eventually, some good news. Dad called to say that he'd raised the money for the tour. I thanked him many times and didn't dare ask how he'd managed the final six hundred dollars. In this case, ignorance is definitely bliss.

Thursday 29th June

I have forgone my daily diary discipline because I've had to focus my full attention on my examinations. Besides, I cannot recall anything of the slightest interest occurring over the last four days. Sparerib did call Rambo in for a "meeting," though. Rambo has refused to let on what it is about, although we think it's *all about Eve* . . . ha ha.

The exams ranged from easy (history, drama, geography, and English) to impossible (maths and science). I doubt very much that I'll be living up to my scholarship billing as a budding genius.

The only other news is that all of Gecko's jocks were stolen last night. Due to our newfound friendship, he told me after dinner that he was hanging loose and he's positive that Julian is behind it. As a precaution I've hidden three pairs of my underpants under the bed and am wearing another three.

Tomorrow is officially the last day of term, although the touring party will be spending the first night of the holidays at school and departing for Cape Town early on Saturday morning. This is my first official tour. I feel like a springbok! (Not that the springboks ever tour.)

Friday 30th June

The entire first rugby team was awarded either colors or honors during the final assembly. The Glock wished our cricket side luck for the tour and then handed out a crapload of ties, badges, and trophies. Think The Glock's cheese might be slipping off his cracker because he spent the whole assembly grinning like an idiot and even made a few lame jokes that only the maths and science teachers laughed at.

12:00 Half the Crazy Eight said their goodbyes and headed off to
their buses or parents' cars. Our touring squad joined The Guv for
an afternoon practice. It was quite weird having the whole place to
ourselves. The staff must love the peace and quiet when us boys
aren't here.

22:00 Rambo slipped back into the dormitory and told us that
he'd just had sex with Eve in the cricket pavilion. Fatty and Mad
Dog pushed him for details, but all he said was that it was the best
feeling he'd ever had. Simon, who had spent the entire evening
bouncing a ball on the edge of his bat, told Rambo to stop his
affair with Eve before things got completely out of hand. Rambo
grinned and cruised off to the showers.

Tomorrow we set off across the country to beautiful Cape Town,
which I haven't seen since I was about five years old. I wonder if
we'll get to go up Table Mountain in the cable car? Last time we
were there, we couldn't go up because Wombat said she got vertigo
and had a premonition that the cable would snap and the cable car
would burst into flames. We went to the Houses of Parliament
instead.

Mad Dog crushed a tea bag, rolled the leaves in a torn-up letter
stolen from Vern's locker, and told us all to smoke it. It tasted vile
and I spent the night with a hacking cough that kept everyone but
Mad Dog awake.

Saturday 1st July

05:00 The rising siren sounded, followed by The Guv's booming
voice ringing out from the quad. "Get up, you miserable fat bastards,
once more unto the bus! All aboard the bus to slay the feckless Cape

swine!" I think he said "feckless," although with The Guv you can never be too sure. (Not sure what "feckless" is anyway, but it sounds bad.)

We sped down Pilgrim's Walk with The Guv leading us in a croaky war cry and some mad screaming from an obscure Shakespearian play called *Simberlina* or something. It suddenly dawned on me that The Guv was as drunk as a skunk and still wearing his academic gown from yesterday's assembly.

Eric Nyathi, the school's bus driver, was thrilled to have the firebrand English teacher sitting next to him and chatted away to our coach in a mixture of English and Zulu. The bus crept its way up the frozen brown hills of the Natal Midlands and then sprinted on the downhill stretches to try and gather pace for the next hill. To keep our spirits up, The Guv asked me to lead the bus in several renditions of the school hymn. Once the singing had died down, The Guv pulled out a series of faxed pages and began telling us about our opponents for the weeklong cricket tournament. Our cunning coach had sent his brother (an estate agent who lives in Cape Town) on a tour of each of the schools we will play, armed with a notepad and a pair of binoculars to spy on our opposition. Our spy reckons the only worrying school is Cardinal College, who "have lethal opening bowlers and a batting lineup as long as a seven-foot tart in high heels"! The Guv carefully read through his information on each school and warned us that if we lose our unbeaten record, we will be walking the 1700 kilometers home.

Sunday 2nd July

Our twenty-five-hour journey eventually ground to a halt outside the community hall in Rondebosch under the famous Table Mountain. (We were told that there was a mountain, but the cloud was so thick and low that it was impossible to see anything at all.) The large hall was packed with mattresses and mini-lockers. It seems the schools have all been thrown in together. We collapsed onto our beds and crashed into a blissful sleep.

14:00 Three other teams have arrived. As per The Guv's instructions, we glared at them with steely-eyed menace as they unpacked and made their beds.

21:45 Mad Dog led our team on a rampaging pillow fight, which resulted in one of the Eastern Province boys bursting into tears and the rest of them screaming with fright and charging off into the rain. We have now drawn first blood and established dominance over our foes.

Monday 3rd July

07:00 Called home to announce my safe arrival in Cape Town. Dad asked how many wickets I'd taken. I told him we only start playing tomorrow. Then there was a lot of shouting and the sound of a chain saw chopping down a tree, and then the line went dead.

After an early morning net session in the drizzle, The Guv and Eric drove us around the Cape Peninsula to Simon's Town. Once again we missed seeing the mountains, but we did see seals, ships, a naval base, and a weird man with a long beard walking across the road stark naked. On the way home The Guv told us that he needed to make a phone call and disappeared with Eric into a pub called the Brass Bell in a small fishing village called Kalk Bay. We had a spectacular view of the ocean until the windows steamed up. We spent the rest of the time playing dice and I Spy. Mad Dog had us guessing for about an hour on something beginning with the letter *l*. After we had all conceded defeat, he told us that he had seen an elf hiding behind the bus. Through gritted teeth Rambo told Mad Dog that even if there was an elf in the middle of Kalk Bay (which was highly unlikely), the word started with the letter *e*. Mad Dog claimed victory all the same and announced himself the I Spy champion.

Some three hours later The Guv and Eric appeared, singing together (although singing different songs in different languages). The pair staggered arm in arm through the mud and stumbled onto the bus. The Guv slurred a short verse of Shakespeare and said that his mother sent us her love. With that, the bus lurched forward and skidded onto the road, narrowly missing an old couple struggling to control their umbrella. As we headed back to base camp, The Guv sang an incredibly long and dirty song about a girl called Amelia. Eventually, he trailed off and fell asleep on Eric's shoulder.

Tuesday 4th July

MATCH 1—TEMPLETON HIGH

09:00 We arrived to find the field waterlogged and, with the rain still belting down, the match was called off and we were taken to the aquarium instead. Leslie and George spent the morning trying to irritate a huge ragged-tooth shark but only succeeded in getting us all kicked out. The Guv then took us to an art gallery where Mad Dog pretended to hump a sculpture, landing us with another eviction—this time from an irate curator who said we were a disgrace to our school. The Guv told the curator to get stuffed and that we were from Templeton High in the Transvaal. The fuming curator

said he would report us. The Guv belched loudly and then
marched us out of the gallery.

After a take out lunch of hamburgers and chips in Sea Point, we
visited the old castle, where, surprisingly, we weren't evicted. I
remember the castle as being deadly boring from my last visit, and
this time proved no different. From there we took a stroll around
the harbor. Through the drizzle, I could just make out the tip of
Robben Island, where Mandela had been imprisoned. It looked
cold and desolate and a horrible place to spend half your life.
Nobody else showed any interest in the island and soon we were
speeding back to base camp.

Thursday 6th July

MATCH 3–CARDINAL COLLEGE

Starting to question why we are at a Cape cricket festival in winter, since winter is when the southern Cape receives all its rain (a
point that I made repeatedly during my geography examination).
Once again our game against Cardinal College wasn't completed
and we didn't get the chance to see the opposition fast bowlers.
The jury's still out on The Guv's infamous intelligence sources.

Friday 7th July

MATCH 4–ORANGE FREE STATE COMBINED

Victory against the Orange Free State Combined! And so endeth the rainy cricket week. Although the weather has been something of a letdown, the good news is that our team is still officially unbeaten.

Saturday 8th July

12:00 The Guv and Eric led us on a wine-tasting tour of Paarl, Stellenbosch, and Franschoek. After the fourth wine farm we were all as drunk as skunks. My head felt like it was swimming with wine. I was staggering everywhere and I had a throbbing headache. After the eighth farm, I joined Leslie, Simon, and Steven George in a communal vomiting session around the back of a chicken run. Meanwhile Fatty had gorged himself on over a kilogram of flavored goats' cheese. The Guv bought four cases of wine and seemed hell-bent on drinking as much as he could on the bus before getting back to base camp. He didn't seem at all worried that we were drunk and mostly vomiting, slurring, and in a general state of chaos. He led us in yet another emotional rendition of all five verses of the school hymn. The low point of the day was when Eric ran over a dog somewhere near Wynberg and pretended not to notice. The sight of the poor animal on the side of the road set off another round of vomiting as well as a few snivels and tears. By now, though, The Guv was unstoppable and he launched into "The Lord's My Shepherd" as a eulogy for the dead dog. (Not the first dog a vehicle carrying a Milton has slain this year.)

We got back to base camp, packed our goods, and got back onto the bus for the long journey home. We were meant to leave tomorrow, but The Guv announced that we were leaving immediately and hailed our unbeaten march through the tournament. We were all feeling too rancid to point out that we'd only completed one game. And so we set off again through the mist and wind and the blinding rain.

Sunday 9th July

From a deep and splendid dream (although for the life of me, I cannot recall what it was all about) I was shaken awake and ordered off the bus. Suddenly my head was throbbing like never before. The Guv handed out four aspirins to each boy and told us to wash them down with a swig from his bottle of Meerlust Cabernet 1985. Before my watch face froze, I managed to see that the time was 03:15. Our bus had a puncture and Eric was pulling out our bags and searching for the spare tire and repair kit. It was bitterly cold and we stood huddled in a group on the tarmac while Eric worked away at the wheel. After some time we were allowed back on the bus—but the damage had been done. I was chilled to the bone and struggled to sleep for the rest of the trip.

17:30 When at last we arrived at school after twenty-three hours of cold, cramped misery, stinking of wine, sweat, and vomit, I spotted the green station wagon parked at the school entrance, but my father was nowhere to be seen. I set about looking for my dad around the empty school buildings, but nothing—everything was locked up and silent—except for the cooing of rock pigeons settling down for the night. I longed for home, for a bath, my own room . . . all I wanted was to leave this place.

After waving the last of my cricket team away, I sat down on the school steps and tried to read *A Dry White Season* in the dim light of the fading sunset. The words were garbage; my brain was a washing machine. I closed the book and sulked.

Then, to my absolute horror, about ten minutes later the front gate to The Glock's mansion clicked open. There was the sound of laughter and cheery goodbyes. Dad shook The Glock's hand, waltzed over to me, and gave me a great bear hug. I was too amazed to remember to sulk. With an impressive explosion, the station wagon roared to life and we sped down Pilgrim's Walk. I was going home.

Wednesday 12th July

I awoke from what seemed like (and was) days of sleeping and felt completely refreshed. After a solid breakfast of eggs, bacon, and a bubble gum shake, I headed off to the Mermaid's with that sinking feeling.

My worst fears were confirmed when I arrived to find the Mermaid sitting in the living room watching television. She hardly seemed to notice me, and while I tried to make conversation, she kept her eyes fixed on a soap opera rerun. Then Marge came in with two suitcases and explained that the Mermaid was going to visit her aunt in England for a while. The Mermaid didn't say anything and just kept watching the television.

Marge beckoned me into the kitchen and explained that the Mermaid was heavily sedated to prevent her from becoming anxious about leaving. Her psychiatrist had suggested that a change of scenery would be good for her, and so she was sending her overseas for a while. I nodded like an idiot and then left because I felt awkward and in the way.

Once I got home, I began to feel angry with the Mermaid. Why had she gone mad? It's not like every kid whose parents get divorced has a license to madness. If that were the case, most of the kids at school would also be mad. Hang on . . . most of the boys at school *are* mad. I gave up thinking, ran a hot bath, and practiced singing my *Oliver* solos to Larry (my old red rubber bath snake).

Thursday 13th July

Mom looks wickedly worried. Wombat's doctor has told her to have the cataracts in her eyes removed. The operation will take

SPUD   217

place on Monday. It was at the exact moment she was telling me
that Dad leapt through the door with an old fishing rod and told
us that we were all going away fishing next weekend. This set off a
ferocious argument, which I avoided by slipping out into the garden to gather my thoughts.

Tried not to think about the Mermaid, who must be in England
by now. Does this mean that we have broken up? Is it all over? Is
she still my girlfriend?

Friday 14th July

My school report arrived in the post. Four As, three Bs, and a C.
Sparerib reckons I need to apply myself. The Guv called me a genius.
I'm on The Guv's side! Dad called me a rocket scientist and cracked
open a bottle of champagne "to celebrate my results and a swift end
to Wombat." After a few sips I poured the rest of my glass down the
sink. I think my liver's on its last legs after our wine tasting.

Saturday 15th July

Got a surprise call from Gecko, who said he was in Durban with
his uncle and aunt for the weekend and wanted to know if I was
keen to go to the beach. Before I could answer, he said he'd pick
me up in half an hour.

10:00 A huge black Mercedes limousine cruised up the driveway
and came to a stop next to the station wagon. A black man in a
dark suit got out and opened the back door. Out jumped Gecko,

grinning like an idiot, and shook hands with me and my folks, who'd gathered around to inspect the vehicle.

I thought chauffeurs were only used by the royal family and movie stars—not pale-faced dormitory mates with rich uncles. While we zoomed along the freeway, I asked Gecko how he knew where I lived. He just smiled and said, "Gladstone knows everything." Gladstone doffed his cap without so much as taking an eye off the road.

The black Mercedes may have been a major drawing card with the girls, but Gecko's gigantic pink swimming trunks were certainly not. With his shockingly white skin, which turned crimson after about ten minutes in the watery winter sun, and what with my skinny body and straggly hair, we were undoubtedly the biggest nerds on the beach. Gladstone waited patiently in the car while we swam and tanned. Gecko bought us Eskimo Pie ice creams and even tried to chat up a group of girls, who told him to take a long walk off a short pier. It's hard to believe that this crazy dude is the same vomiting coward who was terrified of rugby balls and anything else that was thrown at him. I suspect he might be schizophrenic because he's a radically different person out of the dormitory. I like Gecko and I'm no longer ashamed to call him my friend.

Sunday 16th July

Had Wombat for lunch. (Not literally—I doubt she would be very tasty anyway!) She seemed totally paranoid about her eye operation and told us that she refused to be operated on by an Indian doctor. She said he would probably kill her and run off with her purse before she'd regained consciousness. After lunch she announced that she wasn't afraid of dying and then burst into tears. Mom tried to reassure Wombat by saying that she would personally look after her belongings while she was in the hospital. Wombat then did a Gollum and accused Mom of planning to steal her jewelry. Mom stormed into the house in a rage, leaving Dad and me to take Wombat back to her flat.

Monday 17th July

09:00 Wombat went under the knife. The (white) surgeon said that everything was fine and that there were no complications. Mom (who has forgiven her mother for accusing her of theft) was hugely relieved, burst into tears, and gave me a hug and a sloppy kiss in front of a number of people in the waiting room. Some other people waiting for news were less lucky—the doctor took them aside and spoke to them in a hushed whisper. After he'd finished, one lady burst into tears and ran into the toilet with her spindly little husband trailing helplessly behind—not sure whether to follow her in. I was tempted to ask them what had happened but thought it might be a bit callous, so instead I hid behind a big flowerpot and tried to eavesdrop. Unfortunately, they were speaking in Afrikaans, so I gave up and read *Getaway* magazine instead.

Tuesday 18th July

Mandela's birthday. There was a huge dedication to him on television showing his cell on Robben Island and how he had to hammer away at limestone in a quarry for fifteen years. I cannot believe that he doesn't want to wipe out every white person in sight. To celebrate, I religiously slogged away at *A Dry White Season* but kept losing my concentration. At one stage I went through seven pages without reading a word. I wonder if this brings my standing as a young freedom fighter into question? Maybe the point is that these struggle books are meant to be a struggle to read.

Wednesday 19th July

Wombat was in fine form, perched up on her pillows in her hospital bed. With her eye patch she looked a dead ringer for Captain Hook. She verbally abused the nurses and threatened to sue the pants off the hospital if they didn't install a television in her ward. The surgeon reckons she can go home tomorrow. Mom has decided to skip the fishing trip to Lake St. Lucia and stay at Wombat's for the weekend.

Friday 21st July

06:00 The intrepid Miltons braved the freezing pre-dawn wind and sat ready and waiting at the mouth for the tide to start pushing in. Suddenly all hell broke loose as a long bony fish launched itself out of the water like a torpedo. My reel screamed in warning, Dad screamed with excitement, and I screamed with fright. The fish (later identified as a skipjack) kept launching itself out of the water until it finally succeeded in wrapping itself around the anchor rope, the motor propeller, and three other fishing lines. It launched itself again and there was a loud snap as the line broke.

In truth, I was actually quite relieved that the skipjack had escaped. It would have been a shame to kill such a beautiful fish after it had put up such a brilliant performance.

Our luck seemed to be running this morning. Dad caught a spotted grunter and a bream and I landed a prehistoric-looking dude called a sand shark. (Despite its name it had no teeth and looked more scared of us than we of it.)

Unfortunately, the wind picked up at around nine and our good fishing was over. We returned to our holiday flat for a hearty break-fast. It started raining, so we spent the rest of the day in a bar, playing dominoes and cards with some old local guys (called salt dogs). We heard many tales about St. Lucia, most of them dating back to before I was born. The wind continued to howl and the rain to beat against the windows. The barman served more ale, and my dad began to slip into a sorry sort of melancholy. Sometime in the afternoon he began to weep about somebody called Webster. The salt dogs looked at each other and then bade us farewell, saying it was time for home. I didn't have the heart to tell Dad that I could see them piling into the pub across the street.

Sunday 23rd July

06:00 Our early morning fishing was a waste of time. Because of the heavy rain, there was so much debris in the water that our bait was soon covered in seaweed and other nasty-looking gunk. Dad looked a little hung over and resorted to casting over his shoulder in the opposite direction to which he was facing to try and save his energy. This seemed to work rather well until a seagull caught his bait in midair and set off toward its nest on the far bank of the estu-ary. Dad thought he had hooked a whopper and screamed with delight, striking viciously and cackling to himself like a maniac. The poor seagull plummeted into the water with a screech and must have wondered what this nasty slice of sardine was all about.

Dad reeled the seagull in slowly, pretending not to enjoy the tussle. Once aboard, the seagull played dead. Dad removed the hook and released the bird. The seagull opened its eyes, pecked Dad's hand, and flew off squawking. Dad swore at the bird and tried to hit it with a lead sinker. His hand was spurting blood, his mood had soured, and he called the fishing off. I lifted the anchor and we headed back toward the jetty.

After lunch we hitched the boat onto the trailer (with the help of a few lurking salt dogs) and made our way home. The journey was freezing, thanks to the great big gaping hole where the station wagon's back window used to be.

Monday 24th July

Mom has taken Dad to the doctor because his hand has turned blue. The doctor gave him a tetanus shot and told him to lay off the booze.

Tomorrow it's back to school again. I can't wait to get back into *Oliver* rehearsals. When I think about the opening night, my stomach tightens into a knot. The only way to ease the panic is to take a bath and work through the entire play from top to bottom, saying every line and singing every song. After the bath I felt exhausted and drifted into a long and troubled sleep.

Tuesday 25th July

Have been reading back over my diary and realize that my personal life is a mess. My relationship with the Mermaid is on the rocks (mainly because she has turned into a nutcase). I dream about Amanda all the time despite the fact that she's made it obvious that she has no interest in me whatsoever. Mom reckons that the Mermaid is a lost cause and that I should consider our relationship over. (My mother has no respect for people who are unstable—she believes they're hiding something.)

For once, the bus trip back to school isn't fraught with two and a half hours of feeling homesick. I've kind of missed the old dog-eats-dog world of the dorm. And hell, there's nothing like the Crazy Eight for sheer entertainment value.

HOLIDAY SCORECARD:

Rambo	Broke his nose in a fight with a nightclub bouncer in Hillbrow, Johannesburg. He reckons that the bouncer was worse off than him. (Yeah, right, pull the other one.) Rambo's mother insisted that her darling son have plastic surgery to keep his sleek Roman profile intact.
Simon	Broke his ankle in a game of soccer. It took ages for him to make it up the stairs with his crutches. Pike followed the invalid up the stairs making nasty comments and broke into thunderous applause once he'd reached the top.
Vern	Is now completely bald on the left side of his head. He also seems a bit slowed up, a bit like one of those tree sloths that you see on *National Geographic*.

Gecko	Didn't contract one virus or disease during the holidays. To celebrate, his folks took him out to a seafood restaurant. He ate five king prawns and now has a bad case of gastro. He's determined not to go to the sanatorium and has elected to keep running to the toilet instead.
Boggo	Got a hand job from a prostitute in Amsterdam. (She apparently refused him sex because he was only fourteen. It cost him thirty dollars.)
Fatty	Says he picked up a bad case of food poisoning after eating what looked like beef but turned out to be dog food.
Mad Dog	Shot his dog (called Rickets) by mistake. Mad Dog reckons he was aiming at a rabbit, but Rickets attacked the rabbit at the crucial moment. He says the death of Rickets was a relief because he was old and had mange.
Spud	Said goodbye to his nutcase girlfriend and went on an eventful fishing trip with his dad.

Wednesday 26th July

The Glock stalked into assembly wearing his savage face. He said the third term is traditionally known as the "silly season." He went on to say that for the last five years, at least one boy has been expelled during the dreaded third term. According to the experts (Boggo and Rambo), this is because there is no rugby and cricket and no exams, which leads to dodgy behavior.

First rehearsal was a complete dog show. Everybody seems to have taken a giant leap backward. Viking and Kojak took turns at screaming at us. As always, the more they screamed, the worse we all got.

Thursday 27th July

The Guv has turned over a new leaf. He's shaved his beard, stopped drinking, and his wife has returned. His old sparkle and wit are back and his abuse during our first English class was out of the top drawer.

Earthworm's beginning to stress about his final exams (which only begin in November). He's chewed the ends off all his stationery and regularly drools on his pillow (at least I hope it's drool).

Friday 28th July

22:00 Fatty lit the candles and called the rest of us into his cubicle for the first "gathering" of the term. After he had completed his traditional rituals (which get longer every time), he addressed us in his usual formal way. The gathering was ruined by a foul smell that somebody had brought along with them. Rambo accused Roger, Boggo accused Vern, and Simon accused Mad Dog. Eventually, everyone just blamed Gecko, who was viciously doused in Fatty's antiperspirant deodorant.

Sunday 30th July

Full-day rehearsal with the girls. Amanda and I practiced our song together during the lunch break and then got into a serious debate about politics. She seemed impressed that I was planning to be a freedom fighter and told me that her father is an activist and a lecturer at the university in Pietermaritzburg. She didn't look too impressed when I told her my dad ran a small dry-cleaning business.

The play is back on track and Kojak didn't scream at me once today. It's easy to perform well when you're trying to impress someone.

Monday 31st July

08:00 For the second time this year Mad Dog was called up during assembly. (This time his fly was up.) The Glock shook his hand warmly to thunderous applause and whistling (none of it genuine).

Splendid lunch with The Guv, who is like a new man. We devoured a succulent roast beef between us, and The Guv sipped on a ginger ale. He and his wife were like teenagers and kissed and giggled every time they laid eyes on each other. After lunch The Guv shouted at me for not reading anything in ages.

"Stop trying to be a f@)!#$%* freedom fighter and read something you enjoy! For God's sakes, man, you're divorcing yourself from literature to try and impress some private school slapper!"

I was angry. How dare he call her . . . I stopped. I took a moment to unclench my teeth and my fists. Why was I angry? Am I perhaps . . . ?

I can't even bear to write it. I may need to see a psychiatrist myself!

Tuesday 1st August

Rambo's birthday. The day we've all been dreading. The question is, do we turn a blind eye like cowards and pretend we don't know? Or do we brave the storm and give Rambo his birthday present? Through a series of secret negotiations led by Boggo, it was decided that something must be done. At the very least, a dunking in the fountain.

And so dinnertime came along. An army of boys were rounded up and lay in ambush for the rippling Rambo. As he sauntered back from dinner, Boggo issued the call to arms and we all swarmed into the quad, dived on Rambo, and chucked him in the fish pond. Mission successful. In fact, he took it with fairly good grace (apart from hurling his shoe into the face of a third-year called Whittaker).

20:45 Rambo was absent from the house meeting. Sparerib made a note on his clipboard before beginning a long-winded story about toilet roll conservation.

Rambo reckoned that he'd missed the house meeting because he had to get his birthday present from Eve. He didn't say what it was. We could all imagine.

Wednesday 2nd August

Dad has caught Innocence in the act of selling booze. He is still deciding what to do with her. Innocence apparently threw herself on the ground in front of him and begged for her job.

Mad Dog's first cross-country practice ended up a total farce. After a few hill sprints under the guidance of Mr. Williamson, the idiot vomited and collapsed. Sister Collins put it down to too much lunch and gave him the all clear for Saturday's inter-school cross-country meeting.

Thursday 3rd August

Gavin, the prefect under the stairs, beat Rambo for letting Victoria the house snake out of her cage. The greedy reptile devoured an entire box full of cockroaches and died.

The stench in the dormitory is Vern. He confessed that he hasn't showered since returning from the holidays and is adamant that he will never shower again. In typical Rain Man form he wouldn't explain why. Rambo threatened him with death if he didn't shower. Vern made a funny noise and then disappeared for the rest of the day. The trapdoor under the crypt where Vern has spent many of his nights has been sealed, so I would assume that he's searching for other accommodation. Trust my luck to have a stinky psychopath sharing my cubicle.

Friday 4th August

Julian skipped across the quad, squealing and waving a bright pink envelope.

"Guess who's the lover boy? Looks like you don't have to have ball hairs to be a Romeo!" He slapped my bum and dropped the shocking pink envelope into my hands.

"What's his name?" Pike smirked. "Another one of your bum rusher buddies, Spud?" Devries cackled like a hyena and sprayed bits of his sandwich all over Gecko, who he had ordered to tie his shoelace. One look at the handwriting and I knew . . .

Dear Baby,
    So here I am in a different country. It's like another world here. The good news is that I am feeling more like myself again. My doctor here in Nottingham says that I was on the wrong medicine and that it only made my condition worse.
    I'm sure u must be wondering what happened to me and to be honest, I'm not so sure myself. The last few months have been like a nightmare and I can't really remember much of what happened. I think the term used is a nervous breakdown. Anyway, the important thing is that I'm getting better. I go out for walks and see things. Last week I took a train to London with my aunt and we went to Buckingham Palace and St. Paul's Cathedral. (Maybe one day u will sing there.)
    Anyway, what I really wanted to say was that I know it must have been hard for u to see me like I was and that I'm sorry I wasn't myself. I love u. I think about u all the time and u are the one thing in my life that gives me a reason to get better. I wanted u to know that as far as I am concerned, u are my boyfriend and I love u. Please wait for me and then I will be your Mermaid forever.

                    Love,
                    Mermaid

Saturday 5th August

    Barely slept and when I did, I dreamed that I was lying in bed with Amanda and the Mermaid and they were both screaming at me. My mind is in turmoil—could I be on the verge of a breakdown as well? Spent the morning deep in thought and then fell asleep.

Mad Dog pulled out of the inter-school cross-country race at Kings College with a strained hamstring. If only Mr. Williamson had seen Mad Dog sprinting across the quad to the dining hall for supper . . .

Sunday 6th August

Amanda barely gave me the time of day at rehearsals. She spent lunchtime talking and laughing with Geoff Lawson. I confess I was jealous and hardly spoke to either of them in the afternoon.

Monday 7th August

I have taken an enormous step and made an appointment with the school counselor, Dr. Zoodenberg. 14:30 tomorrow. I refuse to have a nervous breakdown!

Lunch The Guv has given me Hemingway's *The Old Man and the Sea* and ordered it read by next Monday. It's not a very thick book. (Obviously he thinks that I've slipped into cretindom!)

Mom phoned and told me that Dad felt sorry for Innocence and let her stay. However, he's charging her a levy of twenty cents on every bottle sold. Innocence agreed and immediately put her price up by twenty-five percent.

Tuesday 8th August

14:30   Dr. Zoodenberg is a complete weirdo. He has a thick hedge of knotted brown hair, a huge wooly beard, and owl glasses from behind which his beady little eyes peer out. He also has the irritating habit of whistling all his *s*'s and *c*'s. Rumor has it that he used to work at the Town Hill nuthouse near Pietermaritzburg. Before we began, he told me that he was a Freudian by training and asked if I had a problem with that. Not knowing what a Freudian was, I told him it was fine by me. He seemed relieved and jotted something down on a pad of paper.

There was silence. I suddenly wished that I hadn't come. It seemed the silence would last forever, so I started telling him about my relationship problems. He jumped up immediately with his hands raised and ordered me to stop.

"Now, Mr. Milton," he said mysteriously, "you will learn that every action has a cause and effect and every action has a reaction."

I nodded a little nervously. Zoodenberg closed the curtains, took off his jacket, and settled into an armchair with a notepad and a fountain pen poised to scribble down my psychological disorder. His beady little eyes were blazing with excitement and he licked his lips repeatedly like he was about to devour a double cheeseburger.

"Mr. Milton, let us start at the beginning. What is your earliest childhood memory?"

By 16:00 we hadn't progressed past 1979! (Which was no help to my problems of 1990.) Dr. Zoo, as he asked me to call him, seemed very pleased with my first session and scheduled me for the same time next week. As I left, he told me that he was working on a sociology thesis and that since he was now moving on to studying group behavior, I should try and persuade the Crazy Eight to join me next week. The words "sociology thesis" produced enough whistles to attract Roger, who meowed loudly and scuttled along the corridor with his tail raised. I noticed a huge bald spot just above Roger's tail. This is a strange place indeed.

Wednesday 9th August

Gecko and I took an afternoon stroll up to our warm rock and vantage point. Gecko has called it Hell's View. (As far as he's concerned, school is hell and this is the best place to view it from.) I told him about my relationship trouble and my visit to Dr. Zoo. He laughed uproariously, with his shrill cackling laugh, as I imitated the nutty psychologist. Gecko reckons that Zoo was once admitted to a nuthouse in Siberia but managed to escape to South Africa. He says that most boys are too scared to go to him for counseling and the only other boy who has seen him is Vern—enough said.

Gecko reckoned that I should play "hard to get" with Amanda and be friendly with the Mermaid, without laying it on too thick. Gecko (in all his wisdom) has pinned Amanda as a man-eating flirt and, like Glenn Close in *Fatal Attraction*, will screw me and then boil my rabbit. (I don't have a rabbit—I suppose she would have to settle for Roger.)

I shall write a friendly letter to the Mermaid and play the cold fish on Sunday (not that Amanda will even notice). My path is clear, and hopefully before long she will fall madly in love with me and become a threat to my friends' domestic pets!

A cold wind picked up and the mist swirled around us before sinking into the valley. Gecko and I ended our discussions on breasts and ball hairs and strolled back down to school.

Thursday 10th August

Posted a friendly letter to the Mermaid that was warm and comforting. I signed it *me* and took special care to leave out anything that looked remotely encouraging. Phase one complete.

Returned to the house after a singing rehearsal to find the dormitories in an uproar. While I was practicing "Consider Yourself at Home," the prefects had launched a house search and found eleven pairs of underpants in Vern's laundry bag. The problem was that none of them were his! After the discovery Vern was marched off to Sparerib's office, where he spent the next hour. Presumably the time was spent trying to make some sense out of Vern's behavior.

Upstairs Luthuli, Bert, and Earthworm were having some difficulty trying to stop a riot. For the first time ever, Pike and Rambo were in agreement—Vern is a nasty little poof and needs to be destroyed, or at the very least maimed. Rambo was particularly miffed because two pairs of his underpants were in the laundry bag. Pike just liked the idea of maiming the poor demented Rain Man. Greg Anderson seemed to be the only person springing to his defense. He was wickedly brave in defending Rain Man. Then again it's probably easy to be brave when you're a first-team rugby god.

22:00 Vern still hasn't returned. Boggo, Simon, and Rambo have held a court case and have already found him guilty of theft, pervy behavior, being mad, being odd, and abusing the cat. (Boggo reckons Vern is pulling Roger's fur out.)

Friday 11th August

It's official. Rain Man is still at school. Gecko was able to get some info out of him before maths. Apparently, he's staying with Dr.

Zoo for a while until things calm down. Luthuli warned the house that should anyone lay a finger on Vern, they will be mutilated and desecrated. (Not sure what that involves, but it sounds nasty.)

Earthworm informed me that he has exactly twelve weeks until his final examinations start. He looked terribly rattled and had to breathe deeply into a plastic bag to avoid a panic attack. When he'd recovered, he pulled out the bottom drawer of his desk and ordered me to sharpen his pencils. Upon closer inspection, I realized the drawer was filled with black and red pencils. Ninety minutes later I had sharpened all forty-eight of them. Earthworm studied each of them in turn before letting me go to supper. Have a feeling that Earthworm could also be on the way to a breakdown.

Saturday 12th August

Spent a rainy day in bed and read the whole of *The Old Man and the Sea*. (By the end I confess to having watery eyes.) Mad Dog asked me what was wrong—I told him I have allergies.

Man, what a book! I couldn't believe those sharks noshed the old man's marlin. Imagine trying to catch a fish for days and then getting home with a skeleton! The injustice of it is unacceptable. I shall have this out with The Guv tomorrow. How dare he give me such a brilliant but unsatisfying story!

Lay awake thinking of our fishing trip and how it would have felt to pull in a giant marlin.

Sunday 13th August

I put my plan into action and gave Amanda the cold shoulder.

It was tough, but I thought it was successful. I refused to look at her, and when she came to talk to me during lunch, I told her I had work to do and left. I returned to the dormitory immediately and reported to Gecko on the morning's events. He congratulated me on my nerves of steel and told me to stay strong during the afternoon session. (For a moment it sounded like one of The Guv's team talks minus the Shakespeare and the swearing.) During the afternoon I turned up the heat. At one stage Amanda flashed me a smile that made my hand tremble. I instantly looked at my script and pretended to be engrossed.

The critical moment happened at the end of the rehearsal, when I warmly embraced a number of girls and then walked off without saying anything to Amanda. Think I have mastered the art of "playing hard to get." Gecko warned me about taking it too far, saying that I just had to *look* disinterested, not act like a complete asshole. I think I did splendidly. What will next Sunday bring? Phase two complete!

Monday 14th August

13:30 Had a great brainstorming lunch with The Guv. We had a huge debate on the Hemingway book without either of us budging an inch. To settle the argument, The Guv played the movie of *The Old Man and the Sea*, which looked like it was filmed in 1880 Unfortunately, he fell asleep after ten minutes, and after half an hour there was a wretched screeching sound and then a bang. The Guv flew from his rocking chair and thumped his old video machine on the head. Like the sharks in the book, the video machine had devoured the tape and strangled itself in the process. The Guv threw a tantrum and I took the hint, excused myself, and headed back toward the school, still wondering how big the sharks would be and what the marlin skeleton would look like.

I came across Rain Man, who was having a long and involved conversation with Roger outside the chapel. I tried to talk to him, but he didn't seem to recognize me and gave very little away. I noticed that Roger's bald spot has spread to the right side of his head now, and unless I'm mistaken, the pair share the same psycho-demented look in the eyes. Apart from one being a human and the other a cat, you could hardly tell them apart. Still nobody knows why he stole the underpants.

Tuesday 15th August

14:30 Second session with Dr. Zoo. Today he explored the issue of me being an only child and how this has affected my development. At one stage I became so frustrated with his incessant whistling and dodgy questions that I demanded that he stop talking about my folks and help me with my relationship troubles. He smiled and told me that my little outburst was "telling" and then made about a page of scribbled notes on his pad. At the end of the session I tried to squirm out of returning, but he told me that I was "bound to continue" and marked me down for another session. Another couple more of these and I'll be following Vern into the loony bin!

Feeling depressed. My relationships are a mess. My acting is crap, my cubicle mate has gone completely crackers, and I'm seeing a weirdo psychiatrist who's delving into my inner workings. My hair is as long as a girl's, and seldom do five minutes pass by without some sort of lewd comment from a teacher or senior boy. Thanks to my girlish look, Julian always seems to follow me into the showers and washes his genitals while talking to me. Problem is that he doesn't seem to wash anything else.

I wonder what suicide must be like.

I had a dream that the Mermaid and I jumped off a cliff. She died when she hit the ground, but I just gently floated downward. When I landed, Amanda was waiting for me. She opened her bag, pulled out her lunch box, and offered me a bite of her hamburger. I must be slipping into madness.

Wednesday 16th August

By some cruel twist of fate we've been allocated Wednesday first lesson for physical education—otherwise known as physical torture! Our master is the crazed Mr. Lambert (nickname Mongrel, which actually means a mixed-breed dog but best describes an animal with no brains, no fear, and no mercy). Mongrel fought for Ian Smith in the Zimbabwean bush war in 1980 and still harbors a hatred for black people, all of whom he thinks are terrorists. Poor Blade Nkosi, a friendly but overweight classmate, received some wicked abuse from Mongrel, who accused him of being a thief, lazy, dumb, and fat and made him drop for twenty push-ups. Mongrel took one look at my hair and told me I was a fairy (much to the delight of the class). I was ordered to run on the spot until further notice—further notice being the end of the class. Mongrel seemed hugely impressed with Rambo and Mad Dog and told us to try and imitate them in everything that they do. Mad Dog immediately scratched his balls and so did the rest of the class. Mongrel flew into a rage and ordered Mad Dog to swim ten lengths of the swimming pool. At sunrise in midwinter this is as close to a death sentence as you can get. Mad Dog swam incredibly quickly and then pulled himself out of the water (having turned an impressive bright blue) and limped into the showers looking very sorry for himself and his manhood, which, he said, had become ingrown.

Thursday 17th August

23:00 We skulked out of the dormitory window (Fatty risked the stairs), took the usual path through the chapel, and met at The Glock's lemon tree. This time we weren't heading toward the dam for a midnight swim and instead circled his house and sprinted across three cricket fields, finally coming to rest behind the maintenance shed beside the cricket oval. Boggo lit a cigarette that smelled really weird and passed it around the group. Gecko kicked off with a coughing fit and I had to breathe heavily to avoid doing likewise. After a while everything became a bit weird and dreamy.

Boggo lit another cigarette. I could feel myself taking another drag but could feel nothing but . . . floating. Then I realized my dream was coming true—I could float. Where was Amanda and her hamburger? Hamburger! God, I felt hungry.

Suddenly Rambo threw himself on top of me. Everywhere was panic and harsh whispering. Torchlight was coming closer, scanning across the field. My snare drum was thumping. I felt faint, dizzy—it was all too dreamlike. The light came closer and closer, dancing this way and that. I found myself hypnotized by the jagging light. In fact, it wasn't a torch. It was a giant firefly coming to carry me away. Coming to carry me home. Rambo's hand clamped my mouth shut. Had I really just been singing "Swing Low, Sweet Chariot"?

Then we were running; legs were everywhere. I could hear snuffling right behind me. The guards had released their dogs. Any moment now a beast would drag me to the ground and sink its teeth into my throat. I was crying and running, trying to scream but making no sound. I couldn't turn to look. But if I didn't, I would never know what killed me. At least if I looked into the dog's eyes and he could see me weeping, he might stop, cock his head to one side, and maybe whimper in sympathy. Die like a man, Milton, a voice was shouting—was it me? I steeled myself and then turned around. There was no dog, only a gecko—my friend Gecko, his eyes blazing red and tears streaming down his face.

There we stood, clasping onto each other, holding each other. Sobbing, sobbing.

Friday 18th August

Awoke feeling refreshed and happy. Until I looked down and realized that I'd slept all night in my running shoes. Glimpses of last night filtered back, like a nightmarish dream that returns piece by piece. I shot a glance at Gecko just before roll call; he looked away. Last night was no dream. The memories kept coming back: the torchlight, the stinking cigarettes, and the dogs that weren't.

I caught up with Gecko just before English. Before I could say anything, he slapped me on the back and said, "It's okay. Spud, I also don't remember anything." We shook hands and went our separate ways. When all else fails, try the ostrich technique and bury your head in the sand.

18:00 Vern arrived at dinner and sat down with the rest of us. He seemed to be much improved, didn't dribble, and even asked Simon to pass the tomato sauce. Perhaps Dr. Zoo is at last proving his worth. I could tell that Rambo was itching to have a go at him but thought better of it after checking Luthuli's hawklike stare from the top table.

Had my recurring dream about floating through the air and meeting Amanda with her hamburger. I'm sure it must mean something. Maybe I'll tell Dr. Zoo about it next week. This may finally force him to talk about my relationships.

Saturday 19th August

Boggo has denied that his cigarettes were dodgy. All he told us was that they were homemade by his brother and contained an herbal remedy that could be a cure for cancer. Mad Dog reckons it could have been pot, while Simon says it was probably wild bush tea. (Simon's uncle smokes wild bush tea every evening—he's an astrologer.) In truth, very little has been said about Thursday night's excursion. Maybe everybody else is also having a little trouble separating fiction from reality.

Sunday 20th August

Today's rehearsal was spot on, both onstage and off. I did a faultless Act One in the morning and then succeeded in avoiding Amanda without looking rude or foolish. During lunch, a pretty girl called Christine plonked herself down next to me and began crapping on about the last twelve years of her life. She was in the middle of explaining to me how she was the best kisser in town when suddenly she stopped talking as she caught the icy stare of Amanda glaring down from the balcony above. Looks like the plan could be working. Gecko will be thrilled to hear about this one!

Monday 21st August

11:00 Julian skipped around the house singing, "Why don't you fill me up, buttercup . . ." and handing out letters. I received a small white envelope. The handwriting was familiar, but it wasn't

the Mermaid's, and I noticed that the letter had no stamp. I ran up
to my bed before opening it.

*As you have probably noticed, this letter has no stamp. I'm writ-
ing it as I watch you singing onstage and wondering how such a
pure and beautiful voice can emerge out of such a dark and cruel
soul. I'm not angry, just a little sad that somebody who seemed so
true can really be so false.*

*Contrary to what you may think, I am not a bitch—in fact, my
greatest affliction is that I am shy and have very little self-confidence.
I am not popular because people are suspicious of me because I like
to be alone. I generally feel apprehensive in a group situation. I'm not
asking you to like me, all I ask is that you treat me like the decent
human being that I am. Don't be cruel, just try and be pleasant
(you're a good actor, I'm sure you can manage it).*

*If we are to work together (onstage, I mean), there has to be
some level of respect and humanity in your dealings with me.
Perhaps it's the attention that you're receiving from all the girls who
are queuing up to try and "score" you—maybe that's made you arrogant. It's just you're not the person I met three months ago.*

Please think about this.
Amanda

After canceling lunch with The Guv (because of too much
work) I marched Gecko up to Hell's View. I showed him the letter
and filled him in on the unfolding events He read the letter a
number of times, whistled to himself, and shook his head. He
then held the letter up toward the sun (checking if it was counter-
feit?) before reading it again. I asked him what he thought. He
ignored me completely, pulled out a small notebook, and jotted
down some notes for about ten minutes. I became quite excited
because it looked like Gecko was working out a complicated for-
mula to solve my relationship problems. Unfortunately, all it
amounted to was a short list of the positives and the negatives of

my situation. I tried not to look disappointed as my girl guru read out his scribblings:

POSITIVES

The situation with the Mermaid is under control. (Could have fooled me!)
There are a number of women who like me. (And this is a positive?)
Amanda wouldn't act like this if she didn't have some feelings for me. (Feelings of malicious hatred and psychosis?)
This weekend is half term, so time is on my side. (It just gives me longer to agonize over it!)

NEGATIVES

I could have at least two girlfriends, maybe more. (More? This is worse than I thought, and where are the others hiding?)
Life is about to get dangerously complicated. (Life is already dangerously complicated!)
I will break at least one heart in the near future. (Probably mine!)
The Mermaid is making a recovery. (And this is a negative?)
I have behaved like an asshole. (Thanks to my adviser!)

I folded the list in my diary and made a mental note to grill it in the prefects' toaster. Unfortunately, while I was reading Gecko's positives and negatives, he was busy scribbling out my way forward.

WAY FORWARD

Keep responding to the Mermaid in a friendly fashion.
Write a letter of apology to Amanda.
Play it cool with all other females.

These at least seemed reasonable. We agreed to keep monitoring the situation and, like two businessmen, we shook hands, put away our notes, and strode down the mountain.

21:15 I stared at myself in the bathroom mirror. Long shaggy brown hair, greeny brown, olive eyes. Small button nose, roundish face, skinny body. No muscles, no facial hair, no ball hair. God must be laughing at me.

Tuesday 22nd August

14:30 Dr. Zoo became incredibly excited when I told him about my recurring dream. He made me repeat the dream over and over while he paced around the office mumbling to himself in a language that sounded alarmingly like Vern's cat talk. (Maybe Vern has consumed Dr. Zoo's mind.) Suddenly he smacked his thigh with delight and shouted something that sounded like "presto" but wasn't.

"I have the answer, Milton," he said feverishly. "Or rather I have two answers!" He licked his thin lips with a pale pink tongue. He eyed me closely and then began. "This Mermaid woman is part fish, yes?" I shook my head and tried to correct him, but it was hopeless.

"She is the fish out of water. The water is your soul. Your soul is asking you to risk, to jump in. Mermaids are a symbol of childhood . . . of make-believe. You are still holding on to your childhood, but your mother wants you to become a man, to take the great plunge into adulthood. You resist her, you jump but float. . . . She jumps, knowing she will die. She dies to see her boy become a man. Such is the Oedipal link between the boy and his mother."

I wanted to run, but the door was locked.

"This other woman, Amanda, you say . . . that could be your own construction of your father. Your father is feminine because you undermine him. You weaken him in the continual struggle for your mother's affections. The hamburger is a strange symbol, perhaps a symbol of material goods. Your father is buying your compliance, but should you accept that hamburger, you will be ceding your mother to your father. The erotic link will be broken. It also foreshadows the Eve complex—Eve offers you the apple, and with that one single action, she controls you. Your father is Eve and your mother is Adam. I don't believe in God. I believe in Freud, Mr. Milton."

I nodded and mumbled pathetically, wishing I had the balls to stand up and tell this idiot what I thought of his theories and then march out the door, never to return. After a long pause, Dr. Zoo rose to his feet and strolled toward the window. He pulled the curtain aside slightly and stared out at the quad before beginning again.

"There is of course another explanation." He turned to me and smiled warmly. I couldn't help smiling politely back. "I can see that perhaps my Freudian analysis does not strike the key? How about this one, then?" He began to pace slowly again, staring at the floor and then now and again lifting his gaze to me before lowering it once more.

"You're an adolescent boy who doesn't know who he loves and what he wants. Your mind is awash with visions, dreams, and metaphors. In the movies they seem to work things out so easily, but real life is a hell of a lot more complicated. The images are unimportant, the hamburger is just a hamburger, and the dream is just a dream."

Now he was at the window again, peering out at Pissing Pete. "It's okay to make mistakes, you know. It's okay to experiment—nobody is going to hate a fourteen-year-old for two-timing his girlfriend. At least not for long. You're too young to take your relationships so seriously—go out there, burn or be burned. If you don't bite into Eve's apple now, you may never get the chance again."

I strolled along the old redbrick cloisters back to the house with my head swimming with crazy thoughts. A prefect from another house told me my hair was a disgrace. I apologized and walked on to the safety of the dormitory.

Wednesday 23rd August

06:40 PE with Mongrel again. True to form, he ordered me to drop for forty push-ups because my hair hadn't been cut. He seems to have forgotten that I have permission and he refused to read my note from Viking, which I now have to produce at least twice a day. (Have a suspicion that Mongrel can't read.) We spent the lesson playing "stingers" with a wet tennis ball. Basically, you chase some-one and then hurl the ball at them as hard as you can and then that person gets a chance. All in all, a brainless game that leads to the small people getting hurt. Steven George had to be taken to the san when Simon nailed him in the goolies.

11:00 Another letter delivered by Julian in a bright red envelope. My heart now sinks every time he flits across the quad with his bundle. Once again the writing was foreign:

> *Dear Johnny,*
>
> *Hello, you naughty boy. Whachya up to? Just sitting here at school thinking about you. It was really great to chat on Sunday. I really like you and hope we can get to know each other better.*
>
> *I know where you live and I have your school and home num-bers. Clever me—found a school calendar, which gives me all the details about each boy. I see you are born on the 20 April, which makes you an Aries. I love Aries. Anyway I'm only six months older than you, which is basically nothing at all.*
>
> *Anyway, as I told you, I also live in Durban and thought maybe we could get together over the midterm weekend. I'll call you and won't take no for an answer.*
>
> > *Lots of love,*
> > *Christine*
>
> *PS We all want to know why you're called Spud. Is it something to do with a potato?*

Thursday 24th August

15:00   Back at Hell's View, Gecko studied Christine's letter. I could see that he was relishing the job of being my personal adviser. Although he has never had a relationship himself, he has read more than a couple of his sister's *Cosmopolitan*s, so he judges himself well educated in matters of the heart. He also had the privilege of that brief meeting with Elton John on the stairs. (Not great credentials, I admit, but still better than nothing.)

He looked up and whistled to himself as if he were surveying the devastation of some horrendous earthquake. "You've got trouble, Spuddy! Looks like you've got one too many eggs in your basket. And this Christine, she looks real feisty. My guess is that she'll get you sooner rather than later."

I told Gecko that the way I see it is that the major problem with me is that I don't know what I want. I like them all and they are all so different. I was madly in love with the Mermaid until she went crackers and now she seems to be coming back to normal. Amanda is beautiful and mysterious and I dream about her . . . and now Christine.

My guru stood on the rock and gazed out over the valley. He turned to me and said, "Spuddy, as your adviser, I say go for it. Live for the moment and sort the rest out later. No regrets, mate. Carpe diem, seize the day. You never know when it will be your last!"

Friday 25th August

LONG WEEKEND

It feels like I just left home yesterday. The last month has flown.

Another month and *Oliver* will be a thing of the past.

Mom and Dad are considering emigrating to Malta. I had to consult my atlas before discovering that Malta is a small island in the Mediterranean. More confirmation that my folks are a couple of loons! Dad is very much of the opinion that South Africa is about to explode.

Does everybody in Malta have a Maltese poodle?

Phone call from guess who . . . Christine invited me to a Saturday night beach barbecue with her friends. She told me to bring a sweater and some marshmallows. I shook my head to decline the invitation. Unfortunately, while my head was shaking my mouth was saying, "Thank you, that will be great!" I sink ever further into the abyss!

Saturday 26th August

Does one ever reach the bottom of the abyss? I guess I always knew it would be dodgy, right from the moment that a bright red BMW 740i roared up our driveway. I confess feeling embarrassed at the old station wagon (still without a rear window) standing under the tree it had once charged into. There was only one way that the evening would end. Christine was affectionate—very affectionate. Surprisingly, there were so many people there. Her brother, who is in matric, had invited his friends, and everywhere you looked were crates of beer and bottles of booze. It was like something out of a surfing movie. I drank two beers and felt horribly drunk. I feebly blathered on about my girlfriend and other lame excuses, but before I knew it Christine was lying on top of me and her tongue was ripping around my mouth like a hungry eel. I wish I could say that I hated every minute of it but, dear diary, you know I could never lie to you.

Sunday 27th August

12:00 Wombat, wearing a black eye patch like some debauched old pirate, was at her crazy best at the infamous Milton family barbecue. She has somehow convinced herself that Dad is trying to kill her with poison (not a totally absurd idea). She made me taste a piece of each item of food on her plate before wolfing it down herself. As you might imagine, nothing kills a friendly gathering of family faster than the belief that your son-in-law is trying to assassinate you.

15:15 Telephone call from the Mermaid. I got such a fright that I panicked and hung up. I took the phone off the hook for half an hour.

After half an hour I replaced the telephone on the receiver and it rang instantly. The shrill noise sent a shock wave through my body. I looked around desperately before hesitantly lifting the receiver and bending my head to listen to the voice on the line: "Hello, lover boy." It was Christine. I decided to take the bull by the horns and break things off. I told her I didn't want a relationship with her because I wanted to focus on the play and because I would be leaving for Malta shortly (a lie, but it sounded good). Besides, I also have a girlfriend. Christine burst into tears and hung up. I contemplated grilling the telephone in the oven for a few hours but finally decided that the pleasure of watching the wretched thing melt would pale against the punishment that followed.

16:10 Christine called in hysterics and begged me to stay with her. I said I'd think about it. Once again the famous limp-wristed Spud was unable to say what he feels and as a result he rockets all the way back to square one. Hopefully, when I finally grow some ball hairs, I'll grow some courage as well.

16:30 Called Gecko and told him my troubles. He did that whistle again and then asked me which one I most wanted to shag. I said none, because I'm still a spud. There was a long pause, and then he told me to pick a name out of the hat and rang off. So much for my personal adviser.

Monday 28th August

Had another variation of my dream: this time Amanda offered me the hamburger, which became Christine. I decided that the only way to solve this madness is to pull a Gecko and write out some pros and cons.

MERMAID

PROS
First love
Bewitching (when not crackers)
Beautiful and enchanting (when not crackers)
Is still technically my girlfriend
I know her mom
My parents like her

CONS
Mentally unstable
Is in England
Prone to depression

CHRISTINE

PROS
Very affectionate
Very forward
Father has a BMW

CONS   Probably also crackers
Prone to hysteria
Huge mood swings
Could be a slut (this would be a pro if I
wasn't a spud)

AMANDA
PROS   Beautiful
Sexy
Mysterious
Intelligent
Catlike (?)
Reads books
Poetic
I can't take my eyes off her
Can't stop dreaming about her

CONS   She is older than me
She is cleverer than me
Despite what Gecko says—not sure if she
likes me
Could also be crackers

I must admit, seeing my thoughts scrawled out in front of me made things a little clearer. With nine pros against four cons, Amanda was the winner. There it was in black and white—I must be in love with Amanda. I found some of Mom's pale blue writing paper with a bowl of fruit at the top and began composing.

Dear Amanda
I apologize for my behavior lately. I have been under strain what with my possible emigration to Malta, the play, my work, and try-ing to find the school ghost. From the first moment I saw you, I found it very difficult to be myself in your presence. I can't explain

*it, but I always feel so lame around you. I'm sorry I have been cruel.
I didn't intend to make you feel bad. See you on Sunday. Looking
forward to having you at school permanently.*

*Love,
Johnny (Spud)*

I sent the letter—she should get it tomorrow. (I suddenly realized
that when I wake up tomorrow, I'll open my eyes to those spooky
old wooden rafters and hear Pissing Pete still trying to finish his
never-ending piss.) It's amazing how time flies by when you're having women trouble. Over a steaming hot bath I decided to focus
on the play and let my relationships take care of themselves.

I kissed Mom goodbye for about the twentieth time this year
and stepped onto the old creaky bus that would take me back to
school.

WEEKEND SCORECARD:

Rambo	Stole a ladies' watch from a jewelry shop. (He says he'll give it to Eve.)
Boggo	Went camping with his older sister and her friends and said he got laid but was very sketchy about the details.
Vern	Not present. Stayed with Dr. Zoo for the weekend. (Lucky him.)
Simon	Was able to walk without looking like a retard for the first time since breaking his ankle.
Fatty	Went to stay with Geoff Lawson in Johannesburg and practically ate himself to death.
Gecko	Put together a model airplane, which was half eaten by his uncle's two-year-old bull

	mastiff, Falcor. (In his short life Falcor has also eaten a cutting board, a trash can, three buckets, and a few small children.)
Mad Dog	Killed a bush pig with a shotgun. (He says it tastes like bacon.) He has been re-nicknamed Obelix.
Spud	Was teased mercilessly by the others for raping and pillaging poor little Christine. Despite his spudness he was accused of being a womanizing, two-timing maniac. Spud smiled and tried to look embarrassed but was really flushed with pride and, for the first time ever, felt like a real man in the dormitory.

Tuesday 29th August

05:00 The dormitory woke to complete their English homework, which The Guv had set for the weekend. The task was to read a twenty-five-page short story called "The Suit" by a South African writer called Can Themba. Thankfully, the homework was remembered by Gecko halfway through one of Boggo's hilarious impersonations of The Guv around midnight last night. Fatty was the only class member from our dormitory who was unable to stir himself from his deep sleep. He told us he would bluff his way through it.

12:00 The Guv cunningly worked out that Fatty hadn't done his homework. He asked him why the writer had set the story in a brothel and gambling hall. Fatty fell into the trap and said it was all about prostitutes! (It's actually about this guy's wife who has an affair with another man, which made me feel guilty about the Mermaid.) The Guv lambasted Fatty in French (or what sounded like French) and he ordered our obese friend to eat his copy of the short story. It took about four seconds for poor Fatty to realize that The Guv was being deadly serious and about 1.4 seconds for Fatty to devour twenty-five pages of print. Unsurprisingly, Fatty didn't seem too concerned about his second breakfast and chomped away while The Guv continued his lesson on South African short story writing.

Other than some serious tummy rumbling, Fatty showed no side effects of devouring his literature. (He did say that the illustrations were more difficult to swallow than the ordinary print.)

14:30 Back in the office of Dr. Zoo. I've come to dread these sessions. Whatever possessed me to volunteer myself as a human guinea pig to this Freudian lunatic? I considered very seriously feigning some illness and heading for the sanatorium but then thought that I might have to miss rehearsals and so decided to face down the bearded whistling beast.

Thankfully, we spent the session discussing Vern. Dr. Zoo is clearly perplexed by Rain Man's behavior and wanted to know what he was like inside the dormitory. I took up as much time as possible with stories about my loony cubicle mate. I described in great detail his running away saga, his unnatural fondness for Roger, his bald spot, and, of course, his conviction as the underpants thief.

Dr Zoo made pages of notes, often grunting and snorting (sometimes simultaneously). He explained that contrary to popular opinion, he thinks Vern was using the underpants to create a nest for Roger under the bicycle shed and there was nothing sexually deviant about his actions. (It will take a lot of explaining to convince the school that a nest of boys' underpants isn't a bit pervy!) He explained that there was enormous pressure from above to have Vern sent to a psychological facility. However, his mother is adamant that he should stay at school and follow in the footsteps of his late father. Rumor has it that his career at school was all but finished until his mom deposited a small fortune into the school building fund. Suddenly The Glock did an about-face and stated that Vern would leave only over his dead body. I left the session with a skip and a jump—freedom for another week.

Wednesday 30th August

Viking whisked me away from my geography lesson and together we cruised down to Pietermaritzburg in his old Jaguar. Away from the school, Viking was relaxed and funny and there was no sign of his infamous temper as he quizzed me about my family and various other things. The occasion was my first visit to the hairdresser's. Today my long scraggly bits of hair are to be permed into *Oliver*-like locks of beauty. (Next Friday, I return for the blond highlights.)

The stylist's name was Bernadette and she seemed to know Viking rather well. In fact, for the first ten minutes after our arrival Viking's hand was glued to her bum. Every time he squeezed it, she would squeal and giggle and call him a naughty boy.

Bernadette set about wrapping my hair up in tiny rollers before applying some smelly concoction and then placing my head in what looked like a giant toaster. After a few minutes in the toaster the excitement of it all wore off and I rifled through a few ladies' magazines. An old woman (also with her head in a toaster) interrupted an article on something called women's monthly flow to ask me if I was a homosexual. I blushed terribly and tried my best to sound outraged. I explained the *Oliver* story and after a few questions she seemed satisfied that I was innocent.

Her stylist—a thin guy called Anton, with leather pants, floral shirt, and many rings and bangles—came over and adjusted her toaster settings. While he was working, she leaned across and said, "You never know nowadays—these homosexuals are on the loose, you know. You can never tell who's at it. Some of them look and sound normal and then suddenly—" Her speech became a squeal of agony. Anton apologized profusely for nicking her with his scissors.

After hours under the toaster I was ready to see my new look. The result was shocking. I looked completely . . . *weird* is the word. Long brown curly locks! Viking seemed happy and squeezed Bernadette's breasts in gratitude. He told me I looked halfway to the perfect Oliver. With that we were back in the Jag and hurtling through traffic into the heart of the Natal Midlands.

18:00 The dining hall. I gathered my tray and joined the queue for roast pork, mashed potatoes, and vegetables. Around me came the murmuring of boys, a few giggles, a swallowed comment. This wasn't going to be easy. I received my dinner and stepped out into the open dining hall and was met with a wall of sound. Three-hundred-odd boys were bleating at me like deranged sheep. Linton Austin, the prefect on duty, leapt to his feet and thumped the gavel on the table. After he threatened to have our condiments removed, the chaos settled into whispered jibes and hideous sniggers. The rest of the Crazy Eight were beside themselves with glee. Simon ordered me not to look so sheepish, which, predictably, had Rambo on the floor in hysterics. The bad news is that I have to look like a sheep for nearly four weeks. Beginning to wonder if it's worth it.

Thursday 31st August

11:00 Received another letter from the Mermaid saying that she's getting better and that she misses me and is nearly ready to come home. For the first time my pulse didn't start pumping and my palms stayed as dry as the Kalahari desert. What with the play opening in less than three weeks and looking like a sheep, the curse of women problems has been put on the back burner.

Rambo reckons that Gavin, the prefect under the stairs, has returned to school with a deadly venomous puff adder called Celeste. Rambo has to feed it a rat every second day, which the snake swallows whole. Gavin, the prefect under the stairs, is breeding rats now instead of cockroaches.

Still being called "Laaaaaaambert" wherever I go. Hoping it will wear off soon.

Sunday 3rd September

I apologize, dear diary, for two days of desertion, but it's been two days of slogging rehearsals. Viking's convinced that the first act isn't up to scratch, so we've been repeating it over and over. If I have to sing "Food, Glorious Food" one more time, I might just move in with Dr. Zoo (his house is now known as the funny farm).

10:00 The girls have arrived and they all made a big fuss over my new sheepy hairstyle. Amanda was as cryptic as ever. Gecko and I were expecting her to give me the cold shoulder and very possibly some stinging looks and glares, but being her weird self, she smiled and chatted warmly to me, completely confusing my personal adviser and me. This display continued through our duet, when the former ice queen looked at me with such love and devotion that I thought my heart would tear into pieces.

Christine, on the other hand, was all over me like a sticky dog's blanket. She gave me a huge hug and started sniveling on my shoulder. Gecko's advised me to stay clear of her because she looks solidly unstable.

Gecko's taken up the menial job of assistant stage manager so that he can stay close to the action and keep an eye on the girls.

Monday 4th September

Awoke refreshed after a thrilling dream about walking down a white sandy beach with Amanda. When I looked down, I realized that her feet weren't making any footprints in the sand. I tried to tell her this, but when I looked up, she was gone.

I told Gecko about the dream over breakfast, but I was unfortunately overheard by Boggo, who gave me his own unique interpretation of it. Needless to say, it involved rape, foot fetishes, and the loss of Amanda's virginity. Boggo then leaned in maliciously and said, "Although I heard Emberton popped her virginity last night."

The mere idea of it was impossible. She had never once mentioned Emberton, nor had I seen her with him before. Still, I found it difficult to get the idea of it out of my mind.

The girls have now officially moved into various teachers' homes and will be joining us for classes each day. During English, Christine made a determined effort to sit next to me, but Gecko swiftly cut her off and plonked himself down in his chair. He then winked at me and said, "Just doing my job, Spuddy."

English was sheer comedy. Eight girls elected to take The Guv's class, and half of them nearly fell off their chairs with his first volley of foul swearing. We studied the Andrew Marvell poem "To His Coy Mistress," in which the poet is trying to get his girlfriend to have sex with him. The Guv made Angela (small, shy, and mousy) read the poem out loud. The poor girl looked like an overripe tomato, especially after Rambo and Boggo started chortling in the back row. The Guv hurled a blackboard duster at Boggo and then tried to strangle Rambo with his tie. The girls looked terrified—welcome to the jungle!

Tuesday 5th September

It's official. Emberton and Amanda are an item. I saw them holding hands in the quad on my way back to the house after lunch. I ducked behind a pillar before she could notice me. (There is no way she was going to see me in pain.) I ran back to the dormitory and tried to read a cricket magazine, but I couldn't concentrate. I decided to spend the afternoon in bed—a session with Dr. Zoo is too much for this heartbroken fourteen-year-old to handle right now.

16:30 Mom phoned in a panic to say that Dad is considering quitting the dry cleaner's and going into illegal alcohol full time. She said it's only a matter of time until my father is arrested again.

Wednesday 6th September

22:00 After rehearsal, Christine and Jenny Sparrow asked me to walk them back to Mr. van Vuuren's house, where they are both staying. Somewhere along the walk Jenny disappeared and Christine stopped me at Cartwright's gate and kissed me. I didn't object and surrendered my tongue for dishwashing. The more I see Christine, the more I like Amanda. I walked back to the house shaking my head and wondering what Amanda and Emberton were up to right now. Jealousy is a terrible disease. At least I know for certain that Christine isn't the girl of my dreams and that I won't let her kiss me again.

Thursday 7th September

19:30 Our first rehearsal with the full stage set was a complete disaster. Mrs. Lennox (playing the part of Widow Corney) stepped back off a platform and fell. She had to be stretchered to the sanatorium with a suspected broken ankle. Viking was so enraged that he kicked one of the chairs in the auditorium and spent the rest of the rehearsal limping around in a foul mood. He was later seen limping off in the general direction of the san.

The set itself is fairly impressive, with a high platform that is able to lift up and down. Viking reckons that with some intelligent lighting, the platform will look like Tower Bridge in London. Unless it's genius lighting I can't see a two-meter-high block of wood being confused with one of the world's great bridges.

Starting to get nervous. In less than two weeks I'll be standing onstage and performing to five hundred people. The realization that after months of work it's all coming down to one single moment is terrifying!

Have a gum boil. Wondering if Christine passed on some terrible mouth disease. From now on I'll carry my toothpaste in my pencil case as a precaution against bad breath. Still no sign of Amanda and Emberton.

Friday 8th September

14:00 Sitting in the hairdresser's reading ladies' magazines with my curly locks covered in blue gunk. I'm trying my best to blend in, but it's a little difficult to when you are a fourteen-year-old boy in full school uniform with permed hair getting blond highlights thrown in for good measure. A Lincoln schoolboy came in with his mother and smirked when he saw me. No doubt he thought I was a poof.

The end result, I think, is slightly less catastrophic than I thought. I now look a bit more like a girl—but a pretty girl at least. Unfortunately, I also look far more like a sheep than I did before. I avoided dinner and asked Gecko to bring me a peanut butter sandwich instead. The first person I saw when coming out of the house was Julian, whose jaw dropped. He then looked me up and down like a hamburger and said, "Oh, hello, Olly!" Unfortunately, things got worse and soon the whole house was taking turns to look me up and down before bleating loudly and then sniggering into their prep books.

19:30 The girls crowded around to examine my hair. There were all sorts of questions about roots, conditioners, moisturizers, and color codes that I was completely unable to answer, but I loved being the center of attention. Viking examined me under bright lights in the dressing room. After some time he said, "Splendid," thumped me on the back, and screamed at Gecko for his cup of coffee.

Mrs. Lennox has fractured her ankle. Viking has cracked a bone in his heel. Both have vowed to fight on and see this monstrosity through to its end.

Saturday 9th September

Sparerib strode into the theater during our morning run-
through and whispered something to Viking. Viking nodded seriously and then Sparerib left. Viking then screamed in agony,
brought the rehearsal to a stop, and ordered me back to the house.
Luthuli was waiting for me when I arrived and told me to wait by
the telephone. My heart was thumping. I knew by all the expres-
sions that something was wrong—badly wrong. I could taste the bile
rise in my throat. I ran to the toilet and vomited. While I was vomiting, the telephone rang. I spat and ran back to the phone booth,
saliva still dribbling down my chin. It was Mom. She was safe, but
her voice sounded sad. In the background I could hear whistling.
Dad was safe. I started breathing again. Through her sobs I worked
out that Wombat had had a stroke overnight and that things
looked bad. I tried to hide the relief in my voice, but it was useless.
They were safe; that's all that counted. Mom said she would phone
later and keep me updated.

I went back to the bathroom. My face was white and my eyes
were red. Somebody had left his toiletry bag on the basin. I stole
some toothpaste and squeezed a finger-full into my mouth. As I
walked back to the theater, I sang the song that Dad was whistling
in the background. It was from *The Wizard of Oz*—the song "Ding
Dong! The Witch Is Dead."

Back at the theater, Viking had told the cast that my grandmother
was on the verge of death. When I returned, I was swamped with
emotional hugs from various girls and a few thumps on the back from
the guys. I got straight back into it, singing my solo "Where Is Love?"
to tumultuous applause. (Cross fingers I get that in a fortnight.)

17:00 No change in Wombat's condition.

Sunday 10th September

For the umpteenth time this year, I'm pleased to announce that Vern is back. At first glance, he looks well. His hair has grown back a bit and his eyes look clear and less demented. He seemed very pleased to see me and shook my hand formally, saying, "How do you do?" like a programmed robot.

Luthuli has asked us to be nice to Vern for as long as we can. He even bribed us by saying that if Vern hasn't flipped out by the end of term, we can all have tea and snackwiches in the prefects' room. Fatty got so excited he offered to make Rain Man's bed and gave Roger a piece of salami.

Wombat still hanging on.

Monday 11th September

Boggo has smelled blood. With great glee he informed me that he saw Emberton and Amanda in a clinch under a tree near the dam. He also told me that the giant first-team rugby prop Richard Moolman is infatuated with Christine, who has told him that she's in love with me. Boggo reckons it's only a matter of hours until I'm assassinated. (Apparently, Moolman was nearly expelled two years ago for sticking a shampoo bottle up a first-year's bum.)

20:00 Debra Whittaker (ironically playing a London prostitute) has been sent home. She was discovered in Ben Cotterel's room in her underwear. Cotterel has been de-prefected and beaten six. Viking gave the cast a savage speech about discipline before shouting, "From the top with gusto!" and hobbling back into the auditorium with his cigar, coffee, and clipboard. Every day the plot thickens.

Fatty reckons that Geoff Lawson is suicidal because of Amanda and Emberton. I laughed loudly—misery loves company.

Tuesday 12th September

Wombat no worse than yesterday.

Christine was playing footsie with me during Lennox's history class on the Great Trek. The Afrikaners celebrate the Trek as a cornerstone of their civilization, and the great Voortrekker monument was built in memory of these brave Boers who traveled across the wild and savage country to get away from the English. Because the Afrikaners run the country, we are expected to get all excited about ox wagons and "the volk." If you ask me, I find the messages scratched into the toilet doors a far better read. Lennox reckons that the truth of it is that many of these trekkers were actually on the run from the law and took the break and hoofed it across the great Karoo! Although he said if we want to pass our final exams and one day get a matric, then it would be best not to mention this. Unfortunately, I missed half the lesson while trying to avoid Christine, who seems to have more legs than an octopus.

Wednesday 13th September

Dad called and sounded very down and depressed. He reckons that Wombat's condition has improved and that it looks like she's going to pull through. I tried to cheer him up by saying that she's probably on her last legs and can't have too many years left. He snorted and said something about Wombat outliving us all. Felt wickedly guilty when I hung up. Hope my grandchildren don't talk about me like that when I'm a Wombat.

Viking stopped us in the middle of a run-through and told Kojak that the band sounded like an inbred cat being dismembered by Cape hunting dogs. Kojak didn't take this lying down and said it was impossible for the band to play when the actors had no feel for pitch and tempo. Rehearsal was temporarily suspended while the heavyweights slugged it out in the theater green room. After half an hour they returned all smiles and the rehearsal continued with the band sounding exactly as it did before the interruption.

During the break I couldn't help but notice Amanda looking terribly distressed. I asked her if she was okay; she squeezed my hand and said she was fine. My hand tingled for half an hour and I acted like a dynamo for the rest of the evening. My temporary elation was destroyed after the rehearsal when I saw Emberton hanging around the stage door with an armful of flowers. I'm beginning to despise this idiot—part of me wishes that he had been expelled for sodomizing The Glock's car with a banana.

Thursday 14th September

14:30 Despite the thick mist and the chilly wind, Gecko and I scuttled up the hill to Hell's View. We had important things on our minds and hardly noticed the steep climb to our lookout. In fact, Gecko's health has been so good of late that he didn't even miss a breath. His skin is now a healthier yellow beige color (instead of its usual transparent milky white). When I congratulated him on his health, he beamed broadly and announced that he hadn't been to the sanatorium all term and hadn't vomited in over two weeks. He's vowed that he will never take another pill again in his life. He reckons whenever he takes pills and medicine, he gets sick.

Gecko says I'm wasting my time on Amanda. I told him that I'm in love with her and dream about her all the time. (The problem with my dreams is that she always ends up kissing me and then when I wake up, I'm gutted by the reality.) Dr. Gecko shook his head, whistled to himself, and then prescribed me a double-strength sleeping pill.

Friday 15th September

19:00 Our first rehearsal in full costume. I begin looking like a girl in rags in the first act and progress to resembling a complete fruit bat in the second. My second-act costume is a green suit and something called a ruff or a fluff around my neck. Viking assured me that's what aristocratic boys would have worn in that time.

More bad news is that Dodge is losing his voice. At present he is speaking/singing in a husky groan. Viking is a wreck.

Saturday 16th September

Amanda has split up with Emberton. Boggo was spreading the news at breakfast. Apparently, Emberton is suicidal and has permission to go home for the weekend. To say that I'm bouncing off the walls is an understatement.

Dodge's voice is now a heavy whisper.

Sunday 17th September

Tried to get the gossip out of Amanda during the lunch break, but she showed absolutely no emotion. Either she didn't give a damn about Emberton or she's the ultimate ice queen. I invited her to African Affairs tonight and she accepted. Does this count as our first date?

Dodge's voice is gone. Viking has taken to the bottle.

20:00 Linton Austin took a dim view of me bringing a girl to the society meeting. He stood up and stated that he wanted his objection noted in the minutes. The rest of the group told him that he was being an idiot, but the genius was adamant that he wanted his objection lodged in the minutes of the meeting. I felt embarrassed for Amanda, who looked like she wanted to punch his lights out. Once the hostilities had died down, we settled down to this week's topic, which was focusing on Buthelezi's Inkatha Freedom Party (IFP), which is made up mostly of Zulus and is very powerful in our province, Natal, and its connections with the Nationalist government (known in our meetings as the apartheid government or "the bastards").

We watched a scratchy home video on how "the bastards" were funding the IFP (although even Lennox admitted it was terribly biased and a classic piece of ANC propaganda). Lennox also read us articles from various magazines and newspapers.

Luthuli led a stinging attack on Buthelezi and accused them (the IFP) of being a bunch of traditional, land-grabbing, rural, traitorous Zulus. (This coming from a Zulu!) Linton Austin sucked on the back of his engraved fountain pen and then rambled on about how urbanized blacks turning against their tribal authorities is the first step in the communist revolution. Once he had finished, he scratched down one of his points on his notepad and looked smug.

I wish I could remember what followed, but in truth, most of the words flew over my head like a flock of frightened fruit bats. Amanda attacked Linton with the most savage array of academic jargon imaginable. I was able to remember: *pedagogue, discourse, racial integration,* and *paradigm.* (Have no idea what these words mean but think I will call somebody a pedagogue or a paradigm and see how they react.) Austin watched Amanda with a mixture of disbelief and awe. She concluded by accusing Austin of being "an apartheid sympathizer, a closet capitalist, and a sexist intellectual misogynist with no understanding or ability to dissect a humanist society from any other construct other than the utilitarian perspective." (The only reason I had that bit is because I scribbled it down on the back of my *Oliver* script.)

The group of eleven put down their coffee and biscuits and applauded the stunning Julia Roberts look-alike. Amanda smiled and took a triumphant sip of coffee. Poor Austin, who has obviously never been attacked by an intellectual equal before (especially a woman), shook his head lamely and for the first time had nothing to say. At the end of the meeting Lennox nodded toward Bruce Henderson (the secretary noting the minutes) and asked him to record how the society meeting had been enriched by Amanda's presence. He then proposed that she be made an honorary member of the society. (This was hastily seconded and voted in by the whole group, except Linton, of course.)

Afterward the society all shook hands with her and just about everybody offered to walk her home. She smiled sweetly and said, "It's okay—Spuddy will take me." I felt myself melting with pride.

We chatted and walked for ages. There was none of the usual small talk. Amanda always went straight for the jugular. This is how I like to remember the conversation (and don't tell me this wouldn't make the perfect scene from a movie).

Walking underneath a long avenue of leafless trees. The night is cold and still. In the distance a train chugs its way toward the station on its long, winding journey from Durban to Johannesburg.

AMANDA	So are you in love with Christine?
SPUD	No, of course not.
AMANDA	She loves you, you know.
SPUD	Really?
AMANDA	She loves anything with a penis.

Pause. Spud squeezes his thigh as he tries to ask the question.

SPUD	What about you and . . . I heard . . . I mean, somebody told me that—
AMANDA	We broke up on Thursday. I suppose you want to know why?

Spud shrugs casually and then nods like an idiot.

AMANDA	He's nice. He's a great guy, but we're just on different levels. He wants to talk about practical jokes and rugby and . . . I want to talk about. . . well, you know what I talk about.
SPUD	You know, you're almost perfect. You have everything.

Pause.

AMANDA	That's your opinion. In my opinion I don't have many things that I want—
SPUD	Such as?
AMANDA	That would be telling.

They reach Mr. Cartwright's old gray gate.

AMANDA   Thank you. That was an interesting night. It's good to flex the old brain muscles now and again.

Pause. An awkward moment as Amanda stares intently at Spud. Spud inspects his shoelaces.

AMANDA   John, come here.

Wedding bells, choirs of angels, wild horses galloping across the prairie. They kiss. Fade to blackout.

I don't remember the kiss. I only remember my left leg shaking and the thud of the snare drum. I think I might have skipped back to the house singing "Ding Dong! The Witch Is Dead."

Monday 18th September

19:00 Full dress rehearsal, including makeup (applied by various teachers' wives and girls from the show). At last everything seems to have fallen into place. The orchestra sounds great, the singing is superb, and the play looks splendid. Dodge's voice is improving but still sounds like the guy who does the voice-overs for the Hollywood movie trailers. The only blemish was that Alf Little, who plays the part of Master Bates (now known as Wanker), was chatting up some girls and forgot to come onstage. After the show Viking struck him savagely on the head with his walking stick and Kojak threw a musical score at him. After the violence was over, Viking gave us a most inspiring speech before bidding us a good night of rest.

After undressing and removing my makeup (I managed to get cream in my eye and Eve made me wash it out with milk), I tried to find Amanda, but she was gone.

Sat for hours on my window ledge above my bed looking at the stars and listening to the sounds of the night. I don't feel nervous, just concerned that I'll never feel this happy again.

Tuesday 19th September

Well, this is it, dear diary. Hours and hours of rehearsing, months of preparation, and it all comes down to tonight. There's a real buzz of expectation around the school. Received calls from the folks, who wished me well, and a telegram from the Mermaid:

Good luck baby stop Mermaid stop

(Not sure why she has written *stop* twice—maybe the madness is back.)

Everywhere people were patting my shoulder and asking me if I was nervous. The answer—no. (One can't be nervous if this is going to become one's life and career.)

18:00 Sitting on the toilet. The world feels like it's fallen out of my bottom. Am terrified and shivering like a leaf. The theater will be packed to the rafters. (The first three nights are already sold out!) All the first, second, and third years will be attending, as well as a whole host of teachers and locals. Everywhere people are hugging and exchanging cards and flowers. I hide away in the boys' change room, unable to face anyone.

19:55 The audience is in. All I can hear is the dull roar of hundreds of excited voices. Viking, dressed in a catastrophic green suit
and a red bow tie (nearly as bad as my second-act costume), wished
us all chukkas (good luck). Amanda blew me a kiss and said,
"You're amazing." Since that moment my nerves have steeled—I'm
ready to seize the day!

20:00 The workhouse boys skulk around the back of the theater
and wait in the foyer to make our grand entrance through the auditorium on "Food, Glorious Food."

Suddenly—applause.

Kojak bows and settles into his place. The band kicks into the
overture.

The opening bars to "Food, Glorious Food." I can feel the fear
around me but not in me. The curtain rises . . . and then suddenly
there is a terrible screech. The curtain stops only a meter off the
ground. We can see Widow Corney up to the waist (her unflattering
half). There is a gasp, then a few giggles and an ironic cheer. Viking,
followed by a few others, hurtles past us, broken heel and all. Kojak
and his band repeat the overture . . . and then again and again. There
we wait for fifteen minutes, maybe longer, until suddenly there is a
whir and the curtain is up. Applause and cheering. We're on!

I reached the stage and looked out at the sea of smiling faces
before me. I have never felt such adoration . . . such . . . God, there
are no words to describe the feeling of being watched by so many
people.

Suddenly it was over, two hours shot by in a blur. All I can
remember was applause and laughter and more applause. Once
again hugs and thumps on the back were passed around like jelly
beans at a Sunday school picnic.

Then I was at Amanda's gate and we were kissing. This time I
was relishing every single moment. This has gotta be as good as it
gets!

Wednesday 20th September

07:30 I was surrounded by well-wishers at breakfast. Teachers and boys stopped me in the quad and in the dining hall to shake my hand. I could get used to this!

23:30 Tonight I was able to digest every moment of the play. It's hard to imagine how many laughs The Guv gets. He should have been a great comedic actor instead of our English master (although for my sake, I'm so glad that he isn't). My solos, particularly "Who Will Buy?" get a lot of applause. The boys get a great kick out of seeing The Glock as a bloodthirsty villain. Eve (playing Nancy) gets loud support, although I think this has more to do with her sexy prostitute costume than the quality of her performance. Overall it feels like the crowd favorite is Dodge, who's a real natural onstage with his voice now fully restored.

Got caught up in a long discussion with Viking and Eve about acting and performance and missed my walk home with Amanda. After I escaped, I sprinted to Mr. Cartwright's house, but her light was already off and I was frightened of waking up the old biology teacher and his infamously crabby wife.

There is a song from *My Fair Lady* that I should have sung. Something about the street where she lives . . . but I couldn't remember it, so I waltzed back to the dormitory whistling "I'll Do Anything" instead.

Thursday 21st September

07:30 This time it was the older boys who were queuing up to shake my hand at breakfast. Earthworm made me coffee while I resharpened his pencils and he asked me hundreds of questions about the play. He seemed incredibly proud that Oliver was his slave. I later heard him bragging to Julian and Gavin, the prefect under the stairs, that he had the most famous slave in the school.

Even Pike didn't try and hit me or spit on me today.

23:30 Tonight, midway through the second act, a woman from the audience got up and started staggering across the stage toward the chorus. We kept singing until the stage manager guided the confused woman off into the wings. It turned out that she was Richard van Zyl's mother, who's been undergoing treatment for seizures. Apparently, when she saw Richard dressed in his rags and begging for money, she thought he needed help. Seems like wherever I go, madness isn't far behind.

Spud and Amanda walk slowly across the fields taking the long route home. They sing their duet hand in hand and then dissolve into giggling weakness. The night is thick and misty.

AMANDA   You know, Spud, I think I might just love you.
SPUD   I know I love you. I've loved you since the first time I saw you.
AMANDA   At that awful social. God, what a start!
SPUD   I saw you and just thought . . . Wow!
AMANDA   And I saw you and thought . . . What a scrawny little chap they've cast as Oliver!

They laugh—she more than him.

AMANDA   You know, you really are special on that stage. When you sing, the audience goes so quiet. It's as if they are waiting for a flaw—a tiny

	blemish in your voice. But there never is. Just perfect.
SPUD	Thank you.
AMANDA	Don't get too cocky. Soon it will break and you'll sound like any other oaf—sentenced to sing in the bath for the rest of your days.
SPUD	Don't think I'll mourn for too long.
AMANDA	You can leave that to everyone else.

Silence. Then a frantic rustle in the trees above as roosting birds are disturbed by the happy couple. Suddenly the atmosphere is different. She looks at him. Like a moth to the flame, he raises his head and stares into her beautiful face.

AMANDA	You do know that you can never be my boyfriend?
SPUD	(*breathless*) Wha . . . what?
AMANDA	You heard me.
SPUD	(*cue snare drum in chest*) But why?
AMANDA	You know why, my darling. You've always known why.
SPUD	I do?
AMANDA	Of course. Good night, Sir Oliver. (*She kisses him.*) Don't follow me—I need some time to think.

He watches her go, his mouth agape, searching to say something. Nothing. She disappears into the darkness.

Friday 22nd September

I wander around the school like the nowhere man, hardly even noticing the well-wishers. I fall asleep in the afternoon, but my dreams are tortured. Last night has flattened me, made me want to stop and rewind the tape a couple of days and then press pause forever. The weather is gray and cold. I wrap my scarf around my neck and try and hide from this cruel, unfriendly world.

20:00 My performance tonight was as bland as a bowl of Jungle Oats porridge without salt, sugar, milk, and butter. My voice was hollow and my singing sounded flat. It was like eating cardboard for two hours. The laughter, applause, and endless hugs bounced off me like black magic. Amanda was smiling but distant. Nothing can be as bitter as watching the most beautiful girl in the world slip through your fingers.

Saturday 23rd September

07:00 I rise like a phoenix from the ashes. (Not sure what a phoenix is, but it sounds impressive.) I'll be damned if a girl (admittedly a gorgeous, clever, perfect girl) is going to ruin my week of fame! I'll be damned if my last performance of *Oliver* is going to be anything but brilliant. Besides, tonight my parents will be in the audience and I'm going to blow their socks off.

17:00 I spent the afternoon watching the inter-house athletics day, which I've somehow avoided being involved in. It seems that over the last week of school, I've lost touch with all its characters and their dealings. Wherever I go, I seem to be followed by a group of new friends and other hangers-on. This feeling of popularity is remarkably easy to live with. After the 100-meters final Gecko pulled me aside and asked me if it would hurt my feelings if he tried to score Christine. I thumped him on the back and said that it would be a favor to have her off my hands. He looked mightily relieved and then confessed to grabbing her last night! I thought about telling him about Amanda but didn't feel like dredging it all up in case the phoenix groveled back into the fireplace or wherever phoenixes hang out. I slapped him on the back again and congratulated him on his first kiss. He looked wickedly proud and we started back toward the house, only to see Christine and Greg Anderson holding hands and walking toward the swimming pool. Gecko looked the other way and pretended not to see them.

20:00 The final performance of *Oliver* roared into life. Everybody was giving their one-hundred percent and whatever was left after that. As soon as I hit the stage, I scanned the audience for my parents (who booked their tickets in March). I nearly shouted in fright when I saw them sitting in the front row. I completely lost my words when I saw who was sitting next to them. There she was, blond hair, blue eyes—as gorgeous as ever. The Mermaid! She smiled her beautiful smile. God almighty . . .

I caught up with the song. Luckily, it was sung with the entire chorus, so I was saved from a major catastrophe. I focused my mind and lost myself in old London town and gave my best performance. Predictably, my parents made their mark. Dad either sneezed or blew his nose loudly during all the quiet bits and they both stood up for a resounding ovation and loud calls for more at what they thought was the end but turned out to be midway through act two. But tonight I was bulletproof. Nothing could stop me, nothing could make me feel shame, embarrassment, or anything other than absolute pride and sheer joy.

Mom, Dad, and the Mermaid were all in tears when I finally got to see them. They all hugged and kissed me so many times that I was soon covered in lipstick. The Mermaid held on to me for so long I thought she might have to be prized away with a chisel. She was back (and I don't just mean from England). Her sparkle, her eyes, her energy, and her beauty.

My folks had to tear her away. (No doubt she was dreading the long drive home in the station wagon.) Once more the snare drum was thumping away in my chest. How much more complicated can the life of a fourteen-year-old boy get?

"Who was that?"

I turned around to find Amanda looking like a black cloud. What should I say? My girlfriend? My friend? My sister . . . My ex . . .

"My ex-girlfriend." (Coward!)

Amanda strolled up to me and then said, "I don't want to hang around the cast party. Will you spend the night with me?"

And so the dream continued.

The noise of people stops. Amanda takes his hand and leads Spud through the excited groups of people chatting and laughing. They watch them go and whisper to each other. Amanda and Spud walk out of the theater, down the steps, past the sanatorium, and onto the rugby field. The night is clear—full moon.

SPUD   Follow me—I know where to go.

He leads her by the hand, past the dam. If it were summer, he would have suggested a night swim. Over a gate, through two barbed wire fences, and up a steep hill.

AMANDA   (*puffing*) What's this—a cross-country course?
SPUD   Just about, actually.
AMANDA   Very romantic, Sir Spud!
SPUD   Thank you. Now save your breath and follow
                me.

He leads her up to a large flat rock. He then stops and looks out over the valley. She looks around and gasps slightly.

AMANDA   It's beautiful.

Below are the twinkling lights of the school. Above the great African sky.

SPUD	Gecko and I call it Hell's View.
AMANDA	Well, if this is hell, then I'd like to see your heaven.
SPUD	So would I.
AMANDA	I'm sorry for dragging you away from the party. I suppose it's a bit selfish.
SPUD	I think if I get another hug, I'll vomit.
AMANDA	I'll bear that in mind.

A great cheer from the direction of the theater.

AMANDA	Funny that I should end up here with you . . . on this night.
SPUD	It's a great . . .

A long silence. Spud sees a falling star. Amanda doesn't look up in time. More silence.

SPUD	(*voice shaking*) Why can we never be together?
AMANDA	Because this is a fairy tale. This is a teen movie—*Romeo and Juliet*.
SPUD	What do you mean?
AMANDA	I don't live in this world, Johnny. I live somewhere else. I'm sixteen, you're fourteen. I'm a woman—you're a boy. And besides, you have a beautiful girlfriend.
SPUD	She's not . . .
AMANDA	Don't say it. Let's just sit and . . . Let's just sit together.

They sit and watch as the night rolls on. Very slowly the lights of the school flicker out before them. The night is cold, but the moment is

*strong. They doze. When Spud awakes, Amanda is watching the
dawn. Around them is the sound of bird life. In the distance a dog
barks. They hold hands and watch the orange sun creep over the hills
and light up the valley.*

Monday 25th September

I seem to have skipped yesterday. Despite eighteen hours of
sleep I still feel like I've been run over by a combine harvester. My
energy reserves are nil and I can't wait for 21:00 and another trip
to dreamland.

The girls are gone, the great London set has been dismantled,
and the theater is now just a dark empty space where something
wonderful once happened. My curly blond locks lie in a pile on the
bathroom floor. (Julian volunteered to give them the chop.) I now
look like a weedy leopard with pale spots all over my head. All talk
of the play and girls and dangerous love triangles has dried up. I'm
now just another first-year with as much status as a crusty old dog
turd.

Friday is the start of the holidays. I plan to sleep for ten days.

Tuesday 26th September

Earthworm has flown to Johannesburg to represent the school at
the Maths Olympiad. (He's only elected to take fifteen pencils with
him, which he sees as a dangerous and potentially fatal gamble.)

Gecko's back in the sanatorium with food poisoning. When I
arrived in the san, he shouted, "Well, it's about bloody time!" and

then gave me a cracking high-five that seemed to rupture the muscles in his side. I apologized for my absence and explained my version of Saturday night. Gecko's eyes were alive with excitement as he explained his "night of passion" with Christine. He drew me closer and whispered into my ear:

"We were snogging behind your cricket pavilion, but then we got cold, so we snuck into the locker room and there was Rambo and Eve . . . doing it. Well, at least it looked like they were doing it—her legs seemed to be wrapped around Rambo's neck. We escaped before they saw us and went to the cricket nets instead."

Gecko swore me to secrecy before adding that some dodgy sausage rolls that had been passed around at the cast party caused his food poisoning. Apparently, The Guv got so drunk that he stripped down to his undies and played a rhythm-and-blues version of "Amazing Grace" on the tuba.

We arranged to spend some time together over the holidays and to discuss things further. Gecko's spending the holidays with his aunt and uncle so that he can see his new love. I didn't have the heart to tell him his new love also has a new love in first-team rugby player Greg Anderson.

Wednesday 27th September

Lunch with The Guv. We watched a rough uncut video of the final night of the play and laughed ourselves sick at how silly we all looked. The Guv reckons I looked like a parakeet and I said that he looked like a cross between a blue fly and a scarecrow. When I saw Amanda (who looked gorgeous), I couldn't help but feel a sharp pang. It was the first time that I'd really thought of her since Saturday, but seeing her again brought everything back. The Guv noticed my change and sighed.

"Oh, to be young and in love."

He's given me Charles Dickens's *Oliver Twist* to read for the holidays.

Thursday 28th September

There's nothing quite like the last two days before the holidays at boarding school. Everybody's wrapped up in their own plans. Violence and bullying are minimal and boys are packing their trunks and bags and discussing their holidays. This is as close to harmony as things will ever get.

20:00 A huge commotion after supper was a sure indication that it was somebody's birthday. A group of boys had pinned a struggling third-year on the carpet while Fatty lowered his gigantic trousers and let loose a revolting fifteen-second fart on his head. The boy screamed throughout the ordeal and then broke loose and charged toward the bogs with his hand over his mouth. It was Pike! With any luck he'll will be scarred for life!

Friday 29th September

LAST DAY OF TERM!

Since there were no classes scheduled, I took a morning stroll around the school, beginning with a stop at the san to see Gecko. He looked in fine fettle and said his uncle's chauffeur was due shortly. I continued my walk and was excited to see that spring had at last broken through. Small green leaves were covering the trees and green shoots were popping out of the dry brown grass. Everything seemed alive and happy. Even the birds were chirping like they knew it was the holidays.

09:00 Assembly. The Glock gave special mention to the cast and crew of *Oliver* and asked Viking to take a bow. The school applauded warmly. Luthuli was awarded honors for service to the school and Linton Austin was given honors for academic achievement. Earthworm wasn't present to accept his academic colors, so Julian wafted onto the stage and collected the tie and badge on his behalf.

As I boarded the old rusty bus for home, I noticed Linton Austin getting into his parents' silver Rolls Royce. Hardly a great advert for a Marxist economist!

As the bus wound its way through the brown hills (with the odd patch of green), I felt the most overwhelming sense of relief. This term has been a whirlwind of excitement and emotions. I can't wait to get back home and see the usual happy faces, but most of all I want to see that girl with the blue, blue eyes and blond locks—the girl who used to swim in my pool.

Saturday 30th September

10:30 Dad returned home with a beautiful Labrador pup. He said it's mine. I had a dog when I was small, but it got run over when it was a puppy. Apparently, I cried so much that Dad vowed never to buy me one again. The true reason for the dog is that Dad wants to prove to the neighborhood that he isn't a dog hater—but also wants a watchdog to bite black people trying to break into the house. (Not sure how the poor dog is supposed to tell the difference between thieves and the liquor clientele.) Dad reckons that Labradors are clever and can therefore tell the difference.

The new dog sniffed around the garden a bit and then caught sight of my mother lying spread-eagled on her tanning bed and galloped up to her like a greyhound. Mom didn't see the fluffy black missile until it was already in midair and by then her terrible scream was utterly useless. The dog landed on her with a thud. Bright red scratch marks appeared as if by magic. Mom screamed again and thrashed wildly at the now confused animal with her industrial mega-size flyswatter that Dad made out of stainless steel and gazelle hide. The poor dog was terrified. It yelped and galloped off down the driveway and disappeared.

11:30 Still searching the neighborhood for my new dog. Mom is too distraught to help search and has retired to her bedroom with an ice pack and a bottle of wine. Our greatest problem is that the dog has no name. There was no time for a christening before it ran away. Dad says that he called it Blacky once or twice during the car journey home. We wander around the streets shouting "Blacky!" at every tree, bush, garden, and water drain.

12:30 The Mermaid arrives and joins the search. She looks as beautiful as ever. Tears sprang to her eyes when I told her about Blacky and she immediately started whistling and calling in a high, sweet voice. I couldn't help but notice how much her breasts have grown over the last few months. I think she caught me staring at them, so I stuck my head down a water drain until my face was no longer beet red.

16:10 Blacky has been found happily rummaging through some garbage bags a few kilometers from our house. Dad picked him up and carried him all the way home. Blacky licked his face and barked happily like he thought it was all a game.

With Blacky snoring in his basket and the Mermaid and I wrapped up under my duvet, I began to relive all the stories of the last few months (although I was careful to skip a couple completely). The Mermaid and I talked late into the night. I had forgotten how perfect she is and how easy she is to talk to when she's not depressed. Despite my happiness I couldn't help feeling that creeping wave of terrible guilt every time I mentioned the play. I pushed it to the back of my mind and made her laugh instead. Perhaps it's my imagination but life seems so normal and simple and happy at home—nothing ever changes and my room is always exactly how I left it.

Sunday 1st October

11:00 Visited Wombat at the Stillwaters Convalescent Home for the Aged. She's been living there since the stroke. She looked wickedly scary—the left side of her face has sagged since the stroke, exposing her set of yellow false teeth. She still wears her eye patch (she reckons that she falls over without it) and now looks like Captain Hook's granny. She's also developed really bad breath, a result of her diet of tinned sardines and boiled eggs.

Wombat was just as chatty as ever, but because of the stroke nobody could understand a word she was saying. Mom tried to act as a translator, but even she seemed to be guessing half the time. (No doubt Wombat was accusing her nurse of some sort of scandalous pillage.) After about half an hour we had to leave because Wombat was becoming overwrought at not being understood. She tried to write something down, but her hands shook so much that she ended up missing the paper and scribbling on the sheet. The doctor has assured Mom that Wombat's speech and writing will improve over time.

The Stillwaters Home has its own hospital, doctors, nurses, and pharmacist. It's an ideal place for Gecko's retirement! I shall show him the printed pamphlet—no doubt he'll be impressed.

Tuesday 3rd October

Dreamed about Amanda again last night. I was just beginning to think that I'd cured myself but . . . there she was again, trying to force her hamburger on me. I'm trying not to think about any girls at the moment—it only leads to confusion, heartache, and madness. Instead I'll concentrate on bowling cricket balls, reading books, and playing with Blacky (who, like the rest of the family, also seems a little touched by madness).

Mom and Dad spent the afternoon poring over atlases and travel guides on Malta while Blacky gnawed on somebody's sandal in the corner. Dad is determined that Malta's the place to be since South Africa is about to explode into flames and all the white people chopped into tiny pieces and thrown into the sea. I've tried to tell them about my African Affairs meetings, but before I can say anything, Dad shouts, "Commie brainwashing!" I've also tried to tell them about Luthuli and how good a leader he is (if he is the type of leader South Africa will have in the future—we could become one of the world's leading nations). Unfortunately, they refuse to listen to me and are adamant that the blacks are out to kill us.

17:00 The Mermaid and I took a stroll around the block with Blacky (who continually tried to strangle himself with his leash). She reckons Malta is a terrible place (full of Mafia people who jabber away in a bizarre foreign accent). When I got home, I told my parents what the Mermaid had said and they seemed shocked that nobody spoke English on the island.

17:45 Malta has been canceled. Dad is now looking at Madagascar.

Gecko called and invited me to a party tomorrow night with Christine and her friends. Gladstone, his chauffeur, will pick me up at 18:00. So much for not thinking about girls!

Wednesday 4th October

Gladstone arrived perfectly on time and opened the car door for me. Dad charged out to have another look at the Mercedes limousine. To my horror, he whipped out his old automatic camera and started taking pictures of the vehicle. He then asked me to take a picture of him standing with Gladstone. Once the photos had been taken, I slunk into the back of the car. Gladstone offered me a drink and I helped myself to an orange juice from the minibar. Blacky chased the limo all the way down the street, barking wildly before giving up and trotting into somebody's yard to rifle through their garbage. I felt like a movie star as we cruised through the suburbs. Everywhere heads turned to watch us. Unfortunately, the windows were tinted so nobody could see the great Spud Milton hanging cool in the back of his limo!

I tried to get some conversation going with Gladstone, but he wasn't very responsive, so I read the evening newspaper instead. After about fifteen minutes we arrived at some impressive-looking electric gates. We cruised up the paved driveway toward an ivy-coated mansion. I skipped out the door before Gladstone could help me and walked into a kitchen that was nearly as big as our whole house. A number of African servants were busy cleaning and preparing snacks and drinks.

"Spuddy—at last! I thought you'd never arrive!" Gecko, dressed in a ridiculous Hawaiian shirt and straw hat, led me into an even more ridiculous living room. It had everything from sofas and rocking chairs to the finest electronic equipment imaginable. Before I had a chance to take it all in, I was shaking hands with boys and hugging girls—some of them from the play and others I'd never met before. Suddenly I was swamped by Christine, who was wearing the shortest miniskirt possible.

"Johnny, darling, welcome to my house. And guess what—my parents are away for the weekend!" She spun me around and snapped her fingers. An African servant appeared. "Get Johnny a beer, Simpiwe!" Before I could argue, Simpiwe was gone. Soon I was collapsing into a love seat with an ice-cold beer in one hand and a handful of strange nuts in the other. This would be my first whole Castle Lager.

It all seemed like a bit of a dream or a scene from a movie. Christine's older brother, who was meant to be in control, had disappeared with some surfing buddies, leaving his sister in charge. Christine already looked drunk. She gave Gecko a kiss on his cheek before charging out of the room with some of her friends. Gecko blushed and gushed and sank down into the love seat.

"My girlfriend sure knows how to party." I could see that the words "my girlfriend" made him feel proud.

Then the group of girls swarmed back into the lounge and dragged Gecko off to the Jacuzzi. He squealed with laughter and disappeared amid bikinis, sarongs, and much giggling. I took a manly sip of beer, tried to swallow, and sank even deeper into the love seat. Hands crept over my shoulders and massaged my neck. It was Christine.

"How you doing, Johnny? Come see my room."

Before I could say anything, she was leading me along a never-ending carpeted passage. (I reckon you could have quite a game of indoor cricket in that passageway.) She led me up a staircase and into a massive room with a stunning view of the ocean.

"What you think?"

"Wow," I said rather lamely.

"You've got to feel my bed; it's the softest ever," she purred while closing the door. Like a fish, I took the bait and flopped onto her bed. Then she was on top of me—her tongue already squirming around my mouth.

I'm sure I tried to resist or say something. I remember her breathing heavily, like one of those murderers in horror movies. She was pulling my shirt off, licking my chest, biting my nipples. Her hands were holding me down. I felt myself kissing her.

I thought of my friend Gecko and my strength returned. I managed to push her off me.

"What about Gecko?" I gasped. "He's my friend . . . he's your boyfriend!"

"I love you," she said, without answering the question. "I only ever want you. I don't care if you want me or not . . . let me make you happy. I've done this before."

She started trying to unzip my jeans. I was terrified. I grabbed my shirt, leapt off the bed, and sprinted off back down the passage. I wish I could say that I did it for Gecko, but in truth, all that went through my mind at that moment was what she would say when she saw my spudness!

I found Gecko in the Jacuzzi drinking champagne and orange juice with some girls and a Maltese poodle, which was also enjoying the warm bubbles. I shook his hand and excused myself, saying that I wasn't feeling well. Everyone groaned and called me a loser.

Gladstone drove me home. As I was getting out of the car, he said, "You're a good boy, Master Spuddy. You take care of him."

"I promise," I said, and burning with guilt, I stumbled up the driveway with the foul taste of beer in my throat.

Thursday 5th October

Feeling wickedly guilty about yesterday. I wonder if I should tel l
Gecko that his girlfriend is actually a psychopathic slut. I looked u_
the word *slut* in the thesaurus. It gave me the options of *wanton*, *la-*
civious, and *nymphomaniac*. Convinced that Christine is a nymphc-
maniac. Must I tell my friend? Will he believe me? Does he really
want to know?

Spent the afternoon with the Mermaid flitting around the shopping mall. Had another attack of guilt when she dragged me into
Natal Wholesale Jewelers to try on a wedding ring. She was only
joking (I hope).

18:00 Mom asked me to take some empty plastic bottles out to
Innocence's quarters. I knocked on the door. I could hear loud
African music coming from inside. Nobody answered. I pushed the
door open and found Innocence and another lady sitting around a
pot in the middle of the floor. She was stirring the liquid with a
spoon. She smiled at me and offered me a taste of her brew. It was
awful. I sat awhile and listened to her jabbering away to her friend
in Zulu. I know they were talking about me because at one point
they looked at me and then burst into fits of laughter. I didn t
mind. The room was small and hot, but the smells made it comforting. I often used to visit Innocence when I was small, but then
Mom said it wasn't a good idea, so I stopped. On the way out I had
a look at her toilet—a hole in the ground. Dad says she's happier
with the hole than a real toilet. She must be crackers as well.

Friday 6th October

It's official. Charles Dickens is a boring old fart and I have every intention of alerting The Guv to this fact before he tries to foist another snoring old masterpiece on me.

Had a call from Amanda. Spent the entire conversation in shocked silence. I then thought of something to say, but she'd obviously had enough of my bumbling idiocy and abruptly said goodbye and hung up. She didn't even tell me why she called in the first place. Once again my mind is in turmoil—girls occupy just about every waking hour of my life and they never seem to make me happy. The worst part about it is that I'm still a spud. What will happen when my balls drop? Will these girls still like me? Is it wrong to love two girls differently? Am I in love? And with which one? I need to speak to Gecko, but I feel ashamed. I guess it's back to Dickens, then.

Saturday 7th October

The house was woken up in the early hours by some furious barking and snarling in the back garden. Blacky had trapped an intruder and was determined to keep the criminal covered until somebody arrived. Dad stalked out into the yard with his club and his torch, which kept fizzling out on him. Mom and I watched from the dining room window as he crept out toward the pool with the club poised to strike a savage blow.

Suddenly there was shouting and whining and then Dad was chasing Blacky around the pool. Dad swore bitterly at the puppy, who thought that Dad was playing a rather splendid game and yapped delightedly as they galloped around and around. The source of the trouble was the Kreepy Krauly (pool-cleaning device), which had automatically switched itself on at 02:00. Blacky's convinced that the Kreepy is some nasty electronic intruder hell-bent on escaping the pool and creating widespread devastation on the house.

Sometime later Blacky got involved in another rowdy confrontation with the Kreepy Krauly. I heard Dad shouting from his window and then swearing before storming out into the garden. He must have thrown something at the dog because there was a crash and a squeal. Dad switched off the Kreepy and returned to bed muttering about drowning poor Blacky.

It now appears that Blacky's completely obsessed with the Kreepy Krauly. Aware that a bark or growl could be fatal, he follows the machine around the edge of the pool as the Kreepy goes about its job of sucking up leaves. The poor animal whimpers and salivates, hardly able to contain himself. Dad reckons he needs to be neutered.

Sunday 8th October

Visited Wombat at the Stillwaters Home. The place is wickedly creepy—everywhere you look, there are old wrinklies sitting and talking to their families or some other old wrinkly. We found Wombat watching the Zulu news with her African maid (Doreen) in her room. Mom gasped and stifled a sob. Dad gasped and stifled a guffaw. I have to admit, the sight of Wombat in her eye patch watching the news in Zulu was pretty trippy. After the news, she stood up and introduced herself to us. She then introduced Doreen as her mother, excused herself, and began watching the weather.

It took some time for Mom to convince Wombat that we are family and that she in fact knows us. Wombat became agitated and clung onto her bag, suspecting that we could be a gang of con men. The tension was only broken when an old gent sidled into the room and introduced himself as Lord Batty. He then told Wombat a lame joke that had her roaring with laughter. The old fossil bowed, straightened his cravat, opened the door, and strode into the closet. After some grunting and thrashing about he was able to free himself from Wombat's raincoats and make it out the door. Dad and I were hysterical and flopped about on the floor in stitches. Suddenly Wombat became confused and agitated, so Mom decided to cut her losses and we left.

Monday 9th October

The Mermaid and I spent the morning in the Japanese gardens. We walked and talked and held hands and kissed. She was wearing a bikini top and I couldn't help staring at her breasts, which are enormous. I touched them by mistake while I was trying to put my arm around her and immediately felt all fuzzy inside. My willy felt weird, as if I was about to wet myself. Luckily I didn't and the moment passed. I wonder if this is a sign of my body changing. Up until last night there were still no ball hairs, although my voice felt a bit deeper when I sang a few hymns in the bath!

Tomorrow it's back to school. No *Oliver* to look forward to this time and no more girls at school. At least it's cricket season again— I plan to mesmerize everyone with my crafty moves and make sure we remain unbeaten. I often find myself wondering what the rest of the Crazy Eight have been up to. All shall be revealed tomorrow.

Came home to find Mom in a flat spin. Lord Batty (the old codger who walked into the closet last time we visited Wombat) has asked Wombat to marry him. Apparently, Wombat agreed and she now wants a priest to come to the old age home to seal the deal. Mom was highly distressed at the news. Having a senile stepfather and a nutty mother could be a disaster. Mom called Wombat to try and discourage her from getting married again, but Wombat thought Mom was trying to sell her something, so she hung up.

Tuesday 10th October

07:30 The Stillwaters Home called to say that they have organized a priest and the wedding will take place tomorrow morning in the rose garden. Never a dull moment with the Miltons!

17:30 The bus back to school was the slowest yet. While creeping up Town Hill into the Midlands, it appeared at one stage to be moving backward. Beside me, a first-year from another house was sobbing but trying to make it look like he was looking for something in his bag. I pretended not to notice and stared at the same page of Dickens until it became too dark to read.

HOLIDAY SCORECARD:

Rambo	Met Eve at a swanky Johannesburg hotel for a weekend of sex. Eve told Sparerib she was going to a drama conference.
Fatty	Did nothing but eat, watch videos, and play Dungeons and Dragons with some of his mates from primary school. Since the Macarthur mystery died, Fatty seems to have become even more lethargic, lazy, and cynical.
Vern	Is back and looking fairly sane. His mother bought him a cat over the holidays. He has called it Roger.
Boggo	Cannot remember a single thing he did over the holidays. Said he was wickedly bored and even contemplated suicide at

one point. He claims his sex drive has also disappeared.

Simon   Has been practicing his batting for up to four hours a day. He has been receiving physiotherapy on his ankle from a gorgeous blonde called Veronica.

Gecko   Reckons he nearly shagged Christine at her love nest. (Not sure what "nearly" means.) He refused to explain until Rambo threatened to fart on his head. Then he confessed to seeing her naked but not doing anything.

Mad Dog   Was arrested with his brother and some friends for vandalism and damage to state property. After a late night-party on the Natal south coast they ripped out a series of road signs and displayed them on the roof of the chalet in which they were staying. The next morning there was a knock on the door. It turned out to be the police, and they were arrested. They each received four lashes from the cops. Mad Dog showed us his arse, which looked hideous (not that it normally looks good). It was wickedly bruised with welts where the cane had broken the skin.

Spud   Got a new dog and hung out with his girlfriend. His nutty grandmother and his narrow escape from his best friend's girlfriend weren't mentioned.

Wednesday 11th October

07:30 Mom called to say that Wombat's wedding has been called off. It turns out that Lord Batty forgot that he was married and only realized this morning that his wife has been living with him for fifty-one years. The Stillwaters Home have apologized for the misunderstanding. They were also under the impression that Lord Batty was living with his sister. It also turns out that Lord Batty isn't a lord after all. He was a journalist and he used the name Lord Batty as a pseudonym. Talk about a con man!

Mom said that Wombat didn't care much for him anyway and she had been considering breaking off the engagement because he had no chin and close-together eyes like a monkey and was most probably after her money.

14:30 Earthworm has lost the plot completely. He's quit the first cricket team, and a possible spot in the Natal schools team, so that he can focus on his studies. He has his heart set on becoming an actuary. (Not sure what that is—but he assured me that it doesn't involve dead bodies.) Since his dismal trial results (five As and two Bs), he has locked himself in his room and devoted himself to his studies. He survives on Lucozade and tinned tuna fish (brain food) sleeping only at odd hours. He looks thinner than ever and by the smell of things doesn't shower that often either.

Thursday 12th October

Eve called Rambo "Baby" by mistake during our drama lesson on ancient Greek theater and the plays of Sophocles. Boggo sniggered and jabbed Rambo in the ribs. Rambo blushed and giggled and then stabbed Boggo in the leg with his fountain pen. One wonders how long it will be until this whole affair blows up into a monumental scandal. The whole school seems to know—Sparerib must be the thickest teacher ever. Then again, maybe he's just like Gecko and is pretending not to know.

Friday 13th October

A letter in the post. I knew straightaway who the author was.

Dear John (you must get a lot of letters that start with that. . . .),

I'm not actually sure why I'm writing this and what exactly I'm going to say. I guess I just wanted you to know that you are in my thoughts constantly—I can't seem to get you out of my mind. In my rational way, I thought it would be an easy thing to walk away from you and carry on regardless, but it isn't. I still think of that last week of the play and our time together—perhaps I'm just being a hopeless romantic. Anyway, I miss you and just wanted you to know that.

Write to me if you care to share your feelings.

Love,
Amanda

Just when I thought I had everything under control and the whole female thing worked out.

I stalked around asking myself questions, most of which don't make any sense.

Am I in love with Amanda?
What about the Mermaid?
Should I tell Amanda about the Mermaid?

Should I tell the Mermaid about Amanda?
Should I take the easy option?
What *is* the easy option?
Should I hang myself in the chapel?
Should I pretend that I didn't get the letter?
Should I try to have two girlfriends at once?

Sunday 15th October

Free bounds. Gecko and I took advantage of the warmer weather and headed up to Hell's View with our workbooks. (Teachers have been warning us that our examinations are less than a month away.) As per usual we didn't so much as open a book and spent four hours talking about girls.

Gecko is still madly in love with Christine and seems blissfully unaware that she has been rumored to be sleeping with every guy in the province (and, if rumors are to be believed, the odd girl as well).

Together we composed a letter to Amanda declaring my love for her but leaving the whole relationship thing in the air. Gecko felt it was important to make the relationship vague enough to prevent anything dramatic from happening. I then felt bad, so I wrote another letter to the Mermaid telling her about our disastrous cricket match yesterday. I told her that I loved her too.

There's a wicked rumor tearing around the dining hall that Julian and somebody called Warren Normington were busted "playing with each other" in the forest behind the dam during free bounds. All the stories are different—no doubt all shall be revealed.

Boggo reckoned that they were seen from a distance to be playing with each other, but Julian has insisted that Normington was attempting to make a hole in his belt buckle. It certainly sounds more than a little dodgy.

Monday 16th October

06:15   Staggered down to the showers by feel, as my eyes were still stuck fast together with sleep. (In fact, I think I was still dreaming when I walked into the showers. Either that or I had somehow been transported to New York!) My eyes opened up fairly quickly after I realized that Pike was pissing on my leg. My initial instinct was to attack him; anger was pumping through my body. Thankfully, I was able to restrain myself because no doubt I would have been beaten to a pulp. Pike then trained his weapon on Boggo and pissed on his back, which was rewarded with much laughter from the older boys in the showers. Boggo swore at Pike, who then made Boggo eat a bar of soap for using foul language in the showers. Boggo coughed and choked as he tried to chew on the soap. (Just as well Boggo didn't see what Pike had done with the soap beforehand!)

13:30   The day certainly improved after a roaring lunch with The Guv, who has regained his composure and humor since Saturday. I told him that Dickens is "a boring old fart with no writing ability." I thought The Guv's eyes would blow straight out of his head. How was I to know that I was insulting one of his top ten great writers of all time?

The Guv fired back by calling me a "malnourished whining cretin!"

I countered this by accusing Dickens of being a snoring old colonialist! (Linton Austin uses the word *colonialist* as a swear word.)

This was too much for The Guv, who threw a spoon of broccoli at me and stalked off into his study. He returned with a pile of books and another bottle of merlot. There followed a series of passages from various Dickens novels.

I continued to remain unimpressed, which further stoked The Guv's outrage. By the end of lunch, my English teacher seemed convinced that my reading age is in single figures. To illustrate his point, he produced a copy of Enid Blyton's *Famous Five* and ordered it read within the week. I could see that the old loony was dead serious, so with my straightest face I thanked him for lunch and strode back to the house, enjoying the spring sunshine while sliding the book under my shirt for fear of discovery.

Tuesday 17th October

15:10 Boggo and I sat together on our lockers shining our shoes and all the while complaining about our harsh treatment from the revolting Pike. I was in full swing, saying, "Pike is a childish, brainless prat who ought to be used as a science experiment . . ." when there was a sudden pause. Boggo didn't answer. I looked up from my black shoes to see a pale-faced Boggo staring past me in horror. I turned to see Pike grinning maliciously behind me. His hands played with something red and shiny—a Swiss army knife.

"So I'm a childish, brainless prat, am I?" he asked, still twirling his knife around in his hands.

I froze. I was in trouble, big trouble. If Rambo or Mad Dog were here, I would be fine, but just Boggo and me . . . I could see in Pike's green slitty eyes that he wanted me to beg and grovel. Every part of me was telling me to do it—but I couldn't. I despised this pig too much even to pretend to worship him.

"You *are* a childish, brainless prat, Pike," I said in a desperately squeaky voice. I wished I could have sounded more convincing, but it was the best that I could do with zero confidence, maximum terror, and the voice of a girl.

Pike spat a greeny onto Mad Dog's duvet and started walking slowly toward me, watching me like a hawk. He was covering the exit—there was no escape. There was a flick as the blade of his knife shot out. I jumped down from the locker and faced him down—a ludicrous mismatch.

Boggo was mumbling and moaning now, trying to discourage the psychopath from doing what he loves most. My legs were trembling but I stood my ground.

"You know, Milton, insulting a senior is a serious offense." I stared at him, the snare drum thumping but everything else still.

"Boggo, get lost," said Pike with a scary calmness, like he had planned the whole thing down to the last word. Boggo scuttled out of the dormitory, glad to be free of this horrible maniac. I prayed he would find Rambo or Mad Dog.

In one swift motion, Pike ripped my T-shirt off and threw me back onto my bed. He jumped on top of me, the blade millimeters from my throat. I could smell his foul breath and hear him panting. His knife slid down the side of my body. As if by magic a long red line appeared. I heard him gasp as he saw the blood. He was breathing heavily now like Christine did that day in her bedroom. My hands were pinned down, but even if I had been free, I'm not sure I could have moved. In horror, I watched him run his tongue over the long red line of blood. The blood disappeared instantly and then, as if by more magic, appeared again. Now he was looking at me, his mouth full of blood. He moved slowly toward me—was this monster really going to . . . ? His right hand let go of my hand and started moving over my body. He licked my chest, his breathing becoming louder. His hand slid down toward my groin. I screamed and lunged at him with all my power. I could hear voices on the stairway. Pike reared back and spat my blood on the floor.

"Tell anyone and I'll kill you, Milton," he whispered.

Then he was gone.

Boggo, Gecko, and Vern arrived at the door, hardly a terrifying prospect for any attacker. I quickly threw on a sweater and swung my Good Knight duvet over me to cover the blood trickling down my side. I knew then and there that Pike's attack would remain a secret.

Wednesday 18th October

It seems as if Pike is now ignoring me completely and has decided to torment Vern instead. He pushed Rain Man into the urinal after breakfast this morning. Thankfully, my cut is not serious, just a deep scratch. Looks like Pike and I will both pretend that nothing ever happened.

Earthworm said that he hadn't slept for days and may wake me up in the middle of the night to talk to him and make him sleep. His hands shake terribly and he speaks too fast—I pick up the odd word but continually have to ask him to repeat himself. I wonder if everyone in this place has had enough and is now cracking apart at the seams? What with Vern, Earthworm, and Pike losing their marbles, it's surely a matter of time before I strip my clothes off and gallop around the quad neighing and frothing at the mouth like a rabid donkey.

Gavin, the prefect under the stairs, must have been doing something vile in his room because some sweet-smelling smoke crept through the door and hung around the stairwell all afternoon. Couldn't put my finger on it, but the smell was vaguely familiar. Nobody was brave enough to go in and see what he was doing in case they were bitten by Celeste the puff adder. Rambo said he wouldn't be surprised if his prefect was cooking a rat.

I have come to the realization that my life is a sane island in a sea of madness. Then again, that sounds like something an insane person would say. I look at myself in the mirror all the time just to check for signs of mad eye movements and frothing at the mouth.

Thursday 19th October

As promised, Earthworm woke me up in the middle of the night and ordered me to remake his bed and talk to him until he dropped off to sleep. I didn't quite know what to talk about, so I rattled on about cricket and The Guv. I then made up a whole lot of cricket matches that never really existed. Earthworm would always stop me and ask me technical questions like, "What were your bowling figures?" or, "Who was umpiring?" So I had to be on my toes. Eventually, he became quiet and, in the middle of a particularly exciting match of my own creation, he fell asleep.

I shuffled back to the dormitory only to find that now I couldn't sleep myself. I spent the night reliving exciting cricket matches that never really happened. It's surely a bad sign when your imagination is far more exciting than your real life.

Friday 20th October

It's that time of year again, folks. The weather is warmer, summer is on its way, and Rambo is planning another night swim. There were the predictable arguments over the breakfast table, but as usual Rambo won through. Boggo pointed out that both our night swims thus far have been utter disasters. He said the first introduced Fatty's backside to the school, the second introduced Sparerib to our backsides. Rambo's response—third time lucky!

23:00 It almost seemed too easy. Out the window, into the chapel, along the aisle, down the steps into the crypt, through the rose garden, over the gate, across The Glock's garden—under the lemon tree . . .

Fatty was waiting, already shivering in his shorts and T-shirt. The night was chilly, but nobody dared to say so in case they were accused of cowardice. We set off behind Rambo—the Crazy Eight on another crazy mission.

This time there was no snare drum, no terror. In fact, I didn't give a damn. The water was icy. Even Rambo was in and out. Soon we were sprinting back across the field, not because of the guard dogs but because of hypothermia.

The rest was easy.

Saturday 21st October

10:00 Our cricket team thumped Fenston High and the game was over before lunch! I didn't have to bowl because Steven George and Mad Dog finished them off in fourteen overs. The game was over before lunch.

The Mermaid came up with my folks, and while they drank up a storm with various teachers, I walked her around the school. Everywhere boys would shout or bark or make rude comments, but I didn't care. The Mermaid is beautiful and she's my girlfriend. She wanted to see my dormitory, but I didn't take her up—no doubt Boggo would be caught in some obscene position with one of his porno mags.

The Mermaid loved the chapel, especially when I showed her the beam where Macarthur hanged himself. We climbed up to the top of the bell tower, from where we surveyed the entire school and looked down on the valley where fields of cows and rich pastures shone in the warm afternoon sun. We kissed until some rude hooting from the quad broke us apart. Walking down the chapel steps, I suddenly had the most overwhelming desire to tell the Mermaid about the Pike attack. I'm sure the memory of it would disappear quicker if I was able to talk to someone about it. The problem is, it's impossible to describe it without making it sound like some perverted psychopathic movie!

The Mermaid cried when we said goodbye and so did Dad—but that was because he had had a couple too many bottles of wine. The station wagon roared off in a puff of smoke and I watched it until it disappeared and then ambled back toward the house wondering if I was feeling happy or not.

Sunday 22nd October

I've been crowned Stud Milton. The general consensus is that the Mermaid is one of the hottest pieces of ass ever to step on the hallowed grounds of this school. Boggo's furious that a spud can actually be a stud and has offered me one hundred bucks for a picture of the Mermaid naked and two hundred bucks for her in a leather biker's outfit. Even Luthuli congratulated me on my catch. I tried to be modest, but good things seldom happen around here, so you might as well enjoy them while they last.

20:00 I carried my newfound arrogance into the African Affairs meeting and was extremely vocal about the issue of corrupt black African dictators. Unfortunately, it was unanimously agreed that I was way out of my league and I was ordered to sit down and shut up. Nothing like some stinging criticism from Linton Austin to put you in your place!

Gavin, the prefect under the stairs, has been rushed to the hospital after Celeste the puff adder bit him on the bum. Rambo reckons his prefect was sleeping with it in his bed and rolled on it by mistake during his afternoon nap. He told Sister Collins that he sat on it during free bounds!

Monday 23rd October

13:30 The Guv and his wife must have just had a savage fight. As I arrived at his house, her car sped down the driveway and then screeched down the road. Inside, The Guv was picking up the last few pieces of the broken plates. An empty bottle of wine lay smashed on the kitchen floor and a freshly opened bottle of red lay waiting on the table.

I offered to help and then to leave, but The Guv insisted that I stay. We sat down and began a bizarre conversation about Enid Blyton. I've finished *Famous Five* but had to read it in secrecy. (It wouldn't do for the major scholarship winner to be caught reading Enid Blyton, never mind the fact that it nearly crept into the Milton top ten!) The Guv drank heavily and continued to sing Blyton's praises until he admitted to having a bizarre attraction to the old bat.

He then became totally morbid, predicting the end of his marriage (his third). He looked at me with his bulging bloodshot eyes and said, "Milton, if I can offer you one piece of advice in your dealings with the unfairer sex—honesty, honesty, honesty, honesty! Avoid it at all costs! Lie through your teeth at every turn and you'll get away with it. When you finally get caught out, pretend you're mad and develop a drinking problem."

Now this is the kind of advice I'd been waiting for! I downed my last few sips of wine and sank back into the couch feeling relieved—damn, life's good when you aren't dragging a huge burden of guilt around on your back!

We watched the first (of many hours) of *Lawrence of Arabia* until The Guv fell asleep in his rocker. I switched off the TV, covered him with a blanket, and left quietly by the back door.

Tuesday 24th October

01:15 Seems like Earthworm can no longer fall asleep without me. I have convinced him that midnight showers are the surest way to bring on sleep. While he showers, I throw his rancid clothes into the laundry bag, make his bed, prepare some toast—and then when he returns, I talk to him until he nods off. This little ritual works a treat for him but is playing havoc with my own sleeping patterns.

Gecko paraded some ghastly-looking capsules in front of us and told us that this was his anti-malaria medication. He reckons he has to take them because Mozambique (where he's going for the long weekend) is a mosquito and malaria cesspool. There was some debate over whether the giant pills were capsules or suppositories. Julian, who was on lights-out duty, told us that they were suppositories and offered to apply the dose to Gecko's butt. Gecko politely declined and quickly hid the hideous-looking pills in a shoe box at the bottom of his footlocker.

Wednesday 25th October

Gavin, the prefect under the stairs, has returned to school looking a bit yellow. He's decided not to share his bed with Celeste the puff adder any longer. Rambo's so scared of it that he's trying to poison it with dead lizards soaked in rat poison. So far the snake hasn't shown any negative side effects and looks quite happy in its cage.

Boggo reckons that Sparerib has threatened to divorce Eve unless she stops shagging Rambo. Apparently Eve broke the news to Rambo last night before their final bonk. Boggo reckons Eve could get thrown in jail for having sex with a minor.

Thursday 26th October

I have been asked to sing the solo from *Once in Royal David's City* at the carol service at the end of the year. Judging by the huge applause from the rest of the choir, this must be some sort of unique honor! I shook hands with people and tried my best to look blown away. (I'm still secretly hoping that my voice will break by then and I can then put my girl's voice to bed for good.)

Mom phoned to tell me that Blacky has finally captured the Kreepy Krauly and has eaten most of it (including the pipe). Dad rushed the mutt to the vet to have its stomach pumped. Mom said the vet also found a small yo-yo, a child's rattle, and three whiskey bottle tops in its belly as well. Apparently Blacky looks as happy as Larry, sitting in his basket chewing one of my old school shoes. Mom held the phone out and I could hear crunching noises and then Blacky licking the phone. I called his name and he barked loudly. I think he may just have recognized my voice!

Mom said Wombat also seems to be improving. She's speaking better and is far more sane than before. She's now walking steadily without her eye patch, but she still wears it when she goes out as some sort of warped fashion statement.

Friday 27th October

Although nowhere near the same intensity of the rugby match, the eve of the Kings College cricket game still brings out the butterflies. These are nights when it's impossible to sleep, so the Crazy Eight end up horsing around until the early hours. The evening's events began rather controversially when Fatty's attempt to better his own farting record quite literally backfired rather badly. About six seconds into his first attempt there was a terrible squeaking noise, Fatty's mouth fell open, and he galloped out of the dormitory.

We moved on to the topic of girls and sex. Despite still being a spud, I feel more confident in these areas now after the last few months, and after parading the Mermaid around the school, I'm regarded as something of a dormitory expert on the topic of sex and seduction.

Boggo produced a theory about my recent success with gorgeous women. He reckons I sing like a girl and, with my blond locks, looked like a girl, thus attracting other girls to me—which, according to the wise Lord Boggo, makes all girls lesbians. (Only Boggo and Mad Dog felt that this theory had any merit.)

Rambo said that my success had more to do with the fact that my willy is two inches long and that I'm not a real man—which makes the girls feel confident and less afraid. Rambo then went on to demonstrate the art of cunnilingus using a close-up of a picture from one of Boggo's porno mags as a demonstration dummy, after which Boggo slipped the porno mag into his dressing gown, said he needed the toilet, and disappeared. Mad Dog then jumped in and instructed a horrified Vern on the four different ways to skin a cat. This time Roger was used as the demonstration dummy. Mad Dog carefully traced the lines where he would make his incisions over Roger's belly with his pocketknife. The sight of the knife sliding across the cat's fur made me shiver slightly. I ran my fingers down my side and felt the scab that had formed over my own long thin cut.

Sunday 29th October

Gecko decided that he needed to prepare himself for his long weekend in darkest Africa, so he hauled me out of bed at an ungodly hour for an "uncensored day of adventure!"

Before reaching Hell's View, we managed to startle a rock rabbit that charged off down the hill whistling in panic. We devoured our packed breakfast on our favorite vantage point and then set off for some wild adventuring.

DISCOVERIES ON OUR DAY OF ADVENTURE:

A green bush snake (non-poisonous, I think)
Three blue-headed lizards
A pheasant (Gecko said it was a partridge)
Vern (who was walking on all fours with Roger in the forest)

We also discovered a grouping of rocks covered in white markings. Gecko was convinced it was an undiscovered painting by the early (and now extinct) San bushmen. I reckoned they were ibis droppings. The debate still rages.

Bert has put his back out after giving Julian a piggyback ride to dinner. Simon says Julian was seen rubbing Bert's back with deep heat in the common room.

Monday 30th October

The moment was quite unbelievable. A crowd of boys in the bathroom. In the middle lay Pike, dazed and mumbling in agony. His left eye had swelled to the size of a cricket ball and Julian (fast becoming the house Florence Nightingale) was about to apply an ice pack. Standing to one side was a drenched Vern (looking like Rain Man) with a trickle of blood running from his knuckles on his right hand. At his feet Roger was meowing and head butting his ankle.

It didn't take a brain surgeon to work out that Vern had just knocked Pike's lights out.

16:00 As a reward, I bought Vern a hot dog at the school canteen. He was thrilled and shook my hand formally. He then took the sausage out of the roll and broke it up into tiny bits for Roger to eat. Finally, my mad cubicle mate scarfed down his plain roll and, without uttering another word, shook my hand again and walked off with Roger trailing behind with his tail raised heavenward.

Wednesday 1st November

Rambo was thrilled to report that he had finally killed Celeste the puff adder. He fed it Albert the rat, who had been soaked in a combination of paraffin, metal polish, and wood glue. Gavin, the prefect under the stairs, is beside himself at the double killing (although he doesn't suspect any foul play) and has refused to get rid of the dead snake. Rambo reckons he hasn't left his room in days and spends his time making strange noises with his didgeridoo.

Thursday 2nd November

08:30 Simon has made school history by being the first first-year to be awarded school colors for cricket.

Amanda has invited me to the St. Catherine's end-of-year dance. I couldn't help the snare drum blasting off in my chest, but that was closely followed by a near fatal stab of guilt as a vision of the Mermaid shot through my brain. Why has Amanda invited me? She's made it clear that I'm too young and she's too old. Does she still like me? Will I kiss her? Will she kiss me? What about the Mermaid? Feeling terrified (and excited). I ticked the box to say I was coming. My fingers were trembling.

Unfortunately, it looks like Christine has invited Greg Anderson instead of her boyfriend, Gecko. My poor friend tried to look unfazed by it, but I could see he was heartbroken.

Friday 3rd November

SPEECH DAY
AND . . .
THE LONG WEEKEND.

09:30 Unbelievably, the folks brought Wombat up to one of the most important days in the school calendar. In front of a crowd of boys, she screeched loudly, threw her arms around me, and proclaimed, "David, you do look handsome!" I felt my cheeks reddening as I heard the loud sniggers around me. I heard Boggo saying, "Check, Spud's granny is a pirate!"

Before reaching the school amphitheater (decked out with a huge red-and-white marquee), just about every boy who passed me called me David and reminded me how handsome I was. Why was I, of all people, born of a line of lunatics?

The guest speaker was a former British chancellor of the exchequer (The Glock assured us that he is important). Wombat was over the moon and clapped every time the poor man paused. Unfortunately, he sounded like an accountant and warbled on about global fiscal discipline and the nurturing of market economies. No doubt Linton Austin was tearing his hair out somewhere in the crowd.

Then came the awards and prizes. I made off with two prizes (English and History) and the award for best performance by a new actor. Dodge received performance of the year. Rambo got the drama prize, although I think that this has more to do with his performances after hours!

The highlight of the ceremony was the announcement of next year's head prefect. A school tradition is that the position is offered to a post-matric boy. This year's head boy, Marshall Martin, stood up to announce the name. There was a hushed silence over the enormous crowd.

"And the position of head prefect goes to . . . Mbulelo Paul Johannes Luthuli."

There was a shocked silence and then polite applause. Luthuli will be the first black person to fill the position. He grinned for about the second time this year and shook hands with all the big shots. I felt my chest swelling with pride. Next year Luthuli is the school's main man! Dad shook his head grimly and checked that his wallet was still in his pocket. After the ceremony, the folks and Wombat headed off to free drinks and snacks at Sparerib's house so that they could chat with my housemaster and various other parents. (I reckon it's just an excuse to get drunk on the school account.) I took the time to pack my bags and say farewell to Gecko, who is flying to Mozambique to meet his parents. He promised to bring me something from the jungle and gave me a funny salute before marching out across the quad and disappearing through the archway.

Thankfully Mom didn't try and steal any food from the buffet and Dad only got moderately sozzled. Unfortunately, the spotless Milton record was blemished somewhat when Wombat ended up in the gents' toilet and was hurriedly escorted out by Mr. Lennox.

Eventually the torture was over and we sailed down to Durban in the now supercharged station wagon. The wind blew my hair and stung my face (still the legacy of our fishing trip). Dad says they're still waiting for the back windscreen to be imported from France. On the positive side the roaring wind thankfully drowned out Wombat's endless drivel.

Blacky was so excited to see me when I got home that he fell back into the pool and had to be rescued with the help of Dad's scoop net. He wouldn't let me out of his sight and slept the night at the foot of my bed, now and again licking my toes, just to let me know that he loves me.

Saturday 4th November

Spent the day studying with the Mermaid at her house. (Feeling guilty about going to the dance with Amanda but decided not to say anything.) Her mom and dad are trying to get back together and went off for a picnic, leaving us to work in silence. Unfortunately, we did absolutely no studying and spent most of the day giggling and telling stories. I was especially careful never to mention the name Amanda.

Sunday 5th November

12:00 The trusty old Milton barbecue with Wombat was its usual predictable farce. Wombat took an instant dislike to Blacky. She watched him beadily while he spent the day stalking the Kreepy Krauly and adjudged him to be touched by madness. (A bit like the pot calling the kettle black, if you ask me!) To make matters worse, Wombat told the Mermaid that she had a good set of knockers and that she must use them wisely. As we were saying goodbye, Wombat asked me confidentially if I was close to starting a family. I smiled warmly and told her that a child wasn't likely. She nodded and told me I was very responsible.

Monday 6th November

The Mermaid has asked me to spend Christmas with her family at a place called Wilderness on the Cape Garden Route. She also gave me a silver ring to mark her commitment to me. I locked it in the safe at home and tried not to think about it.

Back at school already. The weekends and holidays shoot by so fast that it seems like I only dreamed them. Unfortunately, the dark looming shadow of exams awaits. I feel the terrible pressure of proving that my scholarship wasn't a mistake.

WEEKEND SCORECARD:

Rambo	Slept and worked
Boggo	Worked
Fatty	Played a thirty-one-hour game of Monopoly
Gecko	Hasn't returned from Mozambique
Mad Dog	Went white-water rafting down the Tugela River
Vern	Couldn't remember what he did
Spud	Played with his dog and his girlfriend

Tuesday 7th November

Still no sign of Gecko. Luthuli says he'll be back tomorrow.

Sparerib called a house meeting to congratulate Luthuli on his grand appointment. The house gave him a standing ovation, which brought yet another broad smile to his serious face.

Also there was an election for a new house sanitation representative. (Earthworm has been the representative for three years but is finding it too much of a strain what with learning for his examinations.) Nobody was quite sure what a house sanitation representative does, although it apparently has something to do with toilets, basins, leaks, and urinals. Rambo nominated Vern (now a traditional joke at all house elections). Nobody else was nominated, so Vern won his first election by a landslide. Vern looked astonished and more than a little humbled at his new position of authority and immediately after the house meeting strode off to make a thorough inspection of the bogs.

Wednesday 8th November

My mate has returned from darkest Africa looking like an old colonial explorer, complete with a pink face, wide-brimmed hat, and many exciting stories loosely based on myth. He reckoned his chartered plane had technical problems and had to make an emergency landing at Lanseria airport near Johannesburg. The fearless Gecko wasn't afraid and continued on his journey into darkest Africa. While we huffed and puffed our way up to Hell's View, he rattled off a long list of strange animals and birds that he saw in the northern Mozambican jungle. He presented me with some red-faced monkey droppings in a small plastic jar. He told me that these monkeys are nearly extinct and that the discovery of these droppings was wickedly rare. I thanked him and then tried to work out where I would keep my rare monkey droppings.

Apparently it hasn't yet been confirmed, but his father may have discovered a new insect. However, various tests have to be carried out before this can be verified.

We spent the afternoon chatting away like we had been apart for months. The afternoons are now so much warmer, and we stayed up on our rock until we could hear the dinner siren echoing around the valley. Down we went, still chatting endlessly about snakes and scorpions as the night crept in behind us.

Thursday 9th November

The folks had a close shave with the police last night. Apparently the cops arrived and demanded to search Innocence's room. Mom kept them busy while Dad hid her illegal booze in his garage. Luckily there was no chance that they would search the house because Mom and Dad are white and therefore presumed innocent. The cops told the folks to call if they noticed something suspicious and then left.

14:30 Practiced my solo for the carol service with Ms. Roberts, who told me that the day my voice breaks should be made a national day of mourning. I told her the day my voice broke would be the finest of my life. She gave me a knowing "you just wait and see" look.

Earthworm is a complete emotional mess. His final exams start on Monday and he's become a gibbering cretin. One minute he's laughing like a maniac and the next hyperventilating and too terrified to leave his room. I tried to assure him that he'd done enough work, but he just shook his head sadly at me like I was the one who'd lost my marbles. I lulled him to sleep with long-winded stories about *Oliver*, which suddenly felt like a lifetime ago.

Dreamed that Amanda kissed me and asked me to be her boyfriend. I said yes.

Friday 10th November

Can't sleep. My mind is awash with visions of Amanda. I suddenly want her to like me again and kiss me and talk to me in that husky voice that says such clever things. Does that make me a lying cheat?

Saturday 11th November

For the first time in my life I am relieved that a cricket match is rained out. I need to study and I need to prepare myself for God knows what awaits me tonight.

ST. CATHERINE'S END-OF-YEAR DANCE

St. Catherine's is a female version of our school. Also redbrick with manicured quadrangles, fountains, and overfed goldfish. However, the buildings seem less intimidating and definitely less haunted.

Amanda looked gorgeous—I felt completely terrified. Her long red locks hung down over her milky white neck. She wore a tight black dress that showed her curvy figure and perfect legs. I found myself struggling to breathe, let alone talk. I felt silly in my school uniform, but we weren't allowed to wear civvies.

Christine pinched my bum before shoving her tongue down

Greg Anderson's throat. Suddenly I felt for Gecko but was glad that he didn't have to witness the love of his life with somebody else—besides, he's better off without her anyway; she'll cause him nothing but pain and embarrassment. She's a bitch.

Oliver came back like a flash (mainly because most of the girls still call me Oliver), and the thrill and excitement of those busy weeks and months was all around the hall.

It happened during U2's "With or Without You." I remember that the room was dark and couples were slow dancing. The rasp of the singer's voice seemed to capture my life in an unexplainable kind of way. Maybe it was the feeling of longing for something that you can't have and not wanting what you have already . . . but it could have been anything.

Then we were kissing. My body was trembling, my knees were shaking. Surely this woman is magical, unreal—more ghostly than Macarthur even!

Then we were outside on an old wooden bench and Amanda was stroking my hair, whispering something into my ear. I stared into her beautiful dark eyes. They were like a fire or the sea. Maybe she was God? Was this another dream? (Nobody was offering me a hamburger, so I assumed it was reality.)

Amanda grinned. "I'm a stupid girl, I know. I just wanted one more night for old times' sake. But this will be it. This will be our last night together—ever."

"I know," I said. And I did know. This was it and I was happy. From tomorrow my heart belongs to the Mermaid. My heart wasn't thumping anymore. It was just me and my fantasy and the night.

Sunday 12th November

02:00 Awoken by the most terrible screaming imaginable. Already Boggo and Mad Dog were standing over Gecko. His bed was drenched. At first I thought that he had wet himself, but then I realized it was sweat. Gecko had a fever and was talking rubbish. Something about an airplane.

You could have fried an egg on Gecko's skin. Mad Dog and I rushed him down to the sanatorium and rang the emergency bell. After a while, Sister Collins unlocked the door in a foul mood. She took one look at Gecko and diagnosed a flu virus. She gave us some medicine, instructed him to drink a liter of water, and sent us all back to the dormitory. We fed Gecko three spoons of medicine and the water. At first he refused to take it, but we kept up the pressure and finally he swallowed it. He said he felt cooler and we all returned to our beds.

03:20 More screaming. This time it was worse. Gecko's bed was wet again, but now he had a nosebleed and was screaming about his head exploding. Mad Dog and I carried Gecko back to the san, ready to face the wrath of Sister Collins. Once again we rang the emergency bell. After what seemed like an age, Sister Collins returned with a "Now what?" She was about to shout at us when she stopped abruptly. There was a thin trickle of blood leaking out of Gecko's ear and down onto my pajamas.

"Christ," she said. "Get him in here—fast!" We laid Gecko down on a bed. Sister Collins called Sparerib and told him to bring his car. She then ordered us back to bed. I tried to argue, but she said whatever Gecko had could be catching. I left reluctantly, knowing that there was no way that I could possibly sleep.

07:00 Gecko is in the hospital. Nobody's sure what disease he's contracted this time. Sparerib wouldn't allow me to visit him. Apparently Gecko has been isolated.

Earthworm is catatonic. He's staring at the wall mumbling to himself with his maths books open in front of him. I asked him rather hopefully if he had heard any news of Gecko, but he just looked at me like I was crackers and continued to mumble things to himself.

Monday 13th November

06:30 Luthuli says Gecko has cerebral malaria. His condition is serious.

After lunch Sparerib called me into his office and said that Gecko's condition is getting worse. He continually slips in and out of delirium but has been awake and calling for me. Sparerib asked if I would mind spending the day with him tomorrow. Without hesitating, I said yes.

20:45 After prep I went to see Sister Collins to find out about cerebral malaria. She looked grave and said that it was a fever that attacked the lining of the brain and that if it wasn't caught in time, it could be serious. She said that she felt terrible—that she should have known straightaway and not sent him back to bed. She made us each a cup of hot chocolate and spoke in her deep voice that almost lulled me to sleep. She put her arm around my shoulders and said that we should expect the worst. She started crying, blew her nose, and then smiled at me.

"Remember, my little one," she said, "the good Lord works in mysterious ways." She kissed me on the forehead and told me it was time to go.

Sat on my window ledge looking at the stars, which looked brighter than ever. Said a prayer for Gecko—hope God heard it and gets to work immediately.

Tuesday 14th November

Gecko looked terrible (not that he ever really looked healthy). His eyes stood out on stalks as he struggled hard to fight against the fever and the delirium. I sat with him while he slept and held his hand when he was awake. I didn't know what else to do.

The day slipped into night. The doctor said I could sleep at the hospital.

Wednesday 15th November

Sometime in the night I was woken by a nurse. "He wants to see you."

I crawled out of bed and staggered into Gecko's ward. There he sat, propped up on the pillows, lucid and in good spirits. I sat next to him and we chatted, me more than him, but I have become used to these long monologues thanks to Earthworm's madness. I chatted on about *Oliver* and Christine and our adventures together up at Hell's View. He fell asleep with a smile on his face.

When he awoke, he looked very scared. He gripped my hand and asked me if he would be okay. I told him we'd be night swimming by next Friday. He grinned and squeezed my hand and asked me to sing to him. Part song, part prayer, I leapt into "Amazing Grace." I think we both knew that Gecko could do with some much needed attention from above. I kept singing more songs. I ran through all the hymns, the entire score of *Oliver,* and then moved on to pop songs. My singing seemed to be having a soothing effect on my friend. He closed his eyes and smiled a bit as the waves of fever shook his body.

Around dawn, I felt a strong hand on my shoulder. I must have fallen asleep with my head on Gecko's bed. I turned to see

Reverend Bishop. He smiled warmly and asked me to leave him with Gecko. I squeezed his hand, but he didn't wake up.

Outside, Sparerib was deep in conversation with two worried-looking people who I figured were Gecko's folks. Sparerib introduced us. His mother hugged me and his dad shook my hand and then rested his arm around my shoulders.

On the way back to school, Sparerib told me the truth about the rumor that a lion had bitten his shoulder. It turns out that he was attacked by something far more savage—bone cancer. As he studied the road ahead with his wonky eye looking sad, I realized I was with a man who knew the true meaning of pain. There was a long silence, then, like Sister Collins, he said we must expect the worst but believe in God's miracles. He ran his fingers over his jaw and stared out at the rolling green hills around us. I felt happy that this man finally had his wife back. He deserves some happiness.

23:40 Another strong hand shook me awake. It was Luthuli. "Come down to the prefects' room," he said. I staggered out of bed, down the stairs, and entered cautiously, half expecting it to be some prank.

Inside the prefects' room a big wood fire was roaring. Luthuli's notes were spread out all over the floor. He motioned me to sit down in an old comfortable chair and plonked a mug of sweet, milky tea down next to me. I stared into the fire, still groggy and disorientated.

"Gecko's gone." Luthuli's voice was strong yet full of sadness. "He died about half an hour ago."

I nodded blankly. My useless brain wouldn't let me believe.

Luthuli continued talking to me, but I didn't listen. I stared into the flames, watching them swallow up thick pieces of wood and burn them into ash.

Thursday 16th November

I launched myself out of bed in the middle of the night and fumbled around in Vern's locker until I gripped his torch. It was impossible—he had huge green anti-malaria tablets. I ripped open Gecko's footlocker and there they were, still in the shoe box. Twelve green capsules in their packet, unopened. Gecko had kept his promise. He would never take another pill again.

Monday 20th November

I wish I could say that I have been constructive. In fact, there isn't much to say about the last few days. I remember a cricket match, I remember trying to work, I remember packing Gecko's trunk. I didn't cry until last night's roll call, when Bert accidentally read out his name, then quickly moved on to the next name. Somehow that was the moment that I knew my friend wasn't coming back. I ran down to the deserted fields, where I could sob in peace—even then it felt wrong, like somebody was about to jump out and snigger at me.

Today I think I failed my first examination ever. Geography is tricky (even more so when you haven't studied). Science was difficult and I'm not sure if I'll pass that either. I don't care. Nothing seems that important anymore.

Tuesday 21st November

Two more exams shot by. Tomorrow I will sing at Gecko's funeral. His mother said it is what he would have wanted, but I knew that already. I remember him saying up at Hell's View that he wanted me to sing at his funeral. We just didn't think it would be so soon.

Wednesday 22nd November

12:00 I didn't listen much at the funeral. It all passed by in a bit of a haze. I couldn't believe that my friend was lying in this polished wooden box with flowers on it. I remember seeing Christine in the congregation and feeling angry. Amanda was there too, but it didn't matter. Girls may have taken up most of our thoughts and conversations, but now they don't seem as important anymore.

The Crazy Seven carried Gecko's coffin in to the strains of the school hymn. The Glock spoke, then Reverend Bishop, and finally Sparerib. I didn't really listen. Everyone was calling him Henry—it seemed like they were talking about a different person. My friend was Gecko and that's how I will remember him.

Reverend Bishop nodded to me. I shuffled up to the altar with my red-faced monkey droppings tucked away in my blazer pocket and sang "Dear Lord" and "Father of Mankind." I remember the drone of the organ and the absolute silence around me apart from the cooing of the rock pigeons in the eaves outside. And there I stood, singing in my girl's voice that everybody loves, to a God that let my friend die without giving him any of his Amazing Grace.

> *"Dear Lord and father of Mankind,*
> *Forgive our foolish ways.*
> *Breathe through the hearts of our desire,*
> *Thy coolness and thy balm.*
> *Let sense be dumb, let flesh retire.*

Breathe through the earthquake, wind, and fire.
Oh, still small voice of calm.
Oh, still small voice of calm."

Thursday 23rd November

There's a certain confidence that you get when writing exams that you haven't studied for. I bumped into Dr. Zoo on the way back from my English exam. He asked me if I needed another session. I shook my head and told him that there's nothing this world can throw at me that I can't take.

Friday 24th November

Exams are over.

The matrics gathered in the quad after their final paper and performed a Zulu war dance, which they have been practicing for weeks. The roar of approval from the rest of us signaled our respect and farewells for the matric class of 1990. In our house, only Luthuli (head boy) and Greg Anderson (hoping to make the Natal schools rugby team) will be returning for post-matric next year. Julian will be coming back for the carol service, when he will lead the choir for the final time.

I shook Earthworm's hand. He smiled and thumped me on the back before giving me twenty bucks and a pile of his old school clothes. He looked hugely relieved that at last his exams were over. He studied me closely and then, throwing caution to the wind, he gave me three of his treasured pencils and told me to use them wisely.

I carried his bags out to his parents' car and was a slave for the last time in my life.

Saturday 25th November

OUR FINAL CRICKET MATCH

10:00 St. Cyprians were never going to match up to our mighty mean machine. Mad Dog, Simon, and I played with black armbands and dedicated the match to Gecko.

I managed to take four wickets and hit the winning runs, so for the first time in a while I felt like I was making a contribution.

The Guv was highly charged in the change room. He made great speeches, sang songs, and verbally abused Kings College. Abruptly, he said his farewells and told us he was off home to get snot-arsed drunk! He bowed like an old Shakespearian actor and strode off across the field without looking back.

Sunday 26th November

09:30 Geoff Lawson promised that it would be the bash of the year and he did his best to keep his promise. Sixty boys swarmed all over his farm. Impromptu cricket and touch rugby matches sprang up everywhere, as did food, music, and a hotly contested fishing competition. Vern was the first thrown into the dam and he was followed by just about everybody else. The Crazy Seven then won another mud fight before losing a boat race, a round of insults, and a water-drinking competition.

After lunch Rambo made a toast to fallen heroes. Everybody grunted in agreement, downed their Cokes, and charged back into the dam to search for the elusive lake monster that's meant to take up residence in a dark hole near the weeds on the far side of the dam. No monster was found.

Monday 27th November

13:30 My final lunch with The Guv. We chatted about death and the afterlife. The Guv read numerous poems and passages from old classics. At one stage, he shouted out, "We cannot fear it, Milton! Death be not proud, man!" I wasn't quite sure what he was on about, but I felt better anyway. My thoughts rambled forward to the long summer holidays. I feel so tired all the time, I spend my life yawning. Four more days and then . . . sleep.

When it was time to go, I shook The Guv's hand and wished him a good holiday and Christmas. He pulled me close and embraced me, saying, "You're almost a son to me, old boy. You'll get over this, you know, and you'll be a greater man for it." Then he thumped me on the back and said, "Do take good care of yourself and remember, when in doubt—keep reading. A book will never die on you."

I said, "Thank you." He nodded, ruffled my hair, and sent me on my way.

Tuesday 28th November

The school seemed a bit weird without matrics and prefects. Luthuli and Greg Anderson have stuck around to keep chaos from erupting in the house. In truth, it seems like everybody's only focused on going home. Trunks are being packed, plans made, and dreams laid out. Even the school buildings seem to be desperately hanging on for three more days.

Wednesday 29th November

19:00 The chapel was bathed in candles. The organ sounded. I moved quietly forward holding the great candle of St. Michael (not the original), its yellow flame flickering gently. I could feel its warmth against my cheeks. Hundreds of people swiveled around in their seats to watch me. This time I wasn't nervous. My voice was no longer disembodied. It came out clear as a bell, echoing around that enormous holy space. As my solo ended and the rest of the choir joined in for the second verse, I looked up at the beam where Macarthur did himself in. I wonder if he was listening to the forty-sixth rendition of *Once in Royal David's City* since his death. I thought about my friend and wondered if his ghost was here with Macarthur. Or maybe they were in heaven somewhere watching me sing, with Gecko telling the old man he was getting goose bumps. That would seem right to me.

Thursday 30th November

While clearing out my footlocker, I found a small package wrapped in Christmas paper with *Milton 20-04-90* scribbled on it. It was The Guv's birthday present, which I'd hidden away and then forgotten about. I tore open the wrapping and there it was:

The Collected Poetry of John Milton, 1608-1664
On the inside cover was an inscription in The Guv's flamboyant handwriting: *Here's to all the beginnings and the possibilities they bring.* Underneath he had written:

> *When I consider how my light is spent,*
> *Ere half my days in this dark world and wide,*
> *And that one talent which is death to hide*
> *Lodged with me useless, though my soul more bent*
> *To serve therewith my Maker, and present*
> *My true account, lest He returning chide . . .*

"On his blindness"

Happy birthday,
The Guv

I've always struggled to understand the hidden meanings in poems, especially ones written in old English style, but somehow I had the feeling that this poem from my namesake meant more now than it did on my birthday.

23:45 No vote was needed. The final night swim needed no debate or argument. The evening was balmy and clear. Perfect. The full moon would surely help our final assault on the holy grail of illegal, after-lights-out entertainment. We could have done it with our eyes closed. The roof, the window, the gallery, the chapel, the crypt, the rose garden, the lemon tree, the great open field, over the fence, and then the warm water washing over us. We were playing again, diving in and splashing each other. There was Rambo chasing a giggling Vern, Boggo creeping up to scare Fatty and Simon, and Mad Dog climbing up the tree to launch himself into the dark water below. We may be one short, but the Crazy Seven is still one helluva collection of nutters!

Then we were running and laughing, still trying to trip one another as we galloped back across the field. Somewhere a big dog barked—Mad Dog barked back at it. There was nothing to be afraid of anymore. We were just a bunch of fourteen-year-olds charging across a rugby field in our underpants in the middle of the night.

Friday 1st December

D-DAY!

09:00 The Glock bade us farewell in the final assembly and dished out scores more awards and certificates. He finished in a booming voice before striding out of the Great Hall with his black academic gown as always billowing out behind him.

We all shook hands and said our goodbyes. Even Pike was in high spirits and told me to have a good holiday before trying to spit on my shoes.

Gradually, the crowd of boys filtered off to their parents' luxury cars. Dad would be an hour late, but that was okay—there was somewhere I wanted to go.

As I clambered up the slope, I felt the sweat gathering in sticky pools around my body. The African summer is ruthless, especially in full school uniform.

I'd been avoiding Hell's View since Gecko's death, but now I wanted one more look before I left. One more chance to check out the valley below me. One more time to watch and remember.

I'd forgotten how beautiful it is up there. Everything was so alive and full of color. Brightly colored birds and butterflies were everywhere, and at last the Christmas beetles were back with their shrill summer screech. Below me the lush green fields and stark redbrick buildings seemed to be magically sculpted out of the landscape. I felt proud to live in a place this beautiful. Away to the right were the cricket fields and Trafalgar, and then the bog stream and Crispo's old house. I could see his arum lilies, little white specks against the green. The old man was right: looking at them did make you feel better. I remembered him in his rocking chair beside the fire. He turned to me and said something I haven't forgotten.

"Remember, boy, God gave us the greatest gift of all. Not love, health, beauty, not even life. But choice . . . God's greatest gift is choice!"

I'm not really sure why I thought of his words at that particular moment. Maybe as I grow older, they will suddenly change the way I look at the world, but it seems to me that God often doesn't give us a choice. He deals the cards and we play them.

Below me an old green station wagon made its way up Pilgrim's Walk. A black-and-white bird with a bright orange crest hopped onto my rock, glared at me rather suspiciously, and then flew off after a locust. I stood up, stretched my back, and took one last look around me. Then I stumbled down the slope to meet my father.